Professional Android™ Application Development

Professional
Android™ Application Development

Reto Meier

WILEY

Wiley Publishing, Inc.

Professional Android™ Application Development

Published by
Wiley Publishing, Inc.
10475 Crosspoint Boulevard
Indianapolis, IN 46256
www.wiley.com

Copyright © 2009 by Wiley Publishing, Inc., Indianapolis, Indiana

Published simultaneously in Canada

ISBN: 978-0-470-34471-2

Manufactured in the United States of America

10 9 8 7 6 5 4 3 2

Library of Congress Cataloging-in-Publication Data is available from the publisher.

To Kris

About the Author

Originally from Perth, Western Australia, **Reto Meier** now lives in London.

Reto is an experienced software developer with more than 10 years of experience in GUI application architecture, design, and development. He's worked in various industries, including offshore oil and gas, before moving to London and into finance.

Always interested in emerging technologies, Reto has been involved in Android since the initial release in 2007. In his spare time, he tinkers with a wide range of development platforms including WPF and Google's plethora of developer tools.

You can check out Reto's web site, The Radioactive Yak, at `http://blog.radioactiveyak.com`.

About the Tech Editor

Dan Ulery is a software engineer with experience in .NET, Java, and PHP development, as well as in deployment engineering. He graduated from the University of Idaho with a bachelor of science degree in computer science and a minor in mathematics.

Credits

Executive Editor
Chris Webb

Development Editor
William Bridges

Technical Editor
Daniel Ulery

Senior Production Editor
Debra Banninger

Copy Editor
Cate Caffrey

Editorial Manager
Mary Beth Wakefield

Production Manager
Tim Tate

Vice President and Executive Group Publisher
Richard Swadley

Vice President and Executive Publisher
Joseph B. Wikert

Project Coordinator, Cover
Lynsey Stanford

Compositor
James D. Kramer, Happenstance Type-O-Rama

Proofreader
Nancy Carrasco

Indexer
Jack Lewis

Acknowledgments

A big thank you goes to the Android team, particularly those of you who've contributed to the Android developer Google Groups, for creating and supporting an exciting new playground.

I also thank Philipp Lenssen for providing an inspiration, and occasional venue, for my blogging efforts; Chris Webb for reading a blog and seeing an author; and Bill Bridges, Dan Ulery, and the Wrox team for helping me along the way.

Thanks also to Paul, Stu, and Mike: Your friendship and inspiration helped me get to where I am.

Most importantly, I'd like to thank Kristy. For everything.

Contents

Contents

Contents

Contents

Contents

Introduction

Now is an exciting time for mobile developers. Mobile phones have never been more popular, and powerful smartphones are now a regular choice for consumers. Stylish and versatile phones packing hardware features like GPS, accelerometers, and touch screens are an enticing platform upon which to create innovative mobile applications.

Android hardware will be designed to tempt consumers, but the real win is for developers. With existing mobile development built on proprietary operating systems that restrict third-party applications, Android offers an open and equal alternative. Without artificial barriers, Android developers are free to write applications that take full advantage of increasingly powerful mobile hardware. As a result, developer interest in Android devices has made their 2008 release a hugely anticipated mobile technology event.

Built on an open source framework, and featuring powerful SDK libraries and an open philosophy, Android has opened mobile phone development to thousands of developers who haven't had access to tools for building mobile applications. Experienced mobile developers can now expand into the Android platform, leveraging the unique features to enhance existing products or create innovative new ones.

This book is a hands-on guide to building mobile applications using version 1.0 of the Android software development kit. Chapter by chapter, it takes you through a series of sample projects, each introducing new features and techniques to get the most out of Android. It covers all the basic functionality as well as exploring the advanced features through concise and useful examples.

Since Android is a brand-new, version 1 product, there are only a small number of handsets currently available that support it. As with any early release, there are likely to be regular changes and improvements to the software and development libraries. The explanations and examples included in this book will give the grounding and knowledge you need to write compelling mobile applications using the current SDK, along with the flexibility to quickly adapt to future enhancements.

Whom This Book Is For

This book is for anyone interested in creating applications for the Android mobile phone platform. It includes information that will be valuable, whether you're an experienced mobile developer or making your first foray, via Android, into writing mobile applications.

It will help if readers have used mobile phones (particularly phones running Android), but it's not necessary, nor is prior experience in mobile phone development. It's expected that you'll have some experience in software development and be familiar with basic development practices. While knowledge of Java is helpful, it's not a necessity.

Chapters 1 and 2 introduce mobile development and contain instructions to get you started in Android. Beyond that, there's no requirement to read the chapters in order, although a good understanding of the core components described in Chapters 3 through 6 is important before you venture into the remaining chapters. Chapters 7 through 11 cover a variety of optional and advanced functionality and can be read in whatever order interest or need dictates.

What This Book Covers

Chapter 1 introduces Android, including what it is and how it fits into existing mobile development. What Android offers as a development platform and why it's an exciting opportunity for creating mobile phone applications are then examined in greater detail.

Chapter 2 covers some best practices for mobile development and explains how to download the Android SDK and start developing applications. It also introduces the Android developer tools and demonstrates how to create new applications from scratch.

Chapters 3 through 6 take an in-depth look at the fundamental Android application components. Starting with examining the pieces that make up an Android application and its life cycle, you'll quickly move on to the application manifest and external resources before learning about "Activities," their lifetimes, and their life cycles.

You'll then learn how to create User Interfaces with layouts and Views, before being introduced to the Intent mechanism used to perform actions and send messages between application components. Internet resources are then covered before a detailed look at data storage, retrieval, and sharing. You'll start with the preference-saving mechanism before moving on to file handling and databases. This section finishes with a look at sharing application data using Content Providers.

Chapters 7 to 10 look at more advanced topics. Starting with maps and location-based services, you'll move on to Services, background Threads, and using Notifications.

Android's communication abilities are next, including sending and receiving messages through instant messaging and SMS. Hardware is then covered, starting with media recording and playback, before introducing the camera, accelerometers, and compass sensors. Chapter 10 concludes with a look at phone and networking hardware, starting with telephony APIs and going on to Bluetooth and network management (both Wi-Fi and mobile data connections).

Chapter 11 includes several advanced development topics, among them security, IPC, advanced graphics techniques, and user–hardware interactions.

How This Book Is Structured

This book is structured in a logical sequence to help readers of different development backgrounds learn how to write advanced Android applications.

There's no requirement to read each chapter sequentially, but several of the sample projects are developed over the course of several chapters, adding new functionality and other enhancements at each stage.

Experienced mobile developers with a working Android development environment can skim the first two chapters — which are an introduction to mobile development and instructions for creating your development environment — and dive in at Chapters 3 to 6. These cover the fundamentals of Android development, so it's important to have a solid understanding of the concepts they describe. With this covered, you can move on to the remaining chapters, which look at maps, location-based Services, background applications, and more advanced topics such as hardware interaction and netwoking.

What You Need to Use This Book

To use the code samples in this book, you will need to create an Android development environment by downloading the Android SDK libraries and developer tools and the Java development kit. You may also wish to download and install Eclipse and the Android Developer Tool plug-in to ease your development, but neither is a requirement.

Android development is supported in Windows, MacOS, and Linux, with the SDK available from the Android web site.

You do not need an Android device to use this book or develop Android applications.

Chapter 2 outlines these requirements in more detail as well as describing where to download and how to install each component.

Conventions

To help you get the most from the text and keep track of what's happening, I've used various conventions throughout the book.

Notes, tips, hints, tricks, and asides to the current discussion are offset and placed in italics like this.

As for styles in the text:

❑ I show URLs and code within the text like so: `persistence.properties`.

❑ I present code in two different ways:

```
I use a monofont type with no highlighting for most code examples.
```

```
I use gray highlighting to emphasize code that's particularly important in
the present context.
```

❑ In some code samples, you'll see lines marked as follows:

```
[… previous code goes here …]
```

or

```
[… implement something here …]
```

This represents an instruction to replace the entire line (including the square brackets) with actual code, either from a previous code snippet in the former case, or your own implementation in the latter.

Source Code

As you work through the examples in this book, you may choose either to type in all the code manually or to use the source code files that accompany the book. All of the source code used in this book is available for download at www.wrox.com. Once at the site, simply locate the book's title (either by using the Search box or by using one of the title lists), and click the Download Code link on the book's detail page to obtain all the source code for the book.

> *Because many books have similar titles, you may find it easiest to search by ISBN; this book's ISBN is 978-0-470-34471-2.*

Once you download the code, just decompress it with your favorite compression tool. Alternatively, you can go to the main Wrox code download page at www.wrox.com/dynamic/books/download.aspx to see the code available for this book and all other Wrox books.

Errata

We make every effort to ensure that there are no errors in the text or in the code. However, no one is perfect, and mistakes do occur. If you find an error in one of our books, like a spelling mistake or faulty piece of code, we would be very grateful for your feedback. By sending in errata you may save another reader hours of frustration, and at the same time you will be helping us provide even higher quality information.

To find the errata page for this book, go to www.wrox.com and locate the title using the Search box or one of the title lists. Then, on the book details page, click the Book Errata link. On this page, you can view all errata that have been submitted for this book and posted by Wrox editors. A complete book list including links to each book's errata is also available at www.wrox.com/misc-pages/booklist.shtml.

If you don't spot "your" error on the Book Errata page, go to www.wrox.com/contact/techsupport.shtml and complete the form there to send us the error you have found. We'll check the information and, if appropriate, post a message to the book's Errata page and fix the problem in subsequent editions of the book.

p2p.wrox.com

For author and peer discussion, join the P2P forums at p2p.wrox.com. The forums are a Web-based system for you to post messages relating to Wrox books and related technologies and interact with other readers and technology users. The forums offer a subscription feature to e-mail you topics of interest of your choosing when new posts are made to the forums. Wrox authors, editors, other industry experts, and your fellow readers are present on these forums.

At http://p2p.wrox.com, you will find a number of different forums that will help you not only as you read this book, but also as you develop your own applications. To join the forums, just follow these steps:

1. Go to p2p.wrox.com and click the Register link.

2. Read the terms of use and click Agree.

3. Complete the required information to join as well as any optional information you wish to provide, and click Submit.

4. You will receive an e-mail with information describing how to verify your account and complete the joining process.

You can read messages in the forums without joining P2P, but in order to post your own messages, you must join.

Once you join, you can post new messages and respond to messages other users post. You can read messages at any time on the Web. If you would like to have new messages from a particular forum e-mailed to you, click the "Subscribe to This Forum" icon by the forum name in the forum listing.

For more information about how to use the Wrox P2P, be sure to read the P2P FAQs for answers to questions about how the forum software works as well as many common questions specific to P2P and Wrox books. To read the FAQs, click the FAQ link on any P2P page.

1

Hello, Android

Whether you're an experienced mobile engineer, a desktop or web developer, or a complete programming novice, Android represents an exciting new opportunity to write innovative applications for mobile devices.

Despite the name, Android will not help you create an unstoppable army of emotionless robot warriors on a relentless quest to cleanse the earth of the scourge of humanity. Instead, *Android* is an open source software stack that includes the operating system, middleware, and key applications along with a set of API libraries for writing mobile applications that can shape the look, feel, and function of mobile handsets.

Small, stylish, and versatile, modern mobile phones have become powerful tools that incorporate cameras, media players, GPS systems, and touch screens. As technology has evolved, mobile devices have become about more than simply making calls, but their software and development platforms have struggled to keep pace.

Until recently, mobile phones were largely closed environments built on proprietary operating systems that required proprietary development tools. The phones themselves often prioritized native applications over those written by third parties. This has introduced an artificial barrier for developers hoping to build on increasingly powerful mobile hardware.

In Android, native and third-party applications are written using the same APIs and executed on the same run time. These APIs feature hardware access, location-based services, support for background services, map-based activities, relational databases, interdevice peer-to-peer messaging, and 2D and 3D graphics.

Using this book, you will learn how to use these APIs to create your own Android applications. In this chapter, you'll learn some mobile development guidelines and be introduced to the features available from the Android development platform.

Android has powerful APIs, excellent documentation, a thriving developer community, and no development or distribution costs. As mobile devices continue to increase in popularity, this is an exciting opportunity to create innovative mobile phone applications no matter what your development background.

A Little Background

In the days before Twitter and Facebook, when Google was still a twinkle in its founders' eyes and dinosaurs roamed the earth, mobile phones were just that — portable phones small enough to fit inside a briefcase, featuring batteries that could last up to several hours; they offered the freedom to make calls without being physically connected to a landline.

Increasingly small, stylish, and powerful mobile phones are now as ubiquitous as they are indispensable. Hardware advancements have made mobiles smaller and more efficient while including an increasing number of peripherals.

Beginning with cameras and media players, mobiles now include GPS systems, accelerometers, and touch screens. While these hardware innovations should prove fertile ground for software development, the applications available for mobile phones have generally lagged behind the hardware.

The Not So Distant Past

Historically, developers, generally coding in low-level C or C++, have needed to understand the specific hardware they were coding for, generally a single device or possibly a range of devices from a single manufacturer. As hardware technology has advanced, this closed approach has struggled to keep pace.

More recently, platforms like Symbian have been created to provide developers a wider target audience. These systems have proved more successful in encouraging mobile developers to provide rich applications that better leverage the hardware available.

These platforms offer some access to the device hardware, but require writing complex C/C++ code and making heavy use of proprietary APIs that are notoriously difficult to use. This difficulty is amplified when developing applications that must work on different hardware implementations and is particularly true when developing for a particular hardware feature like GPS.

In recent years, the biggest advance in mobile phone development has been the introduction of Java-hosted MIDlets. MIDlets are executed on a Java virtual machine, abstracting the underlying hardware and letting developers create applications that run on the wide variety of hardware that supports the Java run time. Unfortunately, this convenience comes at the price of restricted access to the device hardware.

In mobile development, it's considered normal for third-party applications to receive different hardware access and execution rights compared to native applications written by the phone manufacturers, with MIDlets often receiving few of either.

The introduction of Java MIDlets has expanded developers' audiences, but the lack of low-level hardware access and sandboxed execution have meant that most mobile applications are desktop programs designed to run on a smaller screen rather than take advantage of the inherent mobility of the handheld platform.

The Future

Android sits alongside a new wave of mobile operating systems designed for increasingly powerful mobile hardware. Windows Mobile and Apple's iPhone now provide a richer, simplified development environment for mobile applications. However, unlike Android, they're built on proprietary operating systems that often prioritize native applications over those created by third parties and restrict communication among applications and native phone data. Android offers new possibilities for mobile applications by offering an open development environment built on an open source Linux kernel. Hardware access is available to all applications through a series of API libraries, and application interaction, while carefully controlled, is fully supported.

In Android, all applications have equal standing. Third-party and native Android applications are written using the same APIs and are executed on the same run time. Users can remove and replace any native application with a third-party developer alternative; even the dialer and home screens can be replaced.

What It Isn't

As a disruptive addition to a mature field, it's not hard to see why there has been some confusion about what exactly Android is. Android is **not**:

❏   **A Java ME implementation**   Android applications are written using the Java language, but they are not run within a Java ME virtual machine, and Java-compiled classes and executables will not run natively in Android.

❏   **Part of the Linux Phone Standards Forum (LiPS) or the Open Mobile Alliance (OMA)**   Android runs on an open source Linux kernel, but, while their goals are similar, Android's complete software stack approach goes further than the focus of these standards-defining organizations.

❏   **Simply an application layer (like UIQ or S60)**   While it does include an application layer, "Android" also describes the entire software stack encompassing the underlying operating system, API libraries, and the applications themselves.

❏   **A mobile phone handset**   Android includes a reference design for mobile handset manufacturers, but unlike the iPhone, there is no single "Android Phone." Instead, Android has been designed to support many alternative hardware devices.

❏   **Google's answer to the iPhone**   The iPhone is a fully proprietary hardware and software platform released by a single company (Apple), while Android is an open source software stack produced and supported by the Open Handset Alliance and designed to operate on any handset that meets the requirements. There's been a lot of speculation regarding a Google-branded Android phone, but even should Google produce one, it will be just one company's hardware implementation of the Android platform.

An Open Platform for Mobile Development

Google describes Android as:

> *The first truly open and comprehensive platform for mobile devices, all of the software to run a mobile phone but without the proprietary obstacles that have hindered mobile innovation.*
>
> `http://googleblog.blogspot.com/2007/11/wheres-my-gphone.html`

Android is made up of several necessary and dependent parts including the following:

- ❏ A hardware reference design that describes the capabilities required of a mobile device in order to support the software stack

- ❏ A Linux operating system kernel that provides the low-level interface with the hardware, memory management, and process control, all optimized for mobile devices

- ❏ Open source libraries for application development including SQLite, WebKit, OpenGL, and a media manager

- ❏ A run time used to execute and host Android applications, including the Dalvik virtual machine and the core libraries that provide Android specific functionality. The run time is designed to be small and efficient for use on mobile devices.

- ❏ An application framework that agnostically exposes system services to the application layer, including the window manager, content providers, location manager, telephony, and peer-to-peer services

- ❏ A user interface framework used to host and launch applications

- ❏ Preinstalled applications shipped as part of the stack

- ❏ A software development kit used to create applications, including the tools, plug-ins, and documentation

> *At this stage, not all of the Android stack has been released as open source, although this is expected to happen by the time phones are released to market. It's also worth noting that the applications you develop for Android do not have to be open source.*

What really makes Android compelling is its open philosophy, which ensures that any deficiencies in user interface or native application design can be fixed by writing an extension or replacement. Android provides you, as a developer, the opportunity to create mobile phone interfaces and applications designed to look, feel, and function exactly as you image them.

Native Android Applications

Android phones will normally come with a suite of preinstalled applications including, but not limited to:

- ❏ An e-mail client compatible with Gmail but not limited to it

- ❏ An SMS management application

- ❏ A full PIM (personal information management) suite including a calendar and contacts list, both tightly integrated with Google's online services

- ❏ A fully featured mobile Google Maps application including StreetView, business finder, driving directions, satellite view, and traffic conditions
- ❏ A WebKit-based web browser
- ❏ An Instant Messaging Client
- ❏ A music player and picture viewer
- ❏ The Android Marketplace client for downloading thied-party Android applications.
- ❏ The Amazon MP3 store client for purchasing DRM free music.

All the native applications are written in Java using the Android SDK and are run on Dalvik.

The data stored and used by the native applications — like contact details — are also available to third-party applications. Similarly, your applications can handle events such as an incoming call or a new SMS message.

The exact makeup of the applications available on new Android phones is likely to vary based on the hardware manufacturer and/or the phone carrier or distributor. This is especially true in the United States, where carriers have significant influence on the software included on shipped devices.

Android SDK Features

The true appeal of Android as a development environment lies in the APIs it provides.

As an application-neutral platform, Android gives you the opportunity to create applications that are as much a part of the phone as anything provided out of the box. The following list highlights some of the most noteworthy Android features:

- ❏ No licensing, distribution, or development fees
- ❏ Wi-Fi hardware access
- ❏ GSM, EDGE, and 3G networks for telephony or data transfer, allowing you to make or receive calls or SMS messages, or to send and retrieve data across mobile networks
- ❏ Comprehensive APIs for location-based services such as GPS
- ❏ Full multimedia hardware control including playback and recording using the camera and microphone
- ❏ APIs for accelerometer and compass hardware
- ❏ IPC message passing
- ❏ Shared data stores
- ❏ An integrated open source WebKit-based browser
- ❏ Full support for applications that integrate Map controls as part of their user interface
- ❏ Peer-to-peer (P2P) support using Google Talk
- ❏ Mobile-optimized hardware-accelerated graphics including a path-based 2D graphics library and support for 3D graphics using OpenGL ES

❑ Media libraries for playing and recording a variety of audio/video or still image formats

❑ An application framework that encourages reuse of application components and the replacement of native applications

Access to Hardware including Camera, GPS, and Accelerometer

Android includes API libraries to simplify development involving the device hardware. These ensure that you don't need to create specific implementations of your software for different devices, so you can create Android applications that work as expected on any device that supports the Android software stack.

The Android SDK includes APIs for location-based hardware (such as GPS), camera, network connections, Wi-Fi, Bluetooth, accelerometers, touch screen, and power management. You can explore the possibilities of some of Android's hardware APIs in more detail in Chapter 10.

Native Google Maps, Geocoding, and Location-Based Services

Native map support lets you create a range of map-based applications that leverage the mobility of Android devices. Android lets you create activities that include interactive Google Maps as part of your user interface with full access to maps that you can control programmatically and annotate using Android's rich graphics library.

Android's location-based services manage technologies like GPS and Google's GSM cell-based location technology to determine the device's current position. These services enforce an abstraction from specific location-detecting technology and let you specify minimum requirements (e.g., accuracy or cost) rather than choosing a particular technology. It also means that your location-based applications will work no matter what technology the host handset supports.

To combine maps with locations, Android includes an API for forward and reverse geocoding that lets you find map coordinates for an address, and the address of a map position.

You'll learn the details of using maps, the geocoder, and location-based services in Chapter 7.

Background Services

Android supports applications and services designed to run invisibly in the background.

Modern mobiles are by nature multifunction devices; however, their limited screen size means that generally only one interactive application can be visible at any time. Platforms that don't support background execution limit the viability of applications that don't need your constant attention.

Background services make it possible to create invisible application components that perform automatic processing without direct user action. Background execution allows your applications to become event-driven and to support regular updates, which is perfect for monitoring game scores or market prices, generating location-based alerts, or prioritizing and pre-screening incoming calls and SMS messages.

Learn more about how to get the most out of background services in Chapter 8.

SQLite Database for Data Storage and Retrieval

Rapid and efficient data storage and retrieval are essential for a device whose storage capacity is limited by its compact nature.

Android provides a lightweight relational database for each application using SQLite. Your applications can take advantage of the managed relational database engine to store data securely and efficiently.

By default, each application database is *sandboxed* — its content is available only to the application that created it — but Content Providers supply a mechanism for the managed sharing of these application databases.

Databases, Content Providers, and other data persistence options available in Android are covered in detail in Chapter 6.

Shared Data and Interapplication Communication

Android includes three techniques for transmitting information from your applications for use elsewhere: Notifications, Intents, and Content Providers.

Notifications are the standard ways in which a mobile device traditionally alerts users. Using the API, you can trigger audible alerts, cause vibration, and flash the device's LED, as well as control status bar notification icons as shown in Chapter 8.

Intents provide a mechanism for message passing within and between applications. Using Intents, you can broadcast a desired action (such as dialing the phone or editing a contact) system-wide for other applications to handle. Intents are an important core component of Android and are covered in depth in Chapter 5.

Finally, *Content Providers* are a way to give managed access to your application's private database. The data stores for native applications, such as the Contact Manager, are exposed as Content Providers so you can create your own applications that read or modify these data stores. Chapter 6 covers Content Providers in detail, including the native providers and demonstrating how to create and use providers of your own.

P2P Services with Google Talk

Based on earlier SDK versions, it's expected that in later releases you will once again be able to send structured messages from your application to any other Android mobile using Android's peer-to-peer (P2P) communications service.

The Android P2P service uses a specialized version of XMPP (Extensible Messaging and Presence Protocol). Based on Google's Google Talk instant messaging service, it creates a persistent socket connection between your device and any other online Android handset that ensures communication with low latency and rapid response times.

When made available, you'll be able to use the Google Talk service for conventional instant messaging, or an interface to send data between application instances on separate devices. This is strong sauce for creating interactive applications that involve multiple users, such as real-time multiplayer games or social applications.

The P2P service also offers presence notification, which is used to see if a contact is online. While the P2P service is very attractive in itself, it also plays very well with other Android features. Imagine a background service that transmits locations between friends and a corresponding mapping application that displays these locations or alerts you when friends are nearby.

Owing to security concerns, sending data messages with Google Talk isn't possible in Android 1.0. An instant messaging client is available, and it's expected that XMPP-compatible IM and data messaging will be made available to developers in a future SDK release.

Extensive Media Support and 2D/3D Graphics

Bigger screens and brighter, higher-resolution displays have helped make mobiles multimedia devices. To make the most of the hardware available, Android provides graphics libraries for 2D canvas drawing and 3D graphics with OpenGL.

Android also offers comprehensive libraries for handling still images, video, and audio files including the MPEG4, H.264, MP3, AAC, AMR, JPG, PNG, and GIF formats.

2D and 3D graphics are covered in depth in Chapter 11, while Android media management libraries are covered in Chapter 10.

Optimized Memory and Process Management

Android's process and memory management is a little unusual. Like Java and .NET, Android uses its own run time and virtual machine to manage application memory. Unlike either of these frameworks, the Android run time also manages the process lifetimes. Android ensures application responsiveness by stopping and killing processes as necessary to free resources for higher-priority applications.

In this context, priority is determined depending on the application with which the user is interacting. Ensuring that your applications are prepared for a swift death but are still able to remain responsive and update or restart in the background if necessary, is an important consideration in an environment that does not allow applications to control their own lifetimes.

You will learn more about the Android application life cycle in Chapter 3.

Introducing the Open Handset Alliance

The *Open Handset Alliance (OHA)* is a collection of more than 30 technology companies including hardware manufacturers, mobile carriers, and software developers. Of particular note are the prominent mobile technology companies Motorola, HTC, T-Mobile, and Qualcomm. In their own words, the OHA represents:

A commitment to openness, a shared vision for the future, and concrete plans to make the vision a reality. To accelerate innovation in mobile and offer consumers a richer, less expensive, and better mobile experience.

`http://www.openhandsetalliance.com/oha_faq.html`

The OHA hopes to deliver a better mobile software experience for consumers by providing the platform needed for innovative mobile development at a faster rate and a higher quality without licensing fees for software developers or handset manufacturers.

Ultimately the success of Android as a mobile platform will depend largely on the success of OHA partners in releasing desirable handsets and mobile services that encourage the widespread adoption of Android phones. Developers meanwhile have the opportunity to create innovative new mobile applications for Android to encourage more mobile technology companies to become part of the OHA.

What Does Android Run On?

The first Android mobile handset, the T-Mobile G1, was released in the US in October 2008 and in the UK in November 2008. The Open Handset Alliance has further committed to deploying additional handsets and services that support Android early in 2009.

Rather than a mobile OS created for a single hardware implementation, Android is designed to support a large variety of hardware platforms, from touch-screen phones to devices with no screens at all.

Beyond that, with no licensing fees or proprietary software, the cost to handset manufacturers for providing Android-compatible variations of their handsets is comparatively low. It's hoped that once demand for hardware capable of running popular Android applications reaches a critical mass, more device manufacturers will produce increasingly tailored hardware to meet that demand.

Why Develop for Android?

If you have a background in mobile application development, you don't need me to tell you that:

❑   A lot of what you can do with Android is already possible.

❑   But doing it is painful.

Android represents a clean break, a mobile framework based on the reality of modern mobile devices.

With a simple and powerful SDK, no licensing fees, excellent documentation, and a thriving developer community, Android is an excellent opportunity to create software that changes how and why people use their mobile phones.

Android is backed by more than 30 OHA members and is surrounded by significant industry buzz.

In market terms, the growth in portable devices is a worldwide phenomenon, with mobile-phone ownership outstripping computer ownership in many countries. The increasing popularity of *smartphones* — multifunction devices including a phone but featuring cameras, Internet access, media players, Wi-Fi, and GPS services — combined with the increasing availability of mobile broadband and Wi-Fi has created a growth market for advanced mobile applications.

What Will Drive Android Adoption?

Android is targeted primarily at developers, with Google and the OHA betting that the way to deliver better mobile software to consumers is by making it easier for developers to write it themselves.

As a development platform, Android is powerful and intuitive, letting developers who have never programmed for mobile devices create useful applications quickly and easily. It's easy to see how innovative Android applications could create demand for the devices necessary to run them, particularly if developers write applications for Android because they *can't* write them for other platforms.

Open access to the nuts and bolts of the underlying system is what's always driven software development and platform adoption. The Internet's inherent openness and neutrality have seen it become the platform for a multi-billion-dollar industry within 10 years of its inception. Before that, it was open systems like Linux and the powerful APIs provided as part of the Windows operating system that enabled the explosion in personal computers and the movement of computer programming from the arcane to the mainstream.

This openness and power ensure that anyone with the inclination can bring a vision to life at minimal cost. So far, that's not been the case for mobile phones, and that's why there are so few good mobile phone applications and fewer still available for free.

Corporations will also be attracted to Android for the level of control it offers. By using a popular enterprise programming language in Java, no licensing fees, and offering the level of access and control users demand, Android offers an excellent enterprise platform.

What Does It Have That Others Don't?

Many of the features listed previously, such as 3D graphics and native database support, are also available in other mobile SDKs. Here are some of the unique features that set Android apart:

❑ **Google Map Applications**   Google Maps for Mobile has been hugely popular, and Android offers a Google Map as an atomic, reusable control for use in your applications. The MapView widget lets you display, manipulate, and annotate a Google Map within your Activities to build map-based applications using the familiar Google Maps interface.

❑ **Background Services and Applications**   Background services let you create applications that use an event-driven model, working silently while other applications are being used or while your mobile sits ignored until it rings, flashes, or vibrates to get your attention. Maybe it's an application that tracks the stock market, alerting you to significant changes in your portfolio, or a service that changes your ring tone or volume depending on your current location, the time of day, and the identity of the caller.

❑ **Shared Data and Interprocess Communication** Using Intents and Content Providers, Android lets your applications exchange messages, perform processing, and share data. You can also use these mechanisms to leverage the data and functionality provided by the native Android applications. To mitigate the risks of such an open strategy, each application's process, data storage, and files are private unless explicitly shared with other applications using a full permission-based security mechanism detailed in Chapter 11.

❑ **All Applications Are Created Equal** Android doesn't differentiate between native applications and those developed by third parties. This gives consumers unprecedented power to change the look and feel of their devices by letting them completely replace every native application with a third-party alternative that has access to the same underlying data and hardware. Every rule needs an exception and this one has two. The "unlock" and "in-call experience" screens can not be replaced in the initial SDK release.

❑ **P2P Interdevice Application Messaging** Android offers peer-to-peer messaging that supports presence, instant messaging, and interdevice/interapplication communication.

Changing the Mobile Development Landscape

Existing mobile development platforms have created an aura of exclusivity around mobile development. Whether by design or as a side-effect of the cost or complexity involved in developing native applications, most mobile phones will remain nearly identical to what they were when first unwrapped.

In contrast, Android allows, even encourages, radical change. As consumer devices, Android handsets ship with a core set of standard applications that consumers demand on a new phone, but the real power lies in the ability for users to completely change how their device looks, feels, and functions.

Android gives developers a great opportunity. All Android applications are a native part of the phone, not just software that's run in a sandbox on top of it. Rather than writing small-screen versions of software that can be run on low-power devices, you can now write mobile applications that change the way people use their phones.

While Android will still have to compete with existing and future mobile development platforms as an open source developer framework, the strength of use of the development environment is strongly in its favor. Certainly its free and open approach to mobile application development, with total access to the phone's resources, is a giant step in the right direction.

Introducing the Development Framework

With the PR job done, it's time to look at how you can start developing applications for Android. Android applications are written using Java as a programming language but are executed using a custom virtual machine called *Dalvik* rather than a traditional Java VM.

Later in this chapter, you'll be introduced to the framework, starting with a technical explanation of the Android software stack, a look at what's included in the SDK, an introduction to the Android libraries, and a look at the Dalvik virtual machine.

Each Android application runs in a separate process within its own Dalvik instance, relinquishing all responsibility for memory and process management to the Android run time, which stops and kills processes as necessary to manage resources.

Dalvik and the Android run time sit on top of a Linux kernel that handles low-level hardware interaction including drivers and memory management, while a set of APIs provides access to all of the underlying services, features, and hardware.

What Comes in the Box

The Android software development kit (SDK) includes everything you need to start developing, testing, and debugging Android applications. Included in the SDK download are:

❑ **The Android APIs**   The core of the SDK is the Android API libraries that provide developer access to the Android stack. These are the same libraries used at Google to create native Android applications.

❑ **Development Tools**   To turn Android source code into executable Android applications, the SDK includes several development tools that let you compile and debug your applications. You will learn more about the developer tools in Chapter 2.

❑ **The Android Emulator**   The Android Emulator is a fully interactive Android device emulator featuring several alternative skins. Using the emulator, you can see how your applications will look and behave on a real Android device. All Android applications run within the Dalvik VM so that the software emulator is an excellent environment — in fact, as it is hardware-neutral, it provides a better independent test environment than any single hardware implementation.

❑ **Full Documentation**   The SDK includes extensive code-level reference information detailing exactly what's included in each package and class and how to use them. In addition to the code documentation, Android's reference documentation explains how to get started and gives detailed explanations of the fundamentals behind Android development.

❑ **Sample Code**   The Android SDK includes a selection of sample applications that demonstrate some of the possibilities available using Android, as well as simple programs that highlight how to use individual API features.

❑ **Online Support**   Despite its relative youth, Android has generated a vibrant developer community. The Google Groups at `http://code.google.com/android/groups` are active forums of Android developers with regular input from the Android development team at Google.

For those using the popular Eclipse IDE, Android has released a special plug-in that simplifies project creation and tightly integrates Eclipse with the Android Emulator and debugging tools. The features of the ADT plug-in are covered in more detail in Chapter 2.

Understanding the Android Software Stack

The Android software stack is composed of the elements shown in Figure 1-1 and described in further detail below it. Put simply, a Linux kernel and a collection of C/C++ libraries are exposed through an application framework that provides services for, and management of, the run time and applications.

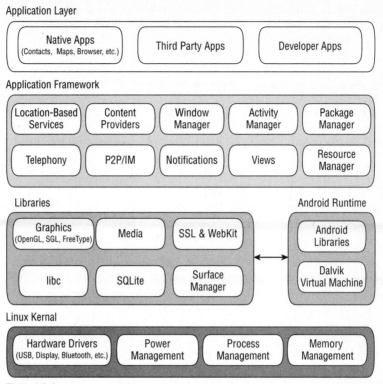

Application Layer

Native Apps
(Contacts, Maps, Browser, etc.) Third Party Apps Developer Apps

Application Framework

| Location-Based Services | Content Providers | Window Manager | Activity Manager | Package Manager |
| Telephony | P2P/IM | Notifications | Views | Resource Manager |

Libraries   **Android Runtime**

Graphics (OpenGL, SGL, FreeType) | Media | SSL & WebKit   Android Libraries

libc | SQLite | Surface Manager   Dalvik Virtual Machine

Linux Kernal

Hardware Drivers (USB, Display, Bluetooth, etc.) | Power Management | Process Management | Memory Management

Figure 1-1

- ❑ **Linux Kernel** Core services (including hardware drivers, process and memory management, security, network, and power management) are handled by a Linux 2.6 kernel. The kernel also provides an abstraction layer between the hardware and the remainder of the stack.

- ❑ **Libraries** Running on top of the kernel, Android includes various C/C++ core libraries such as libc and SSL, as well as:

    - ❑ A media library for playback of audio and video media

    - ❑ A Surface manager to provide display management

    - ❑ Graphics libraries that include SGL and OpenGL for 2D and 3D graphics

    - ❑ SQLite for native database support

    - ❑ SSL and WebKit for integrated web browser and Internet security

- ❑ **Android Run Time** What makes an Android phone an Android phone rather than a mobile Linux implementation is the Android run time. Including the core libraries and the Dalvik virtual machine, the Android run time is the engine that powers your applications and, along with the libraries, forms the basis for the application framework.

    - ❑ **Core Libraries** While Android development is done in Java, Dalvik is not a Java VM. The core Android libraries provide most of the functionality available in the core Java libraries as well as the Android-specific libraries.

❏ **Dalvik Virtual Machine**   Dalvik is a register-based virtual machine that's been optimized to ensure that a device can run multiple instances efficiently. It relies on the Linux kernel for threading and low-level memory management.

❏ **Application Framework**   The application framework provides the classes used to create Android applications. It also provides a generic abstraction for hardware access and manages the user interface and application resources.

❏ **Application Layer**   All applications, both native and third party, are built on the application layer using the same API libraries. The application layer runs within the Android run time using the classes and services made available from the application framework.

The Dalvik Virtual Machine

One of the key elements of Android is the Dalvik virtual machine. Rather than use a traditional Java virtual machine (VM) such as Java ME (Java Mobile Edition), Android uses its own custom VM designed to ensure that multiple instances run efficiently on a single device.

The Dalvik VM uses the device's underlying Linux kernel to handle low-level functionality including security, threading, and process and memory management. It's also possible to write C/C++ applications that run directly on the underlying Linux OS. While you *can* do this, in most cases there's no reason you should need to.

> *This book focuses exclusively on writing applications that run within Dalvik. If your inclinations run toward exploring the Linux kernel and C/C++ underbelly of Android, modifying Dalvik, or otherwise tinkering with things under the hood, check out the Android Internals Google Group at* `http://groups.google.com/group/android-internals`

All Android hardware and system service access is managed using Dalvik as a middle tier. By using a VM to host application execution, developers have an abstraction layer that ensures they never have to worry about a particular hardware implementation.

The Dalvik VM executes Dalvik executable files, a format optimized to ensure minimal memory footprint. The `.dex` executables are created by transforming Java language compiled classes using the tools supplied within the SDK. You'll learn more about how to create Dalvik executables in the next chapter.

Android Application Architecture

Android's architecture encourages the concept of component reuse, allowing you to publish and share activities, services, and data with other applications with access managed by the security restrictions you put in place.

The same mechanism that lets you produce a replacement contact manager or phone dialer can let you expose your application components to let other developers create new UI front ends and functionality extensions, or otherwise build on them.

The following application services are the architectural cornerstones of all Android applications, providing the framework you'll be using for your own software:

❑ **Activity Manager** Controls the life cycle of your activities, including management of the activity stack described in Chapter 3.

❑ **Views** Are used to construct the user interfaces for your activities as described in Chapter 4.

❑ **Notification Manager** Provides a consistent and non-intrusive mechanism for signaling your users as described in Chapter 8.

❑ **Content Providers** Lets your applications share data between applications as described in Chapter 6.

❑ **Resource Manager** Supports non-code resources like strings and graphics to be externalized as shown in Chapter 3.

Android Libraries

Android offers a number of APIs for developing your applications. The following list of core APIs should provide an insight into what's available; all Android devices will offer support for at least these APIs:

❑ **android.util** The core utility package contains low-level classes like specialized containers, string formatters, and XML parsing utilities.

❑ **android.os** The operating system package provides access to basic operating system services like message passing, interprocess communication, clock functions, and debugging.

❑ **android.graphics** The graphics API supplies the low-level graphics classes that support canvases, colors, and drawing primitives, and lets you draw on canvases.

❑ **android.text** The text processing tools for displaying and parsing text.

❑ **android.database** Supplies the low-level classes required for handling cursors when working with databases.

❑ **android.content** The content API is used to manage data access and publishing by providing services for dealing with resources, content providers, and packages.

❑ **android.view** Views are the core user interface class. All user interface elements are constructed using a series of Views to provide the user interaction components.

❑ **android.widget** Built on the View package, the widget classes are the "here's one we created earlier" user-interface elements for you to use in your applications. They include lists, buttons, and layouts.

❑ **com.google.android.maps** A high-level API that provides access to native map controls that you can use within your application. Includes the MapView control as well as the Overlay and MapController classes used to annotate and control your embedded maps.

❑ **android.app**   A high-level package that provides access to the application model. The application package includes the Activity and Service APIs that form the basis for all your Android applications.

❑ **android.provider**   To ease developer access to certain standard Content Providers (such as the contacts database), the Provider package offers classes to provide access to standard databases included in all Android distributions.

❑ **android.telephony**   The telephony APIs give you the ability to directly interact with the device's phone stack, letting you make, receive, and monitor phone calls, phone status, and SMS messages.

❑ **android.webkit**   The WebKit package features APIs for working with Web-based content, including a WebView control for embedding browsers in your activities and a cookie manager.

In addition to the Android APIs, the Android stack includes a set of C/C++ libraries that are exposed through the application framework. These libraries include:

❑ **OpenGL**   The library used to support 3D graphics based on the Open GL ES 1.0 API

❑ **FreeType**   Support for bitmap and vector font rendering

❑ **SGL**   The core library used to provide a 2D graphics engine

❑ **libc**   The standard C library optimized for Linux-based embedded devices

❑ **SQLite**   The lightweight relation database engine used to store application data

❑ **SSL**   Support for using the Secure Sockets Layer cryptographic protocol for secure Internet communications

Advanced Android Libraries

The core libraries provide all the functionality you need to start creating applications for Android, but it won't be long before you're ready to delve into the advanced APIs that offer the really exciting functionality.

Android hopes to target a wide range of mobile hardware, so be aware that the suitability and implementation of the following APIs will vary depending on the device upon which they are implemented.

❑ **android.location**   The location-based services API gives your applications access to the device's current physical location. Location-based services provide generic access to location information using whatever position-fixing hardware or technology is available on the device.

❑ **android.media**   The media APIs provide support for playback and recording of audio and video media files, including streamed media.

❑ **android.opengl**   Android offers a powerful 3D rendering engine using the OpenGL ES API that you can use to create dynamic 3D user interfaces for your applications.

❑ **android.hardware**   Where available, the hardware API exposes sensor hardware including the camera, accelerometer, and compass sensors as shown in Chapter 10.

❑ **android.bluetooth, android.net.wifi, and android.telephony**   Android also provides low-level access to the hardware platform, including Bluetooth, Wi-Fi, and telephony hardware as shown in Chapter 10.

Summary

This chapter explained that despite significant advances in the hardware features available on modern mobile phones, the software available for them has lagged. A lack of openness, hard-to-use development kits, and hardware-specific APIs have stifled innovation in mobile software.

Android offers an opportunity for developers to create innovative software applications for mobile devices without the restrictions generally associated with the existing proprietary mobile development frameworks.

You were shown the complete Android software stack, which includes not only an application layer and development toolkit but also the Dalvik VM, a custom run time, core libraries, and a Linux kernel; all of which will be available as open source.

The Open Handset Alliance was introduced along with the responsibility that developers — as the primary target audience for Android — have to create applications that will make consumers want Android phones on which to run them.

You also learned:

- ❑ How handsets with an expanding range of hardware features have created demand for tools that give developers better access to these features.
- ❑ About some of the features available to developers using Android, including peer-to-peer messaging, native map support, hardware access, background services, interprocess and inter-device messaging, shared databases, and 2D and 3D graphics.
- ❑ That all Android applications are built equal, allowing users to completely replace one application with another, including the replacement of the core native applications.
- ❑ That the Android SDK includes developer tools, APIs, and comprehensive documentation.

The next chapter will help you get started by downloading and installing the Android SDK and setting up an Android development environment in Eclipse.

You'll also learn how to use the Android developer tools plug-in to streamline development, testing, and debugging before creating your first Android application.

After learning about the building blocks of Android applications, you'll be introduced to the different types of applications you can create, and you'll start to understand some of the design considerations that should go into developing applications for mobile devices.

2

Getting Started

All you need to start writing your own Android applications is a copy of the Android SDK and the Java development kit. Unless you're a masochist, you'll probably want a Java IDE — Eclipse is particularly well supported — to make development a little easier.

Versions of the SDK, Java, and Eclipse are available for Windows, Mac OS, and Linux, so you can explore Android from the comfort of whatever OS you favor. The SDK includes an emulator for all three OS environments, and because Android applications are run on a virtual machine, there's no advantage to developing from any particular operating system.

Android code is written using Java syntax, and the core Android libraries include most of the features from the core Java APIs. Before they can be run, though, your projects are first translated into Dalvik byte code. As a result, you get the benefits of using Java, while your applications have the advantage of running on a virtual machine optimized for Android devices.

The SDK download includes all the Android libraries, full documentation, and excellent sample applications. It also includes tools to help you write and debug your applications, like the Android Emulator to run your projects and the Dalvik Debug Monitoring Service (DDMS) to help debug them.

By the end of this chapter, you'll have downloaded the Android SDK, set up your development environment, completed two new applications, and run and debugged them using the emulator and DDMS.

If you've developed for mobile devices before, you already know that their small-form factor, limited power, and restricted memory create some unique design challenges. Even if you're new to the game, it's obvious that some of the things you can take for granted on the desktop or the Web aren't going to work on a mobile.

As well as the hardware limitations, the user environment brings its own challenges. Mobile devices are used on the move and are often a distraction rather than the focus of attention, so your applications need to be fast, responsive, and easy to use.

This chapter examines some of the best practices for writing mobile applications to help overcome the inherent hardware and environmental challenges. Rather than try to tackle the whole topic, we'll focus on using the Android SDK in a way that's consistent with good mobile design principles.

Developing for Android

The Android SDK includes all the tools and APIs you need to write compelling and powerful mobile applications. The biggest challenge with Android, as with any new development toolkit, is learning the features and limitations of its APIs.

If you have experience in Java development, you'll find that the techniques, syntax, and grammar you've been using will translate directly into Android, although some of the specific optimization techniques may seem counterintuitive.

If you don't have experience with Java but have used other object-oriented languages (such as C#), you should find the transition straightforward. The power of Android comes from its APIs, not from Java, so being unfamiliar with all the Java specific classes won't be a big disadvantage.

What You Need to Begin

Because Android applications run within the Dalvik virtual machine, you can write them on any platform that supports the developer tools. This currently includes the following:

❑ Microsoft Windows (XP or Vista)

❑ Mac OS X 10.4.8 or later (Intel chips only)

❑ Linux

To get started, you'll need to download and install the following:

❑ The Android SDK

❑ Java Development Kit (JDK) 5 or 6

You can download the latest JDK from Sun at

```
http://java.sun.com/javase/downloads/index.jsp
```

If you already have a JDK installed, make sure that it meets the version requirements listed above, and note that the Java runtime environment (JRE) is not sufficient.

Downloading and Installing the SDK

The Android SDK is completely open. There's no cost to download and use the API, and Google doesn't charge to allow distribution of your finished programs. You can download the latest version of the SDK for your development platform from the Android development home page at

```
http://code.google.com/android/download.html
```

Unless otherwise noted, the version of the Android SDK used for writing this book was version 1.0 r1.

The SDK is presented as a ZIP file containing the API libraries, developer tools, documentation, and several sample applications and API demos that highlight the use of particular API features. Install it by unzipping the SDK into a new folder. (Take note of this location, as you'll need it later.)

The examples and step-by-step instructions provided are targeted at developers using Eclipse with the Android Developer Tool (ADT) plug-in. Neither is required, though — you can use any text editor or Java IDE you're comfortable with and use the developer tools in the SDK to compile, test, and debug the code snippets and sample applications.

If you're planning to use them, the next sections explain how to set up Eclipse and the ADT plug-in as your Android development environment. Later in the chapter, we'll also take a closer look at the developer tools that come with the SDK, so if you'd prefer to develop without using Eclipse or the ADT plug-in, you'll particularly want to check that out.

The examples included in the SDK are well documented and are an excellent source for full, working examples of applications written for Android. Once you've finished setting up your development environment, it's worth going through them.

Developing with Eclipse

Using Eclipse with the ADT plug-in for your Android development offers some significant advantages.

Eclipse is an open source IDE (integrated development environment) particularly popular for Java development. It's available to download for each of the development platforms supported by Android (Windows, Mac OS, and Linux) from the Eclipse foundation homepage:

```
www.eclipse.org/downloads/
```

There are many variations available when selecting your Eclipse download; the following is the recommended configuration for Android:

❑ Eclipse 3.3, 3.4 (Ganymede)

    ❑ Eclipse JDT plug-in

    ❑ WST

WST and the JDT plug-in are included in most Eclipse IDE packages.

Installing Eclipse consists of uncompressing the download into a new folder. When that's done, run the `Eclipse` executable. When it starts for the first time, create a new workspace for your Android development.

Using the Eclipse Plug-in

The ADT plug-in for Eclipse simplifies your Android development by integrating the developer tools, including the emulator and .class-to-.dex converter, directly into the IDE. While you don't have to use the ADT plug-in, it does make creating, testing, and debugging your applications faster and easier.

The ADT plug-in integrates the following into Eclipse:

❑ An Android Project Wizard that simplifies creating new projects and includes a basic application template

❑ Forms-based manifest, layout, and resource editors to help create, edit, and validate your XML resources

❑ Automated building of Android projects, conversion to Android executables (.dex), packaging to package files (.apk), and installation of packages onto Dalvik virtual machines

❑ The Android Emulator, including control of the emulator's appearance, network connection settings, and the ability to simulate incoming calls and SMS messages

❑ The Dalvik Debug Monitoring Service (DDMS), which includes port forwarding; stack, heap, and thread viewing; process details; and screen capture facilities

❑ Access to the device or emulator's filesystem, allowing you to navigate the folder tree and transfer files

❑ Runtime debugging, so you can set breakpoints and view call stacks

❑ All Android/Dalvik log and console outputs

Figure 2-1 shows the DDMS perspective within Eclipse with the ADT plug-in installed.

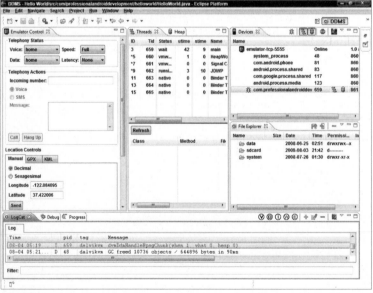

Figure 2-1

Installing the ADT Plug-in

Install the developer tools plug-in by the following steps:

1. Select **Help** ➪ **Software Updates** ➪ **Find and Install** … from within Eclipse.

2. In the resulting dialog box, choose **Search for new features to install**.

3. Select **New Remote Site**, and enter the following address into the dialog box, as shown in Figure 2-2:

```
https://dl-ssl.google.com/android/eclipse/
```

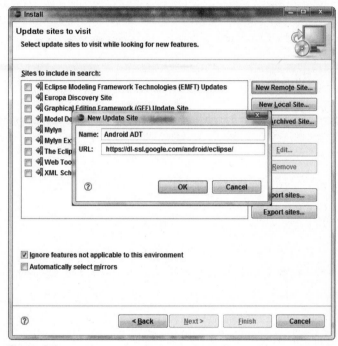

Figure 2-2

4. The new site you entered should now be checked. Click **Finish**.

5. Eclipse will now download the plug-in. When it's finished, select Android **Plugin** ➪ **Developer Tools** from the resulting Search Results dialog box, and click **Next**.

6. Read and then **Accept** the terms of the license agreement, and click **Next** and then **Finish**. As the ADT plug-in is not signed, you'll be prompted before the installation continues.

7. When complete, you'll have to restart Eclipse and update the ADT preferences. Restart and select **Window** ➪ **Preferences** … (or **Eclipse** ➪ **Preferences** for the Mac OS).

8. Then select **Android** from the left panel.

9. Click **Browse** …, and navigate to the folder into which you unzipped the Android SDK, as shown in Figure 2-3; then click **Apply** and **OK**.

Figure 2-3

If you download a new version of the SDK and place it in a different location, you will need to update this preference to reflect the SDK with which the ADT should be building.

Updating the Plug-in

As the Android SDK matures, there are likely to be frequent updates to the ADT plug-in. In most cases, to update your plug-in, you simply:

1. Navigate to **Help** ➪ **Software Updates** ➪ **Find and Install** …

2. Select **Search for updates of the currently installed features**, and click **Finish** …

3. If there are any ADT updates available, they will be presented. Simply select them and choose **Install**.

Sometimes a plug-in upgrade is so significant that the dynamic update mechanism can't be used. In those cases, you may have to remove the previous plug-in completely before installing the newer version as described in the previous section.

Creating Your First Android Activity

You've downloaded the SDK, installed Eclipse, and plugged in the plug-in. You're now ready to start programming for Android. Start by creating a new project and setting up your Eclipse run and debug configurations.

Starting a New Android Project

To create a new Android project using the Android New Project Wizard:

1. Select **File** ➪ **New** ➪ **Project**.

2. Select the **Android Project** application type from the Android folder, and click **Finish**.

3. In the dialog that appears (shown in Figure 2-4), enter the details for your new project. The "Project name" is the name of your project file; the "Package name" specifies its package; the "Activity name" is the name of the class that is your initial Activity; and the "Application name" is the friendly name for your application.

Figure 2-4

4. When you've entered the details, click **Finish**.

The ADT plug-in then creates a new project that includes a new class that extends `Activity`. Rather than being completely empty, the default template implements "Hello World." Before modifying the project, take this opportunity to configure run and debug launch configurations.

Creating a Launch Configuration

Launch configurations let you specify runtime options for running and debugging applications. Using a launch configuration you can specify the following:

❑   The Project and Activity to launch

❑   The emulator options to use

❑   Input/output settings (including console defaults)

You can specify different launch configurations for Run and Debug modes. The following steps show how to create a launch configuration for an Android application:

1. Select **Run ⇨ Open Run Dialog** ... (or **Run ⇨ Open Debug Dialog** ...).

2. Right-click **Android Application** on the project type list, and select **New**.

3. Enter a name for the configuration. You can create multiple configurations for each project, so create a descriptive title that will help you identify this particular setup.

4. Now choose your start-up options. The first (**Android**) tab lets you select the project and Activity that you want to start when you run (or debug) the application. Figure 2-5 shows the settings for the project you created earlier.

Figure 2-5

5. Use the **Target** tab to configure the emulator. There are options to choose the screen size, device skin, and network connection settings. You can also optionally wipe the user data on the emulator and enable or disable the start-up animation. Using the command-line textbox, you can specify additional emulator start-up options if needed.

6. Finally, set any additional properties in the **Common** tab.

7. Click **Apply**, and your launch configuration will be saved.

Running and Debugging Your Android Applications

You've created your first project and created the run and debug configurations for it. Before making any changes, test your installation and configurations by running and debugging the Hello World project.

From the **Run** menu, select **Run** or **Debug** to launch the most recently selected configuration, or select **Open Run Dialog** … or **Open Debug Dialog** … to select a configuration to use.

If you're using the ADT plug-in, running or debugging your application:

❑ Compiles the current project and converts it to an Android executable (.dex).

❑ Packages the executable and external resources into an Android package (.apk).

❑ Starts the emulator (if it's not already running).

❑ Installs your application onto the emulator.

❑ Starts your application.

If you're debugging, the Eclipse debugger will then be attached, allowing you to set breakpoints and debug your code.

If everything is working correctly, you'll see a new Activity running in the emulator, as shown in Figure 2-6.

Figure 2-6

Understanding Hello World

With that confirmed, let's take a step back and have a real look at your first Android application.

`Activity` is the base class for the visual, interactive components of your application; it is roughly equivalent to a Form in traditional desktop development. The following snippet shows the skeleton code for an Activity-based class; note that it extends `Activity`, overriding the `onCreate` method.

```
package com.paad.helloworld;

import android.app.Activity;
import android.os.Bundle;

public class HelloWorld extends Activity {

  /** Called when the activity is first created. */
  @Override
  public void onCreate(Bundle icicle) {
    super.onCreate(icicle);
  }
}
```

What's missing from this template is the layout of the visual interface. In Android, visual components are called *Views*, which are similar to controls in traditional desktop development.

In the Hello World template created by the wizard, the `onCreate` method is overridden to call `setContentView`, which lays out the user interface by inflating a layout resource, as highlighted below:

```
@Override
public void onCreate(Bundle icicle) {
  super.onCreate(icicle);
  setContentView(R.layout.main);
}
```

The resources for an Android project are stored in the `res` folder of your project hierarchy, which includes `drawable`, `layout`, and `values` subfolders. The ADT plug-in interprets these XML resources to provide design time access to them through the `R` variable as described in Chapter 3.

The following code snippet shows the UI layout defined in the `main.xml` file created by the Android project template:

```
<?xml version="1.0" encoding="utf-8"?>
<LinearLayout xmlns:android="http://schemas.android.com/apk/res/android"
  android:orientation="vertical"
  android:layout_width="fill_parent"
  android:layout_height="fill_parent">
  <TextView
    android:layout_width="fill_parent"
    android:layout_height="wrap_content"
    android:text="Hello World, HelloWorld"
  />
</LinearLayout>
```

Defining your UI in XML and inflating it is the preferred way of implementing your user interfaces, as it neatly decouples your application logic from your UI design.

To get access to your UI elements in code, you add identifier attributes to them in the XML definition. You can then use the `findViewById` method to return a reference to each named item. The following XML snippet shows an ID attribute added to the TextView widget in the Hello World template:

```
<TextView
  android:id="@+id/myTextView"
  android:layout_width="fill_parent"
  android:layout_height="wrap_content"
  android:text="Hello World, HelloWorld"
/>
```

And the following snippet shows how to get access to it in code:

```
TextView myTextView = (TextView)findViewById(R.id.myTextView);
```

Alternatively (although it's not considered good practice), if you need to, you can create your layout directly in code as shown below:

```
public void onCreate(Bundle icicle) {
  super.onCreate(icicle);

  LinearLayout.LayoutParams lp;
```

```
    lp = new LinearLayout.LayoutParams(LayoutParams.FILL_PARENT,
                                   LayoutParams.FILL_PARENT);

    LinearLayout.LayoutParams textViewLP;
    textViewLP = new LinearLayout.LayoutParams(LayoutParams.FILL_PARENT,
                                   LayoutParams.WRAP_CONTENT);

    LinearLayout ll = new LinearLayout(this);
    ll.setOrientation(LinearLayout.VERTICAL);
    TextView myTextView = new TextView(this);
    myTextView.setText("Hello World, HelloWorld");
    ll.addView(myTextView, textViewLP);
    this.addContentView(ll, lp);
}
```

All the properties available in code can be set with attributes in the XML layout. As well as allowing easier substitution of layout designs and individual UI elements, keeping the visual design decoupled from the application code helps keep the code more concise.

> *The Android web site (*http://code.google.com/android/documentation.html*) includes several excellent step-by-step guides that demonstrate many of the features and good practices you will be using as an Android developer. They're easy to follow and give a good idea of how Android applications fit together.*

Types of Android Applications

Most of the applications you create in Android will fall into one of the following categories:

- ❑ **Foreground Activity**   An application that's only useful when it's in the foreground and is effectively suspended when it's not visible. Games and map mashups are common examples.

- ❑ **Background Service**   An application with limited interaction that, apart from when being configured, spends most of its lifetime hidden. Examples of this include call screening applications or SMS auto-responders.

- ❑ **Intermittent Activity**   Expects some interactivity but does most of its work in the background. Often these applications will be set up and then run silently, notifying users when appropriate. A common example would be a media player.

Complex applications are difficult to pigeonhole into a single category and include elements of all three. When creating your application, you need to consider how it's likely to be used and then design it accordingly. Let's look more closely at some of the design considerations for each application type described above.

Foreground Activities

When creating foreground applications, you need to consider the Activity life cycle (described in Chapter 3) carefully so that the Activity switches seamlessly between the foreground and the background.

Applications have no control over their life cycles, and a backgrounded application, with no Services, is a prime candidate for cleanup by Android's resource management. This means that you need to save the state of the application when the Activity becomes invisible, and present the exact same state when it returns to the foreground.

It's also particularly important for foreground Activities to present a slick and intuitive user experience.

You'll learn more about creating well-behaved and attractive foreground Activities in Chapter 3.

Background Services

These applications run silently in the background with very little user input. They often listen for messages or actions caused by the hardware, system, or other applications, rather than rely on user interaction.

It's possible to create completely invisible services, but in practice, it's better form to provide at least some sort of user control. At a minimum, you should let users confirm that the service is running and let them configure, pause, or terminate it as needed.

Services, the powerhouse of background applications, are covered in depth in Chapter 8.

Intermittent Activities

Often you'll want to create an application that reacts to user input but is still useful when it's not the active foreground Activity. These applications are generally a union of a visible controller Activity with an invisible background Service.

These applications need to be aware of their state when interacting with the user. This might mean updating the Activity UI when it's visible and sending notifications to keep the user updated when it's in the background, as seen in the section on Notifications and Services in Chapter 8.

Developing for Mobile Devices

Android does a lot to simplify mobile-device software development, but it's still important to understand the reasons behind the conventions. There are several factors to account for when writing software for mobile and embedded devices, and when developing for Android, in particular.

> *In this chapter, you'll learn some of the techniques and best practices for writing efficient Android code. In later examples, efficiency is sometimes compromised for clarity and brevity when introducing new Android concepts or functionality. In the best traditions of "Do as I say, not as I do," the examples you'll see are designed to show the simplest (or easiest-to-understand) way of doing something, not necessarily the best way of doing it.*

Hardware-Imposed Design Considerations

Small and portable, mobile devices offer exciting opportunities for software development. Their limited screen size and reduced memory, storage, and processor power are far less exciting, and instead present some unique challenges.

Compared to desktop or notebook computers, mobile devices have relatively:

- ❑ Low processing power
- ❑ Limited RAM
- ❑ Limited permanent storage capacity

- ❑ Small screens with low resolution
- ❑ Higher costs associated with data transfer
- ❑ Slower data transfer rates with higher latency
- ❑ Less reliable data connections
- ❑ Limited battery life

It's important to keep these restrictions in mind when creating new applications.

Be Efficient

Manufacturers of embedded devices, particularly *mobile* devices, value small size and long battery life over potential improvements in processor speed. For developers, that means losing the head start traditionally afforded thanks to Moore's law. The yearly performance improvements you'll see in desktop and server hardware usually translate into smaller, more power-efficient mobiles without much improvement in processor power.

In practice, this means that you always need to optimize your code so that it runs quickly and responsively, assuming that hardware improvements over the lifetime of your software are unlikely to do you any favors.

Since code efficiency is a big topic in software engineering, I'm not going to try and capture it here. This chapter covers some Android-specific efficiency tips below, but for now, just note that efficiency is particularly important for resource-constrained environments like mobile devices.

Expect Limited Capacity

Advances in flash memory and solid-state disks have led to a dramatic increase in mobile-device storage capacities (although people's MP3 collections tend to expand to fill the available space). In practice, most devices still offer relatively limited storage space for your applications. While the compiled size of your application is a consideration, more important is ensuring that your application is polite in its use of system resources.

You should carefully consider how you store your application data. To make life easier, you can use the Android databases and Content Providers to persist, reuse, and share large quantities of data, as described in Chapter 6. For smaller data storage, such as preferences or state settings, Android provides an optimized framework, as described in Chapter 6.

Of course, these mechanisms won't stop you from writing directly to the filesystem when you want or need to, but in those circumstances, always consider how you're structuring these files, and ensure that yours is an efficient solution.

Part of being polite is cleaning up after yourself. Techniques like caching are useful for limiting repetitive network lookups, but don't leave files on the filesystem or records in a database when they're no longer needed.

Design for Small Screens

The small size and portability of mobiles are a challenge for creating good interfaces, particularly when users are demanding an increasingly striking and information-rich graphical user experience.

Write your applications knowing that users will often only glance at the (small) screen. Make your applications intuitive and easy to use by reducing the number of controls and putting the most important information front and center.

Graphical controls, like the ones you'll create in Chapter 4, are an excellent way to convey dense information in an easy-to-understand way. Rather than a screen full of text with lots of buttons and text entry boxes, use colors, shapes, and graphics to display information.

If you're planning to include touch-screen support (and if you're not, you should be), you'll need to consider how touch input is going to affect your interface design. The time of the stylus has passed; now it's all about finger input, so make sure your Views are big enough to support interaction using a finger on the screen. There's more information on touch-screen interaction in Chapter 11.

Of course, mobile-phone resolutions and screen sizes are increasing, so it's smart to design for small screens, but also make sure your UIs scale.

Expect Low Speeds, High Latency

In Chapter 5, you'll learn how to use Internet resources in your applications. The ability to incorporate some of the wealth of online information in your applications is incredibly powerful.

The mobile Web unfortunately isn't as fast, reliable, or readily available as we'd often like, so when you're developing your Internet-based applications, it's best to assume that the network connection will be slow, intermittent, and expensive. With unlimited 3G data plans and city-wide Wi-Fi, this is changing, but designing for the worst case ensures that you always deliver a high-standard user experience.

This also means making sure that your applications can handle losing (or not finding) a data connection.

The Android Emulator lets you control the speed and latency of your network connection when setting up an Eclipse launch configuration. Figure 2-7 shows the emulator's network connection speed and latency set up to simulate a distinctly suboptimal EDGE connection.

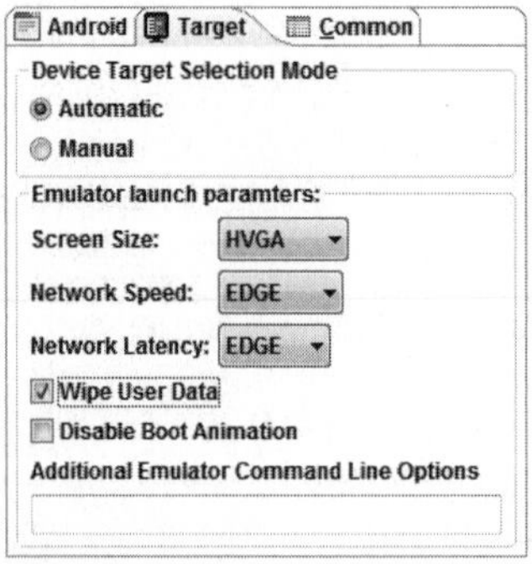

Figure 2-7

Experiment to ensure responsiveness no matter what the speed, latency, and availability of network access. You might find that in some circumstances, it's better to limit the functionality of your application or reduce network lookups to cached bursts, based on the network connection(s) available. Details on how to detect the kind of network connections available at run time, and their speeds, are included in Chapter 10.

At What Cost?

If you're a mobile owner, you know all too well that some of the more powerful features on your mobile can literally come at a price. Services like SMS, GPS, and data transfer often incur an additional tariff from your service provider.

It's obvious why it's important that any costs associated with functionality in your applications are minimized, and that users are aware when an action they perform might result in them being charged.

It's a good approach to assume that there's a cost associated with any action involving an interaction with the outside world. Minimize interaction costs by the following:

❑   Transferring as little data as possible

❑   Caching data and GPS results to eliminate redundant or repetitive lookups

❑   Stopping all data transfers and GPS updates when your activity is not visible in the foreground if they're only being used to update the UI

❑   Keeping the refresh/update rates for data transfers (and location lookups) as low as practicable

❑   Scheduling big updates or transfers at "off peak" times using alarms as shown in Chapter 8

Often the best solution is to use a lower-quality option that comes at a lower cost.

When using the location-based services described in Chapter 7, you can select a location provider based on whether there is an associated cost. Within your location-based applications, consider giving users the choice of lower cost or greater accuracy.

In some circumstances, costs are hard to define, or they're different for different users. Charges for services vary between service providers and user plans. While some people will have free unlimited data transfers, others will have free SMS.

Rather than enforcing a particular technique based on which seems cheaper, consider letting your users choose. For example, when downloading data from the Internet, you could ask users if they want to use any network available or limit their transfers to only when they're connected via Wi-Fi.

Considering the Users' Environment

You can't assume that your users will think of your application as the most important feature of their phones.

Generally, a mobile is first and foremost a phone, secondly an SMS and e-mail communicator, thirdly a camera, and fourthly an MP3 player. The applications you write will most likely be in a fifth category of "useful mobile tools."

That's not a bad thing — it's in good company with others including Google Maps and the web browser. That said, each user's usage model will be different; some people will never use their mobiles to listen to music, and some phones don't include a camera, but the multitasking principle inherent in a device as ubiquitous as it is indispensable is an important consideration for usability design.

It's also important to consider when and how your users will use your applications. People use their mobiles all the time — on the train, walking down the street, or even while driving their cars. You can't make people use their phones appropriately, but you can make sure that your applications don't distract them any more than necessary.

What does this mean in terms of software design? Make sure that your application:

❑ **Is well behaved** Start by ensuring that your Activities suspend when they're not in the foreground. Android triggers event handlers when your Activity is suspended or resumed so you can pause UI updates and network lookups when your application isn't visible — there's no point updating your UI if no one can see it. If you need to continue updating or processing in the background, Android provides a Service class designed to run in the background without the UI overheads.

❑ **Switches seamlessly from the background to the foreground** With the multitasking nature of mobile devices, it's very likely that your applications will regularly switch into and out of the background. When this happens, it's important that they "come to life" quickly and seamlessly. Android's nondeterministic process management means that if your application is in the background, there's every chance it will get killed to free up resources. This should be invisible to the user. You can ensure this by saving the application state and queuing updates so that your users don't notice a difference between restarting and resuming your application. Switching back to it should be seamless with users being shown the exact UI and application state they last saw.

❑ **Is polite** Your application should never steal focus or interrupt a user's current activity. Use Notifications and Toasts (detailed in Chapter 8) instead to inform or remind users that their attention is requested if your application isn't in the foreground. There are several ways for mobile devices to alert users. For example, when a call is coming in, your phone rings; when you have unread messages, the LED flashes; and when you have new voice mail, a small "mail" icon appears in your status bar. All these techniques and more are available through the notification mechanism.

❑ **Presents a consistent user interface** Your application is likely to be one of several in use at any time, so it's important that the UI you present is easy to use. Don't force users to interpret and relearn your application every time they load it. Using it should be simple, easy, and obvious — particularly given the limited screen space and distracting user environment.

❑ **Is responsive** Responsiveness is one of the most important design considerations on a mobile device. You've no doubt experienced the frustration of a "frozen" piece of software; the multifunction nature of a mobile makes it even more annoying. With possible delays due to slow and unreliable data connections, it's important that your application use worker threads and background services to keep your activities responsive and, more importantly, stop them from preventing other applications from responding in a timely manner.

Developing for Android

Nothing covered so far is specific to Android; the design considerations above are just as important when developing applications for any mobile. In addition to these general guidelines, Android has some particular considerations.

To start with, it's worth taking a few minutes to read Google's Android design philosophy at `http://code.google.com/android/toolbox/philosophy.html`.

The Android design philosophy demands that applications be:

- ❑ Fast
- ❑ Responsive
- ❑ Secure
- ❑ Seamless

Being Fast and Efficient

In a resource-constrained environment, being fast means being efficient. A lot of what you already know about writing efficient code will be just as effective in Android, but the limitations of embedded systems and the use of the Dalvik VM mean you can't take things for granted.

The smart bet for advice is to go to the source. The Android team has published some specific guidance on writing efficient code for Android, so rather than rehash their advice, I suggest you visit `http://code.google.com/android/toolbox/performance.html` and take note of their suggestions.

> *You may find that some of these performance suggestions contradict established design practices — for example, avoiding the use of internal setters and getters or preferring virtual over interface. When writing software for resource-constrained systems like embedded devices, there's often a compromise between conventional design principles and the demand for greater efficiency.*

One of the keys to writing efficient Android code is to not carry over assumptions from desktop and server environments to embedded devices.

At a time when 2 to 4 GB of memory is standard for most desktop and server rigs, even advanced smartphones are lucky to feature 32 MB of RAM. With memory such a scarce commodity, you need to take special care to use it efficiently. This means thinking about how you use the stack and heap, limiting object creation, and being aware of how variable scope affects memory use.

Being Responsive

Android takes responsiveness very seriously.

Android enforces responsiveness with the Activity Manager and Window Manager. If either service detects an unresponsive application, it will display the unambiguous Application unresponsive (AUR) message, as shown in Figure 2-8.

This alert is modal, steals focus, and won't go away until you hit a button or your application starts responding — it's pretty much the last thing you ever want to confront a user with.

Android monitors two conditions to determine responsiveness:

- ❑ An application must respond to any user action, such as a key press or screen touch, within 5 seconds.
- ❑ A Broadcast Receiver must return from its `onReceive` handler within 10 seconds.

Figure 2-8

The most likely culprits for causing unresponsiveness are network lookups, complex processing (such as calculating game moves), and file I/O. There are a number of ways to ensure that these actions don't exceed the responsiveness conditions, in particular, using services and worker threads, as shown in Chapter 8.

> *The AUR dialog is a last resort of usability; the generous 5-second limit is a worst-case scenario, not a benchmark to aim for. Users will notice a regular pause of anything more than half a second between key press and action. Happily, a side effect of the efficient code you're already writing will be faster, more responsive applications.*

Developing Secure Applications

Android applications have direct hardware access, can be distributed independently, and are built on an open source platform featuring open communication, so it's not particularly surprising that security is a big concern.

For the most part, users will take responsibility for what applications they install and what permissions they grant them. The Android security model restricts access to certain services and functionality by forcing applications to request permission before using them. During installation, users then decide if the application should be granted the permissions requested. You can learn more about Android's security model in Chapter 11 and at `http://code.google.com/android/devel/security.html`.

This doesn't get you off the hook. You not only need to make sure your application is secure for its own sake, but you also need to ensure that it can't be hijacked to compromise the device. You can use several techniques to help maintain device security, and they'll be covered in more detail as you learn the technologies involved. In particular, you should:

❏ Consider requiring permissions for any services you create or broadcasts you transmit.

❏ Take special care when accepting input to your application from external sources such as the Internet, SMS messages, or instant messaging (IM). You can find out more about using IM and SMS for application messaging in Chapter 9.

❏ Be cautious when your application may expose access to lower-level hardware.

> *For reasons of clarity and simplicity, many of the examples in this book take a fairly relaxed approach to security. When creating your own applications, particularly ones you plan to distribute, this is an area that should not be overlooked. You can find out more about Android security in Chapter 11.*

Ensuring a Seamless User Experience

The idea of a seamless user experience is an important, if somewhat nebulous, concept. What do we mean by *seamless*? The goal is a consistent user experience where applications start, stop, and transition instantly and without noticeable delays or jarring transitions.

The speed and responsiveness of a mobile device shouldn't degrade the longer it's on. Android's process management helps by acting as a silent assassin, killing background applications to free resources as required. Knowing this, your applications should always present a consistent interface, regardless of whether they're being restarted or resumed.

With an Android device typically running several third-party applications written by different developers, it's particularly important that these applications interact seamlessly.

Use a consistent and intuitive approach to usability. You can still create applications that are revolutionary and unfamiliar, but even they should integrate cleanly with the wider Android environment.

Persist data between sessions, and suspend tasks that use processor cycles, network bandwidth, or battery life when the application isn't visible. If your application has processes that need to continue running while your activity is out of sight, use a Service, but hide these implementation decisions from your users.

When your application is brought back to the front, or restarted, it should seamlessly return to its last visible state. As far as your users are concerned, each application should be sitting silently ready to be used but just out of sight.

You should also follow the best-practice guidelines for using Notifications and use generic UI elements and themes to maintain consistency between applications.

There are many other techniques you can use to ensure a seamless user experience, and you'll be introduced to some of them as you discover more of the possibilities available in Android in the coming chapters.

To-Do List Example

In this example, you'll be creating a new Android application from scratch. This simple example creates a new to-do list application using native Android View controls. It's designed to illustrate the basic steps involved in starting a new project.

> *Don't worry if you don't understand everything that happens in this example. Some of the features used to create this application, including ArrayAdapters, ListViews, and KeyListeners, won't be introduced properly until later chapters, where they're explained in detail. You'll also return to this example later to add new functionality as you learn more about Android.*

1. Start by creating a new Android project. Within Eclipse, select **File ➪ New ➪ Project** …, then choose **Android** (as shown in Figure 2-9) before clicking **Next**.

Figure 2-9

2.   In the dialog box that appears (shown in Figure 2-10), enter the details for your new project. The "Application name" is the friendly name of your application, and the "Activity name" is the name of your Activity subclass. With the details entered, click **Finish** to create your new project.

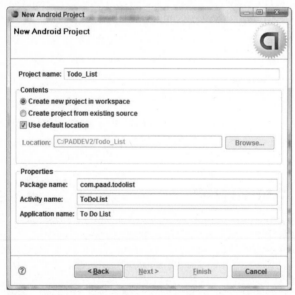

Figure 2-10

3.   Take this opportunity to set up debug and run configurations by selecting **Run ⇨ Open Debug Dialog** … and then **Run ⇨ Open Run Dialog** …, creating a new configuration for each, specifying the Todo_List project. You can leave the launch actions as **Launch Default Activity** or explicitly set them to launch the new ToDoList Activity, as shown in Figure 2-11.

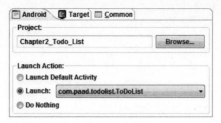

Figure 2-11

4. Now decide what you want to show the users and what actions they'll need to perform. Design a user interface that will make this as intuitive as possible.

In this example, we want to present users with a list of to-do items and a text entry box to add new ones. There's both a list and a text entry control (View) available from the Android libraries. You'll learn more about the Views available in Android and how to create new ones in Chapter 4.

The preferred method for laying out your UI is using a layout resource file. Open the main.xml layout file in the res/layout project folder, as shown in Figure 2-12.

Figure 2-12

5. Modify the main layout to include a `ListView` and an `EditText` within a `LinearLayout`. It's important to give both the `EditText` and `ListView` controls IDs so you can get references to them in code.

```
<?xml version="1.0" encoding="utf-8"?>
<LinearLayout xmlns:android="http://schemas.android.com/apk/res/android"
  android:orientation="vertical"
  android:layout_width="fill_parent"
  android:layout_height="fill_parent">
  <EditText
    android:id="@+id/myEditText"
    android:layout_width="fill_parent"
    android:layout_height="wrap_content"
    android:text="New To Do Item"
  />
  <ListView
```

```
            android:id="@+id/myListView"
            android:layout_width="fill_parent"
            android:layout_height="wrap_content"
        />
    </LinearLayout>
```

6. With your user interface defined, open the `ToDoList.java` Activity class from your project's source folder. In this example, you'll make all your changes by overriding the `onCreate` method. Start by inflating your UI using `setContentView` and then get references to the `ListView` and `EditText` using `findViewById`.

```
public void onCreate(Bundle icicle) {
    // Inflate your view
    setContentView(R.layout.main);

    // Get references to UI widgets
    ListView myListView = (ListView)findViewById(R.id.myListView);
    final EditText myEditText = (EditText)findViewById(R.id.myEditText);
}
```

7. Still within `onCreate`, define an `ArrayList` of Strings to store each to-do list item. You can bind a `ListView` to an `ArrayList` using an `ArrayAdapter`, so create a new `ArrayAdapter` instance to bind the to-do item array to the `ListView`. We'll return to `ArrayAdapters` in Chapter 5.

```
public void onCreate(Bundle icicle) {
    setContentView(R.layout.main);

    ListView myListView = (ListView)findViewById(R.id.myListView);
    final EditText myEditText = (EditText)findViewById(R.id.myEditText);

    // Create the array list of to do items
    final ArrayList<String> todoItems = new ArrayList<String>();
    // Create the array adapter to bind the array to the listview
    final ArrayAdapter<String> aa;
    aa = new ArrayAdapter<String>(this,
                                  android.R.layout.simple_list_item_1,
                                  todoItems);
    // Bind the array adapter to the listview.
    myListView.setAdapter(aa);
}
```

8. The final step to make this to-do list functional is to let users add new to-do items. Add an `onKeyListener` to the `EditText` that listens for a "D-pad center button" click before adding the contents of the `EditText` to the to-do list array and notifying the `ArrayAdapter` of the change. Then clear the `EditText` to prepare for another item.

```
public void onCreate(Bundle icicle) {
    setContentView(R.layout.main);

    ListView myListView = (ListView)findViewById(R.id.myListView);
    final EditText myEditText = (EditText)findViewById(R.id.myEditText);

    final ArrayList<String> todoItems = new ArrayList<String>();
    final ArrayAdapter<String> aa;
    aa = new ArrayAdapter<String>(this,
```

```
                                      android.R.layout.simple_list_item_1,
                                      todoItems);
          myListView.setAdapter(aa);
```

```
          myEditText.setOnKeyListener(new OnKeyListener() {
            public boolean onKey(View v, int keyCode, KeyEvent event) {
              if (event.getAction() == KeyEvent.ACTION_DOWN)
                if (keyCode == KeyEvent.KEYCODE_DPAD_CENTER)
                {
                  todoItems.add(0, myEditText.getText().toString());
                  aa.notifyDataSetChanged();
                  myEditText.setText("");
                  return true;
                }
              return false;
            }
          });
        }
```

9. Run or debug the application, and you'll see a text entry box above a list, as shown in Figure 2-13.

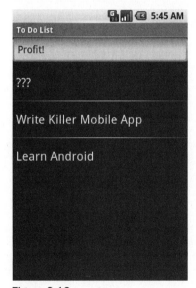

Figure 2-13

10. You've now finished your first "real" Android application. Try adding breakpoints to the code to test the debugger and experiment with the DDMS perspective.

As it stands, this to-do list application isn't spectacularly useful. It doesn't save to-do list items between sessions, you can't edit or remove an item from the list, and typical task list items like due dates and task priority aren't recorded or displayed. On balance, it fails most of the criteria laid out so far for a good mobile application design.

You'll rectify some of these deficiencies when you return to this example in later chapters.

Android Development Tools

The Android SDK includes several tools and utilities to help you create, test, and debug your projects. A detailed examination of each developer tool is outside the scope of this book, but it's worth briefly reviewing what's available. For more detail than is included here, check out the Android documentation at:

```
http://code.google.com/android/intro/tools.html
```

As mentioned earlier, the ADT plug-in conveniently incorporates most of these tools into the Eclipse IDE, where you can access them from the DDMS perspective, including:

- ❑ **The Android Emulator** An implementation of the Android virtual machine designed to run on your development computer. You can use the emulator to test and debug your android applications.

- ❑ **Dalvik Debug Monitoring Service (DDMS)** Use the DDMS perspective to monitor and control the Dalvik virtual machines on which you're debugging your applications.

- ❑ **Android Asset Packaging Tool (AAPT)** Constructs the distributable Android package files (.apk).

- ❑ **Android Debug Bridge (ADB)** The *ADB* is a client-server application that provides a link to a running emulator. It lets you copy files, install compiled application packages (.apk), and run shell commands.

The following additional tools are also available:

- ❑ **SQLite3** A database tool that you can use to access the SQLite database files created and used by Android

- ❑ **Traceview** Graphical analysis tool for viewing the trace logs from your Android application

- ❑ **MkSDCard** Creates an SDCard disk image that can be used by the emulator to simulate an external storage card.

- ❑ **dx** Converts Java `.class` bytecode into Android `.dex` bytecode.

- ❑ **activityCreator** Script that builds Ant build files that you can then use to compile your Android applications without the ADT plug-in

Let's take a look at some of the more important tools in more detail.

The Android Emulator

The emulator is the perfect tool for testing and debugging your applications, particularly if you don't have a real device (or don't want to risk it) for experimentation.

The emulator is an implementation of the Dalvik virtual machine, making it as valid a platform for running Android applications as any Android phone. Because it's decoupled from any particular hardware, it's an excellent baseline to use for testing your applications.

A number of alternative user interfaces are available to represent different hardware configurations, each with different screen sizes, resolutions, orientations, and hardware features to simulate a variety of mobile device types.

Full network connectivity is provided along with the ability to tweak the Internet connection speed and latency while debugging your applications. You can also simulate placing and receiving voice calls and SMS messages.

The ADT plug-in integrates the emulator into Eclipse so that it's launched automatically when you run or debug your projects. If you aren't using the plug-in or want to use the emulator outside of Eclipse, you can telnet into the emulator and control it from its console. For more details on controlling the emulator, check the documentation at http://code.google.com/android/reference/emulator.html.

> At this stage, the emulator doesn't implement all the mobile hardware features supported by Android, including the camera, vibration, LEDs, actual phone calls, the accelerometer, USB connections, Bluetooth, audio capture, battery charge level, and SD card insertion/ejection.

Dalvik Debug Monitor Service (DDMS)

The emulator lets you see how your application will look, behave, and interact, but to really see what's happening under the surface, you need the DDMS. The Dalvik Debug Monitoring Service is a powerful debugging tool that lets you interrogate active processes, view the stack and heap, watch and pause active threads, and explore the filesystem of any active emulator.

The DDMS perspective in Eclipse also provides simplified access to screen captures of the emulator and the logs generated by LogCat.

If you're using the ADT plug-in, the DDMS is fully integrated into Eclipse and is available from the DDMS perspective. If you aren't using the plug-in or Eclipse, you can run DDMS from the command line, and it will automatically connect to any emulator that's running.

The Android Debug Bridge (ADB)

The *Android debug bridge (ADB)* is a client-service application that lets you connect with an Android Emulator or device. It's made up of three components: a daemon running on the emulator, a service that runs on your development hardware, and client applications (like the DDMS) that communicate with the daemon through the service.

As a communications conduit between your development hardware and the Android device/emulator, the ADB lets you install applications, push and pull files, and run shell commands on the target device. Using the device shell, you can change logging settings, and query or modify SQLite databases available on the device.

The ADT tool automates and simplifies a lot of the usual interaction with the ADB, including application installation and update, log files, and file transfer (through the DDMS perspective).

To learn more about what you can do with the ADB, check out the documentation at http://code.google.com/android/reference/adb.html.

Summary

This chapter showed you how to download and install the Android SDK; create a development environment using Eclipse on Windows, Mac OS, or Linux platforms; and how to create run and debug configurations for your projects. You learned how to install and use the ADT plug-in to simplify creating new projects and streamline your development cycle.

You were introduced to some of the design considerations for developing mobile applications, particularly the importance of optimizing for speed and efficiency when increasing battery life and shrinking sizes are higher priorities than increasing processor power.

As with any mobile development, there are considerations when designing for small screens and mobile data connections that can be slow, costly, and unreliable.

After creating an Android to-do list application, you were introduced to the Android Emulator and the developer tools you'll use to test and debug your applications.

Specifically in this chapter, you:

❑ Downloaded and installed the Android SDK.

❑ Set up a development environment in Eclipse and downloaded and installed the ADT plug-in.

❑ Created your first application and learned how it works.

❑ Set up run and debug launch configurations for your projects.

❑ Learned about the different types of Android applications.

❑ Were introduced to some mobile-device design considerations and learned some specific Android design practices.

❑ Created a to-do list application.

❑ Were introduced to the Android Emulator and the developer tools.

The next chapter focuses on Activities and application design. You'll see how to define application settings using the Android manifest and how to externalize your UI layouts and application resources. You'll also find out more about the Android application life cycle and Android application states.

3

Creating Applications and Activities

Before you start writing Android applications, it's important to understand how they're constructed and have an understanding of the Android application life cycle. In this chapter, you'll be introduced to the loosely coupled components that make up Android applications (and how they're bound together using the Android manifest). Next you'll see how and why you should use external resources, before getting an introduction to the Activity component.

In recent years, there's been a move toward development frameworks featuring managed code, such as the Java virtual machine and the .NET Common Language Runtime.

In Chapter 1, you learned that Android uses this model, with each application running in a separate process with its own instance of the Dalvik virtual machine. In this chapter, you'll learn more about the application life cycle and how it's managed by the Android run time. This will lead to an introduction of the process states that represent the application priority, which, in turn, determines the likelihood of an application's being terminated when more resources are required.

Mobile devices now come in many shapes and sizes and are used internationally. In this chapter, you'll learn how to give your applications the flexibility to run seamlessly on different hardware, in different countries, and using multiple languages by externalizing resources.

Next you'll examine the Activity component. Arguably the most important of the Android building blocks, the `Activity` class forms the basis for all your user interface screens. You'll learn how to create new Activities and gain an understanding of their life cycles and how they affect the application lifetime.

Finally, you'll be introduced to some of the Activity subclasses that wrap up resource management for some common user interface components such as maps and lists.

What Makes an Android Application?

Android applications consist of loosely coupled components, bound using a project manifest that describes each component and how they interact.

There are six components that provide the building blocks for your applications:

❑ **Activities**   Your application's presentation layer. Every screen in your application will be an extension of the `Activity` class. Activities use Views to form graphical user interfaces that display information and respond to user actions. In terms of desktop development, an Activity is equivalent to a Form. You'll learn more about Activities later in this chapter.

❑ **Services**   The invisible workers of your application. Service components run invisibly, updating your data sources and visible Activities and triggering Notifications. They're used to perform regular processing that needs to continue even when your application's Activities aren't active or visible. You'll learn how to create Services in Chapter 8.

❑ **Content Providers**   A shareable data store. Content Providers are used to manage and share application databases. Content Providers are the preferred way of sharing data across application boundaries. This means that you can configure your own Content Providers to permit access from other applications and use Content Providers exposed by others to access their stored data. Android devices include several native Content Providers that expose useful databases like contact information. You'll learn how to create and use Content Providers in Chapter 6.

❑ **Intents**   A simple message-passing framework. Using Intents, you can broadcast messages system-wide or to a target Activity or Service, stating your intention to have an action performed. The system will then determine the target(s) that will perform any actions as appropriate.

❑ **Broadcast Receivers**   Intent broadcast consumers. By creating and registering a Broadcast Receiver, your application can listen for broadcast Intents that match specific filter criteria. Broadcast Receivers will automatically start your application to respond to an incoming Intent, making them ideal for event-driven applications.

❑ **Notifications**   A user notification framework. Notifications let you signal users without stealing focus or interrupting their current Activities. They're the preferred technique for getting a user's attention from within a Service or Broadcast Receiver. For example, when a device receives a text message or an incoming call, it alerts you by flashing lights, making sounds, displaying icons, or showing dialog messages. You can trigger these same events from your own applications using Notifications, as shown in Chapter 8.

By decoupling the dependencies between application components, you can share and interchange individual pieces, such as Content Providers or Services, with other applications — both your own and those of third parties.

Introducing the Application Manifest

Each Android project includes a manifest file, `AndroidManifest.xml`, stored in the root of the project hierarchy. The manifest lets you define the structure and metadata of your application and its components.

It includes nodes for each of the components (Activities, Services, Content Providers, and Broadcast Receivers) that make up your application and, using Intent Filters and Permissions, determines how they interact with each other and other applications.

It also offers attributes to specify application metadata (like its icon or theme), and additional top-level nodes can be used for security settings and unit tests as described below.

The manifest is made up of a root `manifest` tag with a `package` attribute set to the project's package. It usually includes an `xmlns:android` attribute that supplies several system attributes used within the file. A typical manifest node is shown in the XML snippet below:

```
<manifest xmlns:android=http://schemas.android.com/apk/res/android
          package="com.my_domain.my_app">
          [ ... manifest nodes ... ]
</manifest>
```

The `manifest` tag includes nodes that define the application components, security settings, and test classes that make up your application. The following list gives a summary of the available `manifest` node tags, and an XML snippet demonstrating how each one is used:

❑　application   A manifest can contain only one application node. It uses attributes to specify the metadata for your application (including its title, icon, and theme). It also acts as a container that includes the Activity, Service, Content Provider, and Broadcast Receiver tags used to specify the application components.

```
<application android:icon="@drawable/icon"
             android:theme="@style/my_theme">
             [ ... application nodes ... ]
</application>
```

❑　activity   An `activity` tag is required for every Activity displayed by your application, using the `android:name` attribute to specify the class name. This must include the main launch Activity and any other screen or dialogs that can be displayed. Trying to start an Activity that's not defined in the manifest will throw a runtime exception. Each Activity node supports `intent-filter` child tags that specify which Intents launch the Activity.

```
<activity android:name=".MyActivity" android:label="@string/app_name">
  <intent-filter>
    <action android:name="android.intent.action.MAIN" />
    <category android:name="android.intent.category.LAUNCHER" />
  </intent-filter>
</activity>
```

❑　service   As with the `activity` tag, create a new `service` tag for each Service class used in your application. (Services are covered in detail in Chapter 8.) Service tags also support `intent-filter` child tags to allow late runtime binding.

```
<service android:enabled="true" android:name=".MyService"></service>
```

❏ provider   Provider tags are used for each of your application's Content Providers. Content Providers are used to manage database access and sharing within and between applications and are examined in Chapter 6.

```
<provider android:permission="com.paad.MY_PERMISSION"
        android:name=".MyContentProvider"
        android:enabled="true"
        android:authorities="com.paad.myapp.MyContentProvider">
</provider>
```

❏ receiver   By adding a receiver tag, you can register a Broadcast Receiver without having to launch your application first. As you'll see in Chapter 5, Broadcast Receivers are like global event listeners that, once registered, will execute whenever a matching Intent is broadcast by an application. By registering a Broadcast Receiver in the manifest, you can make this process entirely autonomous. If a matching Intent is broadcast, your application will be started automatically and the registered Broadcast Receiver will be run.

```
<receiver android:enabled="true"
        android:label="My Broadcast Receiver"
        android:name=".MyBroadcastReceiver">
</receiver>
```

❏ uses-permission   As part of the security model, uses-permission tags declare the permissions you've determined that your application needs for it to operate properly. The permissions you include will be presented to the user, to grant or deny, during installation. Permissions are required for many of the native Android services, particularly those with a cost or security implication (such as dialing, receiving SMS, or using the location-based services). As shown in the item below, third-party applications, including your own, can also specify permissions before providing access to shared application components.

```
<uses-permission android:name="android.permission.ACCESS_LOCATION">
</uses-permission>
```

❏ permission   Before you can restrict access to an application component, you need to define a permission in the manifest. Use the permission tag to create these permission definitions. Application components can then require them by adding the android:permission attribute. Other applications will then need to include a uses-permission tag in their manifests (and have it granted) before they can use these protected components.

Within the permission tag, you can specify the level of access the permission will permit (normal, dangerous, signature, signatureOrSystem), a label, and an external resource containing the description that explain the risks of granting this permission.

```
<permission android:name="com.paad.DETONATE_DEVICE"
          android:protectionLevel="dangerous"
          android:label="Self Destruct"
          android:description="@string/detonate_description">
</permission>
```

❏ instrumentation   Instrumentation classes provide a framework for running tests on your Activities and Services at run time. They provide hooks to monitor your application and its interaction with the system resources. Create a new node for each of the test classes you've created for your application.

```
<instrumentation android:label="My Test"
                 android:name=".MyTestClass"
                 android:targetPackage="com.paad.aPackage">
</instrumentation>
```

A more detailed description of the manifest and each of these nodes can be found at

```
http://code.google.com/android/devel/bblocks-manifest.html
```

The ADT New Project Wizard automatically creates a new manifest file when it creates a new project.

You'll return to the manifest as each of the application components is introduced.

Using the Manifest Editor

The ADT plug-in includes a visual Manifest Editor to manage your manifest, rather than your having to manipulate the underlying XML directly.

To use the Manifest Editor in Eclipse, right-click the AndroidManifest.xml file in your project folder, and select **Open With ⇨ Android Manifest Editor**. This presents the Android Manifest Overview screen, as shown in Figure 3-1. This gives you a high-level view of your application structure and provides shortcut links to the Application, Permissions, Instrumentation, and raw XML screens.

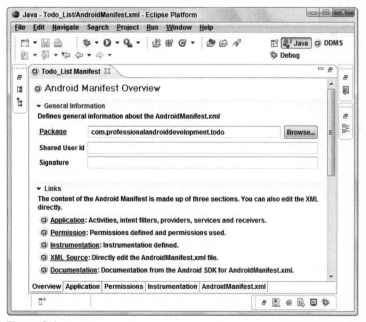

Figure 3-1

Each of the next three tabs contains a visual interface for managing the application, security, and instrumentation (testing) settings, while the last tag (using the manifest's filename) gives access to the raw XML.

Of particular interest is the Application tab, shown in Figure 3-2. Use it to manage the application node and the application component hierarchy, where you specify the application components.

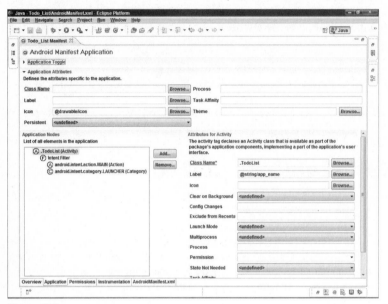

Figure 3-2

You can specify an application's attributes — including its Icon, Label, and Theme — in the Application Attributes panel. The Application Nodes tree beneath it lets you manage the application components, including their attributes and any associated Intent Filter subnodes.

The Android Application Life Cycle

Unlike most traditional environments, Android applications have no control over their own life cycles. Instead, application components must listen for changes in the application state and react accordingly, taking particular care to be prepared for untimely termination.

As mentioned before, by default, each Android application is run in its own process that's running a separate instance of Dalvik. Memory and process management of each application is handled exclusively by the run time.

> *While uncommon, it's possible to force application components within the same application to run in different processes or to have multiple applications share the same process using the* `android:process` *attribute on the affected component nodes within the manifest.*

Android aggressively manages its resources, doing whatever it takes to ensure that the device remains responsive. This means that processes (and their hosted applications) will be killed, without warning if necessary, to free resources for higher-priority applications — generally those that are interacting directly with the user at the time. The prioritization process is discussed in the next section.

Understanding Application Priority and Process States

The order in which processes are killed to reclaim resources is determined by the priority of the hosted applications. An application's priority is equal to its highest-priority component.

Where two applications have the same priority, the process that has been at a lower priority longest will be killed first. Process priority is also affected by interprocess dependencies; if an application has a dependency on a Service or Content Provider supplied by a second application, the secondary application will have at least as high a priority as the application it supports.

All Android applications will remain running and in memory until the system needs its resources for other applications.

Figure 3-3 shows the priority tree used to determine the order of application termination.

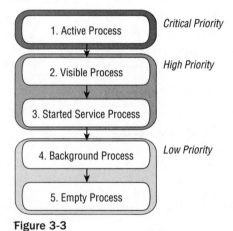

Figure 3-3

It's important to structure your application correctly to ensure that its priority is appropriate for the work it's doing. If you don't, your application could be killed while it's in the middle of something important.

The following list details each of the application states shown in Figure 3-3, explaining how the state is determined by the application components comprising it:

❑ **Active Processes** Active (foreground) processes are those hosting applications with components currently interacting with the user. These are the processes Android is trying to keep responsive by reclaiming resources. There are generally very few of these processes, and they will be killed only as a last resort.

Active processes include:

❑ Activities in an "active" state; that is, they are in the foreground and responding to user events. You will explore Activity states in greater detail later in this chapter.

❑ Activities, Services, or Broadcast Receivers that are currently executing an `onReceive` event handler.

❑ Services that are executing an `onStart`, `onCreate`, or `onDestroy` event handler.

❑ **Visible Processes** Visible, but inactive processes are those hosting "visible" Activities. As the name suggests, visible Activities are visible, but they aren't in the foreground or responding to user events. This happens when an Activity is only partially obscured (by a non-full-screen or transparent Activity). There are generally very few visible processes, and they'll only be killed in extreme circumstances to allow active processes to continue.

❑ **Started Service Processes** Processes hosting Services that have been started. Services support ongoing processing that should continue without a visible interface. Because Services don't interact directly with the user, they receive a slightly lower priority than visible Activities. They are still considered to be foreground processes and won't be killed unless resources are needed for active or visible processes. You'll learn more about Services in Chapter 8.

❑ **Background Processes** Processes hosting Activities that aren't visible and that don't have any Services that have been started are considered background processes. There will generally be a large number of background processes that Android will kill using a last-seen-first-killed pattern to obtain resources for foreground processes.

❑ **Empty Processes** To improve overall system performance, Android often retains applications in memory after they have reached the end of their lifetimes. Android maintains this cache to improve the start-up time of applications when they're re-launched. These processes are routinely killed as required.

Externalizing Resources

No matter what your development environment, it's always good practice to keep non-code resources like images and string constants external to your code. Android supports the externalization of resources ranging from simple values such as strings and colors to more complex resources like images (drawables), animations, and themes. Perhaps the most powerful resources available for externalization are layouts.

By externalizing resources, they become easier to maintain, update, and manage. This also lets you easily define alternative resource values to support different hardware and internationalization.

You'll see later in this section how Android dynamically selects resources from resource trees that let you define alternative values based on a device's hardware configuration, language, and location. This lets you create different resource values for specific languages, countries, screens, and keyboards. When an application starts, Android will automatically select the correct resource values without your having to write a line of code.

Among other things, this lets you change the layout based on the screen size and orientation and customize text prompts based on language and country.

Creating Resources

Application resources are stored under the `res/` folder of your project hierarchy. In this folder, each of the available resource types can have a subfolder containing its resources.

If you start a project using the ADT wizard, it will create a `res` folder that contains subfolders for the `values`, `drawable`, and `layout` resources that contain the default layout, application icon, and string resource definitions, respectively, as shown in Figure 3-4.

Figure 3-4

There are seven primary resource types that have different folders: simple values, drawables, layouts, animations, XML, styles, and raw resources. When your application is built, these resources will be compiled as efficiently as possible and included in your application package.

This process also creates an `R` class file that contains references to each of the resources you include in your project. This lets you reference the resources in your code, with the advantage of design time syntax checking.

The following sections describe the specific resource types available within these categories and how to create them for your applications.

In all cases, the resource filenames should contain only lowercase letters, numbers, and the period (.) and underscore (_) symbols.

Creating Simple Values

Supported simple values include strings, colors, dimensions, and string or integer arrays. All simple values are stored within XML files in the `res/values` folder.

Within each XML file, you indicate the type of value being stored using tags as shown in the sample XML file below:

```
<?xml version="1.0" encoding="utf-8"?>
<resources>
  <string name="app_name">To Do List</string>
  <color name="app_background">#FF0000FF</color>
  <dimen name="default_border">5px</dimen>
  <array name="string_array">
```

```
      <item>Item 1</item>
      <item>Item 2</item>
      <item>Item 3</item>
   </array>
   <array name="integer_array">
      <item>3</item>
      <item>2</item>
      <item>1</item>
   </array>
</resources>
```

This example includes all of the simple value types. By convention, resources are separated into separate files for each type; for example, `res/values/strings.xml` would contain only string resources.

The following sections detail the options for defining simple resources.

Strings

Externalizing your strings helps maintain consistency within your application and makes it much easier to create localized versions.

String resources are specified using the `string` tag as shown in the following XML snippet:

```
<string name="stop_message">Stop.</string>
```

Android supports simple text styling, so you can use the HTML tags <b>, <i>, and <u> to apply bold, italics, or underlining to parts of your text strings as shown in the example below:

```
<string name="stop_message"><b>Stop.</b></string>
```

You can use resource strings as input parameters for the `String.format` method. However, `String.format` does not support the text styling described above. To apply styling to a format string, you have to escape the HTML tags when creating your resource, as shown below:

```
<string name="stop_message">&lt;b>Stop&lt;/b>. %1$s</string>
```

Within your code, use the `Html.fromHtml` method to convert this back into a styled character sequence:

```
String rString = getString(R.string.stop_message);
String fString = String.format(rString, "Collaborate and listen.");
CharSequence styledString = Html.fromHtml(fString);
```

Colors

Use the `color` tag to define a new color resource. Specify the color value using a # symbol followed by the (optional) alpha channel, then the red, green, and blue values using one or two hexadecimal numbers with any of the following notations:

❑   #RGB

❑   #RRGGBB

❏ #ARGB

❏ #ARRGGBB

The following example shows how to specify a fully opaque blue and a partially transparent green:

```
<color name="opaque_blue">#00F</color>
<color name="transparent_green">#7700FF00</color>
```

Dimensions

Dimensions are most commonly referenced within style and layout resources. They're useful for creating layout constants such as borders and font heights.

To specify a dimension resource, use the `dimen` tag, specifying the dimension value, followed by an identifier describing the scale of your dimension:

❏ px   Screen pixels

❏ in   Physical inches

❏ pt   Physical points

❏ mm   Physical millimeters

❏ dp   Density-independent pixels relative to a 160-dpi screen

❏ sp   Scale-independent pixels

These alternatives let you define a dimension not only in absolute terms, but also using relative scales that account for different screen resolutions and densities to simplify scaling on different hardware.

The following XML snippet shows how to specify dimension values for a large font size and a standard border:

```
<dimen name="standard_border">5px</dimen>
<dimen name="large_font_size">16sp</dimen>
```

Styles and Themes

Style resources let your applications maintain a consistent look and feel by specifying the attribute values used by Views. The most common use of themes and styles is to store the colors and fonts for an application.

You can easily change the appearance of your application by simply specifying a different style as the theme in your project manifest.

To create a style, use a `style` tag that includes a `name` attribute, and contains one or more `item` tags. Each `item` tag should include a `name` attribute used to specify the attribute (such as font size or color) being defined. The tag itself should then contain the value, as shown in the skeleton code below:

```
<?xml version="1.0" encoding="utf-8"?>
<resources>
```

```
    <style name="StyleName">
        <item name="attributeName">value</item>
    </style>
</resources>
```

Styles support inheritance using the `parent` attribute on the `style` tag, making it easy to create simple variations.

The following example shows two styles that can also be used as a theme; a base style that sets several text properties and a second style that modifies the first to specify a smaller font.

```
<?xml version="1.0" encoding="utf-8"?>
<resources>
  <style name="BaseText">
    <item name="android:textSize">14sp</item>
    <item name="android:textColor">#111</item>
  </style>
  <style name="SmallText" parent="BaseText">
    <item name="android:textSize">8sp</item>
  </style>
</resources>
```

Drawables

Drawable resources include bitmaps and NinePatch (stretchable PNG) images. They are stored as individual files in the `res/drawable` folder.

The resource identifier for a bitmap resource is the lowercase filename without an extension.

The preferred format for a bitmap resource is PNG, although JPG and GIF files are also supported.

NinePatch (or stretchable) images are PNG files that mark the parts of an image that can be stretched. NinePatch images must be properly defined PNG files that end in `.9.png`. The resource identifier for NinePatches is the filename without the trailing `.9.png`.

A *NinePatch* is a variation of a PNG image that uses a 1-pixel border to define the area of the image that can be stretched if the image is enlarged. To create a NinePatch, draw single-pixel black lines that represent stretchable areas along the left and top borders of your image. The unmarked sections won't be resized, and the relative size of each of the marked sections will remain the same as the image size changes.

NinePatches are a powerful technique for creating images for the backgrounds of Views or Activities that may have a variable size; for example, Android uses NinePatches for creating button backgrounds.

Layouts

Layout resources let you decouple your presentation layer by designing user-interface layouts in XML rather than constructing them in code.

The most common use of a layout is to define the user interface for an Activity. Once defined in XML, the layout is "inflated" within an Activity using `setContentView`, usually within the `onCreate` method.

You can also reference layouts from within other layout resources, such as layouts for each row in a List View. More detailed information on using and creating layouts in Activities can be found in Chapter 4.

Using layouts to create your screens is best-practice UI design in Android. The decoupling of the layout from the code lets you create optimized layouts for different hardware configurations, such as varying screen sizes, orientation, or the presence of keyboards and touch screens.

Each layout definition is stored in a separate file, each containing a single layout, in the `res/layout` folder. The filename then becomes the resource identifier.

A thorough explanation of layout containers and View elements is included in the next chapter, but as an example, the following code snippet shows the layout created by the New Project Wizard. It uses a LinearLayout as a layout container for a TextView that displays the "Hello World" greeting.

```xml
<?xml version="1.0" encoding="utf-8"?>
<LinearLayout xmlns:android="http://schemas.android.com/apk/res/android"
  android:orientation="vertical"
  android:layout_width="fill_parent"
  android:layout_height="fill_parent">
  <TextView
    android:layout_width="fill_parent"
    android:layout_height="wrap_content"
    android:text="Hello World!"
  />
</LinearLayout>
```

Animations

Android supports two types of animation. *Tweened animations* can be used to rotate, move, stretch, and fade a View; or you can create *frame-by-frame animations* to display a sequence of drawable images. A comprehensive overview of creating, using, and applying animations can be found in Chapter 11.

Defining animations as external resources allows you to reuse the same sequence in multiple places and provides you with the opportunity to present an alternative animation based on device hardware or orientation.

Tweened Animations

Each tweened animation is stored in a separate XML file in the project's `res/anim` folder. As with layouts and drawable resources, the animation's filename is used as its resource identifier.

An animation can be defined for changes in `alpha` (fading), `scale` (scaling), `translate` (moving), or `rotate` (rotating).

Each of these animation types supports attributes to define what the sequence will do:

Alpha	fromAlpha and toAlpha	Float from 0 to 1
Scale	fromXScale/toXScale	Float from 0 to 1
	fromYScale/toYScale	Float from 0 to 1
	pivotX/pivotY	String of the percentage of graphic width/height from 0% to 100%

Translate	fromX/toX	Float from 0 to 1
	fromY/toY	Float from 0 to 1
Rotate	fromDegrees/toDegrees	Float from 0 to 360
	pivotX/pivotY	String of the percentage of graphic width/height from 0% to 100%

You can create a combination of animations using the `set` tag. An animation set contains one or more animation transformations and supports various additional tags and attributes to customize when and how each animation within the set is run.

The following list shows some of the set tags available:

❑ **duration**   Duration of the animation in milliseconds.

❑ **startOffset**   Millisecond delay before starting this animation.

❑ **fillBefore**   True to apply the animation transformation before it begins.

❑ **fillAfter**   True to apply the animation transformation after it begins.

❑ **interpolator**   Interpolator to set how the speed of this effect varies over time. Chapter 11 explores the interpolators available. To specify an interpolator, reference the system animation resources at `android:anim/interpolatorName`.

If you do not use the `startOffset` tag, all the animation effects within a set will execute simultaneously.

The following example shows an animation set that spins the target 360 degrees while it shrinks and fades out:

```xml
<?xml version="1.0" encoding="utf-8"?>
<set xmlns:android="http://schemas.android.com/apk/res/android"
     android:interpolator="@android:anim/accelerate_interpolator">
  <rotate
    android:fromDegrees="0"
    android:toDegrees="360"
    android:pivotX="50%"
    android:pivotY="50%"
    android:startOffset="500"
    android:duration="1000" />
  <scale
    android:fromXScale="1.0"
    android:toXScale="0.0"
    android:fromYScale="1.0"
    android:toYScale="0.0"
    android:pivotX="50%"
    android:pivotY="50%"
    android:startOffset="500"
    android:duration="500" />
  <alpha
    android:fromAlpha="1.0"
    android:toAlpha="0.0"
```

```
        android:startOffset="500"
        android:duration="500" />
    </set>
```

Frame-by-Frame Animations

Frame-by-frame animations let you create a sequence of drawables, each of which will be displayed for a specified duration, on the background of a View.

Because frame-by-frame animations represent animated drawables, they are stored in the res/drawble folder, rather than with the tweened animations, and use their filenames (without the xml extension) as their resource IDs.

The following XML snippet shows a simple animation that cycles through a series of bitmap resources, displaying each one for half a second. In order to use this snippet, you will need to create new image resources rocket1 through rocket3.

```
<animation-list
  xmlns:android="http://schemas.android.com/apk/res/android"
  android:oneshot="false">
  <item android:drawable="@drawable/rocket1" android:duration="500" />
  <item android:drawable="@drawable/rocket2" android:duration="500" />
  <item android:drawable="@drawable/rocket3" android:duration="500" />
</animation-list>
```

Using Resources

As well as the resources you create, Android supplies several system resources that you can use in your applications. The resources can be used directly from your application code and can also be referenced from within other resources (e.g., a dimension resource might be referenced in a layout definition).

Later in this chapter, you'll learn how to define alternative resource values for different languages, locations, and hardware. It's important to note that when using resources you cannot choose a particular specialized version. Android will automatically select the most appropriate value for a given resource identifier based on the current hardware and device settings.

Using Resources in Code

You access resources in code using the static R class. R is a generated class based on your external resources and created by compiling your project. The R class contains static subclasses for each of the resource types for which you've defined at least one resource. For example, the default new project includes the R.string and R.drawable subclasses.

> If you are using the ADT plug-in in Eclipse, the R class will be created automatically when you make any change to an external resource file or folder. If you are not using the plug-in, use the AAPT tool to compile your project and generate the R class. R is a compiler-generated class, so don't make any manual modifications to it as they will be lost when the file is regenerated.

Each of the subclasses within R exposes its associated resources as variables, with the variable names matching the resource identifiers — for example, R.string.app_name or R.drawable.icon.

The value of these variables is a reference to the corresponding resource's location in the resource table, *not* an instance of the resource itself.

Where a constructor or method, such as `setContentView`, accepts a resource identifier, you can pass in the resource variable, as shown in the code snippet below:

```
// Inflate a layout resource.
setContentView(R.layout.main);
// Display a transient dialog box that displays the
// error message string resource.
Toast.makeText(this, R.string.app_error, Toast.LENGTH_LONG).show();
```

When you need an instance of the resource itself, you'll need to use helper methods to extract them from the resource table, represented by an instance of the `Resources` class.

Because these methods perform lookups on the application's resource table, these helper methods can't be static. Use the `getResources` method on your application context as shown in the snippet below to access your application's Resource instance:

```
Resources myResources = getResources();
```

The `Resources` class includes getters for each of the available resource types and generally works by passing in the resource ID you'd like an instance of. The following code snippet shows an example of using the helper methods to return a selection of resource values:

```
Resources myResources = getResources();
CharSequence styledText = myResources.getText(R.string.stop_message);
Drawable icon = myResources.getDrawable(R.drawable.app_icon);

int opaqueBlue = myResources.getColor(R.color.opaque_blue);

float borderWidth = myResources.getDimension(R.dimen.standard_border);

Animation tranOut;
tranOut = AnimationUtils.loadAnimation(this, R.anim.spin_shrink_fade);

String[] stringArray;
stringArray = myResources.getStringArray(R.array.string_array);

int[] intArray = myResources.getIntArray(R.array.integer_array);
```

Frame-by-frame animated resources are inflated into `AnimationResources`. You can return the value using `getDrawable` and casting the return value as shown below:

```
AnimationDrawable rocket;
rocket = (AnimationDrawable)myResources.getDrawable(R.drawable.frame_by_frame);
```

> **At the time of going to print, there is a bug in the** `AnimationDrawable` **class. Currently, AnimationDrawable resources are not properly loaded until some time after an Activity's** `onCreate` **method has completed. Current work-arounds use timers to force a delay before loading a frame-by-frame resource.**

Referencing Resources in Resources

You can also reference resources to use as attribute values in other XML resources.

This is particularly useful for layouts and styles, letting you create specialized variations on themes and localized strings and graphics. It's also a useful way to support different images and spacing for a layout to ensure that it's optimized for different screen sizes and resolutions.

To reference one resource from another, use @ notation, as shown in the following snippet:

```
attribute="@[packagename:]resourcetype/resourceidentifier"
```

Android will assume you're using a resource from the same package, so you only need to fully qualify the package name if you're using a resource from a different package.

The following snippet creates a layout that uses color, dimension, and string resources:

```xml
<?xml version="1.0" encoding="utf-8"?>
<LinearLayout
  xmlns:android="http://schemas.android.com/apk/res/android"
  android:orientation="vertical"
  android:layout_width="fill_parent"
  android:layout_height="fill_parent"
  android:padding="@dimen/standard_border">
  <EditText
    android:id="@+id/myEditText"
    android:layout_width="fill_parent"
    android:layout_height="wrap_content"
    android:text="@string/stop_message"
    android:textColor="@color/opaque_blue"
  />
</LinearLayout>
```

Using System Resources

The native Android applications externalize many of their resources, providing you with various strings, images, animations, styles, and layouts to use in your applications.

Accessing the system resources in code is similar to using your own resources. The difference is that you use the native android resource classes available from `android.R`, rather than the application-specific R class. The following code snippet uses the `getString` method available in the application context to retrieve an error message available from the system resources:

```java
CharSequence httpError = getString(android.R.string.httpErrorBadUrl);
```

To access system resources in XML, specify *Android* as the package name, as shown in this XML snippet:

```xml
<EditText
  android:id="@+id/myEditText"
  android:layout_width="fill_parent"
  android:layout_height="wrap_content"
  android:text="@android:string/httpErrorBadUrl"
  android:textColor="@android:color/darker_gray"
/>
```

Referring to Styles in the Current Theme

Themes are an excellent way to ensure consistency for your application's UI. Rather than fully define each style, Android provides a shortcut to let you use styles from the currently applied theme.

To do this, you use `?android:` rather than `@` as a prefix to the resource you want to use. The following example shows a snippet of the above code but uses the current theme's text color rather than an external resource:

```
<EditText
   android:id="@+id/myEditText"
   android:layout_width="fill_parent"
   android:layout_height="wrap_content"
   android:text="@string/stop_message"
   android:textColor="?android:textColor"
/>
```

This technique lets you create styles that will change if the current theme changes, without having to modify each individual style resource.

To-Do List Resources Example

In this example, you'll create new external resources in preparation for adding functionality to the To-Do List example you started in Chapter 2. The string and image resources you create here will be used in Chapter 4 when you implement a menu system for the To-Do List application.

The following steps will show you how to create text and icon resources to use for the add and remove menu items, and how to create a theme to apply to the application:

1. Create two new PNG images to represent adding, and removing, a to-do list item. Each image should have dimensions of approximately 16 × 16 pixels, like those illustrated in Figure 3-5.

Figure 3-5

2. Copy the images into your project's `res/drawable` folder, and refresh your project. Your project hierarchy should appear as shown in Figure 3-6.

Figure 3-6

3. Open the strings.xml resource from the `res/values` folder, and add values for the "add_new," "remove," and "cancel" menu items. (You can remove the default "hello" string value while you're there.)

```xml
<?xml version="1.0" encoding="utf-8"?>
<resources>
  <string name="app_name">To Do List</string>
  <string name="add_new">Add New Item</string>
  <string name="remove">Remove Item</string>
  <string name="cancel">Cancel</string>
</resources>
```

4. Create a new theme for the application by creating a new styles.xml resource in the `res/values` folder. Base your theme on the standard Android theme, but set values for a default text size.

```xml
<?xml version="1.0" encoding="utf-8"?>
<resources>
  <style name="ToDoTheme" parent="@android:style/Theme.Black">
    <item name="android:textSize">12sp</item>
  </style>
</resources>
```

5. Apply the theme to your project in the manifest:

```xml
<activity android:name=".ToDoList"
          android:label="@string/app_name"
          android:theme="@style/ToDoTheme">
```

Creating Resources for Different Languages and Hardware

One of the most powerful reasons to externalize your resources is Android's dynamic resource selection mechanism.

Using the structure described below, you can create different resource values for specific languages, locations, and hardware configurations that Android will choose between dynamically at run time.

This lets you create language-, location-, and hardware-specific user interfaces without having to change your code.

Specifying alternative resource values is done using a parallel directory structure within the `res/` folder, using hyphen (-) separated text qualifiers to specify the conditions you're supporting.

The example hierarchy below shows a folder structure that features default string values, along with a French language alternative with an additional Canadian location variation:

```
Project/
  res/
    values/
      strings.xml
    values-fr/
      strings.xml
    values-fr-rCA/
      strings.xml
```

The following list gives the available qualifiers you can use to customize your resource files:

❑ **Language** Using the lowercase two-letter ISO 639-1 language code (e.g., en)

❑ **Region** A lowercase "r" followed by the uppercase two-letter ISO 3166-1-alpha-2 language code (e.g., rUS, rGB)

❑ **Screen Orientation** One of port (portrait), land (landscape), or square (square)

❑ **Screen Pixel Density** Pixel density in dots per inch (dpi) (e.g., 92dpi, 108dpi)

❑ **Touchscreen Type** One of notouch, stylus, or finger

❑ **Keyboard Availability** Either of keysexposed or keyshidden

❑ **Keyboard Input Type** One of nokeys, qwerty, or 12key

❑ **UI Navigation Type** One of notouch, dpad, trackball, or wheel

❑ **Screen Resolution** Screen resolution in pixels with the largest dimension first (e.g., 320x240)

You can specify multiple qualifiers for any resource type, separating each qualifier with a hyphen. Any combination is supported; however, they must be used in the order given in the list above, and no more than one value can be used per qualifier.

The following example shows valid and invalid directory names for alternative drawable resources.

❑ **Valid:**

```
drawable-en-rUS
drawable-en-keyshidden
drawable-land-notouch-nokeys-320x240
```

❑ **Invalid:**

```
drawable-rUS-en (out of order)
drawable-rUS-rUK (multiple values for a single qualifier)
```

When Android retrieves a resource at run time, it will find the best match from the available alternatives. Starting with a list of all the folders in which the required value exists, it then selects the one with the greatest number of matching qualifiers. If two folders are an equal match, the tiebreaker will be based on the order of the matched qualifiers in the above list.

Runtime Configuration Changes

Android supports runtime changes to the language, location, and hardware by terminating and restarting each application and reloading the resource values.

This default behavior isn't always convenient or desirable, particularly as some configuration changes (like screen orientation and keyboard visibility) can occur as easily as a user rotating the device or sliding out the keyboard. You can customize your application's response to these changes by detecting and reacting to them yourself.

To have an Activity listen for runtime configuration changes, add an android:configChanges attribute to its manifest node, specifying the configuration changes you want to handle.

The following list describes the configuration changes you can specify:

- ❑   `orientation`   The screen has been rotated between portrait and landscape.

- ❑   `keyboardHidden`   The keyboard has been exposed or hidden.

- ❑   `fontScale`   The user has changed the preferred font size.

- ❑   `locale`   The user has chosen a different language setting.

- ❑   `keyboard`   The type of keyboard has changed; for example, the phone may have a 12 keypad that flips out to reveal a full keyboard.

- ❑   `touchscreen` or `navigation`   The type of keyboard or navigation method has changed. Neither of these events should normally happen.

You can select multiple events to handle by separating the values with a pipe (|).

The following XML snippet shows an activity node declaring that it will handle changes in screen orientation and keyboard visibility:

```
<activity android:name=".TodoList"
          android:label="@string/app_name"
          android:theme="@style/TodoTheme"
          android:configChanges="orientation|keyboard"/>
```

Adding this attribute suppresses the restart for the specified configuration changes, instead, triggering the `onConfigurationChanged` method in the Activity. Override this method to handle the configuration changes using the passed-in `Configuration` object to determine the new configuration values, as shown in the following skeleton code. Be sure to call back to the super class and reload any resource values that the Activity uses in case they've changed.

```
@Override
public void onConfigurationChanged(Configuration _newConfig) {
  super.onConfigurationChanged(_newConfig);

  [ ... Update any UI based on resource values ... ]

  if (_newConfig.orientation == Configuration.ORIENTATION_LANDSCAPE) {
    [ ... React to different orientation ... ]
  }

  if (_newConfig.keyboardHidden == Configuration.KEYBOARDHIDDEN_NO) {
    [ ... React to changed keyboard visibility ... ]
  }
}
```

When `onConfigurationChanged` is called, the Activity's Resource variables will have already been updated with the new values so they'll be safe to use.

Any configuration change that you don't explicitly flag as being handled by your application will still cause an application restart without a call to `onConfigurationChanged`.

A Closer Look at Android Activities

To create user-interface screens for your applications, you extend the `Activity` class, using Views to provide user interaction.

Each Activity represents a screen (similar to the concept of a Form in desktop development) that an application can present to its users. The more complicated your application, the more screens you are likely to need.

You'll need to create a new Activity for every screen you want to display. Typically this includes at least a primary interface screen that handles the main UI functionality of your application. This is often supported by secondary Activities for entering information, providing different perspectives on your data, and supporting additional functionality. To move between screens in Android, you start a new Activity (or return from one).

Most Activities are designed to occupy the entire display, but you can create Activities that are semi-transparent, floating, or use dialog boxes.

Creating an Activity

To create a new Activity, you extend the `Activity` class, defining the user interface and implementing your functionality. The basic skeleton code for a new Activity is shown below:

```
package com.paad.myapplication;

import android.app.Activity;
import android.os.Bundle;

public class MyActivity extends Activity {

  /** Called when the activity is first created. */
  @Override
  public void onCreate(Bundle icicle) {
    super.onCreate(icicle);
  }
}
```

The base Activity class presents an empty screen that encapsulates the window display handling functionality. An empty Activity isn't particularly useful, so the first thing you'll want to do is lay out the screen interface using Views and layouts.

Activity UIs are created using Views. Views are the user-interface controls that display data and provide user interaction. Android provides several layout classes, called *View Groups*, that can contain multiple Views to help you design compelling user interfaces.

Chapter 4 examines Views and View Groups in detail, detailing what's available, how to use them, and how to create your own Views and layouts.

To assign a user interface to an Activity, call `setContentView` from the `onCreate` method of your Activity.

In this first snippet, a simple instance of `MyView` is used as the Activity's user interface:

```
@Override
public void onCreate(Bundle icicle) {
  super.onCreate(icicle);
  MyView myView = new MyView(this);
  setContentView(myView);
}
```

More commonly you'll want to use a more complex UI design. You can create a layout in code using layout View Groups, or you can use the standard Android convention of passing a resource ID for a layout defined in an external resource, as shown in the snippet below:

```
@Override
public void onCreate(Bundle icicle) {
  super.onCreate(icicle);
  setContentView(R.layout.main);
}
```

In order to use an Activity in your application, you need to register it in the manifest. Add new `activity` tags within the `application` node of the manifest; the `activity` tag includes attributes for metadata such as the label, icon, required permissions, and themes used by the Activity. An Activity without a corresponding `activity` tag can't be started.

The following XML snippet shows how to add a node for the `MyActivity` class created in the snippets above:

```
<activity android:label="@string/app_name"
          android:name=".MyActivity">
  <intent-filter>
    <action android:name="android.intent.action.MAIN" />
    <category android:name="android.intent.category.LAUNCHER" />
  </intent-filter>
</activity>
```

Within the `activity` tag, you can add `intent-filter` nodes that specify the Intents your Activity will listen for and react to. Each Intent Filter defines one or more actions and categories that your Activity supports. Intents and Intent Filters are covered in depth in Chapter 5, but it's worth noting that to make an Activity available from the main program launcher, it must include an Intent Filter listening for the `Main` action and the `Launcher` category, as highlighted in the snippet below:

```
<activity android:label="@string/app_name"
          android:name=".MyActivity">
  <intent-filter>
    <action android:name="android.intent.action.MAIN" />
    <category android:name="android.intent.category.LAUNCHER" />
  </intent-filter>
</activity>
```

The Activity Life Cycle

A good understanding of the Activity life cycle is vital to ensure that your application provides a seamless user experience and properly manages its resources.

As explained earlier, Android applications do not control their own process lifetimes; the Android run time manages the process of each application, and by extension that of each Activity within it.

While the run time handles the termination and management of an Activity's process, the Activity's state helps determine the priority of its parent application. The application priority, in turn, influences the likelihood that the run time will terminate it and the Activities running within it.

Activity Stacks

The state of each Activity is determined by its position on the Activity stack, a last-in–first-out collection of all the currently running Activities. When a new Activity starts, the current foreground screen is moved to the top of the stack. If the user navigates back using the Back button, or the foreground Activity is closed, the next Activity on the stack moves up and becomes active. This process is illustrated in Figure 3-7.

As described previously in this chapter, an application's priority is influenced by its highest-priority Activity. The Android memory manager uses this stack to determine the priority of applications based on their Activities when deciding which application to terminate to free resources.

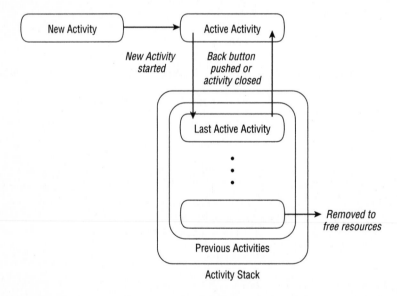

Figure 3-7

Activity States

As activities are created and destroyed, they move in and out of the stack shown in Figure 3-7. As they do so, they transition through four possible states:

❑ **Active**   When an Activity is at the top of the stack, it is the visible, focused, foreground activity that is receiving user input. Android will attempt to keep it alive at all costs, killing Activities further down the stack as needed, to ensure that it has the resources it needs. When another Activity becomes active, this one will be paused.

❑ **Paused**   In some cases, your Activity will be visible but will not have focus; at this point, it's paused. This state is reached if a transparent or non-full-screen Activity is active in front of it. When paused, an Activity is treated as if it were active; however, it doesn't receive user input events. In extreme cases, Android will kill a paused Activity to recover resources for the active Activity. When an Activity becomes totally obscured, it becomes stopped.

❑ **Stopped**   When an Activity isn't visible, it "stops." The Activity will remain in memory retaining all state and member information; however, it is now a prime candidate for execution when the system requires memory elsewhere. When an Activity is stopped, it's important to save data and the current UI state. Once an Activity has exited or closed, it becomes inactive.

❑ **Inactive**   After an Activity has been killed, and before it's been launched, it's inactive. Inactive Activities have been removed from the Activity stack and need to be restarted before they can be displayed and used.

State transitions are nondeterministic and are handled entirely by the Android memory manager. Android will start by closing applications that contain inactive Activities, followed by those that are stopped, and in extreme cases, it will remove those that are paused.

To ensure a seamless user experience, transitions between these states should be invisible to the user. There should be no difference between an Activity moving from paused, stopped, or killed states back to active, so it's important to save all UI state changes and persist all data when an Activity is paused or stopped. Once an Activity does become active, it should restore those saved values.

Monitoring State Changes

To ensure that Activities can react to state changes, Android provides a series of event handlers that are fired when an Activity transitions through its full, visible, and active lifetimes. Figure 3-8 summarizes these lifetimes in terms of the Activity states described above.

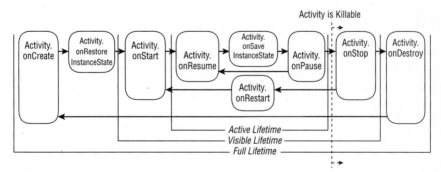

Figure 3-8

The following skeleton code shows the stubs for the state change method handlers available in an Activity. Comments within each stub describe the actions you should consider taking on each state change event.

```java
package com.paad.myapplication;

import android.app.Activity;
import android.os.Bundle;

public class MyActivity extends Activity {

  // Called at the start of the full lifetime.
  @Override
  public void onCreate(Bundle icicle) {
    super.onCreate(icicle);
    // Initialize activity.
  }

  // Called after onCreate has finished, use to restore UI state
  @Override
  public void onRestoreInstanceState(Bundle savedInstanceState) {
    super.onRestoreInstanceState(savedInstanceState);
    // Restore UI state from the savedInstanceState.
    // This bundle has also been passed to onCreate.
  }

  // Called before subsequent visible lifetimes
  // for an activity process.
  @Override
  public void onRestart(){
    super.onRestart();
    // Load changes knowing that the activity has already
    // been visible within this process.
  }

  // Called at the start of the visible lifetime.
  @Override
  public void onStart(){
    super.onStart();
    // Apply any required UI change now that the Activity is visible.
  }

  // Called at the start of the active lifetime.
  @Override
  public void onResume(){
    super.onResume();
    // Resume any paused UI updates, threads, or processes required
    // by the activity but suspended when it was inactive.
  }

  // Called to save UI state changes at the
  // end of the active lifecycle.
  @Override
  public void onSaveInstanceState(Bundle savedInstanceState) {
    // Save UI state changes to the savedInstanceState.
```

```
      // This bundle will be passed to onCreate if the process is
      // killed and restarted.
      super.onSaveInstanceState(savedInstanceState);
    }

    // Called at the end of the active lifetime.
    @Override
    public void onPause(){
      // Suspend UI updates, threads, or CPU intensive processes
      // that don't need to be updated when the Activity isn't
      // the active foreground activity.
      super.onPause();
    }

    // Called at the end of the visible lifetime.
    @Override
    public void onStop(){
      // Suspend remaining UI updates, threads, or processing
      // that aren't required when the Activity isn't visible.
      // Persist all edits or state changes
      // as after this call the process is likely to be killed.
      super.onStop();
    }

    // Called at the end of the full lifetime.
    @Override
    public void onDestroy(){
      // Clean up any resources including ending threads,
      // closing database connections etc.
      super.onDestroy();
    }
  }
```

As shown in the snippet above, you should always call back to the superclass when overriding these event handlers.

Understanding Activity Lifetimes

Within an Activity's full lifetime, between creation and destruction, it will go through one or more iterations of the active and visible lifetimes. Each transition will trigger the method handlers described previously. The following sections provide a closer look at each of these lifetimes and the events that bracket them.

The Full Lifetime

The full lifetime of your Activity occurs between the first call to onCreate and the final call to onDestroy. It's possible, in some cases, for an Activity's process to be terminated *without* the onDestroy method being called.

Use the onCreate method to initialize your Activity: Inflate the user interface, allocate references to class variables, bind data to controls, and create Services and threads. The onCreate method is passed a Bundle object containing the UI state saved in the last call to onSaveInstanceState. You should use this Bundle to restore the user interface to its previous state, either in the onCreate method or by overriding onRestoreInstanceStateMethod.

Override onDestroy to clean up any resources created in onCreate, and ensure that all external connections, such as network or database links, are closed.

As part of Android's guidelines for writing efficient code, it's recommended that you avoid the creation of short-term objects. Rapid creation and destruction of objects forces additional garbage collection, a process that can have a direct impact on the user experience. If your Activity creates the same set of objects regularly, consider creating them in the onCreate method instead, as it's called only once in the Activity's lifetime.

The Visible Lifetime

An Activity's visible lifetimes are bound between calls to onStart and onStop. Between these calls, your Activity will be visible to the user, although it may not have focus and might be partially obscured. Activities are likely to go through several visible lifetimes during their full lifetime, as they move between the foreground and background. While unusual, in extreme cases, the Android run time will kill an Activity during its visible lifetime without a call to onStop.

The onStop method should be used to pause or stop animations, threads, timers, Services, or other processes that are used exclusively to update the user interface. There's little value in consuming resources (such as CPU cycles or network bandwidth) to update the UI when it isn't visible. Use the onStart (or onRestart) methods to resume or restart these processes when the UI is visible again.

The onRestart method is called immediately prior to all but the first call to onStart. Use it to implement special processing that you want done only when the Activity restarts within its full lifetime.

The onStart/onStop methods are also used to register and unregister Broadcast Receivers that are being used exclusively to update the user interface. It will not always be necessary to unregister Receivers when the Activity becomes invisible, particularly if they are used to support actions other than updating the UI. You'll learn more about using Broadcast Receivers in Chapter 5.

The Active Lifetime

The active lifetime starts with a call to onResume and ends with a corresponding call to onPause.

An active Activity is in the foreground and is receiving user input events. Your Activity is likely to go through several active lifetimes before it's destroyed, as the active lifetime will end when a new Activity is displayed, the device goes to sleep, or the Activity loses focus. Try to keep code in the onPause and onResume methods relatively fast and lightweight to ensure that your application remains responsive when moving in and out of the foreground.

Immediately before onPause, a call is made to onSaveInstanceState. This method provides an opportunity to save the Activity's UI state in a Bundle that will be passed to the onCreate and onRestoreInstanceState methods. Use onSaveInstanceState to save the UI state (such as check button states, user focus, and entered but uncommitted user input) to ensure that the Activity can present the same UI when it next becomes active. During the active lifetime, you can safely assume that onSaveInstanceState and onPause will be called before the process is terminated.

Most Activity implementations will override at least the onPause method to commit unsaved changes, as it marks the point beyond which an Activity may be killed without warning. Depending on your application architecture, you may also choose to suspend threads, processes, or Broadcast Receivers while your Activity is not in the foreground.

The onResume method can be very lightweight. You will not need to reload the UI state here as this is handled by the onCreate and onRestoreInstanceState methods when required. Use onResume to re-register any Broadcast Receivers or other processes you may have stopped in onPause.

Android Activity Classes

The Android SDK includes a selection of Activity subclasses that wrap up the use of common user interface widgets. Some of the more useful ones are listed below:

❑ **MapActivity** Encapsulates the resource handling required to support a MapView widget within an Activity. Learn more about MapActivity and MapView in Chapter 7.

❑ **ListActivity** Wrapper class for Activities that feature a ListView bound to a data source as the primary UI metaphor, and exposing event handlers for list item selection

❑ **ExpandableListActivity** Similar to the List Activity but supporting an ExpandableListView

❑ **ActivityGroup** Allows you to embed multiple Activities within a single screen.

Summary

In this chapter, you learned how to design robust applications using loosely coupled application components: Activities, Services, Content Providers, Intents, and Broadcast Receivers bound together using the application manifest.

You were introduced to the Android application life cycle, learning how each application's priority is determined by its process state, which is, in turn, determined by the state of the components within it.

To take full advantage of the wide range of device hardware available and the international user base, you learned how to create external resources and how to define alternative values for specific locations, languages, and hardware configurations.

Next you discovered more about Activities and their role in the application framework. As well as learning how to create new Activities, you were introduced to the Activity life cycle. In particular, you learned about Activity state transitions and how to monitor these events to ensure a seamless user experience.

Finally, you were introduced to some specialized Android Activity classes.

In the next chapter, you'll learn how to create User Interfaces. Chapter 4 will demonstrate how to use layouts to design your UI before introducing some native widgets and showing you how to extend, modify, and group them to create specialized controls. You'll also learn how to create your own unique user interface elements from a blank canvas, before being introduced to the Android menu system.

4

Creating User Interfaces

It's vital to create compelling and intuitive User Interfaces for your applications. Ensuring that they are as stylish and easy to use as they are functional should be a primary design consideration.

To quote Stephen Fry on the importance of style as *part* of substance in the design of digital devices:

> *As if a device can function if it has no style. As if a device can be called stylish that does not function superbly. ... yes, beauty matters. Boy, does it matter. It is not surface, it is not an extra, it is the thing itself.*
>
> — *Stephen Fry,* The Guardian *(October 27, 2007)*

Increasing screen sizes, display resolutions, and mobile processor power has seen mobile applications become increasingly visual. While the diminutive screens pose a challenge for creating complex visual interfaces, the ubiquity of mobiles makes it a challenge worth accepting.

In this chapter, you'll learn the basic Android UI elements and discover how to use Views, View Groups, and layouts to create functional and intuitive User Interfaces for your Activities.

After being introduced to some of the controls available from the Android SDK, you'll learn how to extend and customize them. Using View Groups, you'll see how to combine Views to create atomic, reusable UI elements made up of interacting subcontrols. You'll also learn how to create your own Views to implement creative new ways to display data and interact with users.

The individual elements of an Android User Interface are arranged on screen using a variety of layout managers derived from `ViewGroup`. Correctly using layouts is essential for creating good interfaces; this chapter introduces several native layout classes and demonstrates how to use them and how to create your own.

Android's application and context menu systems use a new approach, optimized for modern touch-screen devices. As part of an examination of the Android UI model, this chapter ends with a look at how to create and use Activity and context menus.

Fundamental Android UI Design

User Interface design, human–computer interaction, and usability are huge topics that aren't covered in great depth in this book. Nonetheless, it's important that you get them right when creating your User Interfaces.

Android introduces some new terminology for familiar programming metaphors that will be explored in detail in the following sections:

❑   **Views**   *Views* are the basic User Interface class for visual interface elements (commonly known as controls or widgets). All User Interface controls, and the layout classes, are derived from Views.

❑   **ViewGroups**   *View Groups* are extensions of the View class that can contain multiple child Views. By extending the `ViewGroup` class, you can create compound controls that are made up of interconnected child Views. The `ViewGroup` class is also extended to provide the layout managers, such as `LinearLayout`, that help you compose User Interfaces.

❑   **Activities**   *Activities*, described in detail in the previous chapter, represent the window or screen being displayed to the user. Activities are the Android equivalent of a Form. To display a User Interface, you assign a View or layout to an Activity.

Android provides several common UI controls, widgets, and layout managers.

For most graphical applications, it's likely that you'll need to extend and modify these standard controls — or create composite or entirely new controls — to provide your own functionality.

Introducing Views

As described above, all visual components in Android descend from the `View` class and are referred to generically as *Views*. You'll often see Views referred to as *controls* or *widgets* — terms you're probably familiar with if you've done any GUI development.

The `ViewGroup` class is an extension of View designed to contain multiple Views. Generally, View Groups are either used to construct atomic reusable components (widgets) or to manage the layout of child Views. View Groups that perform the latter function are generally referred to as *layouts*.

Because all visual elements derive from Views, many of the terms above are interchangeable. By convention, a *control* usually refers to an extension of Views that implements relatively simple functionality, while a *widget* generally refers to both compound controls and more complex extensions of Views.

The conventional naming model is shown in Figure 4-1. In practice, you will likely see both *widget* and *control* used interchangeably with *View*.

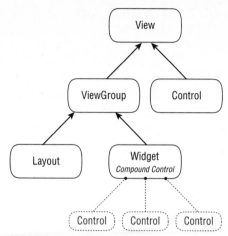

Figure 4-1

You've already been introduced to a layout and two widgets — the `LinearLayout`, a `ListView`, and a `TextView` — when you created the To-Do List example in Chapter 2.

In the following sections, you'll learn how to put together increasingly complex UIs, starting with the Views available in the SDK, before learning how to extend them, build your own compound controls, and create your own custom Views from scratch.

Creating Activity User Interfaces with Views

A new Activity starts with a temptingly empty screen onto which you place your User Interface. To set the User Interface, call `setContentView`, passing in the View instance (typically a layout) to display. Because empty screens aren't particularly inspiring, you will almost always use `setContentView` to assign an Activity's User Interface when overriding its `onCreate` handler.

The `setContentView` method accepts either a layout resource ID (as described in Chapter 3) or a single View instance. This lets you define your User Interface either in code or using the preferred technique of external layout resources.

Using layout resources decouples your presentation layer from the application logic, providing the flexibility to change the presentation without changing code. This makes it possible to specify different layouts optimized for different hardware configurations, even changing them at run time based on hardware changes (such as screen orientation).

The following code snippet shows how to set the User Interface for an Activity using an external layout resource. You can get references to the Views used within a layout with the `findViewById` method. This example assumes that main.xml exists in the project's `res/layout` folder.

```
@Override
public void onCreate(Bundle icicle) {
  super.onCreate(icicle);

  setContentView(R.layout.main);
```

```
        TextView myTextView = (TextView)findViewById(R.id.myTextView);
}
```

If you prefer the more *traditional* approach, you can specify the User Interface in code. The following snippet shows how to assign a new `TextView` as the User Interface:

```
@Override
public void onCreate(Bundle icicle) {
  super.onCreate(icicle);

    TextView myTextView = new TextView(this);
    setContentView(myTextView);
    myTextView.setText("Hello, Android");
}
```

The `setContentView` method accepts a single View instance; as a result, you have to group multiple controls to ensure that you can reference a layout using a single View or View Group.

The Android Widget Toolbox

Android supplies a toolbox of standard Views to help you create simple interfaces. By using these controls (and modifying or extending them as necessary), you can simplify your development and provide consistency between applications.

The following list highlights some of the more familiar toolbox controls:

❑ `TextView`   A standard read only text label. It supports multiline display, string formatting, and automatic word wrapping.

❑ `EditText`   An editable text entry box. It accepts multiline entry and word wrapping.

❑ `ListView`   A View Group that creates and manages a group of Views used to display the items in a List. The standard ListView displays the string value of an array of objects using a Text View for each item.

❑ `Spinner`   Composite control that displays a TextView and an associated ListView that lets you select an item from a list to display in the textbox. It's made from a Text View displaying the current selection, combined with a button that displays a selection dialog when pressed.

❑ `Button`   Standard push-button

❑ `CheckBox`   Two-state button represented with a checked or unchecked box

❑ `RadioButton`   Two-state grouped buttons. Presents the user with a number of binary options of which only one can be selected at a time.

This is only a selection of the widgets available. Android also supports several more advanced View implementations including date-time pickers, auto-complete input boxes, maps, galleries, and tab sheets. For a more comprehensive list of the available widgets, head to
`http://code.google.com/android/reference/view-gallery.html`.

It's only a matter of time before you, as an innovative developer, encounter a situation in which none of the built-in controls meets your needs. Later in this chapter, you'll learn how to extend and combine the existing controls and how to design and create entirely new widgets from scratch.

Introducing Layouts

Layout Managers (more generally, "layouts") are extensions of the `ViewGroup` class designed to control the position of child controls on a screen. Layouts can be nested, letting you create arbitrarily complex interfaces using a combination of Layout Managers.

The Android SDK includes some simple layouts to help you construct your UI. It's up to you to select the right combination of layouts to make your interface easy to understand and use.

The following list includes some of the more versatile layout classes available:

❑ **FrameLayout** The simplest of the Layout Managers, the *Frame Layout* simply pins each child view to the top left corner. Adding multiple children stacks each new child on top of the previous, with each new View obscuring the last.

❑ **LinearLayout** A *Linear Layout* adds each child View in a straight line, either vertically or horizontally. A vertical layout has one child View per row, while a horizontal layout has a single row of Views. The Linear Layout Manager allows you to specify a "weight" for each child View that controls the relative size of each within the available space.

❑ **RelativeLayout** Using the *Relative Layout*, you can define the positions of each of the child Views relative to each other and the screen boundaries.

❑ **TableLayout** The *Table Layout* lets you lay out Views using a grid of rows and columns. Tables can span multiple rows and columns, and columns can be set to shrink or grow.

❑ **AbsoluteLayout** In an *Absolute Layout*, each child View's position is defined in absolute coordinates. Using this class, you can guarantee the exact layout of your components, but at a price. Compared to the previous managers, describing a layout in absolute terms means that your layout can't dynamically adjust for different screen resolutions and orientations.

The Android documentation describes the features and properties of each layout class in detail, so rather than repeating it here, I'll refer you to `http://code.google.com/android/devel/ui/layout.html`.

Later in this chapter, you'll also learn how to create compound controls (widgets made up of several interconnected Views) by extending these layout classes.

Using Layouts

The preferred way to implement layouts is in XML using external resources. A layout XML must contain a single root element. This root node can contain as many nested layouts and Views as necessary to construct an arbitrarily complex screen.

The following XML snippet shows a simple layout that places a `TextView` above an `EditText` control using a `LinearLayout` configured to lay out vertically:

```xml
<?xml version="1.0" encoding="utf-8"?>
<LinearLayout xmlns:android="http://schemas.android.com/apk/res/android"
  android:orientation="vertical"
  android:layout_width="fill_parent"
  android:layout_height="fill_parent">
  <TextView
    android:layout_width="fill_parent"
    android:layout_height="wrap_content"
    android:text="Enter Text Below"
  />
  <EditText
    android:layout_width="fill_parent"
    android:layout_height="wrap_content"
    android:text="Text Goes Here!"
  />
</LinearLayout>
```

Implementing layouts in XML decouples the presentation layer from View and Activity code. It also lets you create hardware-specific variations that are dynamically loaded without requiring code changes.

When it's preferred, or required, you can implement layouts in code. When assigning Views to layouts, it's important to apply `LayoutParameters` using the `setLayoutParams` method, or passing them in to the `addView` call as shown below:

```java
LinearLayout ll = new LinearLayout(this);
ll.setOrientation(LinearLayout.VERTICAL);

TextView myTextView = new TextView(this);
EditText myEditText = new EditText(this);

myTextView.setText("Enter Text Below");
myEditText.setText("Text Goes Here!");

int lHeight = LinearLayout.LayoutParams.FILL_PARENT;
int lWidth = LinearLayout.LayoutParams.WRAP_CONTENT;

ll.addView(myTextView, new LinearLayout.LayoutParams(lHeight, lWidth));
ll.addView(myEditText, new LinearLayout.LayoutParams(lHeight, lWidth));
setContentView(ll);
```

Creating New Views

The ability to extend existing Views, create composite widgets, and create unique new controls lets you create beautiful User Interfaces optimized for your particular workflow. Android lets you subclass the existing widget toolbox and implement your own View controls, giving you total freedom to tailor your User Interface to maximize the user experience.

When you design a User Interface, it's important to balance raw aesthetics and usability. With the power to create your own custom controls comes the temptation to rebuild all of them from scratch. Resist that urge. The standard widgets will be familiar to users from other Android applications. On small screens with users often paying limited attention, familiarity can often provide better usability than a slightly shinier widget.

Deciding on your approach when creating a new View depends on what you want to achieve:

❑ Modify or extend the appearance and/or behavior of an existing control when it already supplies the basic functionality you want. By overriding the event handlers and onDraw, but still calling back to the superclass's methods, you can customize the control without having to reimplement its functionality. For example, you could customize a TextView to display a set number of decimal points.

❑ Combine controls to create atomic, reusable widgets that leverage the functionality of several interconnected controls. For example, you could create a dropdown combo box by combining a TextView and a Button that displays a floating ListView when clicked.

❑ Create an entirely new control when you need a completely different interface that can't be achieved by changing or combining existing controls.

Modifying Existing Views

The toolbox includes a lot of common UI requirements, but the controls are necessarily generic. By customizing these basic Views, you avoid reimplementing existing behavior while still tailoring the User Interface, and functionality, of each control to your application's needs.

To create a new widget based on an existing control, create a new class that extends it — as shown in the following skeleton code that extends TextView:

```
import android.content.Context;
import android.util.AttributeSet;
import android.widget.TextView;

public class MyTextView extends TextView {

  public MyTextView (Context context, AttributeSet attrs, int defStyle)
  {
    super(context, attrs, defStyle);
  }

  public MyTextView (Context context) {
    super(context);
  }

  public MyTextView (Context context, AttributeSet attrs) {
    super(context, attrs);
  }
}
```

To override the appearance or behavior of your new View, override and extend the event handlers associated with the behavior you want to change.

In the following skeleton code, the onDraw method is overridden to modify the View's appearance, and the onKeyDown handler is overridden to allow custom key press handling:

```
public class MyTextView extends TextView {

  public MyTextView (Context context, AttributeSet ats, int defStyle) {
    super(context, ats, defStyle);
  }

  public MyTextView (Context context) {
    super(context);
  }

  public MyTextView (Context context, AttributeSet attrs) {
    super(context, attrs);
  }

  @Override
  public void onDraw(Canvas canvas) {
    [ ... Draw things on the canvas under the text ... ]

    // Render the text as usual using the TextView base class.
    super.onDraw(canvas);

    [ ... Draw things on the canvas over the text ... ]
  }

  @Override
  public boolean onKeyDown(int keyCode, KeyEvent keyEvent) {
    [ ... Perform some special processing ... ]
    [ ... based on a particular key press ... ]

    // Use the existing functionality implemented by
    // the base class to respond to a key press event.
    return super.onKeyDown(keyCode, keyEvent);
  }
}
```

The User Interface event handlers available within Views are covered in more detail later in this chapter.

Customizing Your To-Do List

The To-Do List example from Chapter 2 uses TextViews (within a List View) to display each item. You can customize the appearance of the list by creating a new extension of the Text View, overriding the onDraw method.

In this example, you'll create a new TodoListItemView that will make each item appear as if on a paper pad. When complete, your customized To-Do List should look like Figure 4-2.

Figure 4-2

1. Create a new `TodoListItemView` class that extends TextView. Include a stub for overriding the `onDraw` method, and implement constructors that call a new `init` method stub.

```
package com.paad.todolist;

import android.content.Context;
import android.content.res.Resources;
import android.graphics.Canvas;
import android.graphics.Paint;
import android.util.AttributeSet;
import android.widget.TextView;

public class TodoListItemView extends TextView {

  public TodoListItemView (Context context, AttributeSet ats, int ds) {
    super(context, ats, ds);
    init();
  }

  public TodoListItemView (Context context) {
    super(context);
    init();
  }

  public TodoListItemView (Context context, AttributeSet attrs) {
    super(context, attrs);
    init();
  }

  private void init() {
  }

  @Override
  public void onDraw(Canvas canvas) {
    // Use the base TextView to render the text.
    super.onDraw(canvas);
  }

}
```

2. Create a new `colors.xml` resource in the `res/values` folder. Create new color values for the paper, margin, line, and text colors.

```xml
<?xml version="1.0" encoding="utf-8"?>
<resources>
  <color name="notepad_paper">#AAFFFF99</color>
  <color name="notepad_lines">#FF0000FF</color>
  <color name="notepad_margin">#90FF0000</color>
  <color name="notepad_text">#AA0000FF</color>
</resources>
```

3. Create a new `dimens.xml` resource file, and add a new value for the paper's margin width.

```xml
<?xml version="1.0" encoding="utf-8"?>
<resources>
  <dimen name="notepad_margin">30px</dimen>
</resources>
```

4. With the resources defined, you're ready to customize the `TodoListItemView` appearance. Create new private instance variables to store the `Paint` objects you'll use to draw the paper background and margin. Also create variables for the paper color and margin width values.

   Fill in the `init` method to get instances of the resources you created in the last two steps and create the `Paint` objects.

```java
private Paint marginPaint;
private Paint linePaint;
private int paperColor;
private float margin;

private void init() {
   // Get a reference to our resource table.
   Resources myResources = getResources();

   // Create the paint brushes we will use in the onDraw method.
   marginPaint = new Paint(Paint.ANTI_ALIAS_FLAG);
   marginPaint.setColor(myResources.getColor(R.color.notepad_margin));
   linePaint = new Paint(Paint.ANTI_ALIAS_FLAG);
   linePaint.setColor(myResources.getColor(R.color.notepad_lines));

   // Get the paper background color and the margin width.
   paperColor = myResources.getColor(R.color.notepad_paper);
   margin = myResources.getDimension(R.dimen.notepad_margin);
}
```

5. To draw the paper, override `onDraw`, and draw the image using the Paint objects you created in Step 4. Once you've drawn the paper image, call the superclass's `onDraw` method, and let it draw the text as usual.

```java
@Override
public void onDraw(Canvas canvas) {
   // Color as paper
   canvas.drawColor(paperColor);

   // Draw ruled lines
```

```
canvas.drawLine(0, 0, getMeasuredHeight(), 0, linePaint);
canvas.drawLine(0, getMeasuredHeight(),
                getMeasuredWidth(), getMeasuredHeight(),
                linePaint);

// Draw margin
canvas.drawLine(margin, 0, margin, getMeasuredHeight(), marginPaint);

// Move the text across from the margin
canvas.save();
canvas.translate(margin, 0);

// Use the TextView to render the text.
super.onDraw(canvas);
canvas.restore();
}
```

6. That completes the `TodoListItemView` implementation. To use it in the To-Do List Activity, you need to include it in a new layout and pass that in to the Array Adapter constructor.

Start by creating a new todolist_item.xml resource in the `res/layout` folder. It will specify how each of the to-do list items is displayed. For this example, your layout need only consist of the new `TodoListItemView`, set to fill the entire available area.

```xml
<?xml version="1.0" encoding="utf-8"?>
<com.paad.todolist.TodoListItemView
  xmlns:android="http://schemas.android.com/apk/res/android"
  android:layout_width="fill_parent"
  android:layout_height="fill_parent"
  android:padding="10dp"
  android:scrollbars="vertical"
  android:textColor="@color/notepad_text"
  android:fadingEdge="vertical"
/>
```

7. Now open the `ToDoList` Activity class. The final step is to change the parameters passed in to the `ArrayAdapter` in onCreate. Replace the reference to the default `android.R.layout.simple_list_item_1` with the new `R.layout.todolist_item` layout created in Step 6.

```java
final ArrayList<String> todoItems = new ArrayList<String>();
int resID = R.layout.todolist_item;
final ArrayAdapter<String> aa = new ArrayAdapter<String>(this, resID, todoItems);
myListView.setAdapter(aa);
```

Creating Compound Controls

Compound controls are atomic, reusable widgets that contain multiple child controls laid out and wired together.

When you create a compound control, you define the layout, appearance, and interaction of the Views it contains. Compound controls are created by extending a `ViewGroup` (usually a Layout Manager). To create a new compound control, choose a layout class that's most suitable for positioning the child controls, and extend it as shown in the skeleton code below:

```
public class MyCompoundView extends LinearLayout {

  public MyCompoundView(Context context) {
    super(context);
  }

  public MyCompoundView(Context context, AttributeSet attrs) {
    super(context, attrs);
  }

}
```

As with an Activity, the preferred way to design the UI for a compound control is to use a layout resource. The following code snippet shows the XML layout definition for a simple widget consisting of an Edit Text box and a button to clear it:

```
<?xml version="1.0" encoding="utf-8"?>
<LinearLayout xmlns:android="http://schemas.android.com/apk/res/android"
  android:orientation="vertical"
  android:layout_width="fill_parent"
  android:layout_height="fill_parent">
  <EditText
    android:id="@+id/editText"
    android:layout_width="fill_parent"
    android:layout_height="wrap_content"
  />
  <Button
    android:id="@+id/clearButton"
    android:layout_width="fill_parent"
    android:layout_height="wrap_content"
    android:text="Clear"
  />
</LinearLayout>
```

To use this layout for your new widget, override its constructor to inflate the layout resource using the `inflate` method from the `LayoutInflate` system service. The `inflate` method takes the layout resource and returns an inflated View. For circumstances such as this where the returned View should be the class you're creating, you can pass in a parent and attach the result to it automatically, as shown in the next code sample.

The following code snippet shows the `ClearableEditText` class. Within the constructor it inflates the layout resource created above and gets references to each of the Views it contains. It also makes a call to `hookupButton` that will be used to hookup the *clear text* functionality when the button is pressed.

```
public class ClearableEditText extends LinearLayout {

  EditText editText;
  Button clearButton;

  public ClearableEditText(Context context) {
```

```
        super(context);

        // Inflate the view from the layout resource.
        String infService = Context.LAYOUT_INFLATER_SERVICE;
        LayoutInflater li;
        li = (LayoutInflater)getContext().getSystemService(infService);
        li.inflate(R.layout.clearable_edit_text, this, true);

        // Get references to the child controls.
        editText = (EditText)findViewById(R.id.editText);
        clearButton = (Button)findViewById(R.id.clearButton);

        // Hook up the functionality
        hookupButton();
    }
}
```

If you'd prefer to construct your layout in code, you can do so just as you would for an Activity. The following code snippet shows the ClearableEditText constructor overridden to create the same UI as is defined in the XML used in the earlier example:

```
public ClearableEditText(Context context) {
    super(context);

    // Set orientation of layout to vertical
    setOrientation(LinearLayout.VERTICAL);

    // Create the child controls.
    editText = new EditText(getContext());
    clearButton = new Button(getContext());
    clearButton.setText("Clear");

    // Lay them out in the compound control.
    int lHeight = LayoutParams.WRAP_CONTENT;
    int lWidth = LayoutParams.FILL_PARENT;

    addView(editText, new LinearLayout.LayoutParams(lWidth, lHeight));
    addView(clearButton, new LinearLayout.LayoutParams(lWidth, lHeight));

    // Hook up the functionality
    hookupButton();
}
```

Once the screen has been constructed, you can hook up the event handlers for each child control to provide the functionality you need. In this next snippet, the hookupButton method is filled in to clear the textbox when the button is pressed:

```
private void hookupButton() {
    clearButton.setOnClickListener(new Button.OnClickListener() {
        public void onClick(View v) {
            editText.setText("");
        }
    });
}
```

Creating Custom Widgets and Controls

Creating completely new Views gives you the power to fundamentally shape the way your applications look and feel. By creating your own controls, you can create User Interfaces that are uniquely suited to your users' needs. To create new controls from a blank canvas, you extend either the View or SurfaceView classes.

The View class provides a Canvas object and a series of draw methods and Paint classes, to create a visual interface using raster graphics. You can then override user events like screen touches or key presses to provide interactivity. In situations where extremely rapid repaints and 3D graphics aren't required, the View base class offers a powerful lightweight solution.

The SurfaceView provides a canvas that supports drawing from a background thread and using openGL for 3D graphics. This is an excellent option for graphics-heavy controls that are frequently updated or display complex graphical information, particularly games and 3D visualizations.

This chapter introduces 2D controls based on the View class. To learn more about the SurfaceView class and some of the more advanced Canvas paint features available in Android, see Chapter 11.

Creating a New Visual Interface

The base View class presents a distinctly empty 100×100 pixel square. To change the size of the control and display a more compelling visual interface, you need to override the onMeasure and onDraw methods, respectively.

Within onMeasure, the new View will calculate the height and width it will occupy given a set of boundary conditions. The onDraw method is where you draw on the Canvas to create the visual interface.

The following code snippet shows the skeleton code for a new View class, which will be examined further in the following sections:

```
public class MyView extends View {

  // Constructor required for in-code creation
  public MyView(Context context) {
    super(context);
  }

  // Constructor required for inflation from resource file
  public MyView (Context context, AttributeSet ats, int defaultStyle) {
    super(context, ats, defaultStyle );
  }

  //Constructor required for inflation from resource file
  public MyView (Context context, AttributeSet attrs) {
    super(context, attrs);
  }

  @Override
  protected void onMeasure(int wMeasureSpec, int hMeasureSpec) {
    int measuredHeight = measureHeight(hMeasureSpec);
```

```
      int measuredWidth = measureWidth(wMeasureSpec);

      // MUST make this call to setMeasuredDimension
      // or you will cause a runtime exception when
      // the control is laid out.
      setMeasuredDimension(measuredHeight, measuredWidth);
    }

    private int measureHeight(int measureSpec) {
      int specMode = MeasureSpec.getMode(measureSpec);
      int specSize = MeasureSpec.getSize(measureSpec);

      [ ... Calculate the view height ... ]

      return specSize;
    }

    private int measureWidth(int measureSpec) {
      int specMode = MeasureSpec.getMode(measureSpec);
      int specSize = MeasureSpec.getSize(measureSpec);

      [ ... Calculate the view width ... ]

      return specSize;
    }

    @Override
    protected void onDraw(Canvas canvas) {
      [ ... Draw your visual interface ... ]
    }
  }
```

> Note that the onMeasure **method calls** setMeasuredDimension; **you must always call this method within your overridden** onMeasure **method or your control will throw an exception when the parent container attempts to lay it out.**

Drawing Your Control

The onDraw method is where the magic happens. If you're creating a new widget from scratch, it's because you want to create a completely new visual interface. The Canvas parameter available in the onDraw method is the surface you'll use to bring your imagination to life.

Android provides a variety of tools to help draw your design on the Canvas using various Paint objects. The Canvas class includes helper methods to draw primitive 2D objects including circles, lines, rectangles, text, and Drawables (images). It also supports transformations that let you rotate, translate (move), and scale (resize) the Canvas while you draw on it.

Used in combination with Drawables and the Paint class (which offer a variety of customizable fills and pens), the complexity and detail that your control can render are limited only by the size of the screen and the power of the processor rendering it.

> One of the most important techniques for writing efficient code in Android is to avoid repetitive creation and destruction of objects. Any object created in your onDraw method will be created and destroyed every time the screen refreshes. Improve efficiency by making as many of these objects (in particular, instances of Paint and Drawable) class-scoped and moving their creation into the constructor.

The following code snippet shows how to override the onDraw method to display a simple text string in the center of the control:

```
@Override
protected void onDraw(Canvas canvas) {
  // Get the size of the control based on the last call to onMeasure.
  int height = getMeasuredHeight();
  int width = getMeasuredWidth();

  // Find the center
  int px = width/2;
  int py = height/2;

  // Create the new paint brushes.
  // NOTE: For efficiency this should be done in
  // the widget's constructor
  Paint mTextPaint = new Paint(Paint.ANTI_ALIAS_FLAG);
  mTextPaint.setColor(Color.WHITE);

  // Define the string.
  String displayText = "Hello World!";

  // Measure the width of the text string.
  float textWidth = mTextPaint.measureText(displayText);

  // Draw the text string in the center of the control.
  canvas.drawText(displayText, px-textWidth/2, py, mTextPaint);
}
```

Android offers a rich drawing library for the Canvas. Rather than diverge too far from the current topic, a more detailed look at the techniques available for drawing more complex visuals is included in Chapter 11.

Android does not currently support vector graphics. As a result, changes to any element of your canvas require repainting the entire canvas; modifying the color of a brush will not change your View's display until it is invalidated and redrawn. Alternatively, you can use OpenGL to render graphics; for more details, see the discussion on SurfaceView in Chapter 11.

Sizing Your Control

Unless you conveniently require a control that always occupies 100 × 100 pixels, you will also need to override onMeasure.

The onMeasure method is called when the control's parent is laying out its child controls. It asks the question, "How much space will you use?" and passes in two parameters — widthMeasureSpec and heightMeasureSpec. They specify the space available for the control and some metadata describing that space.

Rather than return a result, you pass the View's height and width into the setMeasuredDimension method.

The following skeleton code shows how to override onMeasure. Note the calls to local method stubs calculateHeight and calculateWidth. They'll be used to decode the widthHeightSpec and heightMeasureSpec values and calculate the preferred height and width values.

```
@Override
protected void onMeasure(int widthMeasureSpec, int heightMeasureSpec) {

    int measuredHeight = measureHeight(heightMeasureSpec);
    int measuredWidth = measureWidth(widthMeasureSpec);

    setMeasuredDimension(measuredHeight, measuredWidth);
}

private int measureHeight(int measureSpec) {
    // Return measured widget height.
}

private int measureWidth(int measureSpec) {
    // Return measured widget width.
}
```

The boundary parameters, widthMeasureSpec and heightMeasureSpec, are passed in as integers for efficiency reasons. Before they can be used, they first need to be decoded using the static getMode and getSize methods from the MeasureSpec class, as shown in the snippet below:

```
int specMode = MeasureSpec.getMode(measureSpec);
int specSize = MeasureSpec.getSize(measureSpec);
```

Depending on the *mode* value, the *size* represents either the maximum space available for the control (in the case of AT_MOST), or the exact size that your control will occupy (for EXACTLY). In the case of UNSPECIFIED, your control does not have any reference for what the size represents.

By marking a measurement size as EXACT, the parent is insisting that the View will be placed into an area of the exact size specified. The AT_MOST designator says the parent is asking what size the View would like to occupy, given an upper bound. In many cases, the value you return will be the same.

In either case, you should treat these limits as absolute. In some circumstances, it may still be appropriate to return a measurement outside these limits, in which case you can let the parent choose how to deal with the oversized View, using techniques such as clipping and scrolling.

The following skeleton code shows a typical implementation for handling View measurement:

```
@Override
protected void onMeasure(int widthMeasureSpec, int heightMeasureSpec) {
    int measuredHeight = measureHeight(heightMeasureSpec);
```

```
    int measuredWidth = measureWidth(widthMeasureSpec);

    setMeasuredDimension(measuredHeight, measuredWidth);
}

private int measureHeight(int measureSpec) {
    int specMode = MeasureSpec.getMode(measureSpec);
    int specSize = MeasureSpec.getSize(measureSpec);

    //  Default size if no limits are specified.
    int result = 500;

    if (specMode == MeasureSpec.AT_MOST) {
        // Calculate the ideal size of your
        // control within this maximum size.
        // If your control fills the available
        // space return the outer bound.
        result = specSize;
    } else if (specMode == MeasureSpec.EXACTLY) {
        // If your control can fit within these bounds return that value.
        result = specSize;
    }
    return result;
}

private int measureWidth(int measureSpec) {
    int specMode = MeasureSpec.getMode(measureSpec);
    int specSize = MeasureSpec.getSize(measureSpec);

    //  Default size if no limits are specified.
    int result = 500;

    if (specMode == MeasureSpec.AT_MOST) {
        // Calculate the ideal size of your control
        // within this maximum size.
        // If your control fills the available space
        // return the outer bound.
        result = specSize;
    } else if (specMode == MeasureSpec.EXACTLY) {
        // If your control can fit within these bounds return that value.
        result = specSize;
    }
    return result;
}
```

Handling User Interaction Events

To make your new widget interactive, it will need to respond to user events like key presses, screen touches, and button clicks. Android exposes several virtual event handlers, listed below, that let you react to user input:

❑   onKeyDown   Called when any device key is pressed; includes the D-pad, keyboard, hang-up, call, back, and camera buttons

❑ onKeyUp   Called when a user releases a pressed key

❑ onTrackballEvent   Called when the device's trackball is moved

❑ onTouchEvent   Called when the touch screen is pressed or released, or it detects movement

The following code snippet shows a skeleton class that overrides each of the user interaction handlers in a View:

```
@Override
public boolean onKeyDown(int keyCode, KeyEvent keyEvent) {
  // Return true if the event was handled.
  return true;
}

@Override
public boolean onKeyUp(int keyCode, KeyEvent keyEvent) {
  // Return true if the event was handled.
  return true;
}

@Override
public boolean onTrackballEvent(MotionEvent event ) {
  // Get the type of action this event represents
  int actionPerformed = event.getAction();
  // Return true if the event was handled.
  return true;
}

@Override
public boolean onTouchEvent(MotionEvent event) {
  // Get the type of action this event represents
  int actionPerformed = event.getAction();
  // Return true if the event was handled.
  return true;
}
```

Further details on using each of these event handlers, including greater detail on the parameters received by each method, are available in Chapter 11.

Creating a Compass View Example

In the following example, you'll create a new Compass View by extending the View class. It uses a traditional compass rose to indicate a heading/orientation. When complete, it should appear as in Figure 4-3.

A compass is an example of a User Interface control that requires a radically different visual display from the textboxes and buttons available in the SDK toolbox, making it an excellent candidate for building from scratch.

In Chapter 10, you'll use this Compass View and the device's built-in accelerometer to display the user's current bearing. Then in Chapter 11, you will learn some advanced techniques for Canvas drawing that will let you dramatically improve its appearance.

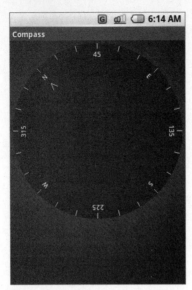

Figure 4-3

1. Create a new `Compass` project that will contain your new Compass View, and an Activity to hold it. Now create a new `CompassView` class that extends `View`. Create constructors that will allow the View to be instantiated in code, or through inflation from a resource layout. Add a new `initCompassView` method that will be used to initialize the control and call it from each constructor.

```
package com.paad.compass;

import android.content.Context;
import android.graphics.*;
import android.graphics.drawable.*;
import android.view.*;
import android.util.AttributeSet;
import android.content.res.Resources;

public class CompassView extends View {

  public CompassView(Context context) {
    super(context);
    initCompassView();
  }

  public CompassView(Context context, AttributeSet attrs) {
    super(context, attrs);
    initCompassView();
  }

  public CompassView(Context context,
                     AttributeSet ats,
                     int defaultStyle) {
    super(context, ats, defaultStyle);
```

```
    initCompassView();
  }

  protected void initCompassView() {
    setFocusable(true);
  }

}
```

2. The compass control should always be a perfect circle that takes up as much of the canvas as this restriction allows. Override the onMeasure method to calculate the length of the shortest side, and use setMeasuredDimension to set the height and width using this value.

```
@Override
protected void onMeasure(int widthMeasureSpec, int heightMeasureSpec) {
  // The compass is a circle that fills as much space as possible.
  // Set the measured dimensions by figuring out the shortest boundary,
  // height or width.
  int measuredWidth = measure(widthMeasureSpec);
  int measuredHeight = measure(heightMeasureSpec);

  int d = Math.min(measuredWidth, measuredHeight);

  setMeasuredDimension(d, d);
}

private int measure(int measureSpec) {
  int result = 0;

  // Decode the measurement specifications.
  int specMode = MeasureSpec.getMode(measureSpec);
  int specSize = MeasureSpec.getSize(measureSpec);

  if (specMode == MeasureSpec.UNSPECIFIED) {
    // Return a default size of 200 if no bounds are specified.
    result = 200;
  } else {
    // As you want to fill the available space
    // always return the full available bounds.
    result = specSize;
  }
  return result;
}
```

3. Create two new resource files that store the colors and text strings you'll use to draw the compass.

3.1. Create the text string resource res/values/strings.xml.

```
<?xml version="1.0" encoding="utf-8"?>
<resources>
  <string name="app_name">Compass</string>
  <string name="cardinal_north">N</string>
  <string name="cardinal_east">E</string>
  <string name="cardinal_south">S</string>
  <string name="cardinal_west">W</string>
</resources>
```

3.2. Create the color resource `res/values/colors.xml`.

```xml
<?xml version="1.0" encoding="utf-8"?>
<resources>
  <color name="background_color">#F555</color>
  <color name="marker_color">#AFFF</color>
  <color name="text_color">#AFFF</color>
</resources>
```

4. Now return to the `CompassView` class. Add a new property for the bearing to display and create `get` and `set` methods for it.

```java
private float bearing;

public void setBearing(float _bearing) {
  bearing = _bearing;
}
public float getBearing() {
  return bearing;
}
```

5. Next, return to the `initCompassView` method, and get references to each resource created in Step 3. Store the String values as instance variables, and use the color values to create new class-scoped `Paint` objects. You'll use these objects in the next step to draw the compass face.

```java
private Paint markerPaint;
private Paint textPaint;
private Paint circlePaint;
private String northString;
private String eastString;
private String southString;
private String westString;
private int textHeight;

protected void initCompassView() {
  setFocusable(true);

  circlePaint = new Paint(Paint.ANTI_ALIAS_FLAG);
  circlePaint.setColor(R.color. background_color);
  circlePaint.setStrokeWidth(1);
  circlePaint.setStyle(Paint.Style.FILL_AND_STROKE);

  Resources r = this.getResources();
  northString = r.getString(R.string.cardinal_north);
  eastString = r.getString(R.string.cardinal_east);
  southString = r.getString(R.string.cardinal_south);
  westString = r.getString(R.string.cardinal_west);

  textPaint = new Paint(Paint.ANTI_ALIAS_FLAG);
  textPaint.setColor(r.getColor(R.color.text_color));

  textHeight = (int)textPaint.measureText("yY");

  markerPaint = new Paint(Paint.ANTI_ALIAS_FLAG);
  markerPaint.setColor(r.getColor(R.color.marker_color));
}
```

6. The final step is drawing the compass face using the `Strings` and `Paint` objects you created in Step 5. The following code snippet is presented with only limited commentary. You can find more detail on how to draw on the Canvas and use advanced Paint effects in Chapter 11.

6.1. Start by overriding the `onDraw` method in the `CompassView` class.

```
@Override
protected void onDraw(Canvas canvas) {
```

6.2. Find the center of the control, and store the length of the smallest side as the compass's radius.

```
int px = getMeasuredWidth() / 2;
int py = getMeasuredHeight() /2 ;

int radius = Math.min(px, py);
```

6.3. Draw the outer boundary, and color the background of the compass face using the `drawCircle` method. Use the `circlePaint` object you created in Step 5.

```
// Draw the background
canvas.drawCircle(px, py, radius, circlePaint);
```

6.4. This compass displays the current heading by rotating the face, so that the current direction is always at the top of the device. To do this, rotate the canvas in the opposite direction to the current heading.

```
// Rotate our perspective so that the 'top' is
// facing the current bearing.
canvas.save();
canvas.rotate(-bearing, px, py);
```

6.5. All that's left is to draw the markings. Rotate the canvas through a full rotation, drawing markings every 15 degrees and the abbreviated direction string every 45 degrees.

```
int textWidth = (int)textPaint.measureText("W");
int cardinalX = px-textWidth/2;
int cardinalY = py-radius+textHeight;

// Draw the marker every 15 degrees and text every 45.
for (int i = 0; i < 24; i++) {
  // Draw a marker.
  canvas.drawLine(px, py-radius, px, py-radius+10, markerPaint);

  canvas.save();
  canvas.translate(0, textHeight);

  // Draw the cardinal points
  if (i % 6 == 0) {
    String dirString = "";
    switch (i) {
      case(0)   : {
                  dirString = northString;
                  int arrowY = 2*textHeight;
                  canvas.drawLine(px, arrowY, px-5, 3*textHeight,
                                  markerPaint);
```

```
                            canvas.drawLine(px, arrowY, px+5, 3*textHeight,
                                           markerPaint);
                            break;
                    }
            case(6)  : dirString = eastString; break;
            case(12) : dirString = southString; break;
            case(18) : dirString = westString; break;
        }
        canvas.drawText(dirString, cardinalX, cardinalY, textPaint);
    }

    else if (i % 3 == 0) {
        // Draw the text every alternate 45deg
        String angle = String.valueOf(i*15);
        float angleTextWidth = textPaint.measureText(angle);

        int angleTextX = (int)(px-angleTextWidth/2);
        int angleTextY = py-radius+textHeight;
        canvas.drawText(angle, angleTextX, angleTextY, textPaint);
    }
    canvas.restore();

    canvas.rotate(15, px, py);
}
canvas.restore();
}
```

7.   To view the compass, modify the main.xml layout resource and replace the `TextView` reference with your new `CompassView`. This process is explained in more detail in the next section.

```xml
<?xml version="1.0" encoding="utf-8"?>
<LinearLayout xmlns:android="http://schemas.android.com/apk/res/android"
  android:orientation="vertical"
  android:layout_width="fill_parent"
  android:layout_height="fill_parent">
  <com.paad.compass.CompassView
     android:id="@+id/compassView"
     android:layout_width="fill_parent"
     android:layout_height="fill_parent"
  />
</LinearLayout>
```

8.   Run the Activity, and you should see the `CompassView` displayed. See Chapter 10 to learn how to bind the `CompassView` to the device's compass.

Using Custom Controls

Having created you own custom Views, you can use them within code and layouts as you would any other Android control. The snippet below shows how to add the `CompassView` created in the above example to an Activity, by overriding the `onCreate` method:

```
@Override
public void onCreate(Bundle icicle) {
```

```
  super.onCreate(icicle);
  CompassView cv = new CompassView(this);
  setContentView(cv);
  cv.setBearing(45);
}
```

To use the same control within a layout resource, specify the fully qualified class name when you create a new node in the layout definition, as shown in the following XML snippet:

```
<com.paad.compass.CompassView
    android:id="@+id/compassView"
    android:layout_width="fill_parent"
    android:layout_height="fill_parent"
/>
```

You can inflate the layout and get a reference to the CompassView as normal, using the following code:

```
@Override
public void onCreate(Bundle icicle) {
  super.onCreate(icicle);
  setContentView(R.layout.main);
  CompassView cv = (CompassView)this.findViewById(R.id.compassView);
  cv.setBearing(45);
}
```

Creating and Using Menus

Menus offer a way to expose application functions without sacrificing valuable screen space. Each Activity can specify its own Activity menu that's displayed when the device's *menu* button is pressed.

Android also supports context menus that can be assigned to any View within an Activity. A View's context menu is triggered when a user holds the middle D-pad button, depresses the trackball, or long-presses the touch screen for around 3 seconds when the View has focus.

Activity and context menus support submenus, checkboxes, radio buttons, shortcut keys, and icons.

Introducing the Android Menu System

If you've ever tried to navigate a mobile phone menu system using a stylus or trackball, you'll know that traditional menu systems are awkward to use on mobile devices.

To improve the usability of application menus, Android features a three-stage menu system optimized for small screens:

❏   **The Icon Menu**   This compact menu (shown in Figure 4-4) appears along the bottom of the screen when the Menu button is pressed. It displays the icons and text for up to six Menu Items (or submenus).

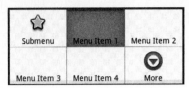

Figure 4-4

This icon menu does *not* display checkboxes, radio buttons, or the shortcut keys for Menu Items, so it's generally good practice not to assign checkboxes or radio buttons to icon menu items, as they will not be available.

If more than six Menu Items have been defined, a *More* item is included that, when selected, displays the expanded menu. Pressing the Back button closes the icon menu.

❏ **The Expanded Menu**   The expanded menu is triggered when a user selects the **More** Menu Item from the icon menu. The expanded menu (shown in Figure 4-5) displays a scrollable list of *only* the Menu Items that weren't visible in the icon menu. This menu displays full text, shortcut keys, and checkboxes/radio buttons as appropriate.

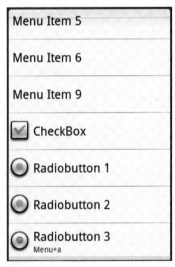

Figure 4-5

It does not, however, display icons. As a result, you should avoid assigning icons to Menu Items that are likely to appear only in the expanded menu.

Pressing Back from the expanded menu returns to the icon menu.

You cannot force Android to display the expanded menu instead of the icon menu. As a result, special care must be taken with Menu Items that feature checkboxes or radio buttons to ensure that they are either available only in the extended menu, or that their state information is also indicated using an icon or change in text.

❑ **Submenus** The traditional "expanding hierarchical tree" can be awkward to navigate using a mouse, so it's no surprise that this metaphor is particularly ill-suited for use on mobile devices. The Android alternative is to display each submenu in a floating window. For example, when a user selects a submenu such as the creatively labeled *Submenu* from Figure 4-5, its items are displayed in a floating menu Dialog box, as shown in Figure 4-6.

Figure 4-6

Note that the name of the submenu is shown in the header bar and that each Menu Item is displayed with its full text, checkbox (if any), and shortcut key. Since Android does not support nested submenus, you can't add a submenu to a submenu (trying will result in an exception).

As with the extended menu, icons are not displayed in the submenu items, so it's good practice to avoid assigning icons to submenu items.

Pressing the Back button closes the floating window without navigating back to the extended or icon menus.

Defining an Activity Menu

To define a menu for an Activity, override its onCreateOptionsMenu method. This method is triggered the first time an Activity's menu is displayed.

The onCreateOptionsMenu receives a Menu object as a parameter. You can store a reference to, and continue to use, the Menu reference elsewhere in your code until the next time that onCreateOptionsMenu is called.

You should always call through to the base implementation as it automatically includes additional system menu options where appropriate.

Use the add method on the Menu object to populate your menu. For each Menu Item, you must specify:

❑ A group value to separate Menu Items for batch processing and ordering

❑ A unique identifier for each Menu Item. For efficiency reasons, Menu Item selections are generally handled by the `onOptionsItemSelected` event handler, so this unique identifier is important to determine which Menu Item was pressed. It is convention to declare each menu ID as a private static variable within the `Activity` class. You can use the `Menu.FIRST` static constant and simply increment that value for each subsequent item.

❑ An order value that defines the order in which the Menu Items are displayed

❑ The menu text, either as a character string or as a string resource

When you have finished populating the menu, return True to allow Android to display the menu.

The following skeleton code shows how to add a single item to an Activity menu:

```
static final private int MENU_ITEM = Menu.FIRST;

@Override
public boolean onCreateOptionsMenu(Menu menu) {
  super.onCreateOptionsMenu(menu);

  // Group ID
  int groupId = 0;
  // Unique menu item identifier. Used for event handling.
  int menuItemId = MENU_ITEM;
  // The order position of the item
  int menuItemOrder = Menu.NONE;
  // Text to be displayed for this menu item.
  int menuItemText = R.string.menu_item;

  // Create the menu item and keep a reference to it.
  MenuItem menuItem = menu.add(groupId, menuItemId,
                               menuItemOrder, menuItemText);

  return true;
}
```

Like the `Menu` object, each Menu Item reference returned by a call to `add` is valid until the next call to `onCreateOptionsMenu`. Rather than maintaining a reference to each item, you can find a particular Menu Item by passing its ID into the `Menu.findItem` method.

Menu Item Options

Android supports most of the traditional Menu Item options you're probably familiar with, including icons, shortcuts, checkboxes, and radio buttons, as described below:

❑ **Checkboxes and Radio Buttons** Checkboxes and radio buttons on Menu Items are visible in expanded menus and submenus, as shown in Figure 4-6. To set a Menu Item as a checkbox, use the `setCheckable` method. The state of that checkbox is controlled using `setChecked`.

A *radio button group* is a group of items displaying circular buttons, where only one item can be selected at any given time. Checking one of these items will automatically unselect any other item in the same group, that is currently checked. To create a radio button group, assign the same group identifier to each item, then call `Menu.setGroupCheckable`, passing in that group identifier and setting the exclusive parameter to True.

Checkboxes are not visible in the icon menu, so Menu Items that feature checkboxes should be reserved for submenus and items that appear only in the expanded menu. The following code snippet shows how to add a checkbox and a group of three radio buttons:

```
// Create a new check box item.
menu.add(0, CHECKBOX_ITEM, Menu.NONE, "CheckBox").setCheckable(true);

// Create a radio button group.
menu.add(RB_GROUP, RADIOBUTTON_1, Menu.NONE, "Radiobutton 1");
menu.add(RB_GROUP, RADIOBUTTON_2, Menu.NONE, "Radiobutton 2");
menu.add(RB_GROUP, RADIOBUTTON_3, Menu.NONE,
          "Radiobutton 3").setChecked(true);
menu.setGroupCheckable(RB_GROUP, true, true);
```

❑ **Shortcut Keys** You can specify a keypad shortcut for a Menu Item using the `setShortcut` method. Each call to `setShortcut` requires two shortcut keys, one for use with the numeric keypad and a second to support a full keyboard. Neither key is case-sensitive.

The code below shows how to set a shortcut for both modes:

```
// Add a shortcut to this menu item, '0' if using the numeric keypad
// or 'b' if using the full keyboard.
menuItem.setShortcut('0', 'b');
```

❑ **Condensed Titles** The icon menu does not display shortcuts or checkboxes, so it's often necessary to modify its display text to indicate its state. The following code shows how to set the icon menu–specific text for a Menu Item:

```
menuItem.setTitleCondensed("Short Title");
```

❑ **Icons** Icon is a drawable resource identifier for an icon to be used in the Menu Item. Icons are only displayed in the icon menu; they are not visible in the extended menu or submenus. The following snippet shows how to apply an icon to a Menu Item:

```
menuItem.setIcon(R.drawable.menu_item_icon);
```

❑ **Menu Item Click Listener** An event handler that will execute when the Menu Item is selected. For efficiency reasons, this is discouraged; instead, Menu Item selections should be handled by the `onOptionsItemSelected` handler as shown later in this section. To apply a click listener to a Menu Item, use the pattern shown in the following code snippet:

```
menuItem.setOnMenuItemClickListener(new OnMenuItemClickListener() {

  public boolean onMenuItemClick(MenuItem _menuItem) {
    [ ... execute click handling, return true if handled ... ]
    return true;
  }

});
```

❑ **Intents**   An Intent assigned to a Menu Item is triggered when clicking a Menu Item isn't handled by either a `MenuItemClickListener` or the Activity's `onOptionsItemSelected` handler. When triggered, Android will execute `startActivity`, passing in the specified Intent. The following code snippet shows how to specify an Intent for a Menu Item:

```
menuItem.setIntent(new Intent(this, MyOtherActivity.class));
```

Dynamically Updating Menu Items

By overriding your activity's `onPrepareOptionsMenu` method, you can modify your menu based on the application state each time it's displayed. This lets you dynamically disable/enable each item, set visibility, and modify text at runtime.

To modify Menu Items dynamically, you can either keep a reference to them when they're created in the `onCreateOptionsMenu` method, or you can use `menu.findItem` as shown in the following skeleton code, where `onPrepareOptionsMenu` is overridden:

```
@Override
public boolean onPrepareOptionsMenu(Menu menu) {
  super.onPrepareOptionsMenu(menu);

  MenuItem menuItem = menu.findItem(MENU_ITEM);

  [ ... modify menu items ... ]

  return true;
}
```

Handling Menu Selections

Android handles all of an Activity's Menu Item selections using a single event handler, the `onOptionsItemSelected` method. The Menu Item selected is passed in to this method as the `MenuItem` parameter.

To react to the menu selection, compare the `item.getItemId` value to the Menu Item identifiers you used when populating the menu, and react accordingly, as shown in the following code:

```
public boolean onOptionsItemSelected(MenuItem item) {
  super.onOptionsItemSelected(item);

  // Find which menu item has been selected
  switch (item.getItemId()) {

    // Check for each known menu item
    case (MENU_ITEM):
      [ ... Perform menu handler actions ... ]
      return true;
  }

  // Return false if you have not handled the menu item.
  return false;
}
```

Submenus and Context Menus

Context menus are displayed using the same floating window as the submenus shown in Figure 4-5. While their appearance is the same, the two menu types are populated differently.

Creating Submenus

Submenus are displayed as regular Menu Items that, when selected, reveal more items. Traditionally, submenus are displayed using a hierarchical tree layout. Android uses a different approach to simplify menu navigation for small-screen devices. Rather than a tree structure, selecting a submenu presents a single floating window that displays all of its Menu Items.

You can add submenus using the `addSubMenu` method. It supports the same parameters as the `add` method used to add normal Menu Items, allowing you to specify a group, unique identifier, and text string for each submenu. You can also use the `setHeaderIcon` and `setIcon` methods to specify an icon to display in the submenu's header bar or the regular icon menu, respectively.

The Menu Items within a submenu support the same options as those assigned to the icon or extended menus. However, unlike traditional systems, Android does not support nested submenus.

The code snippet below shows an extract from an implementation of the `onCreateMenuOptions` code that adds a submenu to the main menu, sets the header icon, and then adds a submenu Menu Item:

```
SubMenu sub = menu.addSubMenu(0, 0, Menu.NONE, "Submenu");
sub.setHeaderIcon(R.drawable.icon);
sub.setIcon(R.drawable.icon);

MenuItem submenuItem = sub.add(0, 0, Menu.NONE, "Submenu Item");
```

Using Context Menus

Context Menus are contextualized by the currently focused View and are triggered by pressing the trackball, middle D-pad button, or the View for around 3 seconds.

You define and populate Context Menus similarly to the Activity menu. There are two options available for creating Context Menus for a particular View.

Creating Context Menus

The first option is to create a generic Context Menu for a `View` class by overriding a View's `onCreateContextMenu` handler as shown below:

```
@Override
public void onCreateContextMenu(ContextMenu menu) {
  super.onCreateContextMenu(menu);
  menu.add("ContextMenuItem1");
}
```

The Context Menu created here will be available from any Activity that includes this `View` class.

The more common alternative is to create Activity-specific Context Menus by overriding the `onCreateContextMenu` method and registering the Views that should use it. Register Views using `registerForContextMenu` and passing them in, as shown in the following code:

```
@Override
public void onCreate(Bundle icicle) {
  super.onCreate(icicle);

  EditText view = new EditText(this);
  setContentView(view);

  registerForContextMenu(view);
}
```

Once a View has been registered, the `onCreateContextMenu` handler will be triggered whenever a Context Menu should be displayed for that View.

Override `onCreateContextMenu` and check which View has triggered the menu creation to populate the menu parameter with the appropriate contextual items, as shown in the following code snippet:

```
@Override
public void onCreateContextMenu(ContextMenu menu, View v,
                                ContextMenu.ContextMenuInfo menuInfo) {
  super.onCreateContextMenu(menu, v, menuInfo);

  menu.setHeaderTitle("Context Menu");
  menu.add(0, menu.FIRST, Menu.NONE,
           "Item 1").setIcon(R.drawable.menu_item);
  menu.add(0, menu.FIRST+1, Menu.NONE, "Item 2").setCheckable(true);
  menu.add(0, menu.FIRST+2, Menu.NONE, "Item 3").setShortcut('3', '3');
  SubMenu sub = menu.addSubMenu("Submenu");
  sub.add("Submenu Item");
}
```

As shown above, the `ContextMenu` class supports the same `add` method as the `Menu` class, so you can populate a Context Menu in the same way as Activity menus — including support for submenus — but icons will never be displayed. You can also specify the title and icon to display in the Context Menu's header bar.

Android supports late runtime population of Context Menus using Intent Filters. This mechanism lets you populate a Context Menu by specifying the kind of data presented by the current View, and asking other Android applications if they support any actions for it. The most common example of this behavior is the cut/copy/paste Menu Items available on EditText controls. This process is covered in detail in the next chapter.

Handling Context Menu Selections

Context Menu Item selections are handled similarly to the Activity menu. You can attach an Intent or Menu Item Click Listener directly to each Menu Item, or use the preferred technique of overriding the `onContextItemSelected` method on the Activity.

This event handler is triggered whenever a Context Menu Item is selected within the Activity. A skeleton implementation is shown below:

```
@Override
public boolean onContextItemSelected(MenuItem item) {
  super.onContextItemSelected(item);

  [ ... Handle menu item selection ... ]

  return false;
}
```

To-Do List Example Continued

In the following example, you'll be adding some simple menu functions to the To-Do List application you started in Chapter 2 and continued to improve previously in this chapter.

You will add the ability to remove items from Context and Activity Menus, and improve the use of screen space by displaying the text entry box only when adding a new item.

1. Start by importing the packages you need to support menu functionality into the ToDoList Activity class.

```
import android.view.Menu;
import android.view.MenuItem;
import android.view.ContextMenu;
import android.widget.AdapterView;
```

2. Then add private static final variables that define the unique IDs for each Menu Item.

```
static final private int ADD_NEW_TODO = Menu.FIRST;
static final private int REMOVE_TODO = Menu.FIRST + 1;
```

3. Now override the onCreateOptionsMenu method to add two new Menu Items, one to add and the other to remove the to-do item. Specify the appropriate text, and assign icon resources and shortcut keys for each item.

```
@Override
public boolean onCreateOptionsMenu(Menu menu) {
  super.onCreateOptionsMenu(menu);

  // Create and add new menu items.
  MenuItem itemAdd = menu.add(0, ADD_NEW_TODO, Menu.NONE,
                              R.string.add_new);
  MenuItem itemRem = menu.add(0, REMOVE_TODO, Menu.NONE,
                              R.string.remove);

  // Assign icons
  itemAdd.setIcon(R.drawable.add_new_item);
  itemRem.setIcon(R.drawable.remove_item);

  // Allocate shortcuts to each of them.
```

```
    itemAdd.setShortcut('0', 'a');
    itemRem.setShortcut('1', 'r');

    return true;
}
```

If you run the Activity, pressing the Menu button should appear as shown in Figure 4-7.

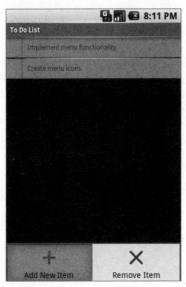

Figure 4-7

4. Having populated the Activity Menu, create a Context Menu. First, modify `onCreate` to register the ListView to receive a Context Menu. Then override `onCreateContextMenu` to populate the menu with a "remove" item.

```
@Override
public void onCreate(Bundle icicle) {

  [ ... existing onCreate method ... ]

  registerForContextMenu(myListView);
}

@Override
public void onCreateContextMenu(ContextMenu menu,
                                View v,
                                ContextMenu.ContextMenuInfo menuInfo) {
  super.onCreateContextMenu(menu, v, menuInfo);

  menu.setHeaderTitle("Selected To Do Item");
  menu.add(0, REMOVE_TODO, Menu.NONE, R.string.remove);
}
```

5. Now modify the appearance of the menu based on the application context, by overriding the onPrepareOptionsMenu method. The menu should be customized to show "cancel" rather than "delete" if you are currently adding a new Menu Item.

```
private boolean addingNew = false;

@Override
public boolean onPrepareOptionsMenu(Menu menu) {
  super.onPrepareOptionsMenu(menu);

  int idx = myListView.getSelectedItemPosition();

  String removeTitle = getString(addingNew ?
                         R.string.cancel : R.string.remove);

  MenuItem removeItem = menu.findItem(REMOVE_TODO);
  removeItem.setTitle(removeTitle);
  removeItem.setVisible(addingNew || idx > -1);

  return true;
}
```

6. For the code in Step 5 to work, you need to increase the scope of the todoListItems and ListView control beyond the onCreate method. Do the same thing for the ArrayAdapter and EditText to support the *add* and *remove* actions when they're implemented later.

```
private ArrayList<String> todoItems;
private ListView myListView;
private EditText myEditText;
private ArrayAdapter<String> aa;

@Override
public void onCreate(Bundle icicle) {
  super.onCreate(icicle);

  // Inflate your view
  setContentView(R.layout.main);

  // Get references to UI widgets
  myListView = (ListView)findViewById(R.id.myListView);
  myEditText = (EditText)findViewById(R.id.myEditText);

  todoItems = new ArrayList<String>();
  int resID = R.layout.todolist_item;
  aa = new ArrayAdapter<String>(this, resID, todoItems);
  myListView.setAdapter(aa);

  myEditText.setOnKeyListener(new OnKeyListener() {
    public boolean onKey(View v, int keyCode, KeyEvent event) {
      if (event.getAction() == KeyEvent.ACTION_DOWN)
        if (keyCode == KeyEvent.KEYCODE_DPAD_CENTER)
        {
          todoItems.add(0, myEditText.getText().toString());
          myEditText.setText("");
```

```
            aa.notifyDataSetChanged();
            return true;
        }
        return false;
    }
});

    registerForContextMenu(myListView);
}
```

7. Next you need to handle Menu Item clicks. Override the `onOptionsItemSelected` and `onContextItemSelected` methods to execute stubs that handle the new Menu Items.

    7.1. Start by overriding `onOptionsItemSelected` to handle the Activity menu selections. For the *remove* menu option, you can use the `getSelectedItemPosition` method on the List View to find the currently highlighted item.

    ```
    @Override
    public boolean onOptionsItemSelected(MenuItem item) {
        super.onOptionsItemSelected(item);

        int index = myListView.getSelectedItemPosition();

        switch (item.getItemId()) {
            case (REMOVE_TODO): {
                if (addingNew) {
                    cancelAdd();
                }
                else {
                    removeItem(index);
                }
                return true;
            }
            case (ADD_NEW_TODO): {
                addNewItem();
                return true;
            }
        }

        return false;
    }
    ```

    7.2. Next override `onContextItemSelected` to handle Context Menu Item selections. Note that you are using the `AdapterView` specific implementation of `ContextMenuInfo`. This includes a reference to the View that triggered the Context Menu and the position of the data it's displaying in the underlying Adapter.

    Use the latter to find the index of the item to remove.

    ```
    @Override
    public boolean onContextItemSelected(MenuItem item) {
        super.onContextItemSelected(item);
        switch (item.getItemId()) {
            case (REMOVE_TODO): {
                AdapterView.AdapterContextMenuInfo menuInfo;
                menuInfo =(AdapterView.AdapterContextMenuInfo)item.getMenuInfo();
    ```

```
      int index = menuInfo.position;

      removeItem(index);
      return true;
    }
  }
  return false;
}
```

7.3.   Create the stubs called in the Menu Item selection handlers you created above.

```
private void cancelAdd() {
}

private void addNewItem() {
}

private void removeItem(int _index) {
}
```

8.   Now implement each of the stubs to provide the new functionality.

```
private void cancelAdd() {
  addingNew = false;
  myEditText.setVisibility(View.GONE);
}

private void addNewItem() {
  addingNew = true;
  myEditText.setVisibility(View.VISIBLE);
  myEditText.requestFocus();
}

private void removeItem(int _index) {
  todoItems.remove(_index);
  aa.notifyDataSetChanged();
}
```

9.   Next you need to hide the text entry box after you've added a new item. In the onCreate method, modify the onKeyListener to call the cancelAdd function after adding a new item.

```
myEditText.setOnKeyListener(new OnKeyListener() {
  public boolean onKey(View v, int keyCode, KeyEvent event) {
    if (event.getAction() == KeyEvent.ACTION_DOWN)
      if (keyCode == KeyEvent.KEYCODE_DPAD_CENTER)
      {
        todoItems.add(0, myEditText.getText().toString());
        myEditText.setText("");
        aa.notifyDataSetChanged();
        cancelAdd();
        return true;
      }
    return false;
  }
});
```

10. Finally, to ensure a consistent UI, modify the main.xml layout to hide the text entry box until the user chooses to add a new item.

```
<EditText
  android:id="@+id/myEditText"
  android:layout_width="fill_parent"
  android:layout_height="wrap_content"
  android:text=""
  android:visibility="gone"
/>
```

Running the application should now let you trigger the Activity menu to add or remove items from the list, and a Context Menu on each item should offer the option of removing it.

Summary

You now know the basics of creating intuitive User Interfaces for Android applications. You learned about Views and layouts and were introduced to the Android menu system.

Activity screens are created by positioning Views using Layout Managers that can be created in code or as resource files. You learned how to extend, group, and create new View-based controls to provide customized appearance and behavior for your applications.

In this chapter, you:

❑ Were introduced to some of the controls and widgets available as part of the Android SDK.

❑ Learned how to use your custom controls within Activities.

❑ Discovered how to create and use Activity Menus and Context Menus.

❑ Extended the To-Do List Example to support custom Views and menu-based functions.

❑ Created a new CompassView control from scratch.

Having covered the fundamentals of Android UI design, the next chapter focuses on binding application components using Intents, Broadcast Receivers, and Adapters. You will learn how to start new Activities and broadcast and consume requests for actions. Chapter 5 also introduces Internet connectivity and looks at the Dialog class.

5

Intents, Broadcast Receivers, Adapters, and the Internet

At first glance, the subjects of this chapter may appear to have little in common; in practice, they represent the glue that binds applications and their components.

Mobile applications on most platforms run in their own sandboxes. They're isolated from each other and have strict limits on their interaction with the system hardware and native components. Android applications are also sandboxed, but they can use Intents, Broadcast Receivers, Adapters, Content Providers, and the Internet to extend beyond those boundaries.

In this chapter, you'll look at Intents and learn how to use them to start Activities, both explicitly and using late runtime binding. Using implicit Intents, you'll learn how to request that an action be performed on a piece of data, letting Android determine which application component can service that request.

Broadcast Intents are used to announce application events system-wide. You'll learn how to transmit these broadcasts and consume them using Broadcast Receivers.

You'll examine Adapters and learn how to use them to bind your presentation layer to data sources, and you'll examine the Dialog-box mechanisms available.

Having looked at the mechanisms for transmitting and consuming local data, you'll be introduced to Android's Internet connectivity model and some of the Java techniques for parsing Internet data feeds.

An earthquake-monitoring example will then demonstrate how to tie all these features together. The earthquake monitor will form the basis of an ongoing example that you'll improve and extend in later chapters.

Introducing Intents

Intents are used as a message-passing mechanism that lets you declare your intention that an action be performed, usually with (or on) a particular piece of data.

You can use Intents to support interaction between any of the application components available on an Android device, no matter which application they're part of. This turns a collection of independent components into a single, interconnected system.

One of the most common uses for Intents is to start new Activities, either *explicitly* (by specifying the class to load) or *implicitly* (by requesting an action be performed on a piece of data).

Intents can also be used to broadcast messages across the system. Any application can register a Broadcast Receiver to listen for, and react to, these broadcast Intents. This lets you create event-driven applications based on internal, system, or third-party application events.

Android uses broadcast Intents to announce system events, like changes in Internet connection status or battery charge levels. The native Android applications, such as the phone dialer and SMS manager, simply register components that listen for specific broadcast Intents — such as "incoming phone call" or "SMS message received" — and react accordingly.

Using Intents to propagate actions — even within the same application — is a fundamental Android design principle. It encourages the decoupling of components, to allow the seamless replacement of application elements. It also provides the basis of a simple model for extending functionality.

Using Intents to Launch Activities

The most common use of Intents is to bind your application components. Intents are used to start, stop, and transition between the Activities within an application.

> *The instructions given in this section refer to starting new Activities, but the same rules generally apply to Services as well. Details on starting (and creating) Services are available in Chapter 8.*

To open a different application screen (Activity) in your application, call `startActivity`, passing in an Intent, as shown in the snippet below.

```
startActivity(myIntent);
```

The `Intent` can either explicitly specify the class to open, or include an action that the target should perform. In the latter case, the run time will choose the Activity to open, using a process known as "Intent resolution."

The `startActivity` method finds, and starts, the single Activity that best matches your Intent.

When using `startActivity`, your application won't receive any notification when the newly launched Activity finishes. To track feedback from the opened form, use the `startActivityForResult` method described in more detail below.

Explicitly Starting New Activities

You learned in Chapter 2 that applications consist of several interrelated screens — Activities — that must be included in the application manifest. To connect them, you may want to explicitly specify which Activity to open.

To explicitly select an Activity class to start, create a new `Intent` specifying the current application context and the class of the Activity to launch. Pass this Intent in to `startActivity`, as shown in the following code snippet:

```
Intent intent = new Intent(MyActivity.this, MyOtherActivity.class);
startActivity(intent);
```

After calling `startActivity`, the new Activity (in this example, `MyOtherActivity`) will be created and become visible and active, moving to the top of the Activity stack.

Calling `finish` programmatically on the new Activity will close it and remove it from the stack. Alternatively, users can navigate to the previous Activity using the device's Back button.

Implicit Intents and Late Runtime Binding

Implicit Intents are a mechanism that lets anonymous application components service action requests.

When constructing a new implicit Intent to use with `startActivity`, you nominate an action to perform and, optionally, supply the data on which to perform that action.

When you use this new *implicit* Intent to start an Activity, Android will — at run time — resolve it into the class best suited to performing the action on the type of data specified. This means that you can create projects that use functionality from other applications, without knowing exactly which application you're borrowing functionality from ahead of time.

For example, if you want to let users make calls from an application, rather than implementing a new dialer you could use an implicit Intent that requests that the action ("dial a number") be performed on a phone number (represented as a URI), as shown in the code snippet below:

```
if (somethingWeird && itDontLookGood) {
  Intent intent = new Intent(Intent.ACTION_DIAL,
                             Uri.parse("tel:555-2368"));
  startActivity(intent);
}
```

Android resolves this Intent and starts an Activity that provides the dial action on a telephone number — in this case, the dialler Activity.

Various native applications provide components to handle actions performed on specific data. Third-party applications, including your own, can be registered to support new actions or to provide an alternative provider of native actions. You'll be introduced to some of the native actions later in this chapter.

Introducing `Linkify`

`Linkify` is a helper class that automagically creates hyperlinks within TextView (and TextView-derived) classes through RegEx pattern matching.

Text that matches a specified RegEx pattern will be converted into a clickable hyperlink that implicitly fires `startActivity(new Intent(Intent.ACTION_VIEW, uri))` using the matched text as the target URI.

You can specify any string pattern you want to turn into links; for convenience, the `Linkify` class provides presets for common content types (like phone numbers and e-mail/web addresses).

The Native Link Types

The static `Linkify.addLinks` method accepts the View to linkify, and a bitmask of one or more of the default content types supported and supplied by the `Linkify` class: WEB_URLS, EMAIL_ADDRESSES, PHONE_NUMBERS, and ALL.

The following code snippet shows how to linkify a TextView to display web and e-mail addresses as hyperlinks. When clicked, they will open the browser or e-mail application, respectively.

```
TextView textView = (TextView)findViewById(R.id.myTextView);
Linkify.addLinks(textView, Linkify.WEB_URLS|Linkify.EMAIL_ADDRESSES);
```

You can linkify Views from within a layout resource using the `android:autoLink` attribute. It supports one or more (separated by |) of the following self-describing values: `none`, `web`, `email`, `phone`, or `all`.

The following XML snippet shows how to add hyperlinks for phone numbers and e-mail addresses:

```
<TextView
  android:layout_width="fill_parent"
  android:layout_height="fill_parent"
  android:text="@string/linkify_me"
  android:autoLink="phone|email"
/>
```

Creating Custom Link Strings

To define your own linkify strings, you create a new RegEx pattern to match the text you want to display as hyperlinks.

As with the native types, you linkify the target view by calling `Linkify.addLinks`, but this time pass in the new RegEx pattern. You can also pass in a prefix that will be prepended to the target URI when a link is clicked.

The following example shows a View being linkified to support earthquake data provided by an Android Content Provider (that you will create in the next Chapter). Rather than include the entire schema, the linkify pattern matches any text that starts with "quake" and is followed by a number. The content schema is then prepended to the URI before the Intent is fired.

```
int flags = Pattern.CASE_INSENSITIVE;
Pattern p = Pattern.compile("\\bquake[0-9]*\\b", flags);
```

```
Linkify.addLinks(myTextView, p,
                 "content://com.paad.earthquake/earthquakes/");
```

Linkify also supports `TransformFilter` and `MatchFilter` interfaces. They offer additional control over the target URI structure and the definition of matching strings, and are used as shown in the skeleton code below:

```
Linkify.addLinks(myTextView, pattern, prefixWith,
                 new MyMatchFilter(), new MyTransformFilter());
```

Using the Match Filter

Implement the `acceptMatch` method in your `MatchFilter` to add additional conditions to RegEx pattern matches. When a potential match is found, `acceptMatch` is triggered, with the match start and end index (along with the full text being searched) passed in as parameters.

The following code shows a `MatchFilter` implementation that cancels any match that is immediately preceded by an exclamation mark.

```
class MyMatchFilter implements MatchFilter {
  public boolean acceptMatch(CharSequence s, int start, int end) {
    return (start == 0 || s.charAt(start-1) != '!');
  }
}
```

Using the Transform Filter

The Transform Filter gives you more freedom to format your text strings by letting you modify the implicit URI generated by the link text. Decoupling the link text from the target URI gives you more freedom in how you display data strings to your users.

To use the Transform Filter, implement the `transformUrl` method in your Transform Filter. When Linkify finds a successful match, it calls `transformUrl`, passing in the RegEx pattern used and the default URI string it creates. You can modify the matched string, and return the URI as a target suitable to be "viewed" by another Android application.

The following `TransformFilter` implementation transforms the matched text into a lowercase URI:

```
class MyTransformFilter implements TransformFilter {
  public String transformUrl(Matcher match, String url) {
    return url.toLowerCase();
  }
}
```

Returning Results from Activities

An Activity started using `startActivity` is independent of its parent and will not provide any feedback when it closes.

Alternatively, you can start an Activity as a sub-Activity that's inherently connected to its parent. Sub-Activities trigger an event handler within their parent Activity when they close. Sub-Activities are perfect for situations in which one Activity is providing data input (such as a user selecting an item from a list) for another.

Sub-Activities are created the same way as normal Activities and must also be registered in the application manifest. Any manifest-registered Activity can be opened as a sub-Activity.

Launching Sub-Activities

The `startActivityForResult` method works much like `startActivity` but with one important difference. As well as the Intent used to determine which Activity to launch, you also pass in a *request code*. This value will be used later to uniquely identify the sub-Activity that has returned a result.

The skeleton code for launching a sub-Activity is shown below:

```
private static final int SHOW_SUBACTIVITY = 1;

Intent intent = new Intent(this, MyOtherActivity.class);
startActivityForResult(intent, SHOW_SUBACTIVITY);
```

As with regular Activities, sub-Activities can be started implicitly or explicitly. The following skeleton code uses an implicit Intent to launch a new sub-Activity to pick a contact:

```
private static final int PICK_CONTACT_SUBACTIVITY = 2;

Uri uri = Uri.parse("content://contacts/people");
Intent intent = new Intent(Intent.ACTION_PICK, uri);
startActivityForResult(intent, PICK_CONTACT_SUBACTIVITY);
```

Returning Results

When your sub-Activity is ready to close, call `setResult` before `finish` to return a result to the calling Activity.

The `setResult` method takes two parameters: the result code and result payload represented as an Intent.

The result code is the "result" of running the sub-Activity — generally either `Activity.RESULT_OK` or `Activity.RESULT_CANCELED`. In some circumstances, you'll want to use your own response codes to handle application-specific choices; `setResult` supports any integer value.

The Intent returned as a result can include a URI to a piece of content (such as the contact, phone number, or media file) and a collection of Extras used to return additional information.

This next code snippet is taken from a sub-Activity's `onCreate` method and shows how an OK button and a Cancel button might return different results to the calling Activity:

```
Button okButton = (Button) findViewById(R.id.ok_button);
  okButton.setOnClickListener(new View.OnClickListener() {

  public void onClick(View view) {
    Uri data = Uri.parse("content://horses/" + selected_horse_id);

    Intent result = new Intent(null, data);
    result.putExtra(IS_INPUT_CORRECT, inputCorrect);
    result.putExtra(SELECTED_PISTOL, selectedPistol);
```

```
        setResult(RESULT_OK, result);

        finish();
    }
});

Button cancelButton = (Button) findViewById(R.id.cancel_button);
cancelButton.setOnClickListener(new View.OnClickListener() {

    public void onClick(View view) {
        setResult(RESULT_CANCELED, null);

        finish();
    }
});
```

Handling Sub-Activity Results

When a sub-Activity closes, its parent Activity's onActivityResult event handler is fired.

Override this method to handle the results from the sub-Activities. The onActivityResult handler receives several parameters:

❑   **The Request Code**   The request code that was used to launch the returning sub-Activity

❑   **A Result Code**   The result code set by the sub-Activity to indicate its result. It can be any integer value, but typically will be either Activity.RESULT_OK or Activity.RESULT_CANCELLED.

If the sub-Activity closes abnormally or doesn't specify a result code before it closes, the result code is Activity.RESULT_CANCELED.

❑   **Data**   An Intent used to bundle any returned data. Depending on the purpose of the sub-Activity, it will typically include a URI that represents the particular piece of data selected from a list. Alternatively, or additionally, the sub-Activity can return extra information as primitive values using the "extras" mechanism.

The skeleton code for implementing the onActivityResult event handler within an Activity is shown below:

```
private static final int SHOW_SUB_ACTIVITY_ONE = 1;
private static final int SHOW_SUB_ACTIVITY_TWO = 2;

@Override
public void onActivityResult(int requestCode,
                             int resultCode,
                             Intent data) {

    super.onActivityResult(requestCode, resultCode, data);

    switch(requestCode) {
      case (SHOW_SUB_ACTIVITY_ONE) : {
        if (resultCode == Activity.RESULT_OK) {
          Uri horse = data.getData();
```

```
                boolean inputCorrect = data.getBooleanExtra(IS_INPUT_CORRECT,
                                                            false);
                String selectedPistol = data.getStringExtra(SELECTED_PISTOL);
            }
            break;
        }
        case (SHOW_SUB_ACTIVITY_TWO) : {
            if (resultCode == Activity.RESULT_OK) {
                // TODO: Handle OK click.
            }
            break;
        }
    }
}
```

Native Android Actions

Native Android applications also use Intents to launch Activities and sub-Activities.

The following noncomprehensive list shows some of the native actions available as static string constants in the `Intent` class. You can use these actions when creating implicit Intents to start Activities and sub-Activities within your own applications.

In the next section you will be introduced to Intent Filters, and you'll learn how to register your own Activities as handlers for these actions.

❑ `ACTION_ANSWER`   Opens an Activity that handles incoming calls. Currently this is handled by the native phone dialer.

❑ `ACTION_CALL`   Brings up a phone dialer and immediately initiates a call using the number supplied in the data URI. Generally, it's considered better form to use the `Dial_Action` if possible.

❑ `ACTION_DELETE`   Starts an Activity that lets you delete the entry currently stored at the data URI location.

❑ `ACTION_DIAL`   Brings up a dialer application with the number to dial prepopulated from the data URI. By default, this is handled by the native Android phone dialer. The dialer can normalize most number schemas; for example, `tel:555-1234` and `tel:(212) 555 1212` are both valid numbers.

❑ `ACTION_EDIT`   Requests an Activity that can edit the data at the URI.

❑ `ACTION_INSERT`   Opens an Activity capable of inserting new items into the cursor specified in the data field. When called as a sub-Activity, it should return a URI to the newly inserted item.

❑ `ACTION_PICK`   Launches a sub-Activity that lets you pick an item from the URI data. When closed, it should return a URI to the item that was picked. The Activity launched depends on the data being picked; for example, passing `content://contacts/people` will invoke the native contacts list.

❑ `ACTION_SEARCH`   Launches the UI for performing a search. Supply the search term as a string in the Intent's extras using the `SearchManager.QUERY` key.

❑ `ACTION_SENDTO`   Launches an Activity to send a message to the contact specified by the data URI.

❏ `ACTION_SEND` Launches an Activity that sends the specified data (the recipient needs to be selected by the resolved Activity). Use `setType` to set the Intent's type as the transmitted data's mime type.

The data itself should be stored as an extra using the key `EXTRA_TEXT` or `EXTRA_STREAM` depending on the type. In the case of e-mail, the native Android applications will also accept extras using the `EXTRA_EMAIL`, `EXTRA_CC`, `EXTRA_BCC`, and `EXTRA_SUBJECT` keys.

❏ `ACTION_VIEW` The most common generic action. View asks that the data supplied in the Intent's URI be viewed in the most reasonable manner. Different applications will handle view requests depending on the URI schema of the data supplied. Natively, `http:` addresses will open in the browser, `tel:` addresses will open the dialer to call the number, `geo:` addresses are displayed in the Google Maps application, and contact content will be displayed in the Contact Manager.

❏ `ACTION_WEB_SEARCH` Opens an activity that performs a Web search based on the text supplied in the data URI.

As well as these Activity actions, Android includes a large number of Broadcast actions that are used to create Intents that the system broadcasts to notify applications of events. These Broadcast actions are described later in this chapter.

Using Intent Filters to Service Implicit Intents

If an Intent is a request for an action to be performed on a set of data, how does Android know which application (and component) to use to service the request? Intent Filters are used to register Activities, Services, and Broadcast Receivers as being capable of performing an action on a particular kind of data.

Using Intent Filters, application components tell Android that they can service action requests from others, including components in the same, native, or third-party applications.

To register an application component as an Intent handler, use the `intent-filter` tag within the component's manifest node.

Using the following tags (and associated attributes) within the Intent Filter node, you can specify a component's supported actions, categories, and data:

❏ `action` Use the `android:name` attribute to specify the name of the action being serviced. Actions should be unique strings, so best practice is to use a naming system based on the Java package naming conventions.

❏ `category` Use the `android:category` attribute to specify under which circumstances the action should be serviced. Each Intent Filter tag can include multiple category tags. You can specify your own categories or use the standard values provided by Android and listed below:

  ❏ `ALTERNATIVE` As you'll see later in this chapter, one of the uses of Intent Filters is to help populate context menus with actions. The `alternative` category specifies that this action should be available as an alternative to the default action performed on an item of this data type. For example, where the default action for a contact is to view it, the alternatives could be to edit or delete it.

❑   SELECTED_ALTERNATIVE   Similar to the alternative category, but where Alternative will always resolve to a single action using the Intent resolution described below, SELECTED_ALTERNATIVE is used when a list of possibilities is required.

❑   BROWSABLE   Specifies an action available from within the browser. When an Intent is fired from within the browser, it will always specify the browsable category.

❑   DEFAULT   Set this to make a component the default action for the data values defined by the Intent Filter. This is also necessary for Activities that are launched using an explicit Intent.

❑   GADGET   By setting the gadget category, you specify that this Activity can run embedded inside another Activity.

❑   HOME   The home Activity is the first Activity displayed when the device starts (the launch screen). By setting an Intent Filter category as home without specifying an action, you are presenting it as an alternative to the native home screen.

❑   LAUNCHER   Using this category makes an Activity appear in the application launcher.

❑   data   The data tag lets you specify matches for data your component can act on; you can include several schemata if your component is capable of handling more than one. You can use any combination of the following attributes to specify the data that your component supports:

❑   android:host   Specifies a valid host name (e.g., com.google).

❑   android:mimetype   Lets you specify the type of data your component is capable of handling. For example, <type android:value="vnd.android.cursor.dir/*"/> would match any Android cursor.

❑   android:path   Valid "path" values for the URI (e.g., /transport/boats/)

❑   android:port   Valid ports for the specified host

❑   android:scheme   Requires a particular scheme (e.g., content or http).

The following code snippet shows how to configure an Intent Filter for an Activity that can perform the SHOW_DAMAGE action as either a primary or alternative action. (You'll create earthquake content in the next chapter.)

```
<activity android:name=".EarthquakeDamageViewer"
          android:label="View Damage">
  <intent-filter>
    <action
      android:name="com.paad.earthquake.intent.action.SHOW_DAMAGE">
    </action>
    <category android:name="android.intent.category.DEFAULT"/>
    <category
      android:name="android.intent.category.ALTERNATIVE_SELECTED"
    />
    <data android:mimeType="vnd.earthquake.cursor.item/*"/>
  </intent-filter>
</activity>
```

How Android Resolves Intent Filters

The anonymous nature of runtime binding makes it important to understand how Android resolves an implicit Intent into a particular application component.

As you saw previously, when using `startActivity`, the implicit Intent resolves to a single Activity. If there are multiple Activities capable of performing the given action on the specified data, the "best" of those Activities will be launched.

The process of deciding which Activity to start is called *Intent resolution*. The aim of Intent resolution is to find the best Intent Filter match possible using the following process:

1. Android puts together a list of all the Intent Filters available from the installed packages.

2. Intent Filters that do not match the action or category associated with the Intent being resolved are removed from the list.

   2.1. Action matches are made if the Intent Filter either includes the specified action or has no action specified.

   An Intent Filter will only fail the action match check if it has one or more actions defined, where none of them match the action specified by the Intent.

   2.2. Category matching is stricter. Intent Filters must include *all* the categories defined in the resolving Intent. An Intent Filter with no categories specified only matches Intents with no categories.

3. Finally, each part of the Intent's data URI is compared to the Intent Filter's `data` tag. If Intent Filter defines the scheme, host/authority, path, or mime type, these values are compared to the Intent's URI. Any mismatches will remove the Intent Filter from the list.

   Specifying no data values in an Intent Filter will match with all Intent data values.

   3.1. The mime type is the data type of the data being matched. When matching data types, you can use wild cards to match subtypes (e.g., `earthquakes/*`). If the Intent Filter specifies a data type, it must match the Intent; specifying no data type resolves to all of them.

   3.2. The scheme is the "protocol" part of the URI — for example, `http:`, `mailto:`, or `tel:`.

   3.3. The host name or "data authority" is the section of the URI between the scheme and the path (e.g., `www.google.com`). For a host name to match, the Intent Filter's scheme must also pass.

   3.4. The data path is what comes after the authority (e.g., `/ig`). A path can only match if the scheme and host-name parts of the `data` tag also match.

4. If more than one component is resolved from this process, they are ordered in terms of priority, with an optional tag that can be added to the Intent Filter node. The highest ranking component is then returned.

Native Android application components are part of the Intent resolution process in exactly the same way as third-party applications. They do not have a higher priority and can be completely replaced with new Activities that declare Intent Filters that service the same action requests.

Responding to Intent Filter Matches

When an application component is started through an implicit Intent, it needs to find the action it is to perform and the data upon which to perform it.

Call the `getIntent` method — usually from within the `onCreate` method — to extract the Intent used to launch a component, as shown below:

```
@Override
public void onCreate(Bundle icicle) {
  super.onCreate(icicle);
  setContentView(R.layout.main);

  Intent intent = getIntent();
}
```

Use the `getData` and `getAction` methods to find the data and action of the Intent. Use the type-safe `get<type>Extra` methods to extract additional information stored in its extras Bundle.

```
String action = intent.getAction();
Uri data = intent.getData();
```

Passing on Responsibility

You can use the `startNextMatchingActivity` method to pass responsibility for action handling to the next best matching application component, as shown in the snippet below:

```
Intent intent = getIntent();
if (isAfterMidnight)
  startNextMatchingActivity(intent);
```

This allows you to add additional conditions to your components that restrict their use beyond the ability of the Intent Filter–based Intent resolution process.

In some cases, your component may wish to perform some processing, or offer the user a choice, before passing the Intent on to the native handler.

Select a Contact Example

In this example, you'll create a new sub-Activity that services the `PICK_ACTION` for contact data. It displays each of the contacts in the contact database and lets the user select one, before closing and returning its URI to the calling Activity.

> It's worth noting that this example is somewhat contrived. Android already supplies an Intent Filter for picking a contact from a list that can be invoked by using the `content:/contacts/people/` URI in an implicit Intent. The purpose of this exercise is to demonstrate the form, even if this particular implementation isn't overly useful.

1. Create a new ContactPicker project that includes a `ContactPicker` Activity.

    ```
    package com.paad.contactpicker;

    import android.app.Activity;
    ```

```java
import android.content.Intent;
import android.database.Cursor;
import android.net.Uri;
import android.os.Bundle;
import android.provider.Contacts.People;
import android.view.View;
import android.widget.AdapterView;
import android.widget.ListView;
import android.widget.SimpleCursorAdapter;
import android.widget.AdapterView.OnItemClickListener;

public class ContactPicker extends Activity {
  @Override
  public void onCreate(Bundle icicle) {
    super.onCreate(icicle);
    setContentView(R.layout.main);
  }
}
```

2. Modify the main.xml layout resource to include a single `ListView` control. This control will be used to display the contacts.

```xml
<?xml version="1.0" encoding="utf-8"?>
<LinearLayout xmlns:android="http://schemas.android.com/apk/res/android"
  android:orientation="vertical"
  android:layout_width="fill_parent"
  android:layout_height="fill_parent">
  <ListView
    android:id="@+id/contactListView"
    android:layout_width="fill_parent"
    android:layout_height="wrap_content"
  />
</LinearLayout>
```

3. Create a new listitemlayout.xml layout resource that includes a single Text View. This will be used to display each contact in the List View.

```xml
<?xml version="1.0" encoding="utf-8"?>
<LinearLayout
  xmlns:android="http://schemas.android.com/apk/res/android"
  android:orientation="vertical"
  android:layout_width="fill_parent"
  android:layout_height="fill_parent">
  <TextView
    android:id="@+id/itemTextView"
    android:layout_width="fill_parent"
    android:layout_height="wrap_content"
    android:padding="10px"
    android:textSize="16px"
    android:textColor="#FFF"
  />
</LinearLayout>
```

4. Return to the ContactPicker Activity. Override the onCreate method, and extract the data path from the calling Intent.

```
@Override
public void onCreate(Bundle icicle) {
  super.onCreate(icicle);
  setContentView(R.layout.main);

  Intent intent = getIntent();
  String dataPath = intent.getData().toString();
```

4.1. Create a new data URI for the people stored in the contact list, and bind it to the List View using a SimpleCursorArrayAdapter.

The SimpleCursorArrayAdapter lets you assign Cursor data, used by Content Providers, to Views. It's used here without further comment but is examined in more detail later in this chapter.

```
final Uri data = Uri.parse(dataPath + "people/");
final Cursor c = managedQuery(data, null, null, null, null);

String[] from = new String[] {People.NAME};
int[] to = new int[] { R.id.itemTextView };

SimpleCursorAdapter adapter = new SimpleCursorAdapter(this,
                                        R.layout.listitemlayout,
                                        c,
                                        from,
                                        to);
ListView lv = (ListView)findViewById(R.id.contactListView);
lv.setAdapter(adapter);
```

4.2. Add an ItemClickListener to the List View. Selecting a contact from the list should return a path to the item to the calling Activity.

```
lv.setOnItemClickListener(new OnItemClickListener() {

  public void onItemClick(AdapterView<?> parent, View view, int pos,
                          long id) {
    // Move the cursor to the selected item
    c.moveToPosition(pos);
    // Extract the row id.
    int rowId = c.getInt(c.getColumnIndexOrThrow("_id"));
    // Construct the result URI.
    Uri outURI = Uri.parse(data.toString() + rowId);
    Intent outData = new Intent();
    outData.setData(outURI);
    setResult(Activity.RESULT_OK, outData);
    finish();
  }
});
```

4.3. Close off the onCreate method.

```
}
```

5. Modify the application manifest and replace the `intent-filter` tag of the Activity to add support for the pick action on contact data.

```xml
<?xml version="1.0" encoding="utf-8"?>
<manifest xmlns:android="http://schemas.android.com/apk/res/android"
  package="com.paad.contactpicker">
  <application android:icon="@drawable/icon">
    <activity android:name="ContactPicker"
            android:label="@string/app_name">
      <intent-filter>
        <action android:name="android.intent.action.PICK"/>
        <category android:name="android.intent.category.DEFAULT"/>
        <data android:path="contacts"
            android:scheme="content">
        </data>
      </intent-filter>
    </activity>
  </application>
</manifest>
```

6. This completes the sub-Activity. To test it, create a new test harness `ContentPickerTester` Activity. Create a new layout resource — `contentpickertester` — that includes a `TextView` to display the selected contact and a `Button` to start the sub-Activity.

```xml
<?xml version="1.0" encoding="utf-8"?>
<LinearLayout
  xmlns:android="http://schemas.android.com/apk/res/android"
  android:orientation="vertical"
  android:layout_width="fill_parent"
  android:layout_height="fill_parent">
  <TextView
    android:id="@+id/selected_contact_textview"
    android:layout_width="fill_parent"
    android:layout_height="wrap_content"
  />
  <Button
    android:id="@+id/pick_contact_button"
    android:layout_width="fill_parent"
    android:layout_height="wrap_content"
    android:text="Pick Contact"
  />
</LinearLayout>
```

7. Override the `onCreate` method of the `ContentPickerTester` to add a Click Listener to the button so that it implicitly starts a new sub-Activity by specifying the `PICK_ACTION` and the contact database URI (`content://contacts/`).

```java
package com.paad.contactpicker;

import android.app.Activity;
import android.content.Intent;
import android.database.Cursor;
import android.net.Uri;
import android.os.Bundle;
import android.provider.Contacts.People;
import android.view.View;
```

```
import android.view.View.OnClickListener;
import android.widget.Button;
import android.widget.TextView;

public class ContentPickerTester extends Activity {

  public static final int PICK_CONTACT = 1;

  @Override
  public void onCreate(Bundle icicle) {
    super.onCreate(icicle);
    setContentView(R.layout.contentpickertester);

    Button button = (Button)findViewById(R.id.pick_contact_button);

    button.setOnClickListener(new OnClickListener() {
      public void onClick(View _view) {
        Intent intent = new Intent(Intent.ACTION_PICK,
                              Uri.parse("content://contacts/"));
        startActivityForResult(intent, PICK_CONTACT);
      }
    });
  }
}
```

8. When the sub-Activity returns, use the result to populate the Text View with the selected contact's name.

```
@Override
public void onActivityResult(int reqCode, int resCode, Intent data) {
  super.onActivityResult(reqCode, resCode, data);

  switch(reqCode) {
    case (PICK_CONTACT) : {
      if (resCode == Activity.RESULT_OK) {
        Uri contactData = data.getData();
        Cursor c = managedQuery(contactData, null, null, null, null);
        c.moveToFirst();
        String name;
        name = c.getString(c.getColumnIndexOrThrow(People.NAME));
        TextView tv;
        tv = (TextView)findViewById(R.id.selected_contact_textview);
        tv.setText(name);
      }
      break;
    }
  }
}
```

9. With your test harness complete, simply add it to your application manifest. You'll also need to add a READ_CONTACTS permission within a uses-permission tag, to allow the application to access the contacts database.

```
<?xml version="1.0" encoding="utf-8"?>
<manifest xmlns:android="http://schemas.android.com/apk/res/android"
```

```
    package="com.paad.contactpicker">
    <application android:icon="@drawable/icon">
      <activity android:name=".ContactPicker"
                android:label="@string/app_name">
        <intent-filter>
          <action android:name="android.intent.action.PICK"/>
          <category android:name="android.intent.category.DEFAULT"/>
          <data android:path="contacts" android:scheme="content"/>
        </intent-filter>
      </activity>
        <activity android:name=".ContentPickerTester"
                  android:label="Contact Picker Test">
        <intent-filter>
          <action android:name="android.intent.action.MAIN"/>
          <category android:name="android.intent.category.LAUNCHER"/>
        </intent-filter>
      </activity>
    </application>
    <uses-permission android:name="android.permission.READ_CONTACTS"/>
  </manifest>
```

When your Activity is running, press the button. The contact picker Activity should be shown as in Figure 5-1.

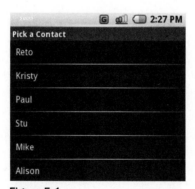

Figure 5-1

Once you select a contact, the parent Activity should return to the foreground with the selected contact name displayed, as shown in Figure 5-2.

Figure 5-2

Using Intent Filters for Plug-ins and Extensibility

So far you've learned how to explicitly create implicit Intents, but that's only half the story. Android lets future packages provide new functionality for existing applications, using Intent Filters to populate menus dynamically at run time.

This provides a plug-in model for your Activities that lets them take advantage of functionality you haven't yet conceived of through new application components, without your having to modify or recompile your projects.

The `addIntentOptions` method available from the `Menu` class lets you specify an Intent that describes the data that is acted upon by this menu. Android resolves this Intent and returns every action specified in the Intent Filters that matches the specified data. A new Menu Item is created for each, with the text populated from the matching Intent Filters' labels.

The elegance of this concept is best explained by example. Say the data your application displays are a list of places. At the moment, the menu actions available might include "view" and "show directions to." Jump a few years ahead, and you've created an application that interfaces with your car, allowing your phone to handle driving. Thanks to the runtime menu generation, by including a new Intent Filter — with a `DRIVE_CAR` action — within the new Activity's node, Android will automagically add this action as a new Menu Item in your earlier application.

Runtime menu population provides the ability to retrofit functionality when you create new components capable of performing actions on a given type of data. Many of Android's native applications use this functionality, giving you the ability to provide additional actions to native Activities.

Supplying Anonymous Actions to Applications

To make actions available for other Activities, publish them using `intent-filter` tags within their manifest nodes.

The Intent Filter describes the `action` it performs and the `data` upon which it can be performed. The latter will be used during the Intent resolution process to determine when this action should be available. The `category` tag must be either or both `ALTERNATIVE` and `SELECTED_ALTERNATIVE`. The text used by Menu Items is specified by the `android:label` attribute.

The following XML shows an example of an Intent Filter used to advertise an Activity's ability to nuke moon bases from orbit.

```xml
<activity android:name=".NostromoController">
  <intent-filter android:label="Nuke From Orbit">
    <action android:name="com.pad.nostromo.NUKE_FROM_ORBIT"/>
    <data android:mimeType="vnd.moonbase.cursor.item/*"/>
    <category android:name="android.intent.category.ALTERNATIVE"/>
    <category
      android:name="android.intent.category.SELECTED_ALTERNATIVE"
    />
  </intent-filter>
</activity>
```

The Content Provider and other code needed for this example to run aren't provided; in the following sections, you'll see how to write the code that will make this action available dynamically from another Activity's menu.

Incorporating Anonymous Actions in Your Activity's Menu

To add menu options to your menus at run time, you use the `addIntentOptions` method on the menu object in question, passing in an Intent that specifies the data for which you want to provide actions. Generally, this will be handled within your Activity's `onCreateOptionsMenu` or `onCreateContextMenu` handlers.

The Intent you create will be used to resolve components with Intent Filters that supply actions for the data you specify. The Intent is being used to find actions, so don't assign it one; it should only specify the data on which to perform actions. You should also specify the category of the action, either `CATEGORY_ALTERNATIVE` or `CATEGORY_SELECTED_ALTERNATIVE`.

The skeleton code for creating an Intent for menu-action resolution is shown below:

```
Intent intent = new Intent();
intent.setData(MyProvider.CONTENT_URI);
intent.addCategory(Intent.CATEGORY_ALTERNATIVE);
```

Pass this Intent into `addIntentOptions` on the menu you wish to populate, as well as any option flags, the name of the calling class, the menu group to use, and menu ID values. You can also specify an array of Intents you'd like to use to create additional Menu Items.

The following code snippet gives an idea of how to dynamically populate an Activity menu that would include the "moonbase nuker" action from the previous section:

```
@Override
public boolean onCreateOptionsMenu(Menu menu) {
  super.onCreateOptionsMenu(menu);

  // Create the intent used to resolve which actions
  // should appear in the menu.
  Intent intent = new Intent();
  intent.setData(MoonBaseProvider.CONTENT_URI);
  intent.addCategory(Intent.CATEGORY_SELECTED_ALTERNATIVE);

  // Normal menu options to let you set a group and ID
  // values for the menu items you're adding.
  int menuGroup = 0;
  int menuItemId = 0;
  int menuItemOrder = Menu.NONE;

  // Provide the name of the component that's calling
  // the action -- generally the current Activity.
  ComponentName caller = getComponentName();

  // Define intents that should be added first.
  Intent[] specificIntents = null;
  // The menu items created from the previous Intents
  // will populate this array.
```

```
       MenuItem[] outSpecificItems = null;

       // Set any optional flags.
       int flags = Menu.FLAG_APPEND_TO_GROUP;

       // Populate the menu
       menu.addIntentOptions(menuGroup,
                             menuItemId,
                             menuItemOrder,
                             caller,
                             specificIntents,
                             intent,
                             flags,
                             outSpecificItems);

       return true;
   }
```

Using Intents to Broadcast Events

As a system-level message-passing mechanism, Intents are capable of sending structured messages across process boundaries.

So far you've looked at using Intents to start new application components, but they can also be used to broadcast messages anonymously *between* components with the `sendBroadcast` method. You can implement Broadcast Receivers to listen for, and respond to, these broadcast Intents within your applications.

Broadcast Intents are used to notify listeners of system or application events, extending the event-driven programming model between applications.

Broadcasting Intents helps make your application more open; by broadcasting an event using an Intent, you let yourself and third-party developers react to events without having to modify your original application. Within your applications, you can listen for Broadcast Intents to replace or enhance native (or third-party) applications or react to system changes and application events.

For example, by listening for the incoming call broadcast, you can modify the ringtone or volume based on the caller.

Android uses Broadcast Intents extensively to broadcast system events like battery-charging levels, network connections, and incoming calls.

Broadcasting Events with Intents

Broadcasting Intents is actually quite simple. Within your application component, construct the Intent you want to broadcast, and use the `sendBroadcast` method to send it.

Set the action, data, and category of your Intent in a way that lets Broadcast Receivers accurately determine their interest. In this scenario, the Intent *action string* is used to identify the event being broadcast, so it should be a unique string that identifies the event. By convention, action strings are constructed using the same form as Java packages, as shown in the following snippet:

```
public static final String NEW_LIFEFORM_DETECTED =
  "com.paad.action.NEW_LIFEFORM";
```

If you wish to include data within the Intent, you can specify a URI using the Intent's data property. You can also include *extras* to add additional primitive values. Considered in terms of an event-driven paradigm, the extras Bundle equates to optional parameters within an event handler.

The skeleton code below shows the basic creation of a Broadcast Intent using the action defined previously, with additional event information stored as extras.

```
Intent intent = new Intent(NEW_LIFEFORM_DETECTED);
intent.putExtra("lifeformName", lifeformType);
intent.putExtra("longitude", currentLongitude);
intent.putExtra("latitude", currentLatitude);

sendBroadcast(intent);
```

Listening for Broadcasts with Broadcast Receivers

Broadcast Receivers are used to listen for Broadcast Intents. To enable a Broadcast Receiver, it needs to be registered, either in code or within the application manifest. When registering a Broadcast Receiver, you must use an Intent Filter to specify which Intents it is listening for.

To create a new Broadcast Receiver, extend the BroadcastReceiver class and override the onReceive event handler as shown in the skeleton code below:

```
import android.content.BroadcastReceiver;
import android.content.Context;
import android.content.Intent;

public class MyBroadcastReceiver extends BroadcastReceiver {

  @Override
  public void onReceive(Context context, Intent intent) {
    //TODO: React to the Intent received.
  }

}
```

The onReceive method will be executed when a Broadcast Intent is received that matches the Intent Filter used to register the receiver. The onReceive handler must complete within 5 seconds, or the *Application Unresponsive* dialog will be displayed.

Applications with registered Broadcast Receivers do not have to be running when the Intent is broadcast for the receivers to execute. They will be started automatically when a matching Intent is broadcast. This is excellent for resource management as it lets you create event-driven applications that can be closed or killed, safe in the knowledge that they will still respond to broadcast events.

Typically, Broadcast Receivers will update content, launch Services, update Activity UI, or notify the user using the Notification Manager. The 5-second execution limit ensures that major processing cannot, as it should not, be done within the Broadcast Receiver directly.

The following example shows how to implement a Broadcast Receiver. In the following sections, you will learn how to register it in code or in your application manifest.

```
public class LifeformDetectedBroadcastReceiver extends BroadcastReceiver {

  public static final String BURN =
    "com.paad.alien.action.BURN_IT_WITH_FIRE";

  @Override
  public void onReceive(Context context, Intent intent) {
    // Get the lifeform details from the intent.
    Uri data = intent.getData();
    String type = intent.getStringExtra("type");
    double lat = intent.getDoubleExtra("latitude", 0);
    double lng = intent.getDoubleExtra("longitude", 0);
    Location loc = new Location("gps");
    loc.setLatitude(lat);
    loc.setLongitude(lng);

    if (type.equals("alien")) {
      Intent startIntent = new Intent(BURN, data);
      startIntent.putExtra("latitude", lat);
      startIntent.putExtra("longitude", lng);

      context.startActivity(startIntent);
    }
  }
}
```

Registering Broadcast Receivers in Your Application Manifest

To include a Broadcast Receiver in the application manifest, add a `receiver` tag within the `application` node specifying the class name of the Broadcast Receiver to register. The receiver node needs to include an `intent-filter` tag that specifies the action string being listened for, as shown in the XML snippet below:

```
<receiver android:name=".LifeformDetectedBroadcastReceiver">
  <intent-filter>
    <action android:name="com.paad.action.NEW_LIFEFORM"/>
  </intent-filter>
</receiver>
```

Broadcast Receivers registered this way are always active.

Registering Broadcast Receivers in Code

You can control the registration of Broadcast Receivers in code. This is typically done when the receiver is being used to update UI elements in an Activity. In this case, it's good practice to unregister Broadcast Receivers when the Activity isn't visible (or active).

The following code snippet shows how to register a Broadcast Receiver using an `IntentFilter`:

```
// Create and register the broadcast receiver.
IntentFilter filter = new IntentFilter(NEW_LIFEFORM_DETECTED);
LifeformDetectedBroadcastReceiver r = new LifeformDetectedBroadcastReceiver();
registerReceiver(r, filter);
```

To unregister a Broadcast Receiver, use the `unregisterReceiver` method on your application context, passing in a Broadcast Receiver instance, as shown below:

```
unregisterReceiver(r);
```

Further examples can also be found in Chapter 8 when you learn to create your own background Services and use Intents to broadcast events back to your Activities.

Native Android Broadcast Actions

Android broadcasts Intents for many of the system Services. You can use these messages to add functionality to your own projects based on system events such as time-zone changes, data-connection status, incoming SMS messages, or phone calls.

The following list introduces some of the native actions exposed as constants in the Intents class; these actions are used primarily to track device status changes:

- ❑ `ACTION_BOOT_COMPLETED`   Fired once when the device has completed its start-up sequence. Requires the `RECEIVE_BOOT_COMPLETED` permission.

- ❑ `ACTION_CAMERA_BUTTON`   Fired when the Camera button is clicked.

- ❑ `ACTION_DATE_CHANGED` and `ACTION_TIME_CHANGED`   These actions are broadcast if the date or time on the device is manually changed (as opposed to them changing through the natural progress of time).

- ❑ `ACTION_GTALK_SERVICE_CONNECTED` and `ACTION_GTALK_SERVICE_DISCONNECTED`   These two actions are broadcast each time a GTalk connection is made or lost. More specific handling of GTalk messaging is discussed in more detail in Chapter 9.

- ❑ `ACTION_MEDIA_BUTTON`   Fired when the Media button is clicked.

- ❑ `ACTION_MEDIA_EJECT`   If the user chooses to eject the external storage media, this event is fired first. If your application is reading or writing to the external media storage, you should listen for this event in order to save and close any open file handles.

- ❑ `ACTION_MEDIA_MOUNTED` and `ACTION_MEDIA_UNMOUNTED`   These two events are broadcast whenever new external storage media are successfully added or removed from the device.

- ❑ `ACTION_SCREEN_OFF` and `ACTION_SCREEN_ON`   Broadcasts when the screen turns off or on.

- ❑ `ACTION_TIMEZONE_CHANGED`   This action is broadcast whenever the phone's current time zone changes. The Intent includes a `time-zone` extra that returns the ID of the new `java.util.TimeZone`.

A comprehensive list of the broadcast actions used and transmitted natively by Android to notify applications of system state changes is available at `http://code.google.com/android/reference/android/content/Intent.html`.

Android also uses Broadcast Intents to monitor application-specific events like incoming SMS messages. The actions and Intents associated with these events are discussed in more detail in later chapters when you learn more about the associated Services.

Introducing Adapters

Adapters are bridging classes that bind data to user-interface Views. The adapter is responsible for creating the child views used to represent each item and providing access to the underlying data.

User-interface controls that support Adapter binding must extend the `AdapterView` abstract class. It's possible to create your own `AdapterView`-derived controls and create new Adapter classes to bind them.

Introducing Some Android-Supplied Adapters

In many cases, you won't have to create your own Adapter from scratch. Android supplies a set of Adapters that pump data into the native user-interface widgets.

Because Adapters are responsible both for supplying the data and selecting the Views that represent each item, Adaptors can radically modify the appearance and functionality of the controls they're bound to.

The following list highlights two of the most useful and versatile native adapters:

❑ `ArrayAdapter` The `ArrayAdapter` is a generic class that binds Adapter Views to an array of objects. By default, the `ArrayAdapter` binds the `toString` value of each object to a `TextView` control defined within a layout. Alternative constructors allow you to use more complex layouts, or you can extend the class to use alternatives to Text View (such as populating an `ImageView` or nested layout) by overriding the `getView` method.

❑ `SimpleCursorAdapter` The `SimpleCursorAdapter` binds Views to cursors returned from Content Provider queries. You specify an XML layout definition and then bind the value within each column in the result set, to a View in that layout.

The following sections will delve into these Adapter classes in more detail. The examples provided bind data to List Views, although the same logic will work just as well for other AdapterView classes such as `Spinners` and `Galleries`.

Using Adapters for Data Binding

To apply an Adapter to an AdapterView-derived class, you call the View's `setAdapter` method, passing in an Adapter instance, as shown in the snippet below:

```
ArrayList<String> myStringArray = new ArrayList<String>();
ArrayAdapter<String> myAdapterInstance;

int layoutID = android.R.layout.simple_list_item_1;
myAdapterInstance = new ArrayAdapter<String>(this, layoutID,
```

```
                                                  myStringArray);

    myListView.setAdapter(myAdapterInstance);
```

This snippet shows the most simplistic case, where the array being bound is a string and the List View items are displayed using a single Text View control.

The first of the following examples demonstrates how to bind an array of complex objects to a List View using a custom layout. The second shows how to use a Simple Cursor Adapter to bind a query result to a custom layout within a List View.

Customizing the To-Do List `ArrayAdapter`

This example extends the To-Do List project, storing each item as a `ToDoItem` object that includes the date each item was created.

You will extend `ArrayAdapter` to bind a collection of `ToDoItem` objects to the `ListView` and customize the layout used to display each List View item.

1. Return to the To-Do List project. Create a new `ToDoItem` class that stores the task and its creation date. Override the `toString` method to return a summary of the item data.

```java
package com.paad.todolist;

import java.text.SimpleDateFormat;
import java.util.Date;

public class ToDoItem {

  String task;
  Date created;

  public String getTask() {
    return task;
  }

  public Date getCreated() {
    return created;
  }

  public ToDoItem(String _task) {
    this(_task, new Date(java.lang.System.currentTimeMillis()));
  }

  public ToDoItem(String _task, Date _created) {
    task = _task;
    created = _created;
  }

  @Override
  public String toString() {
```

```
SimpleDateFormat sdf = new SimpleDateFormat("dd/MM/yy");
String dateString = sdf.format(created);
return "(" + dateString + ") " + task;
    }
}
```

2. Open the `ToDoList` Activity, and modify the `ArrayList` and `ArrayAdapter` variable types to store `ToDoItem` objects rather than Strings. You'll then need to modify the `onCreate` method to update the corresponding variable initialization. You'll also need to update the `onKeyListener` handler to support the `ToDoItem` objects.

```
private ArrayList<ToDoItem> todoItems;
private ListView myListView;
private EditText myEditText;
private ArrayAdapter<ToDoItem> aa;

@Override
public void onCreate(Bundle icicle) {
  super.onCreate(icicle);

  // Inflate your view
  setContentView(R.layout.main);

  // Get references to UI widgets
  myListView = (ListView)findViewById(R.id.myListView);
  myEditText = (EditText)findViewById(R.id.myEditText);

  todoItems = new ArrayList<ToDoItem>();
  int resID = R.layout.todolist_item;
  aa = new ArrayAdapter<ToDoItem>(this, resID, todoItems);
  myListView.setAdapter(aa);

  myEditText.setOnKeyListener(new OnKeyListener() {
    public boolean onKey(View v, int keyCode, KeyEvent event) {
      if (event.getAction() == KeyEvent.ACTION_DOWN)
        if (keyCode == KeyEvent.KEYCODE_DPAD_CENTER) {
          ToDoItem newItem;
          newItem = new ToDoItem(myEditText.getText().toString());
          todoItems.add(0, newItem);
          myEditText.setText("");
          aa.notifyDataSetChanged();
          cancelAdd();
          return true;
        }
      return false;
    }
  });

  registerForContextMenu(myListView);
}
```

3. If you run the Activity, it will now display each to-do item, as shown in Figure 5-3.

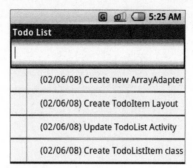

Figure 5-3

4. Now you can create a custom layout to display each to-do item. Start by modifying the custom layout you created in Chapter 4 to include a second `TextView`. It will be used to show the creation date of each to-do item.

```xml
<?xml version="1.0" encoding="utf-8"?>
<RelativeLayout xmlns:android="http://schemas.android.com/apk/res/android"
  android:layout_width="fill_parent"
  android:layout_height="fill_parent"
  android:background="@color/notepad_paper">
  <TextView
    android:id="@+id/rowDate"
    android:layout_width="wrap_content"
    android:layout_height="fill_parent"
    android:padding="10dp"
    android:scrollbars="vertical"
    android:fadingEdge="vertical"
    android:textColor="@color/notepad_text"
    android:layout_alignParentRight="true"
  />
  <TextView
    android:id="@+id/row"
    android:layout_width="fill_parent"
    android:layout_height="fill_parent"
    android:padding="10dp"
    android:scrollbars="vertical"
    android:fadingEdge="vertical"
    android:textColor="@color/notepad_text"
    android:layout_alignParentLeft="@+id/rowDate"
  />
</RelativeLayout>
```

5. Create a new class (`ToDoItemAdapter`) that extends an `ArrayAdapter` with a `ToDoItem`-specific variation. Override `getView` to assign the task and date properties in the `ToDoItem` object to the Views in the layout you created in Step 4.

```java
import java.text.SimpleDateFormat;
import android.content.Context;
import java.util.*;
```

```
import android.view.*;
import android.widget.*;

public class ToDoItemAdapter extends ArrayAdapter<ToDoItem> {

  int resource;

  public ToDoItemAdapter(Context _context,
                         int _resource,
                         List<ToDoItem> _items) {
    super(_context, _resource, _items);
    resource = _resource;
  }

  @Override
  public View getView(int position, View convertView, ViewGroup parent)
  {
    LinearLayout todoView;

    ToDoItem item = getItem(position);

    String taskString = item.getTask();
    Date createdDate = item.getCreated();
    SimpleDateFormat sdf = new SimpleDateFormat("dd/MM/yy");
    String dateString = sdf.format(createdDate);

    if (convertView == null) {
      todoView = new LinearLayout(getContext());
      String inflater = Context.LAYOUT_INFLATER_SERVICE;
      LayoutInflater vi;
      vi = (LayoutInflater)getContext().getSystemService(inflater);
      vi.inflate(resource, todoView, true);
    } else {
      todoView = (LinearLayout) convertView;
    }

    TextView dateView = (TextView)todoView.findViewById(R.id.rowDate);
    TextView taskView = (TextView)todoView.findViewById(R.id.row);

    dateView.setText(dateString);
    taskView.setText(taskString);

    return todoView;
  }
}
```

6. Finally, replace the `ArrayAdapter` declaration with a `ToDoItemAdapter`.

```
private ToDoItemAdapter aa;
```

Within `onCreate`, replace the `ArrayAdapter<String>` instantiation with the new `ToDoItemAdapter`.

```
aa = new ToDoItemAdapter(this, resID, todoItems);
```

7. If you run your Activity, it should appear as shown in the screenshot in Figure 5-4.

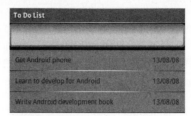

Figure 5-4

Using the `SimpleCursorAdapter`

The `SimpleCursorAdapter` lets you bind columns from a `Cursor` to a List View using a custom layout definition.

The `SimpleCursorAdapter` is constructed by passing in the current context, a layout resource, a Cursor, and two arrays: one that contains the names of the columns to be used and a second (equally sized) array that has resource IDs for the Views to use to display the corresponding column's data value.

The following skeleton code shows how to construct a `SimpleCursorAdapter` to display contact information:

```
String uriString = "content://contacts/people/";
Cursor myCursor = managedQuery(Uri.parse(uriString), null, null, null, null);

String[] fromColumns = new String[] {People.NUMBER, People.NAME};

int[] toLayoutIDs = new int[] { R.id.nameTextView, R.id.numberTextView};

SimpleCursorAdapter myAdapter;
myAdapter = new SimpleCursorAdapter(this,
                                    R.layout.simplecursorlayout,
                                    myCursor,
                                    fromColumns,
                                    toLayoutIDs);

myListView.setAdapter(myAdapter);
```

The Simple Cursor Adapter was used previously in this chapter when creating the Contact Picker example. You'll learn more about Content Providers and Cursors in Chapter 6, where you'll also find more `SimpleCursorAdapter` examples.

Using Internet Resources

With Internet connectivity and WebKit browser, you might well ask if there's any reason to create native Internet-based applications when you could make a web-based version instead.

There are several benefits to creating thick- and thin-client native applications rather than relying on entirely web-based solutions:

❏ **Bandwidth**   Static resources like images, layouts, and sounds can be expensive data consumers on devices with limited and often expensive bandwidth restraints. By creating a native application, you can limit the bandwidth requirements to only data updates.

❏ **Caching**   Mobile Internet access has not yet reached the point of ubiquity. With a browser-based solution, a patchy Internet connection can result in intermittent application availability. A native application can cache data to provide as much functionality as possible without a live connection.

❏ **Native Features**   Android devices are more than a simple platform for running a browser; they include location-based services, camera hardware, and accelerometers. By creating a native application, you can combine the data available online with the hardware features available on the device to provide a richer user experience.

Modern mobile devices offer various alternatives for accessing the Internet. Looked at broadly, Android provides three connection techniques for Internet connectivity. Each is offered transparently to the application layer.

❏ **GPRS, EDGE, and 3G**   Mobile Internet access is available through carriers that offer mobile data plans.

❏ **Wi-Fi**   Wi-Fi receivers and mobile hotspots are becoming increasingly more common.

Connecting to an Internet Resource

While the details of working with specific web services aren't covered within this book, it's useful to know the general principles of connecting to the Internet and getting an input stream from a remote data source.

Before you can access Internet resources, you need to add an `INTERNET uses-permission` node to your application manifest, as shown in the following XML snippet:

```xml
<uses-permission android:name="android.permission.INTERNET"/>
```

The following skeleton code shows the basic pattern for opening an Internet data stream:

```java
String myFeed = getString(R.string.my_feed);
try {
  URL url = new URL(myFeed);

  URLConnection connection = url.openConnection();
  HttpURLConnection httpConnection = (HttpURLConnection)connection;

  int responseCode = httpConnection.getResponseCode();
  if (responseCode == HttpURLConnection.HTTP_OK) {
    InputStream in = httpConnection.getInputStream();
```

```
    [ ... Process the input stream as required ... ]
  }
}
catch (MalformedURLException e) { }
catch (IOException e) { }
```

Android includes several classes to help you handle network communications. They are available in the `java.net.*` and `android.net.*` packages.

Later in this chapter, there is a fully worked example that shows how to obtain and process an Internet feed to get a list of earthquakes felt in the last 24 hours.

Chapter 9 includes further details on Internet-based communications using the GTalk Service. Chapter 10 features more information on managing specific Internet connections, including monitoring connection status and configuring Wi-Fi access point connections.

Leveraging Internet Resources

Android offers several ways to leverage Internet resources.

At one extreme, you can use the `WebView` widget to include a WebKit-based browser control within an Activity. At the other extreme, you can use client-side APIs such as Google's GData APIs to interact directly with server processes. Somewhere in between, you can process remote XML feeds to extract and process data using a Java-based XML parser such as `SAX` or `javax`.

Detailed instructions for parsing XML and interacting with specific web services are outside the scope of this book. That said, the Earthquake example, included later in this chapter, gives a fully worked example of parsing an XML feed using the `javax` classes.

If you're using Internet resources in your application, remember that your users' data connections depend on the communications technology available to them. EDGE and GSM connections are notoriously low bandwidth, while a Wi-Fi connection may be unreliable in a mobile setting.

Optimize the user experience by limiting the quantity of data being transmitted, and ensure that your application is robust enough to handle network outages and bandwidth limitations.

Introducing Dialogs

Dialog boxes are a common UI metaphor in desktop and web applications. They're used to help users answer questions, make selections, confirm actions, and read warning or error messages. An *Android Dialog* is a floating window that partially obscures the Activity that launched it.

As you can see in Figure 5-5, Dialog boxes are not full screen and can be partially transparent. They generally obscure the Activities behind them using a blur or dim filter.

Figure 5-5

There are three ways to implement a Dialog box in Android:

❑   **Using a Dialog-Class Descendent**   As well as the general-purpose `AlertDialog` class, Android includes several specialist classes that extend `Dialog`. Each is designed to provide specific Dialog-box functionality. `Dialog`-class-based screens are constructed entirely within their calling Activity, so they don't need to be registered in the manifest, and their life cycle is controlled entirely by the calling Activity.

❑   **Dialog-Themed Activities**   You can apply the Dialog theme to a regular Activity to give it the appearance of a Dialog box.

❑   **Toasts**   Toasts are special non-modal transient message boxes, often used by Broadcast Receivers and background services to notify users of events. You learn more about Toasts in Chapter 8.

Introducing the `Dialog` Class

The `Dialog` class implements a simple floating window that is constructed entirely within an Activity.

To use the base `Dialog` class, you create a new instance and set the title and layout as shown below:

```
Dialog d = new Dialog(MyActivity.this);

// Have the new window tint and blur the window it
// obscures.
Window window = d.getWindow();
window.setFlags(WindowManager.LayoutParams.FLAG_BLUR_BEHIND,
                WindowManager.LayoutParams.FLAG_BLUR_BEHIND);

d.setTitle("Dialog Title");
d.setContentView(R.layout.dialog_view);

TextView text = (TextView)d.findViewById(R.id.dialogTextView);
text.setText("This is the text in my dialog");
```

Once it's configured to your liking, use the show method to display it.

```
d.show();
```

The AlertDialog Class

The AlertDialog class is one of the most versatile Dialog implementations. It offers various options that let you construct screens for some of the most common Dialog-box use cases, including:

❑   Presenting a message to the user offering one to three options in the form of alternative buttons. This functionality is probably familiar to you if you've done any desktop programming, where the buttons presented are usually a selection of OK, Cancel, Yes, or No.

❑   Offering a list of options in the form of check buttons or radio buttons.

❑   Providing a text entry box for user input.

To construct the Alert Dialog user interface, create a new AlertDialog.Builder object, as shown below:

```
AlertDialog.Builder ad = new AlertDialog.Builder(context);
```

You can then assign values for the title and message to display, and optionally assign values to be used for any buttons, selection items, and text input boxes you wish to display. That includes setting event listeners to handle user interaction.

The following code gives an example of a new Alert Dialog used to display a message and offer two button options to continue. Clicking on either button will automatically close the Dialog after executing the attached Click Listener.

```
Context context = MyActivity.this;
String title = "It is Pitch Black";
String message = "You are likely to be eaten by a grue.";
String button1String = "Go Back";
String button2String = "Move Forward";

AlertDialog.Builder ad = new AlertDialog.Builder(context);
ad.setTitle(title);
ad.setMessage(message);
ad.setPositiveButton(button1String,
                new OnClickListener() {
                    public void onClick(DialogInterface dialog,
                                        int arg1) {
                        eatenByGrue();
                    }
                });
ad.setNegativeButton(button2String,
                new OnClickListener(){
                    public void onClick(DialogInterface dialog,
                                        int arg1) {
                        // do nothing
                    }
                });
ad.setCancelable(true);
ad.setOnCancelListener(new OnCancelListener() {
```

```
                        public void onCancel(DialogInterface dialog) {
                          eatenByGrue();
                        }
                    });
```

To display an Alert Dialog that you've created call `show`.

```
    ad.show();
```

Alternatively, you can override the `onCreateDialog` and `onPrepareDialog` methods within your Activity to create single-instance Dialogs that persist their state. This technique is examined later in this chapter.

Specialist Input Dialogs

One of the major uses of Dialog boxes is to provide an interface for user input. Android includes several specialist Dialog boxes that encapsulate controls designed to facilitate common user input requests. They include the following:

❑   **DatePickerDialog**   Lets users select a date from a `DatePicker` View. The constructor includes a callback listener to alert your calling Activity when the date has been set.

❑   **TimePickerDialog**   Similar to the DatePickerDialog, this Dialog lets users select a time from a `TimePicker` View.

❑   **ProgressDialog**   A Dialog that displays a progress bar beneath a message textbox. Perfect for keeping the user informed of the ongoing progress of a time-consuming operation.

Using and Managing Dialogs

Rather than creating new instances of a Dialog each time it's required, Android provides the `OnCreateDialog` and `onPrepareDialog` event handlers within the Activity class to persist and manage Dialog-box instances.

By overriding the `onCreateDialog` class, you can specify Dialogs that will be created on demand when `showDialog` is used to display a specific Dialog. As shown in this code snippet, the overridden method includes a switch statement that lets you determine which Dialog is required:

```
static final private int TIME_DIALOG = 1;

@Override
public Dialog onCreateDialog(int id) {
  switch(id) {
    case (TIME_DIALOG) :
      AlertDialog.Builder timeDialog = new AlertDialog.Builder(this);
      timeDialog.setTitle("The Current Time Is...");
      timeDialog.setMessage("Now");
      return timeDialog.create();
  }
  return null;
}
```

After the initial creation, each time a `showDialog` is called, it will trigger the `onPrepareDialog` handler. By overriding this method, you can modify a Dialog immediately before it is displayed. This lets you contextualize any of the display values, as shown in the following snippet, which assigns the current time to the Dialog created above:

```
@Override
public void onPrepareDialog(int id, Dialog dialog) {
  switch(id) {
    case (TIME_DIALOG) :
      SimpleDateFormat sdf = new SimpleDateFormat("HH:mm:ss");
      Date currentTime;
      currentTime = new Date(java.lang.System.currentTimeMillis());
      String dateString = sdf.format(currentTime);
      AlertDialog timeDialog = (AlertDialog)dialog;
      timeDialog.setMessage(dateString);

      break;
  }
}
```

Once you've overridden these methods, you can display the Dialogs by calling `showDialog`, as shown below. Pass in the identifier for the Dialog you wish to display, and Android will create (if necessary) and prepare the Dialog before displaying it:

```
showDialog(TIME_DIALOG);
```

As well as improving resource use, this technique lets your Activity handle the persistence of state information within Dialogs. Any selection or data input (such as item selection and text entry) will be persisted between displays of each Dialog instance.

Using Activities as Dialogs

Dialogs offer a simple and lightweight technique for displaying screens, but there will still be times when you need more control over the content and life cycle of your Dialog box.

The solution is to implement it as a full Activity. By creating an Activity, you lose the lightweight nature of the `Dialog` class, but you gain the ability to implement any screen you want and full access to the Activity life-cycle event handlers.

So, when is an Activity a Dialog? The easiest way to make an Activity look like a Dialog is to apply the `android:style/Theme.Dialog` theme when you add it to your manifest, as shown in the following XML snippet:

```
<activity android:name="MyDialogActivity"
          android:theme="@android:style/Theme.Dialog">
</activity>
```

This will cause your Activity to behave like a Dialog, floating on top of, and partially obscuring, the Activity beneath it.

Creating an Earthquake Viewer

In the following example, you'll create a tool that uses a USGS earthquake feed to display a list of recent earthquakes.

> *You will return to this Earthquake application several times, first in Chapter 6 to save and share the earthquake data with a Content Provider, and again in Chapters 7 and 8 to add mapping support and to move the earthquake updates into a background Service.*

In this example, you will create a list-based Activity that connects to an earthquake feed and displays the location, magnitude, and time of the earthquakes it contains. You'll use an Alert Dialog to provide a detail window that includes a linkified Text View with a link to the USGS web site.

1. Start by creating an Earthquake project featuring an `Earthquake` Activity. Modify the main.xml layout resource to include a List View control — be sure to name it so you can reference it from the Activity code.

```xml
<?xml version="1.0" encoding="utf-8"?>
<LinearLayout xmlns:android="http://schemas.android.com/apk/res/android"
    android:orientation="vertical"
    android:layout_width="fill_parent"
    android:layout_height="fill_parent">
    <ListView
        android:id="@+id/earthquakeListView"
        android:layout_width="fill_parent"
        android:layout_height="wrap_content"
    />
</LinearLayout>
```

2. Create a new public `Quake` class. This class will be used to store the details (date, details, location, magnitude, and link) of each earthquake. Override the `toString` method to provide the string that will be used for each quake in the List View.

```java
package com.paad.earthquake;

import java.util.Date;
import java.text.SimpleDateFormat;
import android.location.Location;

public class Quake {
    private Date date;
    private String details;
    private Location location;
    private double magnitude;
    private String link;

    public Date getDate() { return date; }
    public String getDetails() { return details; }
    public Location getLocation() { return location; }
    public double getMagnitude() { return magnitude; }
    public String getLink() { return link; }

    public Quake(Date _d, String _det, Location _loc, double _mag,
                 String _link) {
        date = _d;
```

```
      details = _det;
      location = _loc;
      magnitude = _mag;
      link = _link;
    }

    @Override
    public String toString() {
      SimpleDateFormat sdf = new SimpleDateFormat("HH.mm");
      String dateString = sdf.format(date);
      return dateString + ": " + magnitude + " " + details;
    }


  }
```

3. In the `Earthquake` Activity, override the `onCreate` method to store an ArrayList of `Quake` objects, and bind that to the ListView using an `ArrayAdapter`.

```
package com.paad.earthquake;

import java.io.IOException;
import java.io.InputStream;
import java.net.HttpURLConnection;
import java.net.MalformedURLException;
import java.net.URL;
import java.net.URLConnection;
import java.text.ParseException;
import java.text.SimpleDateFormat;
import java.util.ArrayList;
import java.util.Date;
import java.util.GregorianCalendar;
import javax.xml.parsers.DocumentBuilder;
import javax.xml.parsers.DocumentBuilderFactory;
import javax.xml.parsers.ParserConfigurationException;
import org.w3c.dom.Document;
import org.w3c.dom.Element;
import org.w3c.dom.NodeList;
import org.xml.sax.SAXException;
import android.app.Activity;
import android.app.Dialog;
import android.location.Location;
import android.os.Bundle;
import android.view.Menu;
import android.view.View;
import android.view.WindowManager;
import android.view.MenuItem;
import android.widget.AdapterView;
import android.widget.ArrayAdapter;
import android.widget.ListView;
import android.widget.TextView;
import android.widget.AdapterView.OnItemClickListener;

public class Earthquake extends Activity {

  ListView earthquakeListView;
```

```
        ArrayAdapter<Quake> aa;

        ArrayList<Quake> earthquakes = new ArrayList<Quake>();

        @Override
        public void onCreate(Bundle icicle) {
          super.onCreate(icicle);
          setContentView(R.layout.main);

          earthquakeListView =
            (ListView)this.findViewById(R.id.earthquakeListView);

          int layoutID = android.R.layout.simple_list_item_1;
          aa = new ArrayAdapter<Quake>(this, layoutID , earthquakes);
          earthquakeListView.setAdapter(aa);
        }
      }
```

4. Next, you should start processing the earthquake feed. For this example, the feed used is the 1-day USGS feed for earthquakes with a magnitude greater than 2.5.

   Add the location of your feed as an external string resource. This lets you potentially specify a different feed based on a user's location.

   ```xml
   <?xml version="1.0" encoding="utf-8"?>
   <resources>
     <string name="app_name">Earthquake</string>
     <string name="quake_feed">
       http://earthquake.usgs.gov/eqcenter/catalogs/1day-M2.5.xml
     </string>
   </resources>
   ```

5. Before your application can access the Internet, it needs to be granted permission for Internet access. Add the `uses-permission` to the manifest.

   ```xml
   <uses-permission xmlns:android="http://schemas.android.com/apk/res/android"
     android:name="android.permission.INTERNET">
   </uses-permission>
   ```

6. Returning to the Earthquake Activity, create a new `refreshEarthquakes` method that connects to, and parses, the earthquake feed. Extract each earthquake, and parse the details to obtain the date, magnitude, link, and location. As you finish parsing each earthquake, pass it in to a new `addNewQuake` method.

   The XML parsing is presented here without further comment.

   ```java
   private void refreshEarthquakes() {
     // Get the XML
     URL url;
     try {
       String quakeFeed = getString(R.string.quake_feed);
       url = new URL(quakeFeed);

       URLConnection connection;
   ```

```
connection = url.openConnection();

HttpURLConnection httpConnection = (HttpURLConnection)connection;
int responseCode = httpConnection.getResponseCode();

if (responseCode == HttpURLConnection.HTTP_OK) {
  InputStream in = httpConnection.getInputStream();

  DocumentBuilderFactory dbf;
  dbf = DocumentBuilderFactory.newInstance();
  DocumentBuilder db = dbf.newDocumentBuilder();

  // Parse the earthquake feed.
  Document dom = db.parse(in);
  Element docEle = dom.getDocumentElement();

  // Clear the old earthquakes
  earthquakes.clear();

  // Get a list of each earthquake entry.
  NodeList nl = docEle.getElementsByTagName("entry");
  if (nl != null && nl.getLength() > 0) {
    for (int i = 0 ; i < nl.getLength(); i++) {
      Element entry = (Element)nl.item(i);
      Element title =
        (Element)entry.getElementsByTagName("title").item(0);
      Element g =
        (Element)entry.getElementsByTagName("georss:point").item(0);
      Element when =
        (Element)entry.getElementsByTagName("updated").item(0);
      Element link =
        (Element)entry.getElementsByTagName("link").item(0);

      String details = title.getFirstChild().getNodeValue();
      String hostname = "http://earthquake.usgs.gov";
      String linkString = hostname + link.getAttribute("href");

      String point = g.getFirstChild().getNodeValue();
      String dt = when.getFirstChild().getNodeValue();
      SimpleDateFormat sdf;
      sdf = new SimpleDateFormat("yyyy-MM-dd'T'hh:mm:ss'Z'");
      Date qdate = new GregorianCalendar(0,0,0).getTime();
      try {
        qdate = sdf.parse(dt);
      } catch (ParseException e) {
        e.printStackTrace();
      }

      String[] location = point.split(" ");
      Location l = new Location("dummyGPS");
      l.setLatitude(Double.parseDouble(location[0]));
      l.setLongitude(Double.parseDouble(location[1]));

      String magnitudeString = details.split(" ")[1];
```

```
                int end = magnitudeString.length()-1;
                double magnitude;
                magnitude = Double.parseDouble(magnitudeString.substring(0,
                                                                 end));

                details = details.split(",")[1].trim();

                Quake quake = new Quake(qdate, details, 1,
                                        magnitude, linkString);

                // Process a newly found earthquake
                addNewQuake(quake);
              }
            }
          }
        } catch (MalformedURLException e) {
          e.printStackTrace();
        } catch (IOException e) {
          e.printStackTrace();
        } catch (ParserConfigurationException e) {
          e.printStackTrace();
        } catch (SAXException e) {
          e.printStackTrace();
        }
        finally {
        }
      }

      private void addNewQuake(Quake _quake) {
        // TODO: Add the earthquakes to the array list.
      }
```

7. Update the addNewQuake method so that it takes each newly processed quake and adds it to the Earthquake ArrayList. It should also notify the Array Adapter that the underlying data have changed.

```
      private void addNewQuake(Quake _quake) {
        // Add the new quake to our list of earthquakes.
        earthquakes.add(_quake);

        // Notify the array adapter of a change.
        aa.notifyDataSetChanged();
      }
```

8. Modify your onCreate method to call refreshEarthquakes on start-up.

```
      @Override
      public void onCreate(Bundle icicle) {
        super.onCreate(icicle);
        setContentView(R.layout.main);

        earthquakeListView =
```

```
      (ListView)this.findViewById(R.id.earthquakeListView);

    int layoutID = android.R.layout.simple_list_item_1;
    aa = new ArrayAdapter<Quake>(this, layoutID , earthquakes);
    earthquakeListView.setAdapter(aa);

    refreshEarthquakes();
  }
```

The Internet lookup is currently happening on the main UI thread. This is bad form as the application will become unresponsive if the lookup takes longer than a few seconds. In Chapter 8, you'll learn how to move expensive or time-consuming operations like this onto the background thread.

9. If you run your project, you should see a List View that features the earthquakes from the last 24 hours with a magnitude greater than 2.5, as shown in the screenshot in Figure 5-6.

Figure 5-6

10. There are only two more steps to make this a more useful application. First, create a new menu item to let users refresh the earthquake feed on demand.

   10.1. Start by adding a new external string for the menu option.

   ```
   <string name="menu_update">Refresh Earthquakes</string>
   ```

   10.2 Then override the Activity's onCreateOptionsMenu and onOptionsItemSelected methods to display and handle the *refresh earthquakes* menu item.

   ```
   static final private int MENU_UPDATE = Menu.FIRST;

   @Override
   ```

```java
public boolean onCreateOptionsMenu(Menu menu) {
  super.onCreateOptionsMenu(menu);

  menu.add(0, MENU_UPDATE, Menu.NONE, R.string.menu_update);

  return true;
}

@Override
public boolean onOptionsItemSelected(MenuItem item) {
  super.onOptionsItemSelected(item);

  switch (item.getItemId()) {
    case (MENU_UPDATE): {
      refreshEarthquakes();
      return true;
    }
  }
  return false;
}
```

11. Now add some interaction. Let users find more details by opening a Dialog box when they select an earthquake from the list.

11.1. Creating a new quake_details.xml layout resource for the Dialog box you'll display on an item click.

```xml
<?xml version="1.0" encoding="utf-8"?>
<LinearLayout
  xmlns:android="http://schemas.android.com/apk/res/android"
  android:orientation="vertical"
  android:layout_width="fill_parent"
  android:layout_height="fill_parent"
  android:padding="10sp">
  <TextView
    android:id="@+id/quakeDetailsTextView"
    android:layout_width="fill_parent"
    android:layout_height="fill_parent"
    android:textSize="14sp"
  />
</LinearLayout>
```

11.2. Then modify your onCreate method to add an ItemClickListener to the List View that displays a Dialog box whenever an earthquake item is selected.

```java
static final private int QUAKE_DIALOG = 1;
Quake selectedQuake;

@Override
public void onCreate(Bundle icicle) {
  super.onCreate(icicle);
  setContentView(R.layout.main);

  earthquakeListView =
```

```
                (ListView)this.findViewById(R.id.earthquakeListView);

        earthquakeListView.setOnItemClickListener(new OnItemClickListener() {

            public void onItemClick(AdapterView _av, View _v, int _index,
                                      long arg3) {
              selectedQuake = earthquakes.get(_index);
              showDialog(QUAKE_DIALOG);
            }
        });

        int layoutID = android.R.layout.simple_list_item_1;
        aa = new ArrayAdapter<Quake>(this, layoutID , earthquakes);
        earthquakeListView.setAdapter(aa);

        refreshEarthquakes();
    }
```

11.3. Now override the `onCreateDialog` and `onPrepareDialog` methods to create and populate the Earthquake Details dialog.

```
@Override
public Dialog onCreateDialog(int id) {
    switch(id) {
      case (QUAKE_DIALOG) :
        LayoutInflater li = LayoutInflater.from(this);
        View quakeDetailsView = li.inflate(R.layout.quake_details, null);

        AlertDialog.Builder quakeDialog = new AlertDialog.Builder(this);
        quakeDialog.setTitle("Quake Time");
        quakeDialog.setView(quakeDetailsView);
        return quakeDialog.create();
    }
    return null;
}

@Override
public void onPrepareDialog(int id, Dialog dialog) {
    switch(id) {
      case (QUAKE_DIALOG) :
        SimpleDateFormat sdf;
        sdf = new SimpleDateFormat("dd/MM/yyyy HH:mm:ss");
        String dateString = sdf.format(selectedQuake.getDate());
        String quakeText = "Mangitude " + selectedQuake.getMagnitude() +
                            "\n" + selectedQuake.getDetails()  + "\n" +
                            selectedQuake.getLink();

        AlertDialog quakeDialog = (AlertDialog)dialog;
        quakeDialog.setTitle(dateString);
        TextView tv =
          (TextView)quakeDialog.findViewById(R.id.quakeDetailsTextView);
        tv.setText(quakeText);

        break;
    }
}
```

11.4. The final step is to linkify the Dialog to make the link to the USGS a hyperlink. Adjust the Dialog box's XML layout resource definition to include an `autolink` attribute.

```xml
<?xml version="1.0" encoding="utf-8"?>
<LinearLayout
  xmlns:android="http://schemas.android.com/apk/res/android"
  android:orientation="vertical"
  android:layout_width="fill_parent"
  android:layout_height="fill_parent"
  android:padding="10sp">
  <TextView
    android:id="@+id/quakeDetailsTextView"
    android:layout_width="fill_parent"
    android:layout_height="fill_parent"
    android:textSize="14sp"
    android:autoLink="all"
  />
</LinearLayout>
```

Launch your activity again. When you click on a particular earthquake, a Dialog box will appear, partially obscuring the list, as shown in Figure 5-7.

Figure 5-7

Summary

The focus of this chapter has been on binding your application components.

Intents provide a versatile messaging system that lets you pass intentions between your application and others, to perform actions and signal events. You learned how to use implicit and explicit Intents to start new Activities, and how to populate an Activity menu dynamically through runtime resolution of Activity Intent Filters.

You were introduced to Broadcast Intents and saw how they can be used to send messages throughout the device, particularly to support an event-driven model based on system- and application-specific events.

You learned how to use sub-Activities to pass data between Activities and how to use Dialogs to display information and facilitate user input.

Adapters were introduced and used to bind underlying data to visual components. In particular, you saw how to use an Array Adapter and Simple Cursor Adapter to bind a List View to Array Lists and Cursors.

Finally, you learned the basics behind connecting to the Internet and using remote feeds as data sources for your native client applications.

You also learned:

❑ To use Linkify to add implicit View Intents to TextViews at run time.

❑ Which native Android actions are available for you to extend, replace, or embrace.

❑ How to use Intent Filters to let your own Activities become handlers for completing action requests from your own or other applications.

❑ How to listen for Broadcast Intents using Broadcast Receivers.

❑ How to use an Activity as a Dialog box.

In the next chapter, you will learn how to persist information within your applications. Android provides several mechanisms for saving application data, including files, simple preferences, and fully featured relational databases (using the SQLite database library).

6

Data Storage, Retrieval, and Sharing

In this chapter, you'll be introduced to three of the most versatile data persistence techniques in Android — preferences, local files, and SQLite databases — before looking at Content Providers.

Saving and loading data is an essential requirement for most applications. At a minimum, Activities should save their User Interface (UI) state each time they move out of the foreground. This ensures that the same UI state is presented when it's next seen, even if the process has been killed and restarted before that happens.

It's also likely that you'll need to save preferences, to let users customize the application, and persist data entered or recorded. Just as important is the ability to load data from files, databases, and Content Providers — your own, and those shared by native and third-party applications.

Android's nondeterministic Activity and Application lifetimes make persisting UI state and application data between sessions particularly important. Android offers several alternatives for saving application data, each optimized to fulfill a particular need.

Preferences are a simple, lightweight key/value pair mechanism for saving primitive application data, most commonly a user's application preferences. Android also provides access to the local filesystem, both through specialized methods and the normal `Java.IO` classes.

For a more robust persistence layer, Android provides the SQLite database library. The SQLite database offers a powerful native SQL database over which you have total control.

Content Providers offer a generic interface to any data source. They effectively decouple the underlying data storage technique from the application layer.

By default, access to all files, databases, and preferences is restricted to the application that created them. Content Providers offer a managed way for your applications to share private data with other applications. As a result, your applications can use the Content Providers offered by others, including native providers.

Android Techniques for Saving Data

The data persistence techniques in Android provide options for balancing speed, efficiency, and robustness:

- ❑ **Shared Preferences**   When storing the UI state, user preferences, or application settings, you want a lightweight mechanism to store a known set of values. Shared Preferences let you save groups of key/value pairs of primitive data as named preferences.

- ❑ **Files**   It's not pretty, but sometimes writing to, and reading from, files directly is the only way to go. Android lets you create and load files on the device's internal or external media.

- ❑ **SQLite Databases**   When managed, structured data is the best approach, Android offers the SQLite relational database library. Every application can create its own databases over which it has total control.

- ❑ **Content Providers**   Rather than a storage mechanism in their own right, Content Providers let you expose a well-defined interface for using and sharing private data. You can control access to Content Providers using the standard permission system.

Saving Simple Application Data

There are two lightweight techniques for saving simple application data for Android applications — Shared Preferences and a pair of event handlers used for saving Activity instance details. Both mechanisms use a name/value pair (NVP) mechanism to store simple primitive values.

Using `SharedPreferences`, you can create named maps of key/value pairs within your application that can be shared between application components running in the same Context.

Shared Preferences support the primitive types Boolean, string, float, long, and integer, making them an ideal way to quickly store default values, class instance variables, the current UI state, and user preferences. They are most commonly used to persist data across user sessions and to share settings between application components.

Alternatively, Activities offer the `onSaveInstanceState` handler. It's designed specifically to persist the UI state when the Activity becomes eligible for termination by a resource-hungry run time.

The handler works like the Shared Preference mechanism. It offers a `Bundle` parameter that represents a key/value map of primitive types that can be used to save the Activity's instance values. This Bundle is then made available as a parameter passed in to the `onCreate` and `onRestoreInstanceState` method handlers.

This UI state Bundle is used to record the values needed for an Activity to provide an identical UI following unexpected restarts.

Creating and Saving Preferences

To create or modify a Shared Preference, call `getSharedPreferences` on the application Context, passing in the name of the Shared Preferences to change. Shared Preferences are shared across an application's components but aren't available to other applications.

To modify a Shared Preference, use the `SharedPreferences.Editor` class. Get the Editor object by calling `edit` on the `SharedPreferences` object you want to change. To save edits, call `commit` on the Editor, as shown in the code snippet below.

```
public static final String MYPREFS = "mySharedPreferences";

protected void savePreferences(){
  // Create or retrieve the shared preference object.
  int mode = Activity.MODE_PRIVATE;
  SharedPreferences mySharedPreferences = getSharedPreferences(MYPREFS,
                                                    mode);
  // Retrieve an editor to modify the shared preferences.
  SharedPreferences.Editor editor = mySharedPreferences.edit();

  // Store new primitive types in the shared preferences object.
  editor.putBoolean("isTrue", true);
  editor.putFloat("lastFloat", 1f);
  editor.putInt("wholeNumber", 2);
  editor.putLong("aNumber", 31);
  editor.putString("textEntryValue", "Not Empty");

  // Commit the changes.
  editor.commit();
}
```

Retrieving Shared Preferences

Accessing saved Shared Preferences is also done with the `getSharedPreferences` method. Pass in the name of the Shared Preference you want to access, and use the type-safe `get<type>` methods to extract saved values.

Each getter takes a key and a default value (used when no value is available for that key), as shown in the skeleton code below:

```
public void loadPreferences() {
  // Get the stored preferences
  int mode = Activity.MODE_PRIVATE;
```

```
SharedPreferences mySharedPreferences = getSharedPreferences(MYPREFS,
                                                          mode);

// Retrieve the saved values.
boolean isTrue = mySharedPreferences.getBoolean("isTrue", false);
float lastFloat = mySharedPreferences.getFloat("lastFloat", 0f);
int wholeNumber = mySharedPreferences.getInt("wholeNumber", 1);
long aNumber = mySharedPreferences.getLong("aNumber", 0);
String stringPreference;
stringPreference = mySharedPreferences.getString("textEntryValue",
                                                  "");
}
```

Saving the Activity State

If you want to save Activity information that doesn't need to be shared with other components (e.g., class instance variables), you can call `Activity.getPreferences()` without specifying a preferences name. Access to the Shared Preferences map returned is restricted to the calling Activity; each Activity supports a single unnamed SharedPreferences object.

The following skeleton code shows how to use the Activity's private Shared Preferences:

```
protected void saveActivityPreferences(){
  // Create or retrieve the activity preferences object.
  SharedPreferences activityPreferences =
    getPreferences(Activity.MODE_PRIVATE);

  // Retrieve an editor to modify the shared preferences.
  SharedPreferences.Editor editor = activityPreferences.edit();

  // Retrieve the View
  TextView myTextView = (TextView)findViewById(R.id.myTextView);

  // Store new primitive types in the shared preferences object.
  editor.putString("currentTextValue",
                   myTextView.getText().toString());

  // Commit changes.
  editor.commit();
}
```

Saving and Restoring Instance State

To save Activity instance variables, Android offers a specialized alternative to Shared Preferences.

By overriding an Activity's `onSaveInstanceState` event handler, you can use its `Bundle` parameter to save instance values. Store values using the same `get` and `put` methods as shown for Shared Preferences, before passing the modified `Bundle` into the superclass's handler, as shown in the following code snippet:

```
private static final String TEXTVIEW_STATE_KEY = "TEXTVIEW_STATE_KEY";
```

```
@Override
public void onSaveInstanceState(Bundle outState) {
  // Retrieve the View
  TextView myTextView = (TextView)findViewById(R.id.myTextView);

  // Save its state
  outState.putString(TEXTVIEW_STATE_KEY,
                     myTextView.getText().toString());
  super.onSaveInstanceState(outState);
}
```

This handler will be triggered whenever an Activity completes its Active life cycle, but only when it's not being explicitly finished. As a result, it's used to ensure a consistent Activity state between active life cycles of a single user session.

The saved `Bundle` is passed in to the `onRestoreInstanceState` and `onCreate` methods if the application is forced to restart during a session. The following snippet shows how to extract values from the `Bundle` and use them to update the Activity instance state:

```
@Override
public void onCreate(Bundle icicle) {
  super.onCreate(icicle);
  setContentView(R.layout.main);

  TextView myTextView = (TextView)findViewById(R.id.myTextView);

  String text = "";
  if (icicle != null && icicle.containsKey(TEXTVIEW_STATE_KEY))
    text = icicle.getString(TEXTVIEW_STATE_KEY);

  myTextView.setText(text);
}
```

It's important to remember that onSaveInstanceState *is called only when an Activity becomes inactive, but not when it is being closed by a call to finish or by the user pressing the Back button.*

Saving the To-Do List Activity State

Currently, each time the To-Do List example application is restarted, all the to-do items are lost and any text entered into the text entry box is cleared. In this example, you'll start to save the application state of the To-Do list application across sessions.

The instance state in the `ToDoList` Activity consists of three variables:

❑   Is a new item being added?

❑   What text exists in the new item entry textbox?

❑   What is the currently selected item?

Using the Activity's default Shared Preference, you can store each of these values and update the UI when the Activity is restarted.

Later in this chapter, you'll learn how to use the SQLite database to persist the to-do items as well. This example is a first step that shows how to ensure a seamless experience by saving Activity instance details.

1. Start by adding static String variables to use as preference keys.

```
private static final String TEXT_ENTRY_KEY = "TEXT_ENTRY_KEY";
private static final String ADDING_ITEM_KEY = "ADDING_ITEM_KEY";
private static final String SELECTED_INDEX_KEY = "SELECTED_INDEX_KEY";
```

2. Next, override the onPause method. Get the Activity's private Shared Preference object, and get its Editor object.

Using the keys you created in Step 1, store the instance values based on whether a new item is being added and any text in the "new item" Edit Box.

```
@Override
protected void onPause(){
    super.onPause();

    // Get the activity preferences object.
    SharedPreferences uiState = getPreferences(0);
    // Get the preferences editor.
    SharedPreferences.Editor editor = uiState.edit();

    // Add the UI state preference values.
    editor.putString(TEXT_ENTRY_KEY, myEditText.getText().toString());
    editor.putBoolean(ADDING_ITEM_KEY, addingNew);
    // Commit the preferences.
    editor.commit();
}
```

3. Write a restoreUIState method that applies the instance values you recorded in Step 2 when the application restarts.

Modify the onCreate method to add a call to the restoreUIState method at the very end.

```
@Override
public void onCreate(Bundle icicle) {
    [ ... existing onCreate logic ... ]
    restoreUIState();
}

private void restoreUIState() {
    // Get the activity preferences object.
    SharedPreferences settings = getPreferences(Activity.MODE_PRIVATE);

    // Read the UI state values, specifying default values.
    String text = settings.getString(TEXT_ENTRY_KEY, "");
    Boolean adding = settings.getBoolean(ADDING_ITEM_KEY, false);

    // Restore the UI to the previous state.
    if (adding) {
        addNewItem();
        myEditText.setText(text);
    }
}
```

4. Record the index of the selected item using the `onSaveInstanceState` / `onRestore` `InstanceState` mechanism. It's then only saved and applied if the application is killed without the user's explicit instruction.

```java
@Override
public void onSaveInstanceState(Bundle outState) {
  outState.putInt(SELECTED_INDEX_KEY,
                  myListView.getSelectedItemPosition());

  super.onSaveInstanceState(outState);
}

@Override
public void onRestoreInstanceState(Bundle savedInstanceState) {
  int pos = -1;

  if (savedInstanceState != null)
    if (savedInstanceState.containsKey(SELECTED_INDEX_KEY))
      pos = savedInstanceState.getInt(SELECTED_INDEX_KEY, -1);

  myListView.setSelection(pos);
}
```

When you run the To-Do List application, you should now see the UI state persisted across sessions. That said, it still won't persist the to-do list items — you'll add this essential piece of functionality later in the chapter.

Creating a Preferences Page for the Earthquake Viewer

In Chapter 5, you created an earthquake monitor that showed a list of recent earthquakes based on an Internet feed.

In the following example, you'll create a Preferences page for this earthquake viewer that lets users configure application settings for a more personalized experience. You'll provide the option to toggle automatic updates, control the frequency of updates, and filter the minimum earthquake magnitude displayed.

Later in this chapter, you'll extend this example further by creating a Content Provider to save and share earthquake data with other applications.

1. Open the Earthquake project you created in Chapter 5.

Add new String resources for the labels displayed in the "Preferences" screen. Also, add a String for the new Menu Item that will let users access the Preferences screen.

```xml
<?xml version="1.0" encoding="utf-8"?>
<resources>
  <string name="app_name">Earthquake</string>
  <string name="quake_feed">
    http://earthquake.usgs.gov/eqcenter/catalogs/1day-M2.5.xml
  </string>
  <string name="menu_update">Refresh Earthquakes</string>
```

```
<string name="auto_update_prompt">Auto Update?</string>
<string name="update_freq_prompt">Update Frequency</string>
<string name="min_quake_mag_prompt">Minimum Quake Magnitude</string>
<string name="menu_preferences">Preferences</string>
</resources>
```

2. Create a new preferences.xml layout resource that lays out the UI for the Preferences Activity. Include a checkbox for indicating the "automatic update" toggle, and spinners to select the update rate and magnitude filter.

```xml
<LinearLayout
    xmlns:android="http://schemas.android.com/apk/res/android"
    android:orientation="vertical"
    android:layout_width="fill_parent"
    android:layout_height="fill_parent">
    <TextView
        android:layout_width="fill_parent"
        android:layout_height="wrap_content"
        android:text="@string/auto_update_prompt"
    />
    <CheckBox android:id="@+id/checkbox_auto_update"
        android:layout_width="fill_parent"
        android:layout_height="wrap_content"
    />
    <TextView
        android:layout_width="fill_parent"
        android:layout_height="wrap_content"
        android:text="@string/update_freq_prompt"
    />
    <Spinner
        android:id="@+id/spinner_update_freq"
        android:layout_width="fill_parent"
        android:layout_height="wrap_content"
        android:drawSelectorOnTop="true"
    />
    <TextView
        android:layout_width="fill_parent"
        android:layout_height="wrap_content"
        android:text="@string/min_quake_mag_prompt"
    />
    <Spinner
        android:id="@+id/spinner_quake_mag"
        android:layout_width="fill_parent"
        android:layout_height="wrap_content"
        android:drawSelectorOnTop="true"
    />
    <LinearLayout
        android:orientation="horizontal"
        android:layout_width="fill_parent"
        android:layout_height="wrap_content">
        <Button
```

```
          android:id="@+id/okButton"
          android:layout_width="wrap_content"
          android:layout_height="wrap_content"
          android:text="@android:string/ok"
       />
       <Button
          android:id="@+id/cancelButton"
          android:layout_width="wrap_content"
          android:layout_height="wrap_content"
          android:text="@android:string/cancel"
       />
    </LinearLayout>
  </LinearLayout>
```

3. Create four new array resources in a new `res/values/arrays.xml` file. They will provide the values to use for the update frequency and minimum magnitude filter.

```xml
<?xml version="1.0" encoding="utf-8"?>
<resources>
  <string-array name="update_freq_options">
    <item>Every Minute</item>
    <item>5 minutes</item>
    <item>10 minutes</item>
    <item>15 minutes</item>
    <item>Every Hour</item>
  </string-array>

  <array name="magnitude">
    <item>3</item>
    <item>5</item>
    <item>6</item>
    <item>7</item>
    <item>8</item>
  </array>

  <string-array name="magnitude_options">
    <item>3</item>
    <item>5</item>
    <item>6</item>
    <item>7</item>
    <item>8</item>
  </string-array>

  <array name="update_freq_values">
    <item>1</item>
    <item>5</item>
    <item>10</item>
    <item>15</item>
    <item>60</item>
  </array>
</resources>
```

4. Create the `Preferences` Activity. It will be used to display the application preferences.

Override `onCreate` to inflate the layout you created in Step 2, and get references to the Checkbox and both Spinner controls. Then make a call to the `populateSpinners` stub.

```
package com.paad.earthquake;

import android.app.Activity;
import android.content.SharedPreferences;
import android.content.SharedPreferences.Editor;
import android.os.Bundle;
import android.view.View;
import android.widget.ArrayAdapter;
import android.widget.Button;
import android.widget.CheckBox;
import android.widget.Spinner;

public class Preferences extends Activity {

  CheckBox autoUpdate;
  Spinner updateFreqSpinner;
  Spinner magnitudeSpinner;

  @Override
  public void onCreate(Bundle icicle) {
    super.onCreate(icicle);
    setContentView(R.layout.preferences);

    updateFreqSpinner =
      (Spinner)findViewById(R.id.spinner_update_freq);
    magnitudeSpinner = (Spinner)findViewById(R.id.spinner_quake_mag);
    autoUpdate = (CheckBox)findViewById(R.id.checkbox_auto_update);

    populateSpinners();
  }

  private void populateSpinners() {
  }
}
```

5. Fill in the `populateSpinners` method, using Array Adapters to bind each Spinner to its corresponding array.

```
private void populateSpinners() {
  // Populate the update frequency spinner
  ArrayAdapter<CharSequence> fAdapter;
  fAdapter = ArrayAdapter.createFromResource(this,
                        R.array.update_freq_options,
                        android.R.layout.simple_spinner_item);
  fAdapter.setDropDownViewResource(
    android.R.layout.simple_spinner_dropdown_item);
```

```
        updateFreqSpinner.setAdapter(fAdapter);

        // Populate the minimum magnitude spinner
        ArrayAdapter<CharSequence> mAdapter;
        mAdapter = ArrayAdapter.createFromResource(this,
                                    R.array.magnitude_options,
                                    android.R.layout.simple_spinner_item);
        mAdapter.setDropDownViewResource(
          android.R.layout.simple_spinner_dropdown_item);

        magnitudeSpinner.setAdapter(mAdapter);
    }
```

6. Add public static String values to use to identify the named Shared Preference you're going to create, and the keys it will use to store each preference value. Update the onCreate method to retrieve the named preference and call updateUIFromPreferences. The updateUIFromPreferences method uses the get<type> methods on the Shared Preference object to retrieve each preference value and apply it to the current UI.

```
    public static final String USER_PREFERENCE = "USER_PREFERENCES";

    public static final String PREF_AUTO_UPDATE = "PREF_AUTO_UPDATE";
    public static final String PREF_MIN_MAG = "PREF_MIN_MAG";
    public static final String PREF_UPDATE_FREQ = "PREF_UPDATE_FREQ";

    SharedPreferences prefs;

    @Override
    public void onCreate(Bundle icicle) {
      super.onCreate(icicle);
      setContentView(R.layout.preferences);

      updateFreqSpinner = (Spinner)findViewById(R.id.spinner_update_freq);
      magnitudeSpinner = (Spinner)findViewById(R.id.spinner_quake_mag);
      autoUpdate = (CheckBox)findViewById(R.id.checkbox_auto_update);

      populateSpinners();

      prefs = getSharedPreferences(USER_PREFERENCE, Activity.MODE_PRIVATE);
      updateUIFromPreferences();
    }

    private void updateUIFromPreferences() {
      boolean autoUpChecked = prefs.getBoolean(PREF_AUTO_UPDATE, false);
      int updateFreqIndex = prefs.getInt(PREF_UPDATE_FREQ, 2);
      int minMagIndex = prefs.getInt(PREF_MIN_MAG, 0);

      updateFreqSpinner.setSelection(updateFreqIndex);
      magnitudeSpinner.setSelection(minMagIndex);
      autoUpdate.setChecked(autoUpChecked);
    }
```

7. Still in the `onCreate` method, add event handlers for the OK and Cancel buttons. Cancel should close the Activity, while OK should call `savePreferences` first.

```
@Override
public void onCreate(Bundle icicle) {
  super.onCreate(icicle);
  setContentView(R.layout.preferences);

  updateFreqSpinner = (Spinner)findViewById(R.id.spinner_update_freq);
  magnitudeSpinner = (Spinner)findViewById(R.id.spinner_quake_mag);
  autoUpdate = (CheckBox)findViewById(R.id.checkbox_auto_update);

  populateSpinners();

  prefs = getSharedPreferences(USER_PREFERENCE, Activity.MODE_PRIVATE);
  updateUIFromPreferences();

  Button okButton = (Button) findViewById(R.id.okButton);
  okButton.setOnClickListener(new View.OnClickListener() {

    public void onClick(View view) {
      savePreferences();
      Preferences.this.setResult(RESULT_OK);
      finish();
    }
  });

  Button cancelButton = (Button) findViewById(R.id.cancelButton);
  cancelButton.setOnClickListener(new View.OnClickListener() {

    public void onClick(View view) {
      Preferences.this.setResult(RESULT_CANCELED);
      finish();
    }
  });
}

private void savePreferences() {
}
```

8. Fill in the `savePreferences` method to record the current preferences, based on the UI selections, to the Shared Preference object.

```
private void savePreferences() {
  int updateIndex = updateFreqSpinner.getSelectedItemPosition();
  int minMagIndex = magnitudeSpinner.getSelectedItemPosition();
  boolean autoUpdateChecked = autoUpdate.isChecked();

  Editor editor = prefs.edit();
  editor.putBoolean(PREF_AUTO_UPDATE, autoUpdateChecked);
  editor.putInt(PREF_UPDATE_FREQ, updateIndex);
  editor.putInt(PREF_MIN_MAG, minMagIndex);
  editor.commit();
}
```

9. That completes the `Preferences` Activity. Make it accessible in the application by adding it to the application manifest.

```
<activity android:name=".Preferences"
        android:label="Earthquake Preferences">
</activity>
```

10. Now return to the `Earthquake` Activity, and add support for the new Shared Preferences file and a Menu Item to display the Preferences Activity.

Start by adding the new Menu Item. Extend the `onCreateOptionsMenu` method to include a new item that opens the Preferences Activity.

```
static final private int MENU_PREFERENCES = Menu.FIRST+1;

@Override
public boolean onCreateOptionsMenu(Menu menu) {
  super.onCreateOptionsMenu(menu);

  menu.add(0, MENU_UPDATE, Menu.NONE, R.string.menu_update);
  menu.add(0, MENU_PREFERENCES, Menu.NONE, R.string.menu_preferences);

  return true;
}
```

11. Modify the `onOptionsItemSelected` method to display the Preferences Activity when the new Menu Item is selected. Create an explicit Intent, and pass it in to the `startActivityForResult` method. This will launch the Preferences screen and alert the `Earthquake` class when the preferences are saved through the `onActivityResult` handler.

```
private static final int SHOW_PREFERENCES = 1;

public boolean onOptionsItemSelected(MenuItem item) {
  super.onOptionsItemSelected(item);

  switch (item.getItemId()) {
    case (MENU_UPDATE): {
      refreshEarthquakes();
      return true;
    }
    case (MENU_PREFERENCES): {
      Intent i = new Intent(this, Preferences.class);
      startActivityForResult(i, SHOW_PREFERENCES);
      return true;
    }
  }
  return false;
}
```

12. Launch your application, and select **Preferences** from the Activity menu. The Preferences Activity should be displayed as shown in Figure 6-1.

Figure 6-1

13. All that's left is to apply the preferences to the Earthquake functionality.

Implementing the automatic updates will be left until Chapter 8, when you'll learn how to use Services and background threads. For now, you can put the framework in place and apply the magnitude filter.

14. Start by creating a new `updateFromPreferences` method that reads the Shared Preference values and creates instance variables for each of them.

```
int minimumMagnitude = 0;
boolean autoUpdate = false;
int updateFreq = 0;

private void updateFromPreferences() {
  SharedPreferences prefs =
    getSharedPreferences(Preferences.USER_PREFERENCE,
                         Activity.MODE_PRIVATE);

  int minMagIndex = prefs.getInt(Preferences.PREF_MIN_MAG, 0);
  if (minMagIndex < 0)
    minMagIndex = 0;

  int freqIndex = prefs.getInt(Preferences.PREF_UPDATE_FREQ, 0);
  if (freqIndex < 0)
    freqIndex = 0;

  autoUpdate = prefs.getBoolean(Preferences.PREF_AUTO_UPDATE, false);

  Resources r = getResources();
```

```
      // Get the option values from the arrays.
      int[] minMagValues = r.getIntArray(R.array.magnitude);
      int[] freqValues = r.getIntArray(R.array.update_freq_values);

      // Convert the values to ints.
      minimumMagnitude = minMagValues[minMagIndex];
      updateFreq = freqValues[freqIndex];
  }
```

15. Apply the magnitude filter by updating the `addNewQuake` method to check a new earthquake's magnitude before adding it to the list.

```
private void addNewQuake(Quake _quake) {
  if (_quake.getMagnitude() > minimumMagnitude) {
    // Add the new quake to our list of earthquakes.
    earthquakes.add(_quake);

    // Notify the array adapter of a change.
    aa.notifyDataSetChanged();
  }
}
```

16. Override the `onActivityResult` handler to call `updateFromPreferences` and refresh the earthquakes whenever the Preferences Activity saves changes.

```
@Override
public void onActivityResult(int requestCode, int resultCode,
                             Intent data) {
  super.onActivityResult(requestCode, resultCode, data);

  if (requestCode == SHOW_PREFERENCES)
    if (resultCode == Activity.RESULT_OK) {
      updateFromPreferences();
      refreshEarthquakes();
    }
}
```

17. Finally, call `updateFromPreferences` in `onCreate` (before the call to `refreshEarthquakes`) to ensure that the preferences are applied when the Activity first starts.

```
@Override
public void onCreate(Bundle icicle) {
  super.onCreate(icicle);
  setContentView(R.layout.main);

  earthquakeListView =
    (ListView)this.findViewById(R.id.earthquakeListView);

  earthquakeListView.setOnItemClickListener(new OnItemClickListener() {

    public void onItemClick(AdapterView _av, View _v,
                            int _index, long arg3) {
      selectedQuake = earthquakes.get(_index);
      showDialog(QUAKE_DIALOG);
```

```
            }
        });

        int layoutID = android.R.layout.simple_list_item_1;
        aa = new ArrayAdapter<Quake>(this, layoutID, earthquakes);
        earthquakeListView.setAdapter(aa);

        updateFromPreferences();
        refreshEarthquakes();
    }
```

Saving and Loading Files

It's good practice to use Shared Preferences or a database to store your application data, but there are still times when you'll want to use files directly rather than rely on Android's managed mechanisms.

As well as the standard Java I/O classes and methods, Android offers `openFileInput` and `openFileOuput` to simplify reading and writing streams from and to local files, as shown in the code snippet below:

```
String FILE_NAME = "tempfile.tmp";

// Create a new output file stream that's private to this application.
FileOutputStream fos = openFileOutput(FILE_NAME, Context.MODE_PRIVATE);
// Create a new file input stream.
FileInputStream fis = openFileInput(FILE_NAME);
```

These methods only support files in the current application folder; specifying path separators will cause an exception to be thrown.

If the filename you specify when creating a `FileOutputStream` does not exist, Android will create it for you. The default behavior for existing files is to overwrite them; to append an existing file, specify the mode as `Context.MODE_APPEND`.

By default, files created using the `openFileOutput` method are private to the calling application — a different application that tries to access these files will be denied access. The standard way to share a file between applications is to use a Content Provider. Alternatively, you can specify either `Context.MODE_WORLD_READABLE` or `Context.MODE_WORLD_WRITEABLE` when creating the output file to make them available in other applications, as shown in the following snippet:

```
String OUTPUT_FILE = "publicCopy.txt";
FileOutputStream fos = openFileOutput(OUTPUT_FILE, Context.MODE_WORLD_WRITEABLE);
```

Including Static Files as Resources

If your application requires external file resources, you can include them in your distribution package by placing them in the `res/raw` folder of your project hierarchy.

To access these Read Only file resources, call the `openRawResource` method from your application's `Resource` object to receive an `InputStream` based on the specified resource. Pass in the filename (without extension) as the variable name from the `R.raw` class, as shown in the skeleton code below:

```
Resources myResources = getResources();
InputStream myFile = myResources.openRawResource(R.raw.myfilename);
```

Adding raw files to your resources hierarchy is an excellent alternative for large, preexisting data sources (such as dictionaries) where it's not desirable (or even possible) to convert them into an Android database.

Android's resource mechanism lets you specify alternative resource files for different languages, locations, or hardware configurations. As a result, you could, for example, create an application that dynamically loads a dictionary resource based on the user's current settings.

File Management Tools

Android supplies some basic file management tools to help you deal with the filesystem. Many of these utilities are located within the standard `java.io.File` package.

Complete coverage of Java file management utilities is beyond the scope of this book, but Android does supply some specialized utilities for file management available from the application's Context.

❑ **deleteFile**   Lets you remove files created by the current application.

❑ **fileList**   Returns a `String` array that includes all the files created by the current application.

Databases in Android

Android provides full relational database capabilities through the SQLite library, without imposing any additional limitations.

Using SQLite, you can create independent, relational databases for each application. Use them to store and manage complex, structured application data.

All Android databases are stored in the `/data/data/<package_name>/databases` folder on your device (or emulator). By default, all databases are private, accessible only by the application that created them. To share a database across applications, use Content Providers, as shown later in this chapter.

Database design is a vast topic that deserves more thorough coverage than is possible within this book. However, it's worth highlighting that standard database best practices still apply. In particular, when creating databases for resource-constrained devices, it's important to reduce data redundancy using normalization.

The following sections focus on the practicalities of creating and managing SQLite databases in Android.

Introducing SQLite

SQLite is a relational database management system (RDBMS). It is well regarded, being:

❑ Open source

❑ Standards-compliant

❑ Lightweight

❑ Single-tier

It has been implemented as a compact C library that's included as part of the Android software stack.

By providing functionality through a library, rather than as a separate process, each database becomes an integrated part of the application that created it. This reduces external dependencies, minimizes latency, and simplifies transaction locking and synchronization.

SQLite has a reputation of being extremely reliable and is the database system of choice for many consumer electronic devices, including several MP3 players, the iPhone, and the iPod Touch.

Lightweight and powerful, SQLite differs from many conventional database engines by using a loosely typed approach to column definitions. Rather than requiring column values to conform to a single type, the values in each row for each column are individually typed. As a result, there's no strict type checking when assigning or extracting values from each column within a row.

For more comprehensive coverage of SQLite, including its particular strengths and limitations, check out the official site at www.sqlite.org/.

Cursors and Content Values

ContentValues objects are used to insert new rows into database tables (and Content Providers). Each Content Values object represents a single row, as a map of column names to values.

Queries in Android are returned as Cursor objects. Rather than extracting and returning a copy of the result values, Cursors act as pointers to a subset of the underlying data. Cursors are a managed way of controlling your position (row) in the result set of a database query.

The Cursor class includes several functions to navigate query results including, but not limited to, the following:

❑ moveToFirst   Moves the cursor to the first row in the query result.

❑ moveToNext   Moves the cursor to the next row.

❑ moveToPrevious   Moves the cursor to the previous row.

❑ getCount   Returns the number of rows in the result set.

❑ getColumnIndexOrThrow   Returns an index for the column with the specified name (throwing an exception if no column exists with that name).

❑ getColumnName   Returns the name of the specified column index.

❑ getColumnNames   Returns a String array of all the column names in the current cursor.

❏   moveToPosition   Moves the cursor to the specified row.

❏   getPosition   Returns the current cursor position.

Android provides a mechanism to manage Cursor resources within your Activities. The startManagingCursor method integrates the Cursor's lifetime into the parent Activity's lifetime management. When you've finished with the Cursor, call stopManagingCursor to do just that.

Later in this chapter, you'll learn how to query a database and how to extract specific row/column values from the resulting Cursor objects.

Working with Android Databases

It's good practice to create a helper class to simplify your database interactions.

Consider creating a database adapter, which adds an abstraction layer that encapsulates database interactions. It should provide intuitive, strongly typed methods for adding, removing, and updating items. A database adapter should also handle queries and wrap creating, opening, and closing the database.

It's often also used as a convenient location from which to publish static database constants, including table names, column names, and column indexes.

The following snippet shows the skeleton code for a standard database adapter class. It includes an extension of the SQLiteOpenHelper class, used to simplify opening, creating, and upgrading the database.

```
import android.content.Context;
import android.database.*;
import android.database.sqlite.*;
import android.database.sqlite.SQLiteDatabase.CursorFactory;
import android.util.Log;

public class MyDBAdapter {
  private static final String DATABASE_NAME = "myDatabase.db";
  private static final String DATABASE_TABLE = "mainTable";
  private static final int DATABASE_VERSION = 1;

  // The index (key) column name for use in where clauses.
  public static final String KEY_ID="_id";

  // The name and column index of each column in your database.
  public static final String KEY_NAME="name";
  public static final int NAME_COLUMN = 1;
  // TODO: Create public field for each column in your table.

  // SQL Statement to create a new database.
  private static final String DATABASE_CREATE = "create table " +
    DATABASE_TABLE + " (" + KEY_ID +
    " integer primary key autoincrement, " +
    KEY_NAME + " text not null);";

  // Variable to hold the database instance
  private SQLiteDatabase db;

  // Context of the application using the database.
```

```java
  private final Context context;
  // Database open/upgrade helper
  private myDbHelper dbHelper;

  public MyDBAdapter(Context _context) {
    context = _context;
    dbHelper = new myDbHelper(context, DATABASE_NAME, null,
                              DATABASE_VERSION);
  }

  public MyDBAdapter open() throws SQLException {
    db = dbHelper.getWritableDatabase();
    return this;
  }

  public void close() {
      db.close();
  }

  public long insertEntry(MyObject _myObject) {
    ContentValues contentValues = new ContentValues();
    // TODO fill in ContentValues to represent the new row
    return db.insert(DATABASE_TABLE, null, contentValues);
  }

  public boolean removeEntry(long _rowIndex) {
    return db.delete(DATABASE_TABLE, KEY_ID +
                     "=" + _rowIndex, null) > 0;
  }

  public Cursor getAllEntries () {
    return db.query(DATABASE_TABLE, new String[] {KEY_ID, KEY_NAME},
                    null, null, null, null, null);
  }

  public MyObject getEntry(long _rowIndex) {
    MyObject objectInstance = new MyObject();
    // TODO Return a cursor to a row from the database and
    // use the values to populate an instance of MyObject
    return objectInstance;
  }

  public int updateEntry(long _rowIndex, MyObject _myObject) {
    String where = KEY_ID + "=" + _rowIndex;
    ContentValues contentValues = new ContentValues();
    // TODO fill in the ContentValue based on the new object
    return db.update(DATABASE_TABLE, contentValues, where, null);
  }

  private static class myDbHelper extends SQLiteOpenHelper {

    public myDbHelper(Context context, String name,
                      CursorFactory factory, int version) {
```

```
        super(context, name, factory, version);
    }


    // Called when no database exists in
    // disk and the helper class needs
    // to create a new one.
    @Override
    public void onCreate(SQLiteDatabase _db) {
      _db.execSQL(DATABASE_CREATE);
    }


    // Called when there is a database version mismatch meaning that
    // the version of the database on disk needs to be upgraded to
    // the current version.
    @Override
    public void onUpgrade(SQLiteDatabase _db, int _oldVersion,
                          int _newVersion) {
      // Log the version upgrade.
      Log.w("TaskDBAdapter", "Upgrading from version " +
                             _oldVersion + " to " +
                             _newVersion +
                             ", which will destroy all old data");

      // Upgrade the existing database to conform to the new version.
      // Multiple previous versions can be handled by comparing
      // _oldVersion and _newVersion values.

      // The simplest case is to drop the old table and create a
      // new one.
      _db.execSQL("DROP TABLE IF EXISTS " + DATABASE_TABLE);
      // Create a new one.
      onCreate(_db);
    }
  }
}
```

Using the SQLiteOpenHelper

SQLiteOpenHelper is an abstract class that wraps up the best practice pattern for creating, opening, and upgrading databases. By implementing and using an SQLiteOpenHelper, you hide the logic used to decide if a database needs to be created or upgraded before it's opened.

The code snippet above shows how to extend the SQLiteOpenHelper class by overriding the constructor, onCreate, and onUpgrade methods to handle the creation of a new database and upgrading to a new version, respectively.

> *In the previous example,* onUpgrade *simply drops the existing table and replaces it with the new definition. In practice, a better solution is to migrate existing data into the new table.*

To use an implementation of the helper class, create a new instance, passing in the context, database name, current version, and a CursorFactory (if you're using one).

Call `getReadableDatabase` or `getWriteableDatabase` to open and return a readable/writable instance of the database.

A call to `getWriteableDatabase` can fail because of disk space or permission issues, so it's good practice to provide fallback to the `getReadableDatabase` method as shown below:

```
dbHelper = new myDbHelper(context, DATABASE_NAME, null, DATABASE_VERSION);

SQLiteDatabase db;
try {
  db = dbHelper.getWritableDatabase();
}
catch (SQLiteException ex){
  db = dbHelper.getReadableDatabase();
}
```

Behind the scenes, if the database doesn't exist, the helper executes its `onCreate` handler. If the database version has changed, the `onUpgrade` handler will fire. In both cases, the get<read/write>ableDatabase call will return the existing, newly created, or upgraded database as appropriate.

Opening and Creating Databases without the `SQLiteHelper`

You can create and open databases without using the `SQLiteHelper` class with the `openOrCreateDatabase` method on the application Context.

Setting up a database is a two-step process. First, call `openOrCreateDatabase` to create the new database. Then, call `execSQL` on the resulting database instance to run the SQL commands that will create your tables and their relationships. The general process is shown in the snippet below:

```
private static final String DATABASE_NAME = "myDatabase.db";
private static final String DATABASE_TABLE = "mainTable";

private static final String DATABASE_CREATE =
  "create table " + DATABASE_TABLE +
  " ( _id integer primary key autoincrement," +
  "column_one text not null);";

SQLiteDatabase myDatabase;

private void createDatabase() {
  myDatabase = openOrCreateDatabase(DATABASE_NAME,
                          Context.MODE_PRIVATE, null);
  myDatabase.execSQL(DATABASE_CREATE);
}
```

Android Database Design Considerations

There are several considerations specific to Android that you should consider when designing your database:

❑   Files (such as bitmaps or audio files) are not usually stored within database tables. Instead, use a string to store a path to the file, preferably a fully qualified Content Provider URI.

❑   While not strictly a requirement, it's strongly recommended that all tables include an auto-increment key field, to function as a unique index value for each row. It's worth noting that if you plan to share your table using a Content Provider, this unique ID field is mandatory.

Querying Your Database

All database queries are returned as a Cursor to a result set. This lets Android manage resources more efficiently by retrieving and releasing row and column values on demand.

To execute a query on a database, use the query method on the database object, passing in:

❑ An optional Boolean that specifies if the result set should contain only unique values

❑ The name of the table to query

❑ A projection, as an array of Strings, that lists the columns to include in the result set

❑ A "where" clause that defines the rows to be returned. You can include ? wildcards that will be replaced by the values stored in the selection argument parameter.

❑ An array of selection argument strings that will replace the ?'s in the "where" clause

❑ A "group by" clause that defines how the resulting rows will be grouped

❑ A "having" filter that defines which row groups to include if you specified a "group by" clause

❑ A String that describes the order of the returned rows

❑ An optional String that defines a limit to the returned rows

The following skeleton code shows snippets for returning some, and all, of the rows in a particular table:

```
// Return all rows for columns one and three, no duplicates
String[] result_columns = new String[] {KEY_ID, KEY_COL1, KEY_COL3};

Cursor allRows = myDatabase.query(true, DATABASE_TABLE, result_columns,
                                  null, null, null, null, null, null);

// Return all columns for rows where column 3 equals a set value
// and the rows are ordered by column 5.
String where = KEY_COL3 + "=" + requiredValue;
String order = KEY_COL5;
Cursor myResult = myDatabase.query(DATABASE_TABLE, null, where,
                                   null, null, null, order);
```

In practice, it's often useful to abstract these query commands within an adapter class to simplify data access.

Extracting Results from a Cursor

To extract actual values from a result Cursor, first use the moveTo<location> methods described previously to position the Cursor at the correct row of the result set.

With the Cursor at the desired row, use the type-safe get methods (passing in a column index) to return the value stored at the current row for the specified column, as shown in the following snippet:

```
String columnValue = myResult.getString(columnIndex);
```

Database implementations should publish static constants that provide the column indexes using more easily recognizable variables based on the column names. They are generally exposed within a database adapter as described previously.

The following example shows how to iterate over a result cursor, extracting and summing a column of floats:

```
int GOLD_HOARDED_COLUMN = 2;
Cursor myGold = myDatabase.query("GoldHoards", null, null, null, null,
                                  null, null);

float totalHoard = 0f;

// Make sure there is at least one row.
if (myGold.moveToFirst()) {
  // Iterate over each cursor.
  do {
    float hoard = myGold.getFloat(GOLD_HOARDED_COLUMN);
    totalHoard += hoard;
  } while(myGold.moveToNext());
}

float averageHoard = totalHoard / myGold.getCount();
```

Because SQLite database columns are loosely typed, you can cast individual values into valid types as required. For example, values stored as floats can be read back as Strings.

Adding, Updating, and Removing Rows

The SQLiteDatabase class exposes specialized insert, delete, and update methods to encapsulate the SQL statements required to perform these actions. Nonetheless, the execSQL method lets you execute any valid SQL on your database tables should you want to execute these operations manually.

Any time you modify the underlying database values, you should call refreshQuery on any Cursors that currently have a view on the table.

Inserting New Rows

To create a new row, construct a ContentValues object, and use its put methods to supply values for each column. Insert the new row by passing the Content Values object into the insert method called on the target database object — along with the table name — as shown in the snippet below:

```
// Create a new row of values to insert.
ContentValues newValues = new ContentValues();

// Assign values for each row.
newValues.put(COLUMN_NAME, newValue);
[ ... Repeat for each column ... ]

// Insert the row into your table
myDatabase.insert(DATABASE_TABLE, null, newValues);
```

Updating a Row on the Database

Updating rows is also done using Content Values.

Create a new `ContentValues` object, using the `put` methods to assign new values to each column you want to update. Call `update` on the database object, passing in the table name, the updated Content Values object, and a `where` statement that returns the row(s) to update.

The update process is demonstrated in the snippet below:

```
// Define the updated row content.
ContentValues updatedValues = new ContentValues();

// Assign values for each row.
updatedValues.put(COLUMN_NAME, newValue);
[ ... Repeat for each column ... ]

String where = KEY_ID + "=" + rowId;

// Update the row with the specified index with the new values.
myDatabase.update(DATABASE_TABLE, updatedValues, where, null);
```

Deleting Rows

To delete a row, simply call `delete` on your database object, specifying the table name and a `where` clause that returns the rows you want to delete, as shown in the code below:

```
myDatabase.delete(DATABASE_TABLE, KEY_ID + "=" + rowId, null);
```

Saving Your To-Do List

Previously in this chapter, you enhanced the To-Do List example to persist the Activity's UI state across sessions. That was only half the job; in the following example, you'll create a private database to save the to-do items:

1. Start by creating a new `ToDoDBAdapter` class. It will be used to manage your database interactions.

   Create private variables to store the `SQLiteDatabase` object and the Context of the calling application. Add a constructor that takes the owner application's Context, and include static class variables for the name and version of the database and a name for the to-do item table.

   ```java
   package com.paad.todolist;

   import android.content.ContentValues;
   import android.content.Context;
   import android.database.Cursor;
   import android.database.SQLException;
   import android.database.sqlite.SQLiteException;
   import android.database.sqlite.SQLiteDatabase;
   import android.database.sqlite.SQLiteOpenHelper;
   import android.util.Log;

   public class ToDoDBAdapter {
     private static final String DATABASE_NAME = "todoList.db";
     private static final String DATABASE_TABLE = "todoItems";
     private static final int DATABASE_VERSION = 1;

     private SQLiteDatabase db;
   ```

```
    private final Context context;

    public ToDoDBAdapter(Context _context) {
        this.context = _context;
    }
}
```

2. Create public convenience variables that define the column names and indexes; this will make it easier to find the correct columns when extracting values from query result Cursors.

```
public static final String KEY_ID = "_id";

public static final String KEY_TASK = "task";
public static final int TASK_COLUMN = 1;

public static final String KEY_CREATION_DATE = "creation_date";
public static final int CREATION_DATE_COLUMN = 2;
```

3. Create a new taskDBOpenHelper class within the ToDoDBAdapter that extends SQLiteOpenHelper. It will be used to simplify version management of your database.

   Within it, overwrite the onCreate and onUpgrade methods to handle the database creation and upgrade logic.

```
private static class toDoDBOpenHelper extends SQLiteOpenHelper {

  public toDoDBOpenHelper(Context context, String name,
                          CursorFactory factory, int version) {
    super(context, name, factory, version);
  }

  // SQL Statement to create a new database.
  private static final String DATABASE_CREATE = "create table " +
    DATABASE_TABLE + " (" + KEY_ID +
    " integer primary key autoincrement, " +
    KEY_TASK + " text not null, " + KEY_CREATION_DATE + " long);";

  @Override
  public void onCreate(SQLiteDatabase _db) {
    _db.execSQL(DATABASE_CREATE);
  }

  @Override
  public void onUpgrade(SQLiteDatabase _db, int _oldVersion,
                        int _newVersion) {
    Log.w("TaskDBAdapter", "Upgrading from version " +
                           _oldVersion + " to " +
                           _newVersion +
                           ", which will destroy all old data");

    // Drop the old table.
    _db.execSQL("DROP TABLE IF EXISTS " + DATABASE_TABLE);
    // Create a new one.
    onCreate(_db);
  }
}
```

4. Within the `ToDoDBAdapter` class, add a private instance variable to store an instance of the `toDoDBOpenHelper` class you just created; assign it within the constructor.

```
private toDoDBOpenHelper dbHelper;

public ToDoDBAdapter(Context _context) {
  this.context = _context;
  dbHelper = new toDoDBOpenHelper(context, DATABASE_NAME,
                                  null, DATABASE_VERSION);
}
```

5. Still in the adapter class, create `open` and `close` methods that encapsulate the open and close logic for your database. Start with a `close` method that simply calls close on the database object.

```
public void close() {
  db.close();
}
```

6. The `open` method should use the `toDoDBOpenHelper` class. Call `getWritableDatabase` to let the helper handle database creation and version checking. Wrap the call to try to provide a readable database if a writable instance can't be opened.

```
public void open() throws SQLiteException {
  try {
    db = dbHelper.getWritableDatabase();
  } catch (SQLiteException ex) {
    db = dbHelper.getReadableDatabase();
  }
}
```

7. Add strongly typed methods for adding, removing, and updating items.

```
// Insert a new task
public long insertTask(ToDoItem _task) {
  // Create a new row of values to insert.
  ContentValues newTaskValues = new ContentValues();
  // Assign values for each row.
  newTaskValues.put(KEY_TASK, _task.getTask());
  newTaskValues.put(KEY_CREATION_DATE, _task.getCreated().getTime());
  // Insert the row.
  return db.insert(DATABASE_TABLE, null, newTaskValues);
}

// Remove a task based on its index
public boolean removeTask(long _rowIndex) {
  return db.delete(DATABASE_TABLE, KEY_ID + "=" + _rowIndex, null) > 0;
}

// Update a task
public boolean updateTask(long _rowIndex, String _task) {
  ContentValues newValue = new ContentValues();
  newValue.put(KEY_TASK, _task);
  return db.update(DATABASE_TABLE, newValue,
                   KEY_ID + "=" + _rowIndex, null) > 0;
}
```

8. Now add helper methods to handle queries. Write three methods — one to return all the items, another to return a particular row as a Cursor, and finally, one that returns a strongly typed `ToDoItem`.

```
public Cursor getAllToDoItemsCursor() {
  return db.query(DATABASE_TABLE,
                  new String[] { KEY_ID, KEY_TASK, KEY_CREATION_DATE},
                  null, null, null, null, null);
}

public Cursor setCursorToToDoItem(long _rowIndex) throws SQLException {
  Cursor result = db.query(true, DATABASE_TABLE,
                           new String[] {KEY_ID, KEY_TASK},
                           KEY_ID + "=" + _rowIndex, null, null, null,
                           null, null);
  if ((result.getCount() == 0) || !result.moveToFirst()) {
    throw new SQLException("No to do items found for row: " +
                           _rowIndex);
  }
  return result;
}

public ToDoItem getToDoItem(long _rowIndex) throws SQLException {
  Cursor cursor = db.query(true, DATABASE_TABLE,
                           new String[] {KEY_ID, KEY_TASK},
                           KEY_ID + "=" + _rowIndex,
                           null, null, null, null, null);
  if ((cursor.getCount() == 0) || !cursor.moveToFirst()) {
    throw new SQLException("No to do item found for row: " +
                           _rowIndex);
  }

  String task = cursor.getString(TASK_COLUMN);
  long created = cursor.getLong(CREATION_DATE_COLUMN);

  ToDoItem result = new ToDoItem(task, new Date(created));
  return result;
}
```

9. That completes the database helper class. Return the `ToDoList` Activity, and update it to persist the to-do list array.

Start by updating the Activity's `onCreate` method to create an instance of the `toDoDBAdapter`, and open a connection to the database. Also include a call to the `populateTodoList` method stub.

```
ToDoDBAdapter toDoDBAdapter;

public void onCreate(Bundle icicle) {
  [ ... existing onCreate logic ... ]

  toDoDBAdapter = new ToDoDBAdapter(this);
```

```
    // Open or create the database
    toDoDBAdapter.open();

    populateTodoList();
}

private void populateTodoList() { }
```

10.   Create a new instance variable to store a Cursor over all the to-do items in the database.

Update the `populateTodoList` method to use the `toDoDBAdapter` instance to query the database, and call `startManagingCursor` to let the Activity manage the Cursor. It should also make a call to `updateArray`, a method that will be used to repopulate the to-do list array using the Cursor.

```
Cursor toDoListCursor;

private void populateTodoList() {
    // Get all the todo list items from the database.
    toDoListCursor = toDoDBAdapter.getAllToDoItemsCursor();
    startManagingCursor(toDoListCursor);

    // Update the array.
    updateArray();
}

private void updateArray() { }
```

11.   Now implement the `updateArray` method to update the current to-do list array. Call `requery` on the result Cursor to ensure that it's fully up to date, then clear the array and iterate over the result set. When complete, call `notifyDataSetChanged` on the Array Adapter.

```
private void updateArray() {
    toDoListCursor.requery();

    todoItems.clear();

    if (toDoListCursor.moveToFirst())
      do {
        String task =
          toDoListCursor.getString(ToDoDBAdapter.TASK_COLUMN);
        long created =
          toDoListCursor.getLong(ToDoDBAdapter.CREATION_DATE_COLUMN);

        ToDoItem newItem = new ToDoItem(task, new Date(created));
        todoItems.add(0, newItem);
      } while(toDoListCursor.moveToNext());

    aa.notifyDataSetChanged();
}
```

12. To join the pieces together, modify the OnKeyListener assigned to the text entry box in the onCreate method, and update the removeItem method. Both should now use the toDoDBAdapter to add and remove items from the database rather than modifying the to-do list array directly.

12.1. Start with the OnKeyListener, insert the new item into the database, and refresh the array.

```
public void onCreate(Bundle icicle) {
    super.onCreate(icicle);
    setContentView(R.layout.main);

    myListView = (ListView)findViewById(R.id.myListView);
    myEditText = (EditText)findViewById(R.id.myEditText);

    todoItems = new ArrayList<ToDoItem>();
    int resID = R.layout.todolist_item;
    aa = new ToDoItemAdapter(this, resID, todoItems);
    myListView.setAdapter(aa);

    myEditText.setOnKeyListener(new OnKeyListener() {
        public boolean onKey(View v, int keyCode, KeyEvent event) {
            if (event.getAction() == KeyEvent.ACTION_DOWN)
                if (keyCode == KeyEvent.KEYCODE_DPAD_CENTER) {
                    ToDoItem newItem;
                    newItem = new ToDoItem(myEditText.getText().toString());
                    toDoDBAdapter.insertTask(newItem);
                    updateArray();
                    myEditText.setText("");
                    aa.notifyDataSetChanged();
                    cancelAdd();
                    return true;
                }
            return false;
        }
    });

    registerForContextMenu(myListView);
    restoreUIState();

    toDoDBAdapter = new ToDoDBAdapter(this);

    // Open or create the database
    toDoDBAdapter.open();

    populateTodoList();
}
```

12.2. Then modify the removeItem method to remove the item from the database and refresh the array list.

```
private void removeItem(int _index) {
    // Items are added to the listview in reverse order,
    // so invert the index.
```

```
            toDoDBAdapter.removeTask(todoItems.size()-_index);
            updateArray();
        }
```

13.   As a final step, override the `onDestroy` method of your Activity to close your database connection.

```
        @Override
        public void onDestroy() {

          // Close the database
          toDoDBAdapter.close();

         super.onDestroy();
        }
```

Your to-do items will now be saved between sessions. As a further enhancement, you could change the Array Adapter to a Cursor Adapter and have the List View update dynamically, directly from changes to the underlying database.

By using a private database, your tasks are not available for other applications to view or add to them. To provide access to your tasks for other applications to leverage, you can expose them using a Content Provider.

Introducing Content Providers

Content Providers are a generic interface mechanism that lets you share data between applications. By abstracting away the underlying data source, Content Providers let you decouple your application layer from the data layer, making your applications data-source agnostic.

Content Providers feature full permission control and are accessed using a simple URI model. Shared content can be queried for results as well as supporting write access. As a result, any application with the appropriate permissions can add, remove, and update data from any other applications — including some native Android databases.

Many of the native databases have been made available as Content Providers, accessible by third-party applications. This means that your applications can have access to the phone's Contact Manager, media player, and other native database once they've been granted permission.

By publishing your own data sources as Content Providers, you make it possible for you (and other developers) to incorporate and extend your data in new applications.

Using Content Providers

Access to Content Providers is handled by the `ContentResolver` class.

The following sections demonstrate how to access a Content Resolver and how to use it to query and transact with a Content Provider. They also demonstrate some practical examples using the native Android Content Providers.

Introducing Content Resolvers

Each application Context has a single `ContentResolver`, accessible using the `getContentResolver` method, as shown in the following code snippet:

```
ContentResolver cr = getContentResolver();
```

Content Resolver includes several methods to transact and query Content Providers. You specify the provider to interact using a URI.

A Content Provider's URI is defined by its *authority* as defined in its application manifest node. An authority URI is an arbitrary string, so most providers expose a `CONTENT_URI` property that includes its authority.

Content Providers usually expose two forms of URI, one for requests against all the data and another that specifies only a single row. The form for the latter appends `/<rowID>` to the standard `CONTENT_URI`.

Querying for Content

As in databases, query results are returned as Cursors over a result set. You can extract values from the cursor using the techniques described previously within the database section on "Extracting Results from a Cursor."

Content Provider queries take a very similar form to database queries. Using the `query` method on the `ContentResolver` object, pass in:

❑   The URI of the content provider data you want to query

❑   A projection that represents the columns you want to include in the result set

❑   A `where` clause that defines the rows to be returned. You can include `?` wild cards that will be replaced by the values stored in the selection argument parameter.

❑   An array of selection argument strings that will replace the `?`'s in the `where` clause

❑   A string that describes the order of the returned rows

The following skeleton code demonstrates the use of a Content Resolver to apply a query to a Content Provider:

```
// Return all rows
Cursor allRows = getContentResolver().query(MyProvider.CONTENT_URI,
                                            null, null, null, null);

// Return all columns for rows where column 3 equals a set value
// and the rows are ordered by column 5.
String where = KEY_COL3 + "=" + requiredValue;
String order = KEY_COL5;
Cursor someRows = getContentResolver().query(MyProvider.CONTENT_URI,
                                            null, where, null, order);
```

You'll see some more practical examples of querying for content later in this chapter when the native Android content providers are introduced.

Adding, Updating, and Deleting Content

To perform transactions on Content Providers, use the `delete`, `update`, and `insert` methods on the `ContentResolver` object.

Inserts

The Content Resolver offers two methods for inserting new records into your Content Provider — `insert` and `bulkInsert`. Both methods accept the URI of the item type you're adding; where the former takes a single new `ContentValues` object, the latter takes an array.

The simple `insert` method will return a URI to the newly added record, while `bulkInsert` returns the number of successfully added items.

The following code snippet shows how to use the `insert` and `bulkInsert` methods:

```
// Create a new row of values to insert.
ContentValues newValues = new ContentValues();

// Assign values for each row.
newValues.put(COLUMN_NAME, newValue);
[ ... Repeat for each column ... ]
```

```
Uri myRowUri = getContentResolver().insert(MyProvider.CONTENT_URI,
                                           newValues);
```

```
// Create a new row of values to insert.
ContentValues[] valueArray = new ContentValues[5];

// TODO: Create an array of new rows
```

```
int count = getContentResolver().bulkInsert(MyProvider.CONTENT_URI,
                                            valueArray);
```

Deletes

To delete a single record using the Content Resolver, call `delete`, passing in the URI of the row you want to remove. Alternatively, you can specify a `where` clause to remove multiple rows. Both techniques are shown in the following snippet:

```
// Remove a specific row.
getContentResolver().delete(myRowUri, null, null);
```

```
// Remove the first five rows.
String where = "_id < 5";
getContentResolver().delete(MyProvider.CONTENT_URI, where, null);
```

Updates

Updates to a Content Provider are handled using the `update` method on a Content Resolver. The `update` method takes the URI of the target Content Provider, a `ContentValues` object that maps column names to updated values, and a `where` clause that specifies which rows to update.

When executed, every matching row in the where clause will be updated using the values in the Content Values passed in and will return the number of successful updates.

```
// Create a new row of values to insert.
ContentValues newValues = new ContentValues();

// Create a replacement map, specifying which columns you want to
// update, and what values to assign to each of them.
newValues.put(COLUMN_NAME, newValue);

// Apply to the first 5 rows.
String where = "_id < 5";
```

```
getContentResolver().update(MyProvider.CONTENT_URI, newValues, where,
                            null);
```

Accessing Files in Content Providers

Content Providers represent files as fully qualified URIs rather than raw file data. To insert a file into a Content Provider, or access a saved file, use the Content Resolvers openOutputStream or openInputStream methods, respectively. The process for storing a file is shown in the following code snippet:

```
// Insert a new row into your provider, returning its unique URI.
Uri uri = getContentResolver().insert(MyProvider.CONTENT_URI,
                                      newValues);

try {
  // Open an output stream using the new row's URI.
  OutputStream outStream = getContentResolver().openOutputStream(uri);
  // Compress your bitmap and save it into your provider.
  sourceBitmap.compress(Bitmap.CompressFormat.JPEG, 50, outStream);
}
catch (FileNotFoundException e) { }
```

Native Android Content Providers

Android exposes many Content Providers that supply access to the native databases.

You can use each of these Content Providers natively using the techniques described previously. Alternatively, the android.provider class includes convenience classes that simplify access to many of the most useful providers, including:

❑ **Browser** Use the browser Content Provider to read or modify bookmarks, browser history, or web searches.

❑ **CallLog** View or update the call history including both incoming and outgoing calls together with missed calls and call details, like caller ID and call durations.

❑ **Contacts** Use the Contacts provider to retrieve, modify, or store your contacts' details.

❑ **MediaStore** The Media Store provides centralized, managed access to the multimedia on your device, including audio, video, and images. You can store your own multimedia within the Media Store and make it globally available.

❑ **Settings** You can access the device's preferences using the Settings provider. Using it, you can view and modify Bluetooth settings, ring tones, and other device preferences.

You should use these native Content Providers wherever possible to ensure that your application integrates seamlessly with other native and third-party applications.

While a detailed description of how to use each of these helpers is beyond the scope of this chapter, the following sections describe how to use some of the more useful and powerful native Content Providers.

Using the Media Store Provider

The Android Media Store provides a managed repository for audio, video, and image files. Whenever you add a new multimedia file to the Android filesystem, it should be added to the Media Store to expose it to other applications.

The `MediaStore` class includes a number of convenience methods to simplify inserting files into the Media Store. For example, the following code snippet shows how to insert an image directly into the Media Store:

```
android.provider.MediaStore.Images.Media.insertImage(
  getContentResolver(),
  sourceBitmap,
  "my_cat_pic",
  "Photo of my cat!");
```

Using the Contacts Provider

Access to the Contact Manager is particularly powerful on a communications device. Android does the right thing by exposing all the information available from the contacts database to any application granted the READ_CONTACTS permission.

In the following example, an Activity gets a `Cursor` to every person in the contact database, creating an array of `Strings` that holds each contact's name and phone number.

To simplify extracting the data from the `Cursor`, Android supplies public static properties on the `People` class that expose the column names.

```
// Get a cursor over every contact.
Cursor cursor = getContentResolver().query(People.CONTENT_URI,
                                    null, null, null, null);

// Let the activity manage the cursor lifecycle.
startManagingCursor(cursor);

// Use the convenience properties to get the index of the columns
int nameIdx = cursor.getColumnIndexOrThrow(People.NAME);
```

```
int phoneIdx = cursor. getColumnIndexOrThrow(People.NUMBER);

String[] result = new String[cursor.getCount()];
if (cursor.moveToFirst())
  do {
    // Extract the name.
    String name = cursor.getString(nameIdx);
    // Extract the phone number.
    String phone = cursor.getString(phoneIdx);
    result[cursor.getPosition()] = name + " (" + phone + ")";
  } while(cursor.moveToNext());
```

To run this code snippet, you need to add the READ_CONTACTS *permission to your application.*

As well as querying the contacts database, you can use this Content Provider to modify, delete, or insert contact records.

Creating a New Content Provider

Create a new Content Provider by extending the abstract ContentProvider class. Override the onCreate method to open or initialize the underlying data source you're exposing with this new provider. The skeleton code for a new Content Provider is shown below:

```
import android.content.*;
import android.database.Cursor;
import android.net.Uri;
import android.database.SQLException;
```

```
public class MyProvider extends ContentProvider {

  @Override
  public boolean onCreate() {
    // TODO: Construct the underlying database.
    return true;
  }
}
```

You should also expose a public static CONTENT_URI variable that returns the full URI to this provider. Content URIs must be unique between providers, so it's good practice to base the URI path on your package name. The general form for defining a Content Provider's URI is

```
content://com.<CompanyName>.provider.<ApplicationName>/<DataPath>
```

For example:

```
content://com.paad.provider.myapp/items
```

Content URIs can represent either of two forms. The previous URI represents a request for all values of that type (e.g., all items).

Appending a trailing /<rownumber>, as shown below, represents a request for a single record (e.g., "the fifth item").

```
content://com.paad.provider.myapp/items/5
```

It's good form to support access to your provider using both these forms.

The simplest way to do this is using a UriMatcher. Configure the UriMatcher to parse URIs to determine their form when the provider is being accessed through a Content Resolver. The following snippet shows the skeleton code for this pattern:

```java
public class MyProvider extends ContentProvider {

  private static final String myURI =
    "content://com.paad.provider.myapp/items";
  public static final Uri CONTENT_URI = Uri.parse(myURI);

  @Override
  public boolean onCreate() {
    // TODO: Construct the underlying database.
    return true;
  }

  // Create the constants used to differentiate between the different
  // URI requests.
  private static final int ALLROWS = 1;
  private static final int SINGLE_ROW = 2;

  private static final UriMatcher uriMatcher;

  // Populate the UriMatcher object, where a URI ending in 'items' will
  // correspond to a request for all items, and 'items/[rowID]'
  // represents a single row.
  static {
    uriMatcher = new UriMatcher(UriMatcher.NO_MATCH);
    uriMatcher.addURI("com.paad.provider.myApp", "items", ALLROWS);
    uriMatcher.addURI("com.paad.provider.myApp", "items/#",
                      SINGLE_ROW);
  }
}
```

You can use the same technique to expose alternative URIs for different subsets of data, or different tables within your database from within the same Content Provider.

It's also good practice to expose the names and indexes of the columns available in your provider to simplify extracting information from Cursor results.

Exposing Access to the Data Source

You can expose queries and transactions with your Content Provider by implementing the delete, insert, update, and query methods.

These methods act as a generic interface to the underlying data source, allowing Android applications to share data across application boundaries without having to publish separate interfaces for each application. The most common scenario is to use a Content Provider to expose a private SQLite Database, but within these methods you can access any source of data (including files or application instance variables).

The following code snippet shows the skeleton code for implementing queries and transactions for a Content Provider. Notice that the UriMatcher object is used to refine the transaction and query requests.

```java
@Override
public Cursor query(Uri uri,
                    String[] projection,
                    String selection,
                    String[] selectionArgs,
                    String sort) {

  // If this is a row query, limit the result set to the passed in row.
  switch (uriMatcher.match(uri)) {
    case SINGLE_ROW :
      // TODO: Modify selection based on row id, where:
      // rowNumber = uri.getPathSegments().get(1));
  }
  return null;
}

@Override
public Uri insert(Uri _uri, ContentValues _initialValues) {
  long rowID = [ ... Add a new item ... ]

  // Return a URI to the newly added item.
  if (rowID > 0) {
    return ContentUris.withAppendedId(CONTENT_URI, rowID);
  }
  throw new SQLException("Failed to add new item into " + _uri);
}

@Override
public int delete(Uri uri, String where, String[] whereArgs) {
  switch (uriMatcher.match(uri)) {
    case ALLROWS:
    case SINGLE_ROW:
    default: throw new IllegalArgumentException("Unsupported URI:" +
                                                uri);
  }
}

@Override
public int update(Uri uri, ContentValues values, String where,
                  String[] whereArgs) {
  switch (uriMatcher.match(uri)) {
    case ALLROWS:
    case SINGLE_ROW:
```

```
        default: throw new IllegalArgumentException("Unsupported URI:" +
                                                     uri);
    }
}
```

The final step in creating a Content Provider is defining the MIME type that identifies the data the provider returns.

Override the `getType` method to return a String that uniquely describes your data type. The type returned should include two forms, one for a single entry and another for all the entries, following the forms:

❑ **Single Item**

```
vnd.<companyname>.cursor.item/<contenttype>
```

❑ **All Items**

```
vnd.<companyName>.cursor.dir/<contenttype>
```

The following code snippet shows how to override the `getType` method to return the correct MIME type based on the URI passed in:

```
@Override
public String getType(Uri _uri) {
  switch (uriMatcher.match(_uri)) {
    case ALLROWS: return "vnd.paad.cursor.dir/myprovidercontent";
    case SINGLE_ROW: return "vnd.paad.cursor.item/myprovidercontent";
    default: throw new IllegalArgumentException("Unsupported URI: " +
                                                 _uri);
  }
}
```

Registering Your Provider

Once you have completed your Content Provider, it must be added to the application manifest.

Use the `authorities` tag to specify its address, as shown in the following XML snippet:

```
<provider android:name="MyProvider"
          android:authorities="com.paad.provider.myapp"/>
```

Creating and Using an Earthquake Content Provider

Having created an application that features a list of earthquakes, you have an excellent opportunity to share this information with other applications.

By exposing these data through a Content Provider, you, and others, can create new applications based on earthquake data without having to duplicate network traffic and the associated XML parsing.

Creating the Content Provider

The following example shows how to create an Earthquake Content Provider. Each quake will be stored in an SQLite database.

1. Open the Earthquake project, and create a new `EarthquakeProvider` class that extends `ContentProvider`. Include stubs to override the `onCreate`, `getType`, `query`, `insert`, `delete`, and `update` methods.

```
package com.paad.earthquake;

import android.content.*;
import android.database.Cursor;
import android.database.SQLException;
import android.database.sqlite.SQLiteOpenHelper;
import android.database.sqlite.SQLiteDatabase;
import android.database.sqlite.SQLiteQueryBuilder;
import android.net.Uri;
import android.text.TextUtils;
import android.util.Log;

public class EarthquakeProvider extends ContentProvider {

  @Override
  public boolean onCreate() {
  }

  @Override
  public String getType(Uri url) {
  }

  @Override
  public Cursor query(Uri url, String[] projection, String selection,
                      String[] selectionArgs, String sort) {
  }

  @Override
  public Uri insert(Uri _url, ContentValues _initialValues) {
  }

  @Override
  public int delete(Uri url, String where, String[] whereArgs) {
  }

  @Override
  public int update(Uri url, ContentValues values,
                    String where, String[] wArgs) {
  }
}
```

2. Expose a content URI for this provider. This URI will be used to access the Content Provider from within application components using a `ContentResolver`.

```
public static final Uri CONTENT_URI =
  Uri.parse("content://com.paad.provider.earthquake/earthquakes");
```

3. Create the database that will be used to store the earthquakes. Within the `EathquakeProvider` class, create a new `SQLiteDatabase` instance, and expose public variables that describe the column names and indexes. Include an extension of `SQLiteOpenHelper` to manage database creation and version control.

```java
// The underlying database
private SQLiteDatabase earthquakeDB;

private static final String TAG = "EarthquakeProvider";
private static final String DATABASE_NAME = "earthquakes.db";
private static final int DATABASE_VERSION = 1;
private static final String EARTHQUAKE_TABLE = "earthquakes";

// Column Names
public static final String KEY_ID = "_id";
public static final String KEY_DATE = "date";
public static final String KEY_DETAILS = "details";
public static final String KEY_LOCATION_LAT = "latitude";
public static final String KEY_LOCATION_LNG = "longitude";
public static final String KEY_MAGNITUDE = "magnitude";
public static final String KEY_LINK = "link";

// Column indexes
public static final int DATE_COLUMN = 1;
public static final int DETAILS_COLUMN = 2;
public static final int LONGITUDE_COLUMN = 3;
public static final int LATITUDE_COLUMN = 4;
public static final int MAGNITUDE_COLUMN = 5;
public static final int LINK_COLUMN = 6;

// Helper class for opening, creating, and managing
// database version control
private static class earthquakeDatabaseHelper extends SQLiteOpenHelper {
  private static final String DATABASE_CREATE =
    "create table " + EARTHQUAKE_TABLE + " ("
    + KEY_ID + " integer primary key autoincrement, "
    + KEY_DATE + " INTEGER, "
    + KEY_DETAILS + " TEXT, "
    + KEY_LOCATION_LAT + " FLOAT, "
    + KEY_LOCATION_LNG + " FLOAT, "
    + KEY_MAGNITUDE + " FLOAT, "
    + KEY_LINK + " TEXT);";

  public earthquakeDatabaseHelper(Context context, String name,
                                  CursorFactory factory, int version) {
    super(context, name, factory, version);
  }

  @Override
  public void onCreate(SQLiteDatabase db) {
    db.execSQL(DATABASE_CREATE);
  }

  @Override
  public void onUpgrade(SQLiteDatabase db, int oldVersion,
```

```
                                     int newVersion) {
        Log.w(TAG, "Upgrading database from version " + oldVersion + " to "
                    + newVersion + ", which will destroy all old data");

        db.execSQL("DROP TABLE IF EXISTS " + EARTHQUAKE_TABLE);
        onCreate(db);
      }
    }
```

4. Create a `UriMatcher` to handle requests using different URIs. Include support for queries and transactions over the entire data set (QUAKES) and a single record matching a quake index value (QUAKE_ID).

```
    // Create the constants used to differentiate between the different URI
    // requests.
    private static final int QUAKES = 1;
    private static final int QUAKE_ID = 2;

    private static final UriMatcher uriMatcher;

    // Allocate the UriMatcher object, where a URI ending in 'earthquakes'
    // will correspond to a request for all earthquakes, and 'earthquakes'
    // with a trailing '/[rowID]' will represent a single earthquake row.
    static {
      uriMatcher = new UriMatcher(UriMatcher.NO_MATCH);
      uriMatcher.addURI("com.paad.provider.Earthquake", "earthquakes",
                        QUAKES);
      uriMatcher.addURI("com.paad.provider.Earthquake", "earthquakes/#",
                        QUAKE_ID);
    }
```

5. Override the `getType` method to return a `String` for each of the URI structures supported.

```
    @Override
    public String getType(Uri uri) {
      switch (uriMatcher.match(uri)) {
        case QUAKES:
          return "vnd.android.cursor.dir/vnd.paad.earthquake";
        case QUAKE_ID:
          return "vnd.android.cursor.item/vnd.paad.earthquake";
        default:
          throw new IllegalArgumentException("Unsupported URI: " + uri);
      }
    }
```

6. Override the provider's `onCreate` handler to create a new instance of the database helper class and open a connection to the database.

```
    @Override
    public boolean onCreate() {
      Context context = getContext();

      earthquakeDatabaseHelper dbHelper;
      dbHelper = new earthquakeDatabaseHelper(context, DATABASE_NAME, null,
                                              DATABASE_VERSION);
```

```
        earthquakeDB = dbHelper.getWritableDatabase();
        return (earthquakeDB == null) ? false : true;
    }
```

7. Implement the query and transaction stubs. Start with the `query` method; it should decode the request being made (all content or a single row) and apply the selection, projection, and sort-order criteria parameters to the database before returning a result `Cursor`.

```
@Override
public Cursor query(Uri uri,
                    String[] projection,
                    String selection,
                    String[] selectionArgs,
                    String sort) {
```

```
    SQLiteQueryBuilder qb = new SQLiteQueryBuilder();

    qb.setTables(EARTHQUAKE_TABLE);

    // If this is a row query, limit the result set to the passed in row.
    switch (uriMatcher.match(uri)) {
      case QUAKE_ID:
        qb.appendWhere(KEY_ID + "=" + uri.getPathSegments().get(1));
        break;
      default: break;
    }

    // If no sort order is specified sort by date / time
    String orderBy;
    if (TextUtils.isEmpty(sort)) {
      orderBy = KEY_DATE;
    } else {
      orderBy = sort;
    }

    // Apply the query to the underlying database.
    Cursor c = qb.query(earthquakeDB,
                        projection,
                        selection, selectionArgs,
                        null, null,
                        orderBy);

    // Register the contexts ContentResolver to be notified if
    // the cursor result set changes.
    c.setNotificationUri(getContext().getContentResolver(), uri);

    // Return a cursor to the query result.
    return c;
    }
```

8. Now implement methods for inserting, deleting, and updating content. In this case, the process is largely an exercise in mapping Content Provider transaction requests to database equivalents.

```
@Override
public Uri insert(Uri _uri, ContentValues _initialValues) {
```

```java
      // Insert the new row, will return the row number if
      // successful.
      long rowID = earthquakeDB.insert(EARTHQUAKE_TABLE, "quake",
                                       _initialValues);

      // Return a URI to the newly inserted row on success.
      if (rowID > 0) {
        Uri uri = ContentUris.withAppendedId(CONTENT_URI, rowID);
        getContext().getContentResolver().notifyChange(uri, null);
        return uri;
      }
      throw new SQLException("Failed to insert row into " + _uri);
  }

  @Override
  public int delete(Uri uri, String where, String[] whereArgs) {
    int count;

    switch (uriMatcher.match(uri)) {
      case QUAKES:
        count = earthquakeDB.delete(EARTHQUAKE_TABLE, where, whereArgs);
        break;

      case QUAKE_ID:
        String segment = uri.getPathSegments().get(1);
        count = earthquakeDB.delete(EARTHQUAKE_TABLE, KEY_ID + "="
                               + segment
                               + (!TextUtils.isEmpty(where) ? " AND ("
                               + where + ')' : ""), whereArgs);
        break;

      default: throw new IllegalArgumentException("Unsupported URI: " +
                                                  uri);
    }

    getContext().getContentResolver().notifyChange(uri, null);
    return count;
  }

  @Override
  public int update(Uri uri, ContentValues values, String where,
                    String[] whereArgs) {
    int count;
    switch (uriMatcher.match(uri)) {
      case QUAKES:
        count = earthquakeDB.update(EARTHQUAKE_TABLE, values,
                                    where, whereArgs);
        break;

      case QUAKE_ID:
        String segment = uri.getPathSegments().get(1);
        count = earthquakeDB.update(EARTHQUAKE_TABLE, values, KEY_ID
                               + "=" + segment
                               + (!TextUtils.isEmpty(where) ? " AND ("
```

```
                                            + where + ')' : ""), whereArgs);
        break;

    default: throw new IllegalArgumentException("Unknown URI " + uri);
    }

    getContext().getContentResolver().notifyChange(uri, null);
    return count;
}
```

9. With the Content Provider finished, register it in the manifest by creating a new node within the application tag.

```
<provider android:name=".EarthquakeProvider"
          android:authorities="com.paad.provider.earthquake" />
```

Using the Provider

You can now update the Earthquake Activity to use the Earthquake Provider to store quakes, and use them to populate the List View.

1. Within the Earthquake Activity, update the addNewQuake method. It should use the application's Content Resolver to insert each new earthquake into the provider. Move the existing array control logic into a separate addQuakeToArray method.

```
private void addNewQuake(Quake _quake) {
    ContentResolver cr = getContentResolver();
    // Construct a where clause to make sure we don't already have this
    // earthquake in the provider.
    String w = EarthquakeProvider.KEY_DATE + " = " +
               _quake.getDate().getTime();

    // If the earthquake is new, insert it into the provider.
    Cursor c = cr.query(EarthquakeProvider.CONTENT_URI,
                        null, w, null, null);
    int dbCount = c.getCount();
    c.close();

    if (dbCount > 0) {
      ContentValues values = new ContentValues();

      values.put(EarthquakeProvider.KEY_DATE,
                 _quake.getDate().getTime());
      values.put(EarthquakeProvider.KEY_DETAILS, _quake.getDetails());

      double lat = _quake.getLocation().getLatitude();
      double lng = _quake.getLocation().getLongitude();
      values.put(EarthquakeProvider.KEY_LOCATION_LAT, lat);
      values.put(EarthquakeProvider.KEY_LOCATION_LNG, lng);
      values.put(EarthquakeProvider.KEY_LINK, _quake.getLink());
      values.put(EarthquakeProvider.KEY_MAGNITUDE,
                 _quake.getMagnitude());

      cr.insert(EarthquakeProvider.CONTENT_URI, values);
```

```
            earthquakes.add(_quake);

            addQuakeToArray(_quake);
        }
    }

    private void addQuakeToArray(Quake _quake) {
        if (_quake.getMagnitude() > minimumMagnitude) {
            // Add the new quake to our list of earthquakes.
            earthquakes.add(_quake);

            // Notify the array adapter of a change.
            aa.notifyDataSetChanged();
        }
    }
```

2. Create a new `loadQuakesFromProvider` method that loads all the earthquakes from the Earthquake Provider and inserts them into the array list using the `addQuakeToArray` method created in Step 1.

```
    private void loadQuakesFromProvider() {
    // Clear the existing earthquake array
    earthquakes.clear();

    ContentResolver cr = getContentResolver();

        // Return all the saved earthquakes
        Cursor c = cr.query(EarthquakeProvider.CONTENT_URI,
                            null, null, null, null);

        if (c.moveToFirst())
          {
            do {
               // Extract the quake details.
               Long datems = c.getLong(EarthquakeProvider.DATE_COLUMN);
               String details;
               details = c.getString(EarthquakeProvider.DETAILS_COLUMN);
               Float lat = c.getFloat(EarthquakeProvider.LATITUDE_COLUMN);
               Float lng = c.getFloat(EarthquakeProvider.LONGITUDE_COLUMN);
               Double mag = c.getDouble(EarthquakeProvider.MAGNITUDE_COLUMN);
               String link = c.getString(EarthquakeProvider.LINK_COLUMN);

               Location location = new Location("dummy");
               location.setLongitude(lng);
               location.setLatitude(lat);

               Date date = new Date(datems);

               Quake q = new Quake(date, details, location, mag, link);
               addQuakeToArray(q);
            } while(c.moveToNext());
        }
        c.close();
    }
```

3. Call `loadQuakesFromProvider` from `onCreate` to initialize the Earthquake List View at start-up.

```
@Override
public void onCreate(Bundle icicle) {
  super.onCreate(icicle);
  setContentView(R.layout.main);

  earthquakeListView =
    (ListView)this.findViewById(R.id.earthquakeListView);

  earthquakeListView.setOnItemClickListener(new OnItemClickListener() {

    public void onItemClick(AdapterView _av, View _v,
                            int _index, long arg3) {
      selectedQuake = earthquakes.get(_index);
      showDialog(QUAKE_DIALOG);
    }
  });

  int layoutID = android.R.layout.simple_list_item_1;
  aa = new ArrayAdapter<Quake>(this, layoutID , earthquakes);
  earthquakeListView.setAdapter(aa);

  loadQuakesFromProvider();

  updateFromPreferences();
  refreshEarthquakes();
}
```

4. Finally, make a change to the `refreshEarthquakes` method so that it loads the saved earthquakes from the provider after clearing the array, but before adding any new quakes received.

```
private void refreshEarthquakes() {
  [ ... exiting refreshEarthquakes method ... ]

  // Clear the old earthquakes
  earthquakes.clear();
  loadQuakesFromProvider();

  [ ... exiting refreshEarthquakes method ... ]
}
```

Summary

In this chapter, you learned how to add a persistence layer to your applications.

Starting with the ability to save the Activity instance data between sessions using the save and restore instance state handlers, you were then introduced to Shared Preferences. You used them to save instance values and user preferences that can be used across your application components.

Chapter 6: Data Storage, Retrieval, and Sharing

Android provides a fully featured SQLite RDBMS to all applications. This small, efficient, and robust database lets you create relational databases to persist application data. Using Content Providers, you learned how to share private data, particularly databases, across application boundaries.

All database and Content Provider queries are returned as Cursors; you learned how to perform queries and extract data from the resulting Cursor objects.

Along the way, you also learned to:

❑ Save and load files directly to and from the underlying filesystem.

❑ Include static files as external project resources.

❑ Create new SQLite databases.

❑ Interact with databases to insert, update, and delete rows.

❑ Use the native Content Providers included with Android to access and manage native data like media and contacts.

With a solid foundation in the fundamentals of Android development, the remainder of this book will investigate some of the more interesting optional Android features.

Starting in the next chapter, you'll be introduced to the geographic APIs. Android offers a rich suite of geographical functionality including location-based services (such as GPS), forward and reverse geocoding, as well as a fully integrated Google Maps implementation. Using Google Maps, you can create map-based Activities that feature annotations to develop native map-mashup style applications.

7

Maps, Geocoding, and Location-Based Services

One of the defining features of mobile phones is their portability, so it's not surprising that some of the most enticing Android features are the services that let you find, contextualize, and map physical locations.

You can create map-based Activities using Google Maps as a User Interface element. You have full access to the map, allowing you to control display settings, alter the zoom level, and move the centered location. Using Overlays, you can annotate maps and handle user input to provide map-contextualized information and functionality.

Also covered in this chapter are the location-based services (LBS) — the services that let you find the device's current location. They include technologies like GPS and Google's cell-based location technology. You can specify which location-sensing technology to use explicitly by name, or implicitly by defining a set of criteria in terms of accuracy, cost, and other requirements.

Maps and location-based services use latitude and longitude to pinpoint geographic locations, but your users are more likely to think in terms of an address. Android provides a Geocoder that supports forward and reverse geocoding. Using the Geocoder, you can convert back and forth between latitude/longitude values and real-world addresses.

Used together, the mapping, geocoding, and location-based services provide a powerful toolkit for incorporating your phone's native mobility into your mobile applications.

In this chapter, you'll learn to:

- ❑ Set up your emulator to test location-based services.
- ❑ Find and track the device location.
- ❑ Create proximity alerts.

❑ Turn geographical locations into street addresses and vice versa.

❑ Create and customize map-based Activities using MapView and MapActivity.

❑ Add Overlays to your maps.

Using Location-Based Services

Location-based services (LBS) is an umbrella term used to describe the different technologies used to find the device's current location. The two main LBS elements are:

❑ **LocationManager**   Provides hooks to the location-based services.

❑ **LocationProviders**   Each of which represents a different location-finding technology used to determine the device's current location.

Using the Location Manager, you can:

❑ Obtain your current location.

❑ Track movement.

❑ Set proximity alerts for detecting movement into and out of a specified area.

Setting up the Emulator with Test Providers

Location-based services are dependant on device hardware for finding the current location. When developing and testing with the emulator, your hardware is virtualized, and you're likely to stay in pretty much the same location.

To compensate, Android includes hooks that let you emulate Location Providers for testing location-based applications. In this section, you'll learn how to mock the position of the supported GPS provider.

> If you're planning on doing location-based application development and using the Android emulator, this section will show how to create an environment that simulates real hardware and location changes. In the remainder of this chapter, it will be assumed that you have used the examples in this section to update the location for, the GPS_PROVIDER within the emulator.

Updating Locations in Emulator Location Providers

Use the Location Controls available from the DDMS perspective in Eclipse (shown in Figure 7-1) to push location changes directly into the test GPS_PROVIDER.

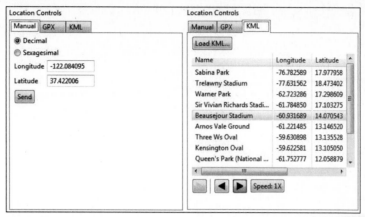

Figure 7-1

Figure 7-1 shows the Manual and KML tabs. Using the Manual tab, you can specify particular latitude/ longitude pairs. Alternatively, the KML and GPX tabs let you load KML (Keyhole Markup Language) and GPX (GPS Exchange Format) files, respectively. Once loaded, you can jump to particular waypoints (locations) or play back each location sequentially.

> *Most GPS systems record track files using GPX, while KML is used extensively online to define geographic information. You can handwrite your own KML file or generate one automatically using Google Earth and finding directions between two locations.*

All location changes applied using the DDMS Location Controls will be applied to the GPS receiver, which must be enabled and active. Note that the GPS values returned by `getLastKnownLocation` will not change unless at least one application has requested location updates.

Create an Application to Manage Test Location Providers

In this example, you'll create a new project to set up the emulator to simplify testing other location-based applications. Running this project will ensure that the GPS provider is active and updating regularly.

1. Create a new Android project, TestProviderController, which includes a
`TestProviderController` Activity.

```
package com.paad.testprovidercontroller;

import java.util.List;
import android.app.Activity;
import android.content.Context;
import android.location.Criteria;
import android.location.Location;
import android.location.LocationManager;
import android.location.LocationListener;
import android.location.LocationProvider;
```

```
import android.os.Bundle;
import android.widget.TextView;

public class TestProviderController extends Activity {

  @Override
  public void onCreate(Bundle icicle) {
    super.onCreate(icicle);
    setContentView(R.layout.main);
  }


}
```

2. Add an instance variable to store a reference to the LocationManager, then get that reference to it from within the onCreate method. Add stubs for creating a new test provider and to enable the GPS provider for testing.

```
LocationManager locationManager;

@Override
public void onCreate(Bundle icicle) {
  super.onCreate(icicle);
  setContentView(R.layout.main);

  String location_context = Context.LOCATION_SERVICE;
  locationManager = (LocationManager)getSystemService(location_context);
  testProviders();
}

public void testProviders() {}
```

3. Add a FINE_LOCATION permission to test the providers.

```
<uses-permission android:name="android.permission.ACCESS_FINE_LOCATION"/>
```

4. Update the testProviders method to check the enabled status of each provider and return the last known location; also request periodic updates for each provider to force Android to start updating the locations for other applications. The methods used here are presented without comment; you'll learn more about how to use each of them in the remainder of this chapter.

```
public void testProviders() {
  TextView tv = (TextView)findViewById(R.id.myTextView);
  StringBuilder sb = new StringBuilder("Enabled Providers:");

  List<String> providers = locationManager.getProviders(true);

  for (String provider : providers) {

    locationManager.requestLocationUpdates(provider, 1000, 0,
                                      new LocationListener() {
      public void onLocationChanged(Location location) {}
      public void onProviderDisabled(String provider){}
```

```
        public void onProviderEnabled(String provider){}
        public void onStatusChanged(String provider, int status,
                                    Bundle extras){}
    });

    sb.append("\n").append(provider).append(": ");

    Location location = locationManager.getLastKnownLocation(provider);
    if (location != null) {
      double lat = location.getLatitude();
      double lng = location.getLongitude();
      sb.append(lat).append(", ").append(lng);
    } else {
      sb.append("No Location");
    }
  }
}
tv.setText(sb);
}
```

5. The final step before you run the application is to update the main.xml layout resource to add an ID for the text label you're updating in Step 4.

```
<?xml version="1.0" encoding="utf-8"?>
<LinearLayout
  xmlns:android="http://schemas.android.com/apk/res/android"
  android:orientation="vertical"
  android:layout_width="fill_parent"
  android:layout_height="fill_parent">
  <TextView
    android:id="@+id/myTextView"
    android:layout_width="fill_parent"
    android:layout_height="wrap_content"
    android:text="@string/hello"
  />
</LinearLayout>
```

6. Run your application, and it should appear as shown in Figure 7-2.

Figure 7-2

7. Android will now update the last known position for any applications using location-based services. You can update the current location using the techniques described in the previous section.

The test provider controller application you just wrote needs to be restarted to reflect any changes in the current location. Below in this chapter, you'll learn how to request updates based on the elapsed time and distance traveled.

Selecting a Location Provider

Depending on the device, there may be several technologies that Android can use to determine the current location. Each technology, or Location Provider, will offer different capabilities including power consumption, monetary cost, accuracy, and the ability to determine altitude, speed, or heading information.

To get an instance of a specific provider, call getProvider, passing in the name:

```
String providerName = LocationManager.GPS_PROVIDER;
LocationProvider gpsProvider;
gpsProvider = locationManager.getProvider(providerName);
```

This is generally only useful for determining the abilities of a particular provider. Most Location Manager methods require only a provider name to perform location-based services.

Finding the Available Providers

The LocationManager class includes static string constants that return the provider name for the two most common Location Providers:

❑   LocationManager.GPS_PROVIDER

❑   LocationManager.NETWORK_PROVIDER

To get a list of names for all the providers available on the device, call getProviders, using a Boolean to indicate if you want all, or only the enabled, providers to be returned:

```
boolean enabledOnly = true;
List<String> providers = locationManager.getProviders(enabledOnly);
```

Finding Providers Based on Requirement Criteria

In most scenarios, it's unlikely that you will want to explicitly choose the Location Provider to use. More commonly, you'll specify the requirements that a provider must meet and let Android determine the best technology to use.

Use the Criteria class to dictate the requirements of a provider in terms of accuracy (fine or coarse), power use (low, medium, high), cost, and the ability to return values for altitude, speed, and bearing.

The following code creates Criteria that require coarse accuracy, low power consumption, and no need for altitude, bearing, or speed. The provider is permitted to have an associated cost.

```
Criteria criteria = new Criteria();
criteria.setAccuracy(Criteria.ACCURACY_COARSE);
criteria.setPowerRequirement(Criteria.POWER_LOW);
criteria.setAltitudeRequired(false);
criteria.setBearingRequired(false);
criteria.setSpeedRequired(false);
criteria.setCostAllowed(true);
```

Having defined the required Criteria, you can use `getBestProvider` to return the best matching Location Provider or `getProviders` to return all the possible matches. The following snippet demonstrates using `getBestProvider` to return the best provider for your criteria where the Boolean lets you restrict the result to a currently enabled provider:

```
String bestProvider = locationManager.getBestProvider(criteria, true);
```

If more than one Location Provider matches your criteria, the one with the greatest accuracy is returned. If no Location Providers meet your requirements, the criteria are loosened, in the following order, until a provider is found:

- ❑   Power use
- ❑   Accuracy
- ❑   Ability to return bearing, speed, and altitude

The criterion for allowing a device with monetary cost is never implicitly relaxed. If no provider is found, null is returned.

To see a list of names for all the providers that match your criteria, you can use `getProviders`. It accepts Criteria and returns a filtered String list of all available Location Providers that match them. As with the `getBestProvider` call, if no matching providers are found, this call returns null.

```
List<String> matchingProviders = locationManager.getProviders(criteria,
                                                              false);
```

Finding Your Location

The purpose of location-based services is to find the physical location of the device.

Access to the location-based services is handled using the Location Manager system Service. To access the Location Manager, request an instance of the `LOCATION_SERVICE` using the `getSystemService` method, as shown in the following snippet:

```
String serviceString = Context.LOCATION_SERVICE;
LocationManager locationManager;
locationManager = (LocationManager)getSystemService(serviceString);
```

Before you can use the Location Manager, you need to add one or more `uses-permission` tags to your manifest to support access to the LBS hardware.

The following snippet shows the *fine* and *coarse* permissions. Of the default providers, the GPS provider requires fine permission, while the Network provider requires only coarse. An application that has been granted fine permission will have coarse permission granted implicitly.

```
<uses-permission android:name="android.permission.ACCESS_FINE_LOCATION"/>
<uses-permission android:name="android.permission.ACCESS_COARSE_LOCATION"/>
```

You can find the last location fix determined by a particular Location Provider using the `getLastKnownLocation` method, passing in the name of the Location Provider. The following example finds the last location fix taken by the GPS provider:

```
String provider = LocationManager.GPS_PROVIDER;
Location location = locationManager.getLastKnownLocation(provider);
```

Note that `getLastKnownLocation` does not ask the Location Provider to update the current position. If the device has not recently updated the current position this value may be be out of date.

The Location object returned includes all the position information available from the provider that supplied it. This can include latitude, longitude, bearing, altitude, speed, and the time the location fix was taken. All these properties are available using `get` methods on the Location object. In some instances, additional details will be included in the extras Bundle.

"Where Am I?" Example

The following example — "Where Am I?" — features a new Activity that finds the device's current location using the GPS Location Provider. You will expand on this example throughout the chapter as you learn new geographic functionality.

This example assumes that you have enabled the `GPS_PROVIDER` Location Provider using the techniques shown previously in this chapter, or that you're running it on a device that supports GPS and has that hardware enabled.

1. Create a new WhereAmI project with a `WhereAmI` Activity. This example uses the GPS provider (either mock or real), so modify the manifest file to include the `uses-permission` tag for `ACCESS_FINE_LOCATION`.

```xml
<?xml version="1.0" encoding="utf-8"?>
<manifest xmlns:android="http://schemas.android.com/apk/res/android"
          package="com.paad.whereami">
  <application
    android:icon="@drawable/icon">
    <activity
      android:name=".WhereAmI"
      android:label="@string/app_name">
      <intent-filter>
        <action android:name="android.intent.action.MAIN" />
        <category android:name="android.intent.category.LAUNCHER" />
      </intent-filter>
    </activity>
  </application>

  <uses-permission android:name="android.permission.ACCESS_FINE_LOCATION"/>

</manifest>
```

2. Modify the main.xml layout resource to include an `android:ID` attribute for the `TextView` control so that you can access it from within the Activity.

```xml
<?xml version="1.0" encoding="utf-8"?>
<LinearLayout
```

```
xmlns:android="http://schemas.android.com/apk/res/android"
android:orientation="vertical"
android:layout_width="fill_parent"
android:layout_height="fill_parent">
<TextView
  android:id="@+id/myLocationText"
  android:layout_width="fill_parent"
  android:layout_height="wrap_content"
  android:text="@string/hello"
/>
</LinearLayout>
```

3. Override the `onCreate` method of the `WhereAmI` Activity to get a reference to the Location Manager. Call `getLastKnownLocation` to get the last location fix value, and pass it in to the `updateWithNewLocation` method stub.

```
package com.paad.whereami;

import android.app.Activity;
import android.content.Context;
import android.location.Location;
import android.location.LocationManager;
import android.os.Bundle;
import android.widget.TextView;

public class WhereAmI extends Activity {
  @Override
  public void onCreate(Bundle icicle) {
    super.onCreate(icicle);
    setContentView(R.layout.main);

    LocationManager locationManager;
    String context = Context.LOCATION_SERVICE;
    locationManager = (LocationManager)getSystemService(context);

    String provider = LocationManager.GPS_PROVIDER;
    Location location = locationManager.getLastKnownLocation(provider);

    updateWithNewLocation(location);
  }

  private void updateWithNewLocation(Location location) {
  }
}
```

4. Fill in the `updateWithNewLocation` method to display the passed-in Location in the Text View by extracting the latitude and longitude values.

```
private void updateWithNewLocation(Location location) {
  String latLongString;
  TextView myLocationText;
  myLocationText = (TextView)findViewById(R.id.myLocationText);
  if (location != null) {
    double lat = location.getLatitude();
    double lng = location.getLongitude();
```

```
        latLongString = "Lat:" + lat + "\nLong:" + lng;
    } else {
        latLongString = "No location found";
    }
    myLocationText.setText("Your Current Position is:\n" +
                          latLongString);
}
```

5. When running, your Activity should look like Figure 7-3.

Figure 7-3

Tracking Movement

Most location-sensitive applications will need to be reactive to user movement. Simply polling the Location Manager will not force it to get new updates from the Location Providers.

Use the `requestLocationUpdates` method to get updates whenever the current location changes, using a `LocationListener`. Location Listeners also contain hooks for changes in a provider's status and availability.

The `requestLocationUpdates` method accepts either a specific Location Provider name or a set of Criteria to determine the provider to use.

To optimize efficiency and minimize cost and power use, you can also specify the minimum time and the minimum distance between location change updates.

The following snippet shows the skeleton code for requesting regular updates based on a minimum time and distance.

```
String provider = LocationManager.GPS_PROVIDER;

int t = 5000; // milliseconds
int distance = 5; // meters

LocationListener myLocationListener = new LocationListener() {

  public void onLocationChanged(Location location) {
    // Update application based on new location.
  }

  public void onProviderDisabled(String provider){
    // Update application if provider disabled.
```

```
  }

  public void onProviderEnabled(String provider){
    // Update application if provider enabled.
  }

  public void onStatusChanged(String provider, int status,
                              Bundle extras){
    // Update application if provider hardware status changed.
  }
};
```

```
locationManager.requestLocationUpdates(provider, t, distance,
                                       myLocationListener);
```

When the minimum time and distance values are exceeded, the attached Location Listener will execute its `onLocationChanged` event.

> *You can request multiple location updates pointing to different Location Listeners and using different minimum thresholds. A common design pattern is to create a single listener for your application that broadcasts Intents to notify other components of location changes. This centralizes your listeners and ensures that the Location Provider hardware is used as efficiently as possible.*

To stop location updates, call `removeUpdates`, as shown below. Pass in the Location Listener instance you no longer want to have triggered.

```
locationManager.removeUpdates(myLocationListener);
```

Most GPS hardware incurs significant power cost. To minimize this, you should disable updates whenever possible in your application, specifically when location changes are being used to update an Activity's User Interface. You can improve performance further by extending the minimum time between updates as long as possible.

Updating Your Location in "Where Am I?"

In the following example, "Where Am I?" is enhanced to track your current location by listening for location changes. Updates are restricted to one every 2 seconds, and only when movement of more than 10 meters has been detected.

Rather than explicitly selecting the GPS provider, in this example, you'll create a set of Criteria and let Android choose the best provider available.

1. Start by opening the `WhereAmI` Activity in the WhereAmI project. Update the `onCreate` method to find the best Location Provider that features high accuracy and draws as little power as possible.

```
@Override
public void onCreate(Bundle icicle) {
  super.onCreate(icicle);
```

```
        setContentView(R.layout.main);

        LocationManager locationManager;
        String context = Context.LOCATION_SERVICE;
        locationManager = (LocationManager)getSystemService(context);

        Criteria criteria = new Criteria();
        criteria.setAccuracy(Criteria.ACCURACY_FINE);
        criteria.setAltitudeRequired(false);
        criteria.setBearingRequired(false);
        criteria.setCostAllowed(true);
        criteria.setPowerRequirement(Criteria.POWER_LOW);

        String provider = locationManager.getBestProvider(criteria, true);

        Location location = locationManager.getLastKnownLocation(provider);

        updateWithNewLocation(location);}
```

2. Create a new `LocationListener` instance variable that fires the existing `updateWithNewLocation` method whenever a location change is detected.

```
        private final LocationListener locationListener = new LocationListener() {
          public void onLocationChanged(Location location) {
            updateWithNewLocation(location);
          }

          public void onProviderDisabled(String provider){
            updateWithNewLocation(null);
          }

          public void onProviderEnabled(String provider){ }
          public void onStatusChanged(String provider, int status,
                                      Bundle extras){ }
        };
```

3. Return to `onCreate` and execute `requestLocationUpdates`, passing in the new Location Listener object. It should listen for location changes every 2 seconds but fire only when it detects movement of more than 10 meters.

```
        @Override
        public void onCreate(Bundle icicle) {
          super.onCreate(icicle);
          setContentView(R.layout.main);

          LocationManager locationManager;
          String context = Context.LOCATION_SERVICE;
          locationManager = (LocationManager)getSystemService(context);

          Criteria criteria = new Criteria();
          criteria.setAccuracy(Criteria.ACCURACY_FINE);
          criteria.setAltitudeRequired(false);
          criteria.setBearingRequired(false);
          criteria.setCostAllowed(true);
```

```
criteria.setPowerRequirement(Criteria.POWER_LOW);

String provider = locationManager.getBestProvider(criteria, true);

Location location = locationManager.getLastKnownLocation(provider);

updateWithNewLocation(location);

locationManager.requestLocationUpdates(provider, 2000, 10,
                                       locationListener);
}
```

If you run the application and start changing the device location, you will see the Text View update accordingly.

Using Proximity Alerts

It's often useful to have your applications react when a user moves toward, or away from, a specific location. Proximity alerts let your applications set triggers that are fired when a user moves within or beyond a set distance from a geographic location.

Internally, Android may use different Location Providers depending on how close you are to the outside edge of your target area. This allows the power use and cost to be minimized when the alert is unlikely to be fired based on your distance from the interface.

To set a proximity alert for a given coverage area, select the center point (using longitude and latitude values), a radius around that point, and an expiry time-out for the alert. The alert will fire if the device crosses over that boundary, both when it moves within the radius and when it moves beyond it.

When triggered, proximity alerts fire Intents, most commonly broadcast Intents. To specify the Intent to fire, you use a `PendingIntent`, a class that wraps an Intent in a kind of method pointer, as shown in the following code snippet:

```
Intent intent = new Intent(MY_ACTIVITY);
PendingIntent pendingIntent = PendingIntent.getBroadcast(this, -1, intent, 0);
```

The following example sets a proximity alert that never expires and triggers when the device moves within 10 meters of its target:

```
private static String TREASURE_PROXIMITY_ALERT = "com.paad.treasurealert";

private void setProximityAlert() {
  String locService = Context.LOCATION_SERVICE;
  LocationManager locationManager;
  locationManager = (LocationManager)getSystemService(locService);

  double lat = 73.147536;
  double lng = 0.510638;
  float radius = 100f; // meters
```

```
long expiration = -1; // do not expire

Intent intent = new Intent(TREASURE_PROXIMITY_ALERT);
PendingIntent proximityIntent = PendingIntent.getBroadcast(this, -1,
                                                           intent,
                                                           0);
locationManager.addProximityAlert(lat, lng, radius, expiration,
                                  proximityIntent);}
```

When the Location Manager detects that you have moved either within or beyond the specified radius, the packaged Intent will be fired with an `extra` keyed as `LocationManager.KEY_PROXIMITY_ENTERING` set to `true` or `false` accordingly.

To handle proximity alerts, you need to create a `BroadcastReceiver`, such as the one shown in the following snippet:

```
public class ProximityIntentReceiver extends BroadcastReceiver {

  @Override
  public void onReceive (Context context, Intent intent) {
    String key = LocationManager.KEY_PROXIMITY_ENTERING;

    Boolean entering = intent.getBooleanExtra(key, false);
    [ ... perform proximity alert actions ... ]
  }

}
```

To start listening for them, register your receiver, as shown in the snippet below:

```
IntentFilter filter = new IntentFilter(TREASURE_PROXIMITY_ALERT);
registerReceiver(new ProximityIntentReceiver(), filter);
```

Using the Geocoder

Geocoding lets you translate between street addresses and longitude/latitude map coordinates. This can give you a recognizable context for the locations and coordinates used in location-based services and map-based Activities.

The `Geocoder` class provides access to two geocoding functions:

❑   **Forward Geocoding**   Finds the latitude and longitude of an address.

❑   **Reverse Geocoding**   Finds the street address for a given latitude and longitude.

The results from these calls will be contextualized using a locale, where a locale is used to define your usual location and language. The following snippet shows how you set the locale when creating your Geocoder. If you don't specify a locale, it will assume your device's default.

```
Geocoder geocoder = new Geocoder(getApplicationContext(),
                                 Locale.getDefault());
```

Both geocoding functions return a list of `Address` objects. Each list can contain several possible results, up to a limit you specify when making the call.

Each Address object is populated with as much detail as the Geocoder was able to resolve. This can include the latitude, longitude, phone number, and increasingly granular address details from country to street and house number.

> *Geocoder lookups are performed synchronously, so they will block the calling thread. For slow data connections, this can lead to an Application Unresponsive dialog. In most cases, it's good form to move these lookups into a Service or background thread, as shown in Chapter 8.*

> *For clarity and brevity, the calls made in the code samples within this chapter are made on the main application thread.*

Reverse Geocoding

Reverse geocoding returns street addresses for physical locations, specified by latitude/longitude pairs. It provides a recognizable context for the locations returned by location-based services.

To perform a reverse lookup, you pass the target latitude and longitude to a Geocoder's `getFromLocation` method. It will return a list of possible matching addresses. If the Geocoder could not resolve any addresses for the specified coordinate, it will return null.

The following example shows how to reverse-geocode your last known location:

```
location = locationManager.getLastKnownLocation(LocationManager.GPS_PROVIDER);

double latitude = location.getLatitude();
double longitude = location.getLongitude();
```

```
Geocoder gc = new Geocoder(this, Locale.getDefault());

List<Address> addresses = null;
try {
  addresses = gc.getFromLocation(latitude, longitude, 10);
} catch (IOException e) {}
```

The accuracy and granularity of reverse lookups are entirely dependent on the quality of data in the geocoding database; as such, the quality of the results may vary widely between different countries and locales.

Forward Geocoding

Forward geocoding (or just geocoding) determines map coordinates for a given location.

> *What constitutes a valid location varies depending on the locale (geographic area) within which you're searching. Generally, it will include regular street addresses of varying granularity (from country to street name and number), postcodes, train stations, landmarks, and hospitals. As a general guide, valid search terms will be similar to the addresses and locations you can enter into the Google Maps search bar.*

To do a forward-geocoding lookup, call `getFromLocationName` on a Geocoder instance. Pass in the location you want the coordinates for and the maximum number of results to return, as shown in the snippet below:

```
List<Address> result = geocoder.getFromLocationName(aStreetAddress, maxResults);
```

The returned list of Addresses can include multiple possible matches for the named location. Each address result will include latitude and longitude and any additional address information available for those coordinates. This is useful to confirm that the correct location was resolved, as well as providing address specifics when searching for landmarks.

As with reverse geocoding, if no matches are found, null will be returned. The availability, accuracy, and granularity of geocoding results will depend entirely on the database available for the area you're searching.

When doing forward lookups, the Locale specified when creating the Geocoder object is particularly important. The Locale provides the geographical context for interpreting your search requests, as the same location names can exist in multiple areas. Where possible, consider selecting a regional Locale to help avoid place name ambiguity.

Additionally, try to use as many address details as possible. For example, the following code snippet demonstrates a forward geocode for a New York street address:

```
Geocoder fwdGeocoder = new Geocoder(this, Locale.US);
String streetAddress = "160 Riverside Drive, New York, New York";

List<Address> locations = null;
try {
   locations = fwdGeocoder.getFromLocationName(streetAddress, 10);
} catch (IOException e) {}
```

For even more specific results, use the `getFromLocationName` overload, that lets you restrict your search to within a geographical bounding box, as shown in the following snippet:

```
List<Address> locations = null;
try {
   locations = fwdGeocoder.getFromLocationName(streetAddress, 10,
                                               n, e, s, w);
} catch (IOException e) {}
```

This overload is particularly useful in conjunction with a MapView as you can restrict the search to within the visible map.

Geocoding "Where Am I?"

Using the Geocoder, you can determine the street address at your current location. In this example, you'll further extend the "Where Am I?" project to include and update the current street address whenever the device moves.

Open the `WhereAmI` Activity. Modify the `updateWithNewLocation` method to instantiate a new Geocoder object, and call the `getFromLocation` method, passing in the newly received location and limiting the results to a single address.

Extract each line in the street address, as well as the locality, postcode, and country, and append this information to an existing Text View string.

```java
private void updateWithNewLocation(Location location) {
  String latLongString;
  TextView myLocationText;
  myLocationText = (TextView)findViewById(R.id.myLocationText);

  String addressString = "No address found";

  if (location != null) {
    double lat = location.getLatitude();
    double lng = location.getLongitude();
    latLongString = "Lat:" + lat + "\nLong:" + lng;

    double latitude = location.getLatitude();
    double longitude = location.getLongitude();

    Geocoder gc = new Geocoder(this, Locale.getDefault());
    try {
      List<Address> addresses = gc.getFromLocation(latitude, longitude, 1);
      StringBuilder sb = new StringBuilder();
      if (addresses.size() > 0) {
        Address address = addresses.get(0);

        for (int i = 0; i < address.getMaxAddressLineIndex(); i++)
          sb.append(address.getAddressLine(i)).append("\n");

        sb.append(address.getLocality()).append("\n");
        sb.append(address.getPostalCode()).append("\n");
        sb.append(address.getCountryName());
      }
      addressString = sb.toString();
    } catch (IOException e) {}
  } else {
    latLongString = "No location found";
  }
  myLocationText.setText("Your Current Position is:\n" +
                         latLongString + "\n" + addressString);
}
```

If you run the example now, it should appear as shown in Figure 7-4.

Figure 7-4

Creating Map-Based Activities

The `MapView` provides a compelling User Interface option for presentation of geographical data.

One of the most intuitive ways of providing context for a physical location or address is to display it on a map. Using a `MapView`, you can create Activities that feature an interactive map.

Map Views support annotation using both Overlays and by pinning Views to geographical locations. Map Views offer full programmatic control of the map display, letting you control the zoom, location, and display modes — including the option to display satellite, street, and traffic views.

In the following sections, you'll see how to use Overlays and the MapController to create dynamic map-based Activities. Unlike online mashups, your map Activities will run natively on the device, allowing you to leverage its hardware and mobility to provide a more customized and personal user experience.

Introducing MapView and MapActivity

This section introduces several classes used to support Android maps:

- ❑ `MapView` is the actual Map View (control).
- ❑ `MapActivity` is the base class you extend to create a new Activity that can include a Map View. The `MapActivity` class handles the application life cycle and background service management required for displaying maps. As a result, you can only use a `MapView` within `MapActivity`-derived Activities.
- ❑ `Overlay` is the class used to annotate your maps. Using Overlays, you can use a Canvas to draw onto any number of layers that are displayed on top of a Map View.
- ❑ `MapController` is used to control the map, allowing you to set the center location and zoom levels.
- ❑ `MyLocationOverlay` is a special overlay that can be used to display the current position and orientation of the device.
- ❑ `ItemizedOverlays` and `OverlayItems` are used together to let you create a layer of map markers, displayed using drawable with associated text.

Creating a Map-Based Activity

To use maps in your applications, you need to create a new Activity that extends `MapActivity`. Within it, add a `MapView` to the layout to display a Google Maps interface element. The Android map library is not a standard package; as an optional API, it must be explicitly included in the application manifest before it can be used. Add the library to your manifest using a `uses-library` tag within the `application` node, as shown in the XML snippet below:

```
<uses-library android:name="com.google.android.maps"/>
```

Google Maps downloads the map tiles on demand; as a result, it implicitly requires permission to use the Internet. To see map tiles in your Map View, you need to add a `uses-permission` tag to your application manifest for `android.permission.INTERNET`, as shown below:

```
<uses-permission android:name="android.permission.INTERNET"/>
```

Once you've added the library and configured your permission, you're ready to create your new map-based Activity.

`MapView` controls can only be used within an Activity that extends `MapActivity`. Override the `onCreate` method to lay out the screen that includes a `MapView`, and override `isRouteDisplayed` to return `true` if the Activity will be displaying routing information (such as traffic directions).

The following skeleton code shows the framework for creating a new map-based Activity:

```
import com.google.android.maps.MapActivity;
import com.google.android.maps.MapController;
import com.google.android.maps.MapView;
import android.os.Bundle;

public class MyMapActivity extends MapActivity {
  private MapView mapView;
  private MapController mapController;

  @Override
  public void onCreate(Bundle icicle) {
    super.onCreate(icicle);
    setContentView(R.layout.map_layout);
    mapView = (MapView)findViewById(R.id.map_view);
  }

  @Override
  protected boolean isRouteDisplayed() {
    // IMPORTANT: This method must return true if your Activity
    // is displaying driving directions. Otherwise return false.
    return false;
  }
}
```

The corresponding layout file used to include the `MapView` is shown below. Note that you need to include a maps API key in order to use a Map View in your application.

```
<?xml version="1.0" encoding="utf-8"?>
<LinearLayout
  xmlns:android="http://schemas.android.com/apk/res/android"
  android:orientation="vertical"
  android:layout_width="fill_parent"
  android:layout_height="fill_parent">
  <com.google.android.maps.MapView
    android:id="@+id/map_view"
    android:layout_width="fill_parent"
```

```
          android:layout_height="fill_parent"
          android:enabled="true"
          android:clickable="true"
          android:apiKey="mymapapikey"
     />
</LinearLayout>
```

> At the time of publication, it was unclear how developers would apply for map keys. Invalid or disabled API keys will result in your `MapView` not loading the map image tiles. Until this process is revealed, you can use any text as your API key value.

Figure 7-5 shows an example of a basic map-based Activity.

Figure 7-5

Android currently recommends that you include no more than one `MapActivity` and one `MapView` in each application.

Configuring and Using Map Views

The `MapView` class is a View that displays the actual map; it includes several options for deciding how the map is displayed.

By default, the Map View will show the standard street map, as shown in Figure 7-5. In addition, you can choose to display a satellite view, StreetView, and expected traffic, as shown in the code snippet below:

```
mapView.setSatellite(true);
mapView.setStreetView(true);
mapView.setTraffic(true);
```

You can also query the Map View to find the current and maximum available zoom level, as well as the center point and currently visible longitude and latitude span (in decimal degrees). The latter (shown below) is particularly useful for performing geographically limited Geocoder lookups:

```
GeoPoint center = mapView.getMapCenter();
int latSpan = mapView.getLatitudeSpan();
int longSpan = mapView.getLongitudeSpan();
```

You can also optionally display the standard map zoom controls. The following code snippet shows how to get a reference to the Zoom Control View and pin it to a screen location. The Boolean parameter lets you assign focus to the controls once they're added.

```
int y = 10;
int x = 10;

MapView.LayoutParams lp;
lp = new MapView.LayoutParams(MapView.LayoutParams.WRAP_CONTENT,
                              MapView.LayoutParams.WRAP_CONTENT,
                              x, y,
                              MapView.LayoutParams.TOP_LEFT);

View zoomControls = mapView.getZoomControls();
mapView.addView(zoomControls, lp);
mapView.displayZoomControls(true);
```

The technique used to pin the zoom controls to the `MapView` is covered in more detail later in this chapter.

Using the Map Controller

You use the Map Controller to pan and zoom a `MapView`. You can get a reference to a `MapView`'s controller using `getController`, as shown in the following code snippet:

```
MapController mapController = myMapView.getController();
```

Map locations in the Android mapping classes are represented by `GeoPoint` objects, which contain latitude and longitude measured in microdegrees (i.e., degrees multiplied by 1E6 [or 1,000,000]).

Before you can use the latitude and longitude values stored in the Location objects used by the location-based services, you'll need to convert them to microdegrees and store them as GeoPoints, as shown in the following code snippet:

```
Double lat = 37.422006*1E6;
Double lng = -122.084095*1E6;
GeoPoint point = new GeoPoint(lat.intValue(), lng.intValue());
```

Re-center and zoom the `MapView` using the `setCenter` and `setZoom` methods available on the `MapView`'s `MapController`, as shown in the snippet below:

```
mapController.setCenter(point);
mapController.setZoom(1);
```

When using `setZoom`, 1 represents the widest (or furthest away) zoom and 21 the tightest (nearest) view.

The actual zoom level available for a specific location depends on the resolution of Google's maps and imagery for that area. You can also use `zoomIn` and `zoomOut` to change the zoom level by one step.

The `setCenter` method will "jump" to a new location; to show a smooth transition, use `animateTo` as shown in the code below:

```
mapController.animateTo(point);
```

Mapping "Where Am I?"

In the following code example, the "Where Am I?" project is extended again. This time you'll add mapping functionality by transforming it into a Map Activity. As the device location changes, the map will automatically re-center on the new position.

1. Start by adding the `uses-permission` tag for Internet access to the application manifest. Also import the Android maps library within the `application` tag.

```xml
<?xml version="1.0" encoding="utf-8"?>
<manifest xmlns:android="http://schemas.android.com/apk/res/android"
          package="com.paad.whereami">
  <application
    android:icon="@drawable/icon">
    <activity
      android:name=".WhereAmI"
      android:label="@string/app_name">
      <intent-filter>
        <action android:name="android.intent.action.MAIN" />
        <category android:name="android.intent.category.LAUNCHER" />
      </intent-filter>
    </activity>
    <uses-library android:name="com.google.android.maps"/>
  </application>

  <uses-permission android:name="android.permission.INTERNET"/>
  <uses-permission android:name="android.permission.ACCESS_FINE_LOCATION"/>

</manifest>
```

2. Change the inheritance of `WhereAmI` to descend from `MapActivity` instead of `Activity`. You'll also need to include an override for the `isRouteDisplayed` method. Because this Activity won't show routing directions, you can return `false`.

```java
public class WhereAmI extends MapActivity {

  @Override
  protected boolean isRouteDisplayed() {
    return false;
  }

  [ ... existing Activity code ... ]

}
```

3. Modify the main.xml layout resource to include a `MapView` using the fully qualified class name. Be sure to include an `android:apikey` attribute within the `com.android.MapView` node. If you have an Android maps API key, use it here.

```xml
<?xml version="1.0" encoding="utf-8"?>
<LinearLayout
  xmlns:android="http://schemas.android.com/apk/res/android"
  android:orientation="vertical"
  android:layout_width="fill_parent"
  android:layout_height="fill_parent">
  <TextView
    android:id="@+id/myLocationText"
    android:layout_width="fill_parent"
    android:layout_height="wrap_content"
    android:text="@string/hello"
  />
  <com.google.android.maps.MapView
    android:id="@+id/myMapView"
    android:layout_width="fill_parent"
    android:layout_height="fill_parent"
    android:enabled="true"
    android:clickable="true"
    android:apiKey="myMapKey"
  />
</LinearLayout>
```

4. Running the application now should display the original geolocation text, with a `MapView` beneath it, as shown in Figure 7-6.

Figure 7-6

5. Configure the Map View and store a reference to its `MapController` as an instance variable. Set up the Map View display options to show the satellite and `StreetView` and zoom in for a closer look.

```java
MapController mapController;

@Override
public void onCreate(Bundle icicle) {
  super.onCreate(icicle);
  setContentView(R.layout.main);

  // Get a reference to the MapView
  MapView myMapView = (MapView)findViewById(R.id.myMapView);
  // Get the Map View's controller
  mapController = myMapView.getController();

  // Configure the map display options
  myMapView.setSatellite(true);
  myMapView.setStreetView(true);
  myMapView.displayZoomControls(false);

  // Zoom in
  mapController.setZoom(17);

  LocationManager locationManager;
  String context = Context.LOCATION_SERVICE;
  locationManager = (LocationManager)getSystemService(context);

  Criteria criteria = new Criteria();
  criteria.setAccuracy(Criteria.ACCURACY_FINE);
  criteria.setAltitudeRequired(false);
  criteria.setBearingRequired(false);
  criteria.setCostAllowed(true);
  criteria.setPowerRequirement(Criteria.POWER_LOW);
  String provider = locationManager.getBestProvider(criteria, true);

  Location location = locationManager.getLastKnownLocation(provider);

  updateWithNewLocation(location);

  locationManager.requestLocationUpdates(provider, 2000, 10,
                                         locationListener);
}
```

6. The final step is to modify the `updateWithNewLocation` method to re-center the map to the current location using the Map Controller.

```java
private void updateWithNewLocation(Location location) {
  String latLongString;
  TextView myLocationText;
  myLocationText = (TextView)findViewById(R.id.myLocationText);
```

```
    String addressString = "No address found";

    if (location != null) {
      // Update the map location.
      Double geoLat = location.getLatitude()*1E6;
      Double geoLng = location.getLongitude()*1E6;
      GeoPoint point = new GeoPoint(geoLat.intValue(),
                                    geoLng.intValue());

      mapController.animateTo(point);

      double lat = location.getLatitude();
      double lng = location.getLongitude();
      latLongString = "Lat:" + lat + "\nLong:" + lng;

      double latitude = location.getLatitude();
      double longitude = location.getLongitude();

      Geocoder gc = new Geocoder(this, Locale.getDefault());
      try {
        List<Address> addresses = gc.getFromLocation(latitude, longitude, 1);
        StringBuilder sb = new StringBuilder();
        if (addresses.size() > 0) {
          Address address = addresses.get(0);

          for (int i = 0; i < address.getMaxAddressLineIndex(); i++)
            sb.append(address.getAddressLine(i)).append("\n");

          sb.append(address.getLocality()).append("\n");
          sb.append(address.getPostalCode()).append("\n");
          sb.append(address.getCountryName());
        }
        addressString = sb.toString();
      } catch (IOException e) {}
    } else {
      latLongString = "No location found";
    }
    myLocationText.setText("Your Current Position is:\n" +
                           latLongString + "\n" + addressString);
  }
```

Creating and Using Overlays

Overlays are a way to add annotations and click handling to `MapViews`. Each Overlay lets you draw 2D primitives including text, lines, images and shapes directly onto a canvas, which is then overlaid onto a Map View.

You can add several Overlays onto a single map. All the Overlays assigned to a Map View are added as layers, with newer layers potentially obscuring older ones. User clicks are passed through the stack until they are either handled by an Overlay or registered as a click on the Map View itself.

Creating New Overlays

Each overlay is a canvas with a transparent background that you can layer on top of a Map View and use to handle map touch events.

To add a new Overlay, create a new class that extends `Overlay`. Override the `draw` method to draw the annotations you want to add, and override `onTap` to react to user clicks (generally when the user taps an annotation added by this overlay).

The following code snippet shows the framework for creating a new Overlay that can draw annotations and handle user clicks:

```
import android.graphics.Canvas;
import com.google.android.maps.MapView;
import com.google.android.maps.Overlay;

public class MyOverlay extends Overlay {

  @Override
  public void draw(Canvas canvas, MapView mapView, boolean shadow) {
    if (shadow == false) {
      [ ... Draw annotations on main map layer ... ]
    }
    else {
      [ ... Draw annotations on the shadow layer ... ]
    }
  }

  @Override
  public boolean onTap(GeoPoint point, MapView mapView) {
   // Return true if screen tap is handled by this overlay
   return false;
  }
}
```

Introducing Projections

The Canvas used to draw Overlay annotations is a standard `Canvas` that represents the visible display surface. To add annotations based on physical locations, you need to convert between geographical points and screen coordinates.

The Projection class lets you translate between latitude/longitude coordinates (stored as `GeoPoints`) and x/y screen pixel coordinates (stored as `Points`).

A map's Projection may change between subsequent calls to draw, so it's good practice to get a new instance each time. Get a Map View's Projection by calling `getProjection`, as shown in the snippet below:

```
Projection projection = mapView.getProjection();
```

Use the `fromPixel` and `toPixel` methods to translate from GeoPoints to Points and vice versa.

For performance reasons, the `toPixel` Projection method is best used by passing a Point object to be populated (rather than relying on the return value), as shown below:

```
Point myPoint = new Point();
```

```
// To screen coordinates
projection.toPixels(geoPoint, myPoint);
```

```
// To GeoPoint location coordinates
projection.fromPixels(myPoint.x, myPoint.y);
```

Drawing on the Overlay Canvas

Canvas drawing for Overlays is handled by overriding the Overlay's `draw` handler.

The passed-in Canvas is the surface on which you draw your annotations, using the same techniques introduced in Chapter 4 when creating custom User Interfaces for Views. The Canvas object includes the methods for drawing 2D primitives on your map (including lines, text, shapes, ellipses, images, etc.). Use `Paint` objects to define the style and color.

The following code snippet uses a Projection to draw text and an ellipse at a given location:

```
@Override
public void draw(Canvas canvas, MapView mapView, boolean shadow) {
  Projection projection = mapView.getProjection();

  Double lat = -31.960906*1E6;
  Double lng = 115.844822*1E6;
  GeoPoint geoPoint = new GeoPoint(lat.intValue(), lng.intValue());

  if (shadow == false) {
    Point myPoint = new Point();
    projection.toPixels(geoPoint, myPoint);

    // Create and setup your paint brush
    Paint paint = new Paint();
    paint.setARGB(250, 255, 0, 0);
    paint.setAntiAlias(true);
    paint.setFakeBoldText(true);

    // Create the circle
    int rad = 5;
    RectF oval = new RectF(myPoint.x-rad, myPoint.y-rad,
                           myPoint.x+rad, myPoint.y+rad);

    // Draw on the canvas
    canvas.drawOval(oval, paint);
    canvas.drawText("Red Circle", myPoint.x+rad, myPoint.y, paint);
  }
}
```

For more advanced drawing features, check out Chapter 11, where gradients, strokes, and filters are introduced that provide powerful tools for drawing attractive and compelling map overlays.

Handling Map Tap Events

To handle map taps (user clicks), override the `onTap` event handler within the Overlay extension class.

The `onTap` handler receives two parameters:

❑   A `GeoPoint` that contains the latitude/longitude of the map location tapped

❑   The `MapView` that was tapped to trigger this event

When overriding `onTap`, the method should return `true` if it has handled a particular tap and `false` to let another overlay handle it, as shown in the skeleton code below:

```
@Override
public boolean onTap(GeoPoint point, MapView mapView) {
  // Perform hit test to see if this overlay is handling the click
  if ([... perform hit test ... ]) {
    [ ... execute on tap functionality ... ]
    return true;
  }

  // If not handled return false
  return false;
}
```

Adding and Removing Overlays

Each `MapView` contains a list of Overlays currently displayed. You can get a reference to this list by calling `getOverlays`, as shown in the snippet below:

```
List<Overlay> overlays = mapView.getOverlays();
```

Adding and removing items from the list is thread safe and synchronized, so you can modify and query the list safely. Iterating over the list should still be done within a synchronization block synchronized on the List.

To add an Overlay onto a Map View, create a new instance of the Overlay, and add it to the list, as shown in the snippet below:

```
List<Overlay> overlays = mapView.getOverlays();

MyOverlay myOverlay = new MyOverlay();
overlays.add(myOverlay);
mapView.postInvalidate();
```

The added Overlay will be displayed the next time the Map View is redrawn, so it's usually good practice to call `postInvalidate` after you modify the list to update the changes on the map display.

Annotating "Where Am I?"

This final modification to "Where Am I?" creates and adds a new Overlay that displays a red circle at the device's current position.

1. Start by creating a new `MyPositionOverlay` Overlay class in the WhereAmI project.

```
package com.paad.whereami;

import android.graphics.Canvas;
import android.graphics.Paint;
import android.graphics.Point;
import android.graphics.RectF;
import android.location.Location;
import com.google.android.maps.GeoPoint;
import com.google.android.maps.MapView;
import com.google.android.maps.Overlay;
import com.google.android.maps.Projection;

public class MyPositionOverlay extends Overlay {

  @Override
  public void draw(Canvas canvas, MapView mapView, boolean shadow) {
  }

  @Override
  public boolean onTap(GeoPoint point, MapView mapView) {
    return false;
  }
}
```

2. Create a new instance variable to store the current Location, and add setter and getter methods for it.

```
Location location;

public Location getLocation() {
  return location;
}
public void setLocation(Location location) {
  this.location = location;
}
```

3. Override the `draw` method to add a small red circle at the current location.

```
private final int mRadius = 5;

@Override
public void draw(Canvas canvas, MapView mapView, boolean shadow) {
  Projection projection = mapView.getProjection();

  if (shadow == false) {
    // Get the current location
    Double latitude = location.getLatitude()*1E6;
    Double longitude = location.getLongitude()*1E6;
    GeoPoint geoPoint;
    geoPoint = new GeoPoint(latitude.intValue(),longitude.intValue());

    // Convert the location to screen pixels
```

```
      Point point = new Point();
      projection.toPixels(geoPoint, point);

      RectF oval = new RectF(point.x - mRadius, point.y - mRadius,
                             point.x + mRadius, point.y + mRadius);

      // Setup the paint
      Paint paint = new Paint();
      paint.setARGB(250, 255, 0, 0);
      paint.setAntiAlias(true);
      paint.setFakeBoldText(true);

      Paint backPaint = new Paint();
      backPaint.setARGB(175, 50, 50, 50);
      backPaint.setAntiAlias(true);

      RectF backRect = new RectF(point.x + 2 + mRadius,
                                 point.y - 3*mRadius,
                                 point.x + 65, point.y + mRadius);

      // Draw the marker
      canvas.drawOval(oval, paint);
      canvas.drawRoundRect(backRect, 5, 5, backPaint);

      canvas.drawText("Here I Am", point.x + 2*mRadius, point.y, paint);
    }
    super.draw(canvas, mapView, shadow);
  }
}
```

4. Now open the WhereAmI Activity class, and add the MyPositionOverlay to the MapView.

    Start by adding a new instance variable to store the MyPositionOverlay, then override onCreate to create a new instance of the class, and add it to the MapView's Overlay list.

```
MyPositionOverlay positionOverlay;

@Override
public void onCreate(Bundle icicle) {
  super.onCreate(icicle);
  setContentView(R.layout.main);

  MapView myMapView = (MapView)findViewById(R.id.myMapView);
  mapController = myMapView.getController();

  myMapView.setSatellite(true);
  myMapView.setStreetView(true);
  myMapView.displayZoomControls(false);

  mapController.setZoom(17);

  // Add the MyPositionOverlay
  positionOverlay = new MyPositionOverlay();
  List<Overlay> overlays = myMapView.getOverlays();
```

```
      overlays.add(positionOverlay);

  LocationManager locationManager;
  String context = Context.LOCATION_SERVICE;
  locationManager = (LocationManager)getSystemService(context);

  Criteria criteria = new Criteria();
  criteria.setAccuracy(Criteria.ACCURACY_FINE);
  criteria.setAltitudeRequired(false);
  criteria.setBearingRequired(false);
  criteria.setCostAllowed(true);
  criteria.setPowerRequirement(Criteria.POWER_LOW);
  String provider = locationManager.getBestProvider(criteria, true);

  Location location = locationManager.getLastKnownLocation(provider);

  updateWithNewLocation(location);

  locationManager.requestLocationUpdates(provider, 2000, 10,
                                         locationListener);
}
```

5. Finally, update the `updateWithNewLocation` method to pass the new location to the overlay.

```
private void updateWithNewLocation(Location location) {
  String latLongString;
  TextView myLocationText;
  myLocationText = (TextView)findViewById(R.id.myLocationText);
  String addressString = "No address found";

  if (location != null) {
    // Update my location marker
    positionOverlay.setLocation(location);

    // Update the map location.
    Double geoLat = location.getLatitude()*1E6;
    Double geoLng = location.getLongitude()*1E6;
    GeoPoint point = new GeoPoint(geoLat.intValue(),
                                  geoLng.intValue());

    mapController.animateTo(point);

    double lat = location.getLatitude();
    double lng = location.getLongitude();
    latLongString = "Lat:" + lat + "\nLong:" + lng;

    double latitude = location.getLatitude();
    double longitude = location.getLongitude();

    Geocoder gc = new Geocoder(this, Locale.getDefault());
    try {
      List<Address> addresses = gc.getFromLocation(latitude, longitude, 1);
      StringBuilder sb = new StringBuilder();
```

```
        if (addresses.size() > 0) {
          Address address = addresses.get(0);

          for (int i = 0; i < address.getMaxAddressLineIndex(); i++)
            sb.append(address.getAddressLine(i)).append("\n");

          sb.append(address.getLocality()).append("\n");
          sb.append(address.getPostalCode()).append("\n");
          sb.append(address.getCountryName());
        }
        addressString = sb.toString();
      } catch (IOException e) {}
    } else {
      latLongString = "No location found";
    }
    myLocationText.setText("Your Current Position is:\n" +
                            latLongString + "\n" + addressString);
  }
```

When run, your application will display your current device location with a red circle and supporting text, as shown in Figure 7-7.

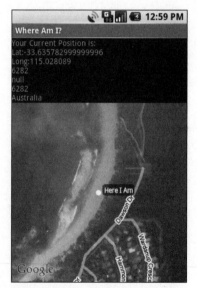

Figure 7-7

It's worth noting that this is not the preferred technique for displaying your current location on a map. This functionality is implemented natively by Android through the MyLocationOverlay *class. If you want to display and follow your current location, you should consider using this class (as shown in the next section) instead of implementing it manually as shown here.*

Introducing MyLocationOverlay

The `MyLocationOverlay` class is a special Overlay designed to show your current location and orientation on a `MapView`.

To use the My Location Overlay, you need to create a new instance, passing in the application Context and target Map View, and add it to the `MapView`'s Overlay list, as shown below:

```
List<Overlay> overlays = mapView.getOverlays();
MyLocationOverlay myLocationOverlay = new MyLocationOverlay(this, mapView);
overlays.add(myLocationOverlay);
```

You can use the My Location Overlay to display both your current location (represented as a flashing blue marker) and orientation (shown as a compass on the map display).

The following snippet shows how to enable both the compass and marker; in this instance, the Map View's `MapController` is also passed in, allowing the overlay to automatically scroll the map if the marker moves off screen.

```
myLocationOverlay.enableCompass();
myLocationOverlay.enableMyLocation(mapView.getMapController());
```

Introducing ItemizedOverlays and OverlayItems

`OverlayItems` are used to supply simple maker functionality to your `MapViews` using the `ItemizedOverlay` class.

You can create your own Overlays that draw markers onto a map, but `ItemizedOverlays` provide a convenient shortcut, letting you assign a marker image and associated text to a particular geographical position. The `ItemizedOverlay` instance handles the drawing, placement, click handling, focus control, and layout optimization of each `OverlayItem` marker for you.

> At the time of going to print, the `ItemizedOverlay`/`OverlayItem` functionality was not fully supported. While it was possible to implement each required class, the markers were not displayed on the map.

To add an `ItemizedOverlay` marker layer to your map, start by creating a new class that extends `ItemizedOverlay<OverlayItem>`, as shown in the skeleton code below:

```
import android.graphics.drawable.Drawable;
import com.google.android.maps.GeoPoint;
import com.google.android.maps.ItemizedOverlay;
import com.google.android.maps.OverlayItem;

public class MyItemizedOverlay extends ItemizedOverlay<OverlayItem> {

  public MyItemizedOverlay(Drawable defaultMarker) {
    super(defaultMarker);
```

```
        // Create each of the overlay items included in this layer.
        populate();
    }

    @Override
    protected OverlayItem createItem(int index) {
        switch (index) {
            case 1:
                Double lat = 37.422006*1E6;
                Double lng = -122.084095*1E6;
                GeoPoint point = new GeoPoint(lat.intValue(), lng.intValue());

                OverlayItem oi;
                oi = new OverlayItem(point, "Marker", "Marker Text");
                return oi;
        }

        return null;
    }

    @Override
    public int size() {
        // Return the number of markers in the collection
        return 1;
    }

}
```

`ItemizedOverlay` *is a generic class that lets you create extensions based on any* `OverlayItem`-*derived subclass.*

Within the implementation, override `size` to return the number of markers to display and `createItem` to create a new item based on the index of each marker. You will also need to make a call to `populate` within the class's constructor. This call is a requirement and is used to trigger the creation of each `OverlayItem`; it must be called as soon as you have the data required to create all the items.

To add an `ItemizedOverlay` implementation to your map, create a new instance (passing in the default drawable marker image to use), and add it to the map's Overlay list, as shown in the following snippet:

```
List<Overlay> overlays = mapView.getOverlays();

MyItemizedOverlay markrs = new MyItemizedOverlay(r.getDrawable(R.drawable.marker));
overlays.add(markrs);
```

Pinning Views to the Map and Map Positions

Previously in this chapter, you saw how to add the Zoom View to a Map View by pinning it to a specific screen location. You can pin any View-derived object to a Map View (including layouts and other View Groups), attaching it to either a screen position or a geographical map location.

In the latter case, the View will move to follow its pinned position on the map, effectively acting as an interactive map marker. As a more resource-intensive solution, this is usually reserved for supplying the detail "balloons" often displayed on mashups to provide further detail when a marker is clicked.

Both pinning mechanisms are implemented by calling `addView` on the `MapView`, usually from the `onCreate` or `onRestore` methods within the `MapActivity` containing it. Pass in the View you want to pin and the layout parameters to use.

The `MapView.LayoutParams` parameters you pass in to `addView` determine how, and where, the View is added to the map.

To add a new View to the map relative to the screen, specify a new `MapView.LayoutParams` including arguments that set the height and width of the View, the x/y screen coordinates to pin to, and the alignment to use for positioning, as shown below:

```
int y = 10;
int x = 10;

MapView.LayoutParams screenLP;
screenLP = new MapView.LayoutParams(MapView.LayoutParams.WRAP_CONTENT,
                                    MapView.LayoutParams.WRAP_CONTENT,
                                    x, y,
                                    MapView.LayoutParams.TOP_LEFT);

EditText editText1 = new EditText(getApplicationContext());
editText1.setText("Screen Pinned");

mapView.addView(editText1, screenLP);
```

To pin a View relative to a physical map location, pass four parameters when constructing the new `MapView LayoutParams`, representing the height, width, GeoPoint to pin to, and the layout alignment.

```
Double lat = 37.422134*1E6;
Double lng = -122.084069*1E6;
GeoPoint geoPoint = new GeoPoint(lat.intValue(), lng.intValue());

MapView.LayoutParams geoLP;
geoLP = new MapView.LayoutParams(MapView.LayoutParams.WRAP_CONTENT,
                                 MapView.LayoutParams.WRAP_CONTENT,
                                 geoPoint,
                                 MapView.LayoutParams.TOP_LEFT);

EditText editText2 = new EditText(getApplicationContext());
editText2.setText("Location Pinned");

mapView.addView(editText2, geoLP);
```

Panning the map will leave the first `TextView` stationary in the upper left corner, while the second `TextView` will move to remain pinned to a particular position on the map.

To remove a View from a `MapView`, call `removeView`, passing in the View instance you wish to remove, as shown below:

```
mapView.removeView(editText2);
```

Mapping Earthquakes Example

The following step-by-step guide demonstrates how to build a map-based Activity for the Earthquake project you started in Chapter 5. The new `MapActivity` will display a map of recent earthquakes using techniques you learned within this chapter.

1. Create a new earthquake_map.xml layout resource that includes a `MapView`, being sure to include an `android:id` attribute and a `android:apiKey` attribute that contains your Android Maps API key.

```
<?xml version="1.0" encoding="utf-8"?>
<LinearLayout
  xmlns:android="http://schemas.android.com/apk/res/android"
  android:orientation="vertical"
  android:layout_width="fill_parent"
  android:layout_height="fill_parent">
  <com.google.android.maps.MapView
    android:id="@+id/map_view"
    android:layout_width="fill_parent"
    android:layout_height="fill_parent"
    android:enabled="true"
    android:clickable="true"
    android:apiKey="myapikey"
  />
</LinearLayout>
```

2. Create a new `EarthquakeMap` Activity that inherits from `MapActivity`. Use `setContentView` within `onCreate` to inflate the earthquake_map resource you created in Step 1.

```
package com.paad.earthquake;

import android.os.Bundle;
import com.google.android.maps.MapActivity;

public class EarthquakeMap extends MapActivity {

  @Override
  public void onCreate(Bundle icicle) {
    super.onCreate(icicle);
    setContentView(R.layout.earthquake_map);
  }

  @Override
  protected boolean isRouteDisplayed() {
    return false;
  }

}
```

3. Update the application manifest to include your new `EarthquakeMap` Activity and import the map library.

```xml
<?xml version="1.0" encoding="utf-8"?>
<manifest xmlns:android="http://schemas.android.com/apk/res/android"
  package="com.paad.earthquake">
  <application android:icon="@drawable/icon">
    <activity
      android:name=".Earthquake"
      android:label="@string/app_name">
      <intent-filter>
        <action android:name="android.intent.action.MAIN" />
        <category android:name="android.intent.category.LAUNCHER" />
      </intent-filter>
    </activity>
    <activity android:name=".Preferences"
              android:label="Earthquake Preferences"/>
    <activity android:name=".EarthquakeMap"
              android:label="View Earthquakes"/>
    <provider android:name=".EarthquakeProvider"
              android:authorities="com.paad.provider.earthquake" />
    <uses-library android:name="com.google.android.maps"/>
  </application>
  <uses-permission android:name="android.permission.INTERNET"/>
</manifest>
```

4. Add a new menu option to the Earthquake Activity to display the EarthquakeMap Activity.

4.1. Start by adding a new string to the strings.xml resource for the menu text.

```xml
<?xml version="1.0" encoding="utf-8"?>
<resources>
  <string name="app_name">Earthquake</string>
  <string name="quake_feed">
    http://earthquake.usgs.gov/eqcenter/catalogs/1day-M2.5.xml
  </string>
  <string name="menu_update">Refresh Earthquakes</string>
  <string name="auto_update_prompt">Auto Update?</string>
  <string name="update_freq_prompt">Update Frequency</string>
  <string name="min_quake_mag_prompt">Minimum Quake Magnitude</string>
  <string name="menu_preferences">Preferences</string>
  <string name="menu_earthquake_map">Earthquake Map</string>
</resources>
```

4.2. Then add a new menu identifier before modifying the `onCreateOptionsMenu` handler to add the new Menu Item. It should use the text defined in Step 4.1, and when selected, it should fire an Intent to explicitly start the `EarthquakeMap` Activity.

```java
static final private int MENU_EARTHQUAKE_MAP = Menu.FIRST+2;

@Override
public boolean onCreateOptionsMenu(Menu menu) {
  super.onCreateOptionsMenu(menu);

  menu.add(0, MENU_UPDATE, Menu.NONE, R.string.menu_update);
  menu.add(0, MENU_PREFERENCES, Menu.NONE, R.string.menu_preferences);
```

```
        Intent startMap = new Intent(this, EarthquakeMap.class);
        menu.add(0, MENU_EARTHQUAKE_MAP,
                    Menu.NONE,
                    R.string.menu_earthquake_map).setIntent(startMap);
    return true;
}
```

5. Now create a new `EarthquakeOverlay` class that extends `Overlay`. It will draw the position and magnitude of each earthquake on the Map View.

```java
package com.paad.earthquake;

import java.util.ArrayList;
import android.database.Cursor;
import android.database.DataSetObserver;
import android.graphics.Canvas;
import android.graphics.Paint;
import android.graphics.Point;
import android.graphics.RectF;
import com.google.android.maps.GeoPoint;
import com.google.android.maps.MapView;
import com.google.android.maps.Overlay;
import com.google.android.maps.Projection;

public class EarthquakeOverlay extends Overlay {

  @Override
  public void draw(Canvas canvas, MapView mapView, boolean shadow) {
    Projection projection = mapView.getProjection();

    if (shadow == false) {
     // TODO: Draw earthquakes
    }
  }
}
```

   5.1. Add a new constructor that accepts a `Cursor` to the current earthquake data, and store that Cursor as an instance variable.

```java
Cursor earthquakes;

public EarthquakeOverlay(Cursor cursor, ContentResolver resolver) {
  super();

  earthquakes = cursor;
}
```

   5.2. Create a new `refreshQuakeLocations` method that iterates over the results Cursor and extracts the location of each earthquake, extracting the latitude and longitude before storing each coordinate in a List of `GeoPoint`s.

```java
ArrayList<GeoPoint> quakeLocations;

private void refreshQuakeLocations() {
  if (earthquakes.moveToFirst())
```

```
    do {
      Double lat;
      lat = earthquakes.getFloat(EarthquakeProvider.LATITUDE_COLUMN) * 1E6;
      Double lng;
      lng = earthquakes.getFloat(EarthquakeProvider.LONGITUDE_COLUMN) * 1E6;

      GeoPoint geoPoint = new GeoPoint(lng.intValue(), lat.intValue());

      quakeLocations.add(geoPoint);

    } while(earthquakes.moveToNext());
}
```

5.3. Call `refreshQuakeLocations` from the Overlay's constructor. Also register a `DataSetObserver` on the results Cursor that refreshes the Earthquake Location list if a change in the Earthquake Cursor is detected.

```
public EarthquakeOverlay(Cursor cursor) {
  super();
  earthquakes = cursor;

    quakeLocations = new ArrayList<GeoPoint>();
    refreshQuakeLocations();
    earthquakes.registerDataSetObserver(new DataSetObserver() {
      @Override
      public void onChanged() {
        refreshQuakeLocations();
      }
    });
}
```

5.4. Complete the `EarthquakeOverlay` by overriding the `draw` method to iterate over the list of `GeoPoints`, drawing a marker at each earthquake location. In this example, a simple red circle is drawn, but it could easily be modified to include additional information, such as by adjusting the size of each circle based on the magnitude of the quake.

```
int rad = 5;

@Override
public void draw(Canvas canvas, MapView mapView, boolean shadow) {
    Projection projection = mapView.getProjection();

    // Create and setup your paint brush
    Paint paint = new Paint();
    paint.setARGB(250, 255, 0, 0);
    paint.setAntiAlias(true);
    paint.setFakeBoldText(true);

    if (shadow == false) {
      for (GeoPoint point : quakeLocations) {

        Point myPoint = new Point();
        projection.toPixels(point, myPoint);
```

```
              RectF oval = new RectF(myPoint.x-rad, myPoint.y-rad,
                                 myPoint.x+rad, myPoint.y+rad);

              canvas.drawOval(oval, paint);
          }
       }
     }
```

6.   Return to the `EarthquakeMap` class. Within the `onCreate` method, create a Cursor that returns the earthquakes you want to display on the map. Use this Cursor to create a new `EarthquakeOverlay` before adding the new instance to the Map View's list of overlays.

```
Cursor earthquakeCursor;

@Override
  public void onCreate(Bundle icicle) {
      super.onCreate(icicle);
      setContentView(R.layout.earthquake_map);

String earthquakeURI = EarthquakeProvider.CONTENT_URI;
      earthquakeCursor = getContentResolver().query(earthquakeURI,
                                         null, null, null, null);

      MapView earthquakeMap = (MapView)findViewById(R.id.map_view);
      EarthquakeOverlay eo = new EarthquakeOverlay(earthquakeCursor);
      earthquakeMap.getOverlays().add(eo);
  }
```

7.   Finally, override `onResume` to call `requery` on the Earthquake result set whenever this Activity becomes visible. Also, override `onPause` and `onDestroy` to optimize use of the Cursor resources.

```
@Override
public void onResume() {
    earthquakeCursor.requery();
    super.onResume();
}

@Override
public void onPause() {
    earthquakeCursor.deactivate();
    super.onPause();
}

@Override
public void onDestroy() {
    earthquakeCursor.close();
    super.onDestroy();
}
```

8.   If you run the application and select Earthquake Map from the main menu, your application should appear as shown in Figure 7-8.

Figure 7-8

Summary

Location-based services, the Geocoder, and MapViews are available to create intuitive, location-aware applications that feature geographical information.

This chapter introduced the Geocoder and showed how to perform forward and reverse geocoding lookups to translate between map coordinates and street addresses. You were introduced to location-based services, used to find the current geographical position of the device. You also used them to track movement and create proximity alerts.

Then you created interactive map applications. Using Overlays and Views, you annotated `MapViews` with 2D graphics, as well as markers in the form of `OverlayItems` and Views (including ViewGroups and layouts).

In Chapter 8, you'll learn how to work from the background. You'll be introduced to the Service component and learn how to move processing onto background threads. To interact with the user while hidden from view, you'll use Toasts to display transient messages and the Notification Manager to ring, vibrate, and flash the phone.

Working in the Background

Because of the limited screen size of most mobile devices, typically only one application is visible and active on a device at any given time. This offers a perfect environment for applications that run in the background without a User Interface — responding to events, polling for data, or updating Content Providers.

Android offers the `Service` class to create application components specifically to handle operations and functionality that should run silently, without a User Interface. Android accords Services a higher priority than inactive Activities, so they're less likely to be killed when the system requires resources. In fact, should the run time prematurely terminate a Service that's been started, it will be restarted as soon as sufficient resources are available. By using Services, you can ensure that your applications continue to run and respond to events, even when they're not in active use.

Services run without a dedicated GUI, but, like Activities and Broadcast Receivers, they still execute in the main thread of the application's process. To help keep your applications responsive, you'll learn to move time-consuming processes (like network lookups) into background threads.

Android offers several techniques for application components (particularly Services) to communicate with users without an Activity providing a direct User Interface. In this chapter, you'll learn how to use Notifications and Toasts to politely alert and update users, without interrupting the active application.

Toasts are a transient, non-modal Dialog-box mechanism used to display information to users without stealing focus from the active application. You'll learn to display Toasts from any application component to send unobtrusive on-screen messages to your users.

Where Toasts are silent and transient, *Notifications* represent a more robust mechanism for alerting users. For many users, when they're not actively using their mobile phones, they sit silent and unwatched in a pocket or on a desk until it rings, vibrates, or flashes. Should a user miss these alerts, status bar icons are used to indicate that an event has occurred. All of these attention-grabbing antics are available within Android as Notifications.

Alarms provide a mechanism for firing Intents at set times, outside the control of your application life cycle. You'll learn to use Alarms to start Services, open Activities, or broadcast Intents based on either the clock time or the time elapsed since device boot. An Alarm will fire even after its owner application has been closed, and can (if required) wake a device from sleep.

Introducing Services

Unlike Activities, which present a rich graphical interface to users, Services run in the background — updating your Content Providers, firing Intents, and triggering Notifications. They are the perfect way to perform regular processing or handle events even after your application's Activities are invisible, inactive, or have been closed.

With no visual interface, Services are started, stopped, and controlled from other application components including other Services, Activities, and Broadcast Receivers. If your application regularly, or continuously, performs actions that don't depend directly on user input, Services may be the answer.

Started Services receive higher priority than inactive or invisible Activities, making them less likely to be terminated by the run time's resource management. The only time Android will stop a Service prematurely is when it's the only way for a foreground Activity to gain required resources; if that happens, your Service will be restarted automatically when resources become available.

Applications that update regularly but only rarely or intermittently need user interaction are good candidates for implementation as Services. MP3 players and sports-score monitors are examples of applications that should continue to run and update without an interactive visual component (Activity) visible.

Further examples can be found within the software stack itself; Android implements several Services including the Location Manager, Media Controller, and the Notification Manager.

Creating and Controlling Services

Services are designed to run in the background, so they need to be started, stopped, and controlled by other application components.

In the following sections, you'll learn how to create a new Service, and how to start and stop it using Intents and the `startService` method. Later you'll learn how to bind a Service to an Activity, providing a richer interface for interactivity.

Creating a Service

To define a Service, create a new class that extends the `Service` base class. You'll need to override `onBind` and `onCreate`, as shown in the following skeleton class:

```
import android.app.Service;
import android.content.Intent;
import android.os.IBinder;

public class MyService extends Service {

  @Override
  public void onCreate() {
```

```
  // TODO: Actions to perform when service is created.
}

@Override
public IBinder onBind(Intent intent) {
  // TODO: Replace with service binding implementation.
  return null;
}
}
```

In most cases, you'll also want to override onStart. This is called whenever the Service is started with a call to startService, so it can be executed several times within the Service's lifetime. You should ensure that your Service accounts for this.

The snippet below shows the skeleton code for overriding the onStart method:

```
@Override
public void onStart(Intent intent, int startId) {
  // TODO: Actions to perform when service is started.
}
```

Once you've constructed a new Service, you have to register it in the application manifest.

Do this by including a service tag within the application node. You can use attributes on the service tag to enable or disable the Service and specify any permissions required to access it from other applications using a requires-permission flag.

Below is the service tag you'd add for the skeleton Service you created above:

```
<service android:enabled="true" android:name=".MyService"></service>
```

Starting, Controlling, and Interacting with a Service

To start a Service, call startService; you can either implicitly specify a Service to start using an action against which the Service is registered, or you can explicitly specify the Service using its class.

If the Service requires permissions that your application does not have, this call will throw a SecurityException. The snippet below demonstrates both techniques available for starting a Service:

```
// Implicitly start a Service
startService(new Intent(MyService.MY_ACTION));
// Explicitly start a Service
startService(new Intent(this, MyService.class));
```

To use this example, you would need to include a MY_ACTION property in the MyService class and use an Intent Filter to register it as a provider of MY_ACTION.

To stop a Service, use stopService, passing an Intent that defines the Service to stop. This next code snippet first starts and then stops a Service both explicitly and by using the component name returned when calling startService:

```
ComponentName service = startService(new Intent(this, BaseballWatch.class));
// Stop a service using the service name.
stopService(new Intent(this, service.getClass()));
```

```
// Stop a service explicitly.
try {
  Class serviceClass = Class.forName(service.getClassName());
  stopService(new Intent(this, serviceClass));
} catch (ClassNotFoundException e) {}
```

If `startService` is called on a Service that's already running, the Service's `onStart` method will be executed again. Calls to `startService` do not nest, so a single call to `stopService` will terminate it no matter how many times `startService` has been called.

An Earthquake Monitoring Service Example

In this chapter, you'll modify the Earthquake example you started in Chapter 5 (and continued to enhance in Chapters 6 and 7). In this example, you'll move the earthquake updating and processing functionality into a separate Service component.

Later in this chapter, you'll build additional functionality within this Service, starting by moving the network lookup and XML parsing to a background thread. Later, you'll use Toasts and Notifications to alert users of new earthquakes.

1. Start by creating a new `EarthquakeService` that extends `Service`.

```
package com.paad.earthquake;

import android.app.Service;
import android.content.Intent;
import android.os.IBinder;
import java.util.Timer;
import java.util.TimerTask;

public class EarthquakeService extends Service {

  @Override
  public void onStart(Intent intent, int startId) {
    // TODO: Actions to perform when service is started.
  }

  @Override
  public void onCreate() {
    // TODO: Initialize variables, get references to GUI objects
  }

  @Override
  public IBinder onBind(Intent intent) {
    return null;
  }
}
```

2. Add this new Service to the manifest by adding a new `service` tag within the `application` node.

```
<service android:enabled="true" android:name=".EarthquakeService"></service>
```

3. Move the `refreshEarthquakes` and `addNewQuake` methods out of the Earthquake Activity and into the `EarthquakeService`.

You'll need to remove the calls to `addQuakeToArray` and `loadQuakesFromProvider` (leave both of these methods in the Earthquake Activity because they're still required). In the `EarthquakeService` also remove all references to the earthquakes ArrayList.

```java
private void addNewQuake(Quake _quake) {
  ContentResolver cr = getContentResolver();
  // Construct a where clause to make sure we don't already have this
  // earthquake in the provider.
  String w = EarthquakeProvider.KEY_DATE + " = " + _quake.getDate().getTime();

  // If the earthquake is new, insert it into the provider.
  Cursor c = cr.query(EarthquakeProvider.CONTENT_URI, null, w, null, null);
  if (c.getCount()==0){
    ContentValues values = new ContentValues();

    values.put(EarthquakeProvider.KEY_DATE, _quake.getDate().getTime());
    values.put(EarthquakeProvider.KEY_DETAILS, _quake.getDetails());

    double lat = _quake.getLocation().getLatitude();
    double lng = _quake.getLocation().getLongitude();
    values.put(EarthquakeProvider.KEY_LOCATION_LAT, lat);
    values.put(EarthquakeProvider.KEY_LOCATION_LNG, lng);
    values.put(EarthquakeProvider.KEY_LINK, _quake.getLink());
    values.put(EarthquakeProvider.KEY_MAGNITUDE, _quake.getMagnitude());

    cr.insert(EarthquakeProvider.CONTENT_URI, values);
  }
  c.close();
}

private void refreshEarthquakes() {
  // Get the XML
  URL url;
  try {
    String quakeFeed = getString(R.string.quake_feed);
    url = new URL(quakeFeed);

    URLConnection connection;
    connection = url.openConnection();

    HttpURLConnection httpConnection = (HttpURLConnection)connection;
    int responseCode = httpConnection.getResponseCode();

    if (responseCode == HttpURLConnection.HTTP_OK) {
      InputStream in = httpConnection.getInputStream();

      DocumentBuilderFactory dbf = DocumentBuilderFactory.newInstance();
      DocumentBuilder db = dbf.newDocumentBuilder();

      // Parse the earthquake feed.
      Document dom = db.parse(in);
      Element docEle = dom.getDocumentElement();

      // Get a list of each earthquake entry.
      NodeList nl = docEle.getElementsByTagName("entry");
      if (nl != null && nl.getLength() > 0) {
```

```java
        for (int i = 0 ; i < nl.getLength(); i++) {
          Element entry = (Element)nl.item(i);
          Element title;
          title = (Element)entry.getElementsByTagName("title").item(0);
          Element g;
          g = (Element)entry.getElementsByTagName("georss:point").item(0);
          Element when;
          when = (Element)entry.getElementsByTagName("updated").item(0);
          Element link = (Element)entry.getElementsByTagName("link").item(0);

          String details = title.getFirstChild().getNodeValue();
          String hostname = "http://earthquake.usgs.gov";
          String linkString = hostname + link.getAttribute("href");

          String point = g.getFirstChild().getNodeValue();
          String dt = when.getFirstChild().getNodeValue();
          SimpleDateFormat sdf;
          sdf = new SimpleDateFormat("yyyy-MM-dd'T'hh:mm:ss'Z'");
          Date qdate = new GregorianCalendar(0,0,0).getTime();
          try {
            qdate = sdf.parse(dt);
          } catch (ParseException e) {
            e.printStackTrace();
          }

          String[] location = point.split(" ");
          Location l = new Location("dummyGPS");
          l.setLatitude(Double.parseDouble(location[0]));
          l.setLongitude(Double.parseDouble(location[1]));

          String magnitudeString = details.split(" ")[1];
          int end =  magnitudeString.length()-1;
          double magnitude;
          magnitude = Double.parseDouble(magnitudeString.substring(0, end));

          details = details.split(",")[1].trim();

          Quake quake = new Quake(qdate, details, l, magnitude, linkString);

          // Process a newly found earthquake
          addNewQuake(quake);
        }
      }
    }
  } catch (MalformedURLException e) {
    e.printStackTrace();
  } catch (IOException e) {
    e.printStackTrace();
  } catch (ParserConfigurationException e) {
    e.printStackTrace();
  } catch (SAXException e) {
    e.printStackTrace();
  }
  finally {
  }
}
```

4. Within the Earthquake Activity, create a new `refreshEarthquakes` method. It should explicitly start the `EarthquakeService`.

```
private void refreshEarthquakes() {
  startService(new Intent(this, EarthquakeService.class));
}
```

5. Return to the `EarthquakeService`. Override the `onStart` and `onCreate` methods to support a new Timer that will be used to update the earthquake list. Use the `SharedPreference` object created in Chapter 6 to determine if the earthquakes should be regularly updated.

```
private Timer updateTimer;
private float minimumMagnitude;

@Override
public void onStart(Intent intent, int startId) {
  // Retrieve the shared preferences
  SharedPreferences prefs = getSharedPreferences(Preferences.USER_PREFERENCE,
                                                 Activity.MODE_PRIVATE);

  int minMagIndex = prefs.getInt(Preferences.PREF_MIN_MAG, 0);
  if (minMagIndex < 0)
    minMagIndex = 0;

  int freqIndex = prefs.getInt(Preferences.PREF_UPDATE_FREQ, 0);
  if (freqIndex < 0)
    freqIndex = 0;

  boolean autoUpdate = prefs.getBoolean(Preferences.PREF_AUTO_UPDATE, false);

  Resources r = getResources();
  int[] minMagValues = r.getIntArray(R.array.magnitude);
  int[] freqValues = r.getIntArray(R.array.update_freq_values);

  minimumMagnitude = minMagValues[minMagIndex];
  int updateFreq = freqValues[freqIndex];

  updateTimer.cancel();
  if (autoUpdate) {
    updateTimer = new Timer("earthquakeUpdates");
    updateTimer.scheduleAtFixedRate(doRefresh, 0, updateFreq*60*1000);
  }
  else
    refreshEarthquakes();
};

private TimerTask doRefresh = new TimerTask() {
  public void run() {
    refreshEarthquakes();
  }
};

@Override
public void onCreate() {
  updateTimer = new Timer("earthquakeUpdates");
}
```

6. The `EarthquakeService` will now update the earthquake provider each time it is asked to refresh, as well as on an automated schedule (if one is specified). This information is not yet passed back to the Earthquake Activity's ListView or the EathquakeMap Activity.

To alert those components, and any other applications interested in earthquake data, modify the `EarthquakeService` to broadcast a new Intent whenever a new earthquake is added.

6.1. Modify the `addNewQuake` method to call a new `announceNewQuake` method.

```java
public static final String NEW_EARTHQUAKE_FOUND = "New_Earthquake_Found";

private void addNewQuake(Quake _quake) {
  ContentResolver cr = getContentResolver();
  // Construct a where clause to make sure we don't already have this
  // earthquake in the provider.
  String w = EarthquakeProvider.KEY_DATE +
          " = " + _quake.getDate().getTime();

  // If the earthquake is new, insert it into the provider.
  Cursor c = cr.query(EarthquakeProvider.CONTENT_URI, null, w, null, null);
  if (c.getCount()==0){
    ContentValues values = new ContentValues();

    values.put(EarthquakeProvider.KEY_DATE, _quake.getDate().getTime());
    values.put(EarthquakeProvider.KEY_DETAILS, _quake.getDetails());

    double lat = _quake.getLocation().getLatitude();
    double lng = _quake.getLocation().getLongitude();
    values.put(EarthquakeProvider.KEY_LOCATION_LAT, lat);
    values.put(EarthquakeProvider.KEY_LOCATION_LNG, lng);
    values.put(EarthquakeProvider.KEY_LINK, _quake.getLink());
    values.put(EarthquakeProvider.KEY_MAGNITUDE, _quake.getMagnitude());

    cr.insert(EarthquakeProvider.CONTENT_URI, values);
    announceNewQuake(_quake);
  }
  c.close();
}

private void announceNewQuake(Quake quake) {
}
```

6.2. Within `announceNewQuake`, broadcast a new Intent whenever a new earthquake is found.

```java
private void announceNewQuake(Quake quake) {
    Intent intent = new Intent(NEW_EARTHQUAKE_FOUND);
    intent.putExtra("date", quake.getDate().getTime());
    intent.putExtra("details", quake.getDetails());
    intent.putExtra("longitude", quake.getLocation().getLongitude());
    intent.putExtra("latitude", quake.getLocation().getLatitude());
    intent.putExtra("magnitude", quake.getMagnitude());

    sendBroadcast(intent);
}
```

7. That completes the `EarthquakeService` implementation. You still need to modify the two Activity components to listen for the Service Intent broadcasts and refresh their displays accordingly.

> **7.1.** Within the Earthquake Activity, create a new internal `EarthquakeReceiver` class that extends `BroadcastReceiver`. Override the `onReceive` method to call `loadFromProviders` to update the earthquake array and refresh the list.

```
public class EarthquakeReceiver extends BroadcastReceiver {

  @Override
  public void onReceive(Context context, Intent intent) {
    loadQuakesFromProvider();
  }
}
```

> **7.2.** Override the `onResume` method to register the new Receiver and update the LiveView contents when the Activity becomes active. Override `onPause` to unregister it when the Activity moves out of the foreground.

```
EarthquakeReceiver receiver;

@Override
public void onResume() {
  IntentFilter filter;
  filter = new IntentFilter(EarthquakeService.NEW_EARTHQUAKE_FOUND);
  receiver = new EarthquakeReceiver();
  registerReceiver(receiver, filter);

  loadQuakesFromProvider();
  super.onResume();
}

@Override
public void onPause() {
  unregisterReceiver(receiver);
  super.onPause();
}
```

> **7.3.** Do the same for the EarthquakeMap Activity, this time calling `requery` on the result Cursor before invalidating the MapView whenever the Intent is received.

```
EarthquakeReceiver receiver;

@Override
public void onResume() {
  earthquakeCursor.requery();

  IntentFilter filter;
  filter = new IntentFilter(EarthquakeService.NEW_EARTHQUAKE_FOUND);
  receiver = new EarthquakeReceiver();
  registerReceiver(receiver, filter);

  super.onResume();
```

```
  }

  @Override
  public void onPause() {
    earthquakeCursor.deactivate();
    super.onPause();
  }

  public class EarthquakeReceiver extends BroadcastReceiver {
    @Override
    public void onReceive(Context context, Intent intent) {
      earthquakeCursor.requery();
      MapView earthquakeMap = (MapView)findViewById(R.id.map_view);
      earthquakeMap.invalidate();
    }
  }
}
```

Now when the Earthquake Activity is launched, it will start the Earthquake Service. This Service will then continue to run, updating the earthquake Content Provider in the background, even after the Activity is suspended or closed.

> *You'll continue to upgrade and enhance the Earthquake Service throughout the chapter, first using Toasts and later Notifications.*

At this stage, the earthquake processing is done in a Service, but it's still being executed on the main thread. Later in this chapter, you'll learn how to move time-consuming operations onto background threads to improve performance and avoid "Application Unresponsive" messages.

Binding Activities to Services

When an Activity is bound to a Service, it maintains a reference to the Service instance itself, allowing you to make method calls on the running Service as you would any other instantiated class.

Binding is available for Activities that would benefit from a more detailed interface with a Service. To support binding for a Service, implement the onBind method as shown in the simple example below:

```
private final IBinder binder = new MyBinder();

@Override
public IBinder onBind(Intent intent) {
  return binder;
}

public class MyBinder extends Binder {
  MyService getService() {
    return MyService.this;
  }
}
```

The connection between the Service and Activity is represented as a ServiceConnection. You'll need to implement a new ServiceConnection, overriding the onServiceConnected and `onServiceDisconnected` methods to get a reference to the Service instance once a connection has been established.

```
// Reference to the service
private MyService serviceBinder;

// Handles the connection between the service and activity
private ServiceConnection mConnection = new ServiceConnection() {

  public void onServiceConnected(ComponentName className, IBinder service) {
    // Called when the connection is made.
    serviceBinder = ((MyService.MyBinder)service).getService();
  }

  public void onServiceDisconnected(ComponentName className) {
    // Received when the service unexpectedly disconnects.
    serviceBinder = null;
  }
};
```

To perform the binding, call `bindService`, passing in an Intent (either explicit or implicit) that selects the Service to bind to and an instance of your new `ServiceConnection` implementation, as shown in this skeleton code:

```
@Override
public void onCreate(Bundle icicle) {
  super.onCreate(icicle);

  // Bind to the service
  Intent bindIntent = new Intent(MyActivity.this, MyService.class);
  bindService(bindIntent, mConnection, Context.BIND_AUTO_CREATE);
}
```

Once the Service has been bound, all of its public methods and properties are available through the `serviceBinder` object obtained from the `onServiceConnected` handler.

Android applications do not (normally) share memory, but in some cases, your application may want to interact with (and bind to) Services running in different application processes.

You can communicate with a Service running in a different process using broadcast Intents or through the extras Bundle in the Intent used to start the Service. If you need a more tightly coupled connection, you can make a Service available for binding across application boundaries using AIDL. AIDL defines the Service's interface in terms of OS level primitives, allowing Android to transmit objects across process boundaries. AIDL definitions are covered in Chapter 11.

Using Background Worker Threads

To ensure that your applications remain responsive, it's good practice to move all slow, time-consuming operations off the main application thread and onto a child thread.

All Android application components — including Activities, Services, and Broadcast Receivers — run on the main application thread. As a result, time-consuming processing in any component will block all other components including Services and the visible Activity.

Using background threads is vital to avoid the "Application Unresponsive" Dialog box described in Chapter 2. Unresponsiveness is defined in Android as Activities that don't respond to an input event (such as a key press) within 5 seconds and Broadcast Receivers that don't complete their onReceive handlers within 10 seconds.

Not only do you want to avoid this scenario, you don't want to even get close. Use background threads for all time-consuming processing, including file operations, network lookups, database transactions, and complex calculations.

Creating New Threads

You can create and manage child threads using Android's Handler class and the threading classes available within java.lang.Thread. The following skeleton code shows how to move processing onto a child thread:

```
// This method is called on the main GUI thread.
private void mainProcessing() {
    // This moves the time consuming operation to a child thread.
    Thread thread = new Thread(null, doBackgroundThreadProcessing, "Background");
    thread.start();
}

// Runnable that executes the background processing method.
private Runnable doBackgroundThreadProcessing = new Runnable() {
    public void run() {
        backgroundThreadProcessing();
    }
};

// Method which does some processing in the background.
private void backgroundThreadProcessing() {
    [ ... Time consuming operations ... ]
}
```

Synchronizing Threads for GUI Operations

Whenever you're using background threads in a GUI environment, it's important to synchronize child threads with the main application (GUI) thread before creating or modifying graphical components.

The Handler class allows you to post methods onto the thread in which the Handler was created. Using the Handler class, you can post updates to the User Interface from a background thread using the Post method. The following example shows the outline for using the Handler to update the GUI thread:

```
// Initialize a handler on the main thread.
private Handler handler = new Handler();

private void mainProcessing() {
    Thread thread = new Thread(null, doBackgroundThreadProcessing, "Background");
```

```
    thread.start();
  }
  private Runnable doBackgroundThreadProcessing = new Runnable() {
    public void run() {
      backgroundThreadProcessing();
    }
  };

  // Method which does some processing in the background.
  private void backgroundThreadProcessing() {
    [ ... Time consuming operations ... ]
    handler.post(doUpdateGUI);
  }

  // Runnable that executes the update GUI method.
  private Runnable doUpdateGUI = new Runnable() {
    public void run() {
      updateGUI();
    }
  };

  private void updateGUI() {
    [ ... Open a dialog or modify a GUI element ... ]
  }
```

The `Handler` class lets you delay posts or execute them at a specific time, using the `postDelayed` and `postAtTime` methods, respectively.

In the specific case of actions that modify Views, the `UIThreadUtilities` class provides the `runOnUIThread` method, which lets you force a method to execute on the same thread as the specified View, Activity, or Dialog.

Within your application components, Notifications and Intents are always received and handled on the GUI thread. In all other cases, operations that explicitly interact with objects created on the GUI thread (such as Views) or that display messages (like Toasts) must be invoked on the main thread.

Moving the Earthquake Service to a Background Thread

The following example shows how to move the network lookup and XML processing done in the `EarthquakeService` onto a background thread:

1. Rename the `refreshEarthquakes` method to `doRefreshEarthquakes`.

```
private void doRefreshEarthquakes() {
  [ ... previous refreshEarthquakes method ... ]
}
```

2. Create a new `refreshEarthquakes` method. It should start a background thread that executes the newly named `doRefreshEarthquakes` method.

```
private void refreshEarthquakes() {
  Thread updateThread = new Thread(null, backgroundRefresh,
                                   "refresh_earthquake");
  updateThread.start();
```

```
}

        private Runnable backgroundRefresh = new Runnable() {
          public void run() {
              doRefreshEarthquakes();
          }
        };
```

Let's Make a Toast

Toasts are transient Dialog boxes that remain visible for only a few seconds before fading out. Toasts don't steal focus and are non-modal, so they don't interrupt the active application.

Toasts are perfect for informing your users of events without forcing them to open an Activity or read a Notification. They provide an ideal mechanism for alerting users to events occurring in background Services without interrupting foreground applications.

The `Toast` class includes a static `makeText` method that creates a standard Toast display window. Pass the application Context, the text message to display, and the length of time to display it (`LENGTH_SHORT` or `LENGTH_LONG`) in to the `makeText` method to construct a new Toast. Once a Toast has been created, display it by calling `show`, as shown in the following snippet:

```
Context context = getApplicationContext();
String msg = "To health and happiness!";
int duration = Toast.LENGTH_SHORT;
Toast toast = Toast.makeText(context, msg, duration);
toast.show();
```

Figure 8-1 shows a Toast. It will remain on screen for around 2 seconds before fading out. The application behind it remains fully responsive and interactive while the Toast is visible.

Figure 8-1

Customizing Toasts

The standard Toast text message window is often sufficient, but in many situations you'll want to customize its appearance and screen position. You can modify a Toast by setting its display position and assigning it alternative Views or layouts.

The following snippet shows how to align a Toast to the bottom of the screen using the `setGravity` method:

```
Context context = getApplicationContext();
String msg = "To the bride an groom!";
int duration = Toast.LENGTH_SHORT;
Toast toast = Toast.makeText(context, msg, duration);
int offsetX = 0;
int offsetY = 0;
toast.setGravity(Gravity.BOTTOM, offsetX, offsetY);
toast.show();
```

When a text message just isn't going to get the job done, you can specify a custom View or layout to use a more complex, or more visual, display. Using `setView` on a Toast object, you can specify any View (including layouts) to display using the transient message window mechanism.

For example, the following snippet assigns a layout, containing the `CompassView` widget from Chapter 4 along with a `TextView`, to be displayed as a Toast.

```
Context context = getApplicationContext();
String msg = "Cheers!";
int duration = Toast.LENGTH_LONG;
Toast toast = Toast.makeText(context, msg, duration);
toast.setGravity(Gravity.TOP, 0, 0);

LinearLayout ll = new LinearLayout(context);
ll.setOrientation(LinearLayout.VERTICAL);

TextView myTextView = new TextView(context);
CompassView cv = new CompassView(context);

myTextView.setText(msg);

int lHeight = LinearLayout.LayoutParams.FILL_PARENT;
int lWidth = LinearLayout.LayoutParams.WRAP_CONTENT;

ll.addView(cv, new LinearLayout.LayoutParams(lHeight, lWidth));
ll.addView(myTextView, new LinearLayout.LayoutParams(lHeight, lWidth));

ll.setPadding(40, 50, 0, 50);

toast.setView(ll);
toast.show();
```

The resulting Toast will appear as shown in Figure 8-2.

Figure 8-2

Using Toasts in Worker Threads

As GUI components, Toasts must be opened on the GUI thread or risk throwing a cross thread exception. In the following example, a Handler is used to ensure that the Toast is opened on the GUI thread:

```
private void mainProcessing() {
  Thread thread = new Thread(null, doBackgroundThreadProcessing, "Background");
  thread.start();
}

private Runnable doBackgroundThreadProcessing = new Runnable() {
  public void run() {
    backgroundThreadProcessing();
  }
};

private void backgroundThreadProcessing() {
  handler.post(doUpdateGUI);
}

// Runnable that executes the update GUI method.
private Runnable doUpdateGUI = new Runnable() {
  public void run() {
    Context context = getApplicationContext();
    String msg = "To open mobile development!";
    int duration = Toast.LENGTH_SHORT;
    Toast.makeText(context, msg, duration).show();
  }
};
```

Introducing Notifications

Notifications are a way for your applications to alert users, without using an Activity. Notifications are handled by the Notification Manger, and currently include the ability to:

❏   Create a new status bar icon.

❏   Display additional information (and launch an Intent) in the extended status bar window.

❏   Flash the lights/LEDs.

❏   Vibrate the phone.

❏   Sound audible alerts (ringtones, media store sounds).

Notifications are the preferred way for invisible application components (Broadcast Receivers, Services, and inactive Activities) to alert users that events have occurred that require attention.

As a User Interface metaphor, Notifications are particularly well suited to mobile devices. It's likely that your users will have their phones with them at all times but quite unlikely that they will be paying attention to them, or your application, at any given time. Generally, users will have several applications open in the background, and they won't be paying attention to any of them.

In this environment, it's important that your applications be able to alert users when specific events occur that require their attention.

Notifications can be persisted through insistent repetition, or (more commonly) by using an icon on the status bar. Status bar icons can be updated regularly or expanded to show additional information using the expanded status bar window shown in Figure 8-3.

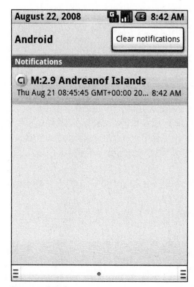

Figure 8-3

To display the expanded status bar view, click a status bar icon and drag it toward the bottom of the screen. To "lock" it in place, ensure that you release your drag only after the window covers the entire screen. To hide it, simply drag it back upward.

Introducing the Notification Manager

The *Notification Manager* is a system Service used to handle Notifications. Get a reference to it using the getSystemService method, as shown in the snippet below:

```
String svcName = Context.NOTIFICATION_SERVICE;

NotificationManager notificationManager;
notificationManager = (NotificationManager)getSystemService(svcName);
```

Using the Notification Manager, you can trigger new Notifications, modify existing ones, or remove those that are no longer needed or wanted.

Creating Notifications

Creating and configuring a new Notification is done in three parts.

Firstly, you create a new Notification object, passing in the icon to display in the status bar, along with the status bar ticker-text, and the time of this Notification, as shown in the following code snippet:

```
// Choose a drawable to display as the status bar icon
int icon = R.drawable.icon;
// Text to display in the status bar when the notification is launched
String tickerText = "Notification";
// The extended status bar orders notification in time order
long when = System.currentTimeMillis();
```

```
Notification notification = new Notification(icon, tickerText, when);
```

The ticker-text will scroll along the status bar when the Notification is fired.

Secondly, configure the appearance of the Notification within the extended status window using the setLatestEventInfo method. This extended status window displays the icon and time defined in the constructor and also shows a title and a details string. Notifications often represent a request for action or attention, so you can specify a PendingIntent that will be fired if a user clicks the Notification item.

The code snippet below uses setLatestEventInfo to set these values:

```
Context context = getApplicationContext();
// Text to display in the extended status window
String expandedText = "Extended status text";
// Title for the expanded status
String expandedTitle = "Notification Title";
// Intent to launch an activity when the extended text is clicked
Intent intent = new Intent(this, MyActivity.class);
PendingIntent launchIntent = PendingIntent.getActivity(context, 0, intent, 0);
```

```
notification.setLatestEventInfo(context,
```

```
                                 expandedTitle,
                                 expandedText,
                                 launchIntent);
```

It's good form to use one Notification icon to represent multiple instances of the same event (e.g., receiving multiple SMS messages). To demonstrate this to users, update the values set by setLatestEventInfo to reflect the most recent message and re-trigger the Notification to update its values.

You can also use the number property to display the number of events a status bar icon represents. Setting this value greater than 1, as shown below, overlays the values as a small number over the status bar icon:

```
notification.number++;
```

As with all changes to a Notification, you will need to re-trigger it to apply the change. To remove the overlay, set the number value to 0 or -1.

Finally, you can enhance Notifications using various properties on the Notification object to flash the device LEDs, vibrate the phone, and play audio files. These advanced features are detailed later in this chapter.

Triggering Notifications

To fire a Notification, pass it in to the notify method on the NotificationManager along with an integer reference ID, as shown in the following snippet:

```
int notificationRef = 1;
notificationManager.notify(notificationRef, notification);
```

To update a Notification that's already been fired, re-trigger, passing the same reference ID. You can pass in either the same Notification object or an entirely new one. As long as the ID values are the same, the new Notification will be used to replace the status icon and extended status window details.

You also use the reference ID to cancel Notifications by calling the cancel method on the Notification Manager, as shown below:

```
notificationManager.cancel(notificationRef);
```

Canceling a Notification removes its status bar icon and clears it from the extended status window.

Adding Notifications to the Earthquake Monitor

In the following example, the EarthquakeService is enhanced to trigger a Notification for each new earthquake. As well as displaying a status bar icon, the expanded Notification view will display the magnitude and location of the latest quake, and selecting it will open the Earthquake Activity.

1. Within the EarthquakeService, start by creating a new Notification instance variable to store the Notification object used to control the status bar icon and extended status window item details.

```
private Notification newEarthquakeNotification;
public static final int NOTIFICATION_ID = 1;
```

2. Extend the `onCreate` method to create this Notification object.

```
@Override
public void onCreate() {
  updateTimer = new Timer("earthquakeUpdates");

    int icon = R.drawable.icon;
    String tickerText = "New Earthquake Detected";
    long when = System.currentTimeMillis();

    newEarthquakeNotification= new Notification(icon, tickerText, when);
}
```

3. Now extend the `announceNewQuake` method to trigger the Notification after each new earthquake is added to the Content Provider. Before initiating the Notification, update the extended details using `setLatestEventInfo`.

```
private void announceNewQuake(Quake quake) {
    String svcName = Context.NOTIFICATION_SERVICE;
    NotificationManager notificationManager;
    notificationManager = (NotificationManager)getSystemService(svcName);

    Context context = getApplicationContext();
    String expandedText = quake.getDate().toString();
    String expandedTitle = "M:" + quake.getMagnitude() + " " +
                           quake.getDetails();
    Intent startActivityIntent = new Intent(this, Earthquake.class);
    PendingIntent launchIntent = PendingIntent.getActivity(context,
                                                  0,
                                                  startActivityIntent,
                                                  0);

    newEarthquakeNotification.setLatestEventInfo(context,
                                              expandedTitle,
                                              expandedText,
                                              launchIntent);
    newEarthquakeNotification.when = java.lang.System.currentTimeMillis();

    notificationManager.notify(NOTIFICATION_ID, newEarthquakeNotification);

    Intent intent = new Intent(NEW_EARTHQUAKE_FOUND);
    intent.putExtra("date", quake.getDate().getTime());
    intent.putExtra("details", quake.getDetails());
    intent.putExtra("longitude", quake.getLocation().getLongitude());
    intent.putExtra("latitude", quake.getLocation().getLatitude());
    intent.putExtra("magnitude", quake.getMagnitude());

    sendBroadcast(intent);
}
```

4. The final step is to clear and disable Notifications within the two Activity classes. This is done to dismiss the status icon when the application is active.

4.1. Starting with the Earthquake Activity, modify the `onCreate` method to get a reference to the Notification Manager.

```
NotificationManager notificationManager;

@Override
public void onCreate(Bundle icicle) {
  [ ... existing onCreate ... ]

  String svcName = Context.NOTIFICATION_SERVICE;
  notificationManager = (NotificationManager)getSystemService(svcName);
}
```

4.2. Modify the `onReceive` method of the `EarthquakeReceiver`. As this is only registered (so it will only execute) when the Activity is active, you can safely cancel all Notification earthquake Notifications here as soon as they're triggered.

```
@Override
public void onReceive(Context context, Intent intent) {
  loadQuakesFromProvider();

  notificationManager.cancel(EarthquakeService.NOTIFICATION_ID);
}
```

4.3. Next, extend the `onResume` method to cancel the Notification when the Activity becomes active.

```
@Override
public void onResume() {
  notificationManager.cancel(EarthquakeService.NOTIFICATION_ID);

  IntentFilter filter;
  filter = new IntentFilter(EarthquakeService.NEW_EARTHQUAKE_FOUND);
  receiver = new EarthquakeReceiver();
  registerReceiver(receiver, filter);
  super.onResume();
}
```

4.4. Repeat the same process with the `EarthquakeMap` Activity.

```
NotificationManager notificationManager;

@Override
public void onCreate(Bundle icicle) {
  super.onCreate(icicle);
  setContentView(R.layout.earthquake_map);

  ContentResolver cr = getContentResolver();
  earthquakeCursor = cr.query(EarthquakeProvider.CONTENT_URI,
                              null, null, null, null);

  MapView earthquakeMap = (MapView)findViewById(R.id.map_view);
  earthquakeMap.getOverlays().add(new EarthquakeOverlay(earthquakeCursor));

  String svcName = Context.NOTIFICATION_SERVICE;
  notificationManager = (NotificationManager)getSystemService(svcName);
```

```
      }

      @Override
      public void onResume() {
        notificationManager.cancel(EarthquakeService.NOTIFICATION_ID);

        earthquakeCursor.requery();

        IntentFilter filter;
        filter = new IntentFilter(EarthquakeService.NEW_EARTHQUAKE_FOUND);
        receiver = new EarthquakeReceiver();
        registerReceiver(receiver, filter);

        super.onResume();
      }

      public class EarthquakeReceiver extends BroadcastReceiver {
        @Override
        public void onReceive(Context context, Intent intent) {
          notificationManager.cancel(EarthquakeService.NOTIFICATION_ID);

          earthquakeCursor.requery();
          MapView earthquakeMap = (MapView)findViewById(R.id.map_view);
          earthquakeMap.invalidate();
        }
      }
```

Advanced Notification Techniques

In the following sections, you'll learn to enhance Notifications to provide additional alerting through hardware, in particular, by making the device ring, flash, and vibrate.

As each enhancement is described, you will be provided with a code snippet that can be added to the Earthquake example to provide user feedback on the severity of each earthquake as it's detected.

To use the Notification techniques described here without also displaying the status bar icon, simply cancel the Notification directly after triggering it. This stops the icon from displaying but doesn't interrupt the other effects.

Making Sounds

Using an audio alert to notify the user of a device event (like incoming calls) is a technique that predates the mobile, and has stood the test of time. Most native phone events from incoming calls to new messages and low battery are announced by an audible ringtone.

Android lets you play any audio file on the phone as a Notification by assigning a location URI to the sound property, as shown in the snippet below:

```
notification.sound = ringURI;
```

To use your own custom audio, push the file onto your device, or include it as a raw resource, as described in Chapter 6.

The following snippet can be added to the `announceNewQuake` method within the Earthquake Service from the earlier example. It adds an audio component to the earthquake Notification, ringing one of the default phone ringtones if a significant earthquake (one with magnitude greater than 6) occurs.

```
if (quake.getMagnitude() > 6) {
  Uri ringURI = Uri.fromFile(new File("/system/media/audio/ringtones/ringer.mp3"));
  newEarthquakeNotification.sound = ringURI;
}
```

Vibrating the Phone

You can use the phone's vibration function to execute a vibration pattern specific to your Notification. Android lets you control the pattern of a vibration; you can use vibration to convey information as well as get the user's attention.

To set a vibration pattern, assign an array of `longs` to the Notification's `vibrate` property. Construct the array so that every alternate number is the length of time (in milliseconds) to vibrate or pause, respectively.

Before you can use vibration in your application, you need to be granted permission. Add a `uses-permission` to your application to request access to the device vibration using the following code snippet:

```
<uses-permission android:name="android.permission.VIBRATE"/>
```

The following example shows how to modify a Notification to vibrate in a repeating pattern of 1 second on, 1 second off, for 5 seconds total.

```
long[] vibrate = new long[] { 1000, 1000, 1000, 1000, 1000 };
notification.vibrate = vibrate;
```

You can take advantage of this fine-grained control to pass information to your users. In the following update to the `announceNewQuake` method, the phone is set to vibrate in a pattern based on the power of the quake. Earthquakes are measured on an exponential scale, so you'll use the same scale when creating the vibration pattern.

For a barely perceptible magnitude 1 quake, the phone will vibrate for a fraction of a second; but for magnitude 10, an earthquake that would split the earth in two, your users will have a head start on the Apocalypse when their devices vibrate for a full 20 seconds. Most significant quakes fall between 3 and 7 on the Richter scale, so the more likely scenario is a more reasonable 200-millisecond to 4-second vibration duration range.

```
double vibrateLength = 100*Math.exp(0.53*quake.getMagnitude());
long[] vibrate = new long[] {100, 100, (long)vibrateLength };
newEarthquakeNotification.vibrate = vibrate;
```

The current Android Emulator does not visually or audibly indicate that the device is vibrating. To confirm that your Notification is behaving appropriately, you can monitor the log for "Vibration On"/"Vibration Off."

Flashing the Lights

Notifications also include properties to configure the color and flash frequency of the device's LED.

The `ledARGB` property can be used to set the LED's color, while the `ledOffMS` and `ledOnMS` properties let you set the frequency and pattern of the flashing LED. You can turn the LED on by setting the `ledOnMS` property to 1 and the `ledOffMS` property to 0, or turn it off by setting both properties to 0.

Once you have configured the LED settings, you must also add the `FLAG_SHOW_LIGHTS` flag to the Notification's `flags` property.

The following code snippet shows how to turn on the red device LED:

```
notification.ledARGB = Color.RED;
notification.ledOffMS = 0;
notification.ledOnMS = 1;
notification.flags = notification.flags | Notification.FLAG_SHOW_LIGHTS;
```

Controlling the color and flash frequency is another opportunity to pass additional information to users.

In the Earthquake monitoring example, you can help your users perceive the nuances of an exponential scale by also using the device's LED to help convey the magnitude. In the snippet below, the color of the LED depends on the size of the quake, and the frequency of the flashing is inversely related to the power of the quake:

```
int color;
if (quake.getMagnitude() < 5.4)
  color = Color.GREEN;
else if (quake.getMagnitude() < 6)
  color = Color.YELLOW;
else
  color = Color.RED;

newEarthquakeNotification.ledARGB = color;
newEarthquakeNotification.ledOffMS = (int)vibrateLength;
newEarthquakeNotification.ledOnMS = (int)vibrateLength;
newEarthquakeNotification.flags = newEarthquakeNotification.flags |
                       Notification.FLAG_SHOW_LIGHTS;
```

The current Android Emulator does not visually illustrate the LEDs. This makes it quite difficult to confirm that your LEDs are flashing correctly. In hardware, each device may have different limitations in regard to setting the color of the LED. In such cases, as close an approximation as possible will be used.

Ongoing and Insistent Notifications

Notifications can be configured as ongoing and/or insistent by setting the `FLAG_INSISTENT` and `FLAG_ONGOING_EVENT` flags.

Notifications flagged as ongoing, as in the snippet below, are used to represent events that are currently in progress (such as an incoming call). Ongoing events are separated from "normal" Notifications within the extended status bar window.

```
notification.flags = notification.flags | Notification.FLAG_ONGOING_EVENT;
```

Insistent Notifications repeat continuously until canceled. The code snippet below shows how to set a Notification as insistent:

```
notification.flags = notification.flags | Notification.FLAG_INSISTENT;
```

Insistent Notifications are handled by continuously repeating the initial Notification effects until the Notification is canceled. Insistent Notifications should be reserved for situations like Alarms, where timely and immediate response is required.

Using Alarms

Alarms are an application independent way of firing Intents at predetermined times.

Alarms are set outside the scope of your applications, so they can be used to trigger application events or actions even after your application has been closed. They can be particularly powerful in combination with Broadcast Receivers, allowing you to set Alarms that launch applications or perform actions without applications needing to be open and active until they're required.

For example, you can use Alarms to implement an alarm clock application, perform regular network lookups, or schedule time-consuming or cost-bound operations at "off peak" times.

> For timing operations that occur only during the lifetime of your applications, the Handler class in combination with Timers and Threads is a better approach as it allows Android better control over system resources.

Alarms in Android remain active while the device is in sleep mode and can optionally be set to wake the device; however, all Alarms are canceled whenever the device is rebooted.

Alarm operations are handled through the AlarmManager, a system Service accessed via getSystemService as shown below:

```
AlarmManager alarms = (AlarmManager)getSystemService(Context.ALARM_SERVICE);
```

To create a new Alarm, use the set method and specify an alarm type, trigger time, and a Pending Intent to fire when the Alarm triggers. If the Alarm you set occurs in the past, it will be triggered immediately.

There are four alarm types available. Your selection will determine if the time value passed in the set method represents a specific time or an elapsed wait:

❑ **RTC_WAKEUP** Wakes up the device to fire the Intent at the clock time specified when setting the Alarm.

❑ **RTC** Will fire the Intent at an explicit time, but will not wake the device.

❑ **ELAPSED_REALTIME** The Intent will be fired based on the amount of time elapsed since the device was booted, but will not wake the device. The elapsed time includes any period of time the device was asleep. Note that the time elapsed is since it was last booted.

❑ **ELAPSED_REALTIME_WAKEUP** Will wake up the device if necessary and fire the Intent after a specified length of time has passed since the device was booted.

The Alarm creation process is demonstrated in the snippet below:

```
int alarmType = AlarmManager.ELAPSED_REALTIME_WAKEUP;
long timeOrLengthofWait = 10000;
String ALARM_ACTION = "ALARM_ACTION";
Intent intentToFire = new Intent(ALARM_ACTION);
PendingIntent pendingIntent = PendingIntent.getBroadcast(this, 0, intentToFire, 0);

alarms.set(alarmType, timeOrLengthofWait, pendingIntent);
```

When the Alarm goes off, the Pending Intent you specified will be fired. Setting a second Alarm using the same Pending Intent replaces the preexisting Alarm.

To cancel an Alarm, call `cancel` on the Alarm Manager, passing in the Pending Intent you no longer wish to trigger, as shown in the snippet below:

```
alarms.cancel(pendingIntent);
```

In the following code snippet, two Alarms are set and the first one is subsequently canceled. The first is explicitly set to a specific time and will wake up the device in order to fire. The second is set for 30 minutes of time elapsed since the device was started, but will not wake the device if it's sleeping.

```
AlarmManager alarms = (AlarmManager)getSystemService(Context.ALARM_SERVICE);

String MY_RTC_ALARM = "MY_RTC_ALARM";
String ALARM_ACTION = "MY_ELAPSED_ALARM";

PendingIntent rtcIntent = PendingIntent.getBroadcast(this, 0,
                                               new Intent(MY_RTC_ALARM),
                                               1);
PendingIntent elapsedIntent = PendingIntent.getBroadcast(this, 0,
                                               new Intent(ALARM_ACTION),
                                               1);

// Wakeup and fire intent in 5 hours.
Date t = new Date();
t.setTime(java.lang.System.currentTimeMillis() + 60*1000*5);
alarms.set(AlarmManager.RTC_WAKEUP, t.getTime(), rtcIntent);

// Fire intent in 30 mins if already awake.
alarms.set(AlarmManager.ELAPSED_REALTIME, 30*60*1000, elapsedIntent);

// Cancel the first alarm.
alarms.cancel(rtcIntent);
```

Using Alarms to Update Earthquakes

In this final modification to the Earthquake example, you'll use Alarms to replace the Timer currently used to schedule Earthquake network refreshes.

1. Start by creating a new `EarthquakeAlarmReceiver` class that extends `BroadcastReceiver`.

```
package com.paad.earthquake;

import android.content.BroadcastReceiver;
import android.content.Context;
import android.content.Intent;

public class EarthquakeAlarmReceiver extends BroadcastReceiver {

}
```

2. Override the onReceive method to explicitly start the EarthquakeService.

```
@Override
public void onReceive(Context context, Intent intent) {
  Intent startIntent = new Intent(context, EarthquakeService.class);
  context.startService(startIntent);
}
```

3. Create a new public static String to define the action that will be used to trigger the Broadcast Receiver.

```
public static final String ACTION_REFRESH_EARTHQUAKE_ALARM =
                  "com.paad.earthquake.ACTION_REFRESH_EARTHQUAKE_ALARM";
```

4. Add the new EarthquakeAlarmReceiver to the manifest, including an intent-filter tag that listens for the action defined in Step 3.

```
<receiver android:name=".EarthquakeAlarmReceiver">
  <intent-filter>
    <action
      android:name="com.paad.earthquake.ACTION_REFRESH_EARTHQUAKE_ALARM"
    />
  </intent-filter>
</receiver>
```

5. Within the EarthquakeService, update the onCreate method to get a reference to the AlarmManager, and create a new PendingIntent that will be fired when the Alarm goes off. You can also remove the timerTask initialization.

```
AlarmManager alarms;
PendingIntent alarmIntent;

@Override
public void onCreate() {
  int icon = R.drawable.icon;
  String tickerText = "New Earthquake Detected";
  long when = System.currentTimeMillis();

  newEarthquakeNotification = new Notification(icon, tickerText, when);

  alarms = (AlarmManager)getSystemService(Context.ALARM_SERVICE);

  String ALARM_ACTION;
  ALARM_ACTION = EarthquakeAlarmReceiver.ACTION_REFRESH_EARTHQUAKE_ALARM;
  Intent intentToFire = new Intent(ALARM_ACTION);
```

```
        alarmIntent = PendingIntent.getBroadcast(this, 0, intentToFire, 0);
    }
```

6. Modify the `onStart` method to set an Alarm rather than use a Timer to schedule the next refresh (if automated updates are enabled). Setting a new Intent with the same action will automatically cancel the previous Alarm.

```
@Override
public void onStart(Intent intent, int startId) {
    SharedPreferences prefs = getSharedPreferences(Preferences.USER_PREFERENCE,
                                                    Activity.MODE_PRIVATE);

    int minMagIndex = prefs.getInt(Preferences.PREF_MIN_MAG, 0);
    if (minMagIndex < 0)
      minMagIndex = 0;

    int freqIndex = prefs.getInt(Preferences.PREF_UPDATE_FREQ, 0);
    if (freqIndex < 0)
      freqIndex = 0;

    boolean autoUpdate = prefs.getBoolean(Preferences.PREF_AUTO_UPDATE, false);

    Resources r = getResources();
    int[] minMagValues = r.getIntArray(R.array.magnitude);
    int[] freqValues = r.getIntArray(R.array.update_freq_values);

    minimumMagnitude = minMagValues[minMagIndex];
    int updateFreq = freqValues[freqIndex];

    if (autoUpdate) {
      int alarmType = AlarmManager.ELAPSED_REALTIME_WAKEUP;
      long timeToRefresh = SystemClock.elapsedRealtime() + updateFreq*60*1000;
      alarms.set(alarmType, timeToRefresh, alarmIntent);
    }
    else
      alarms.cancel(alarmIntent);

    refreshEarthquakes();
};
```

7. You can now remove the `updateTimer` instance variable and the TimerTask instance `doRefresh`.

Summary

Services are one of the most compelling reasons to develop applications on the Android platform. In this chapter, you learned how to use these invisible application components to perform processing while your applications are hidden in the background.

You were introduced to Toasts, a transient message box that lets you display information to users without stealing focus or interrupting their workflow.

You used the Notification Manager to send alerts to your users from within Services and Activities using customized LEDs, vibration patterns, and audio files to convey detailed event information.

Using Alarms, you were able to preset events and actions on the device using Intents to broadcast actions or start Activities or Services.

This chapter also demonstrated how to:

❑　Bind a Service to an Activity to make use of a more detailed, structured interface.

❑　Ensure that your applications remain responsive by moving time-consuming processing like network lookups onto worker threads.

❑　Use handlers to synchronize child threads with the main application GUI when performing operations using visual controls and Toasts.

❑　Create insistent and ongoing Notifications.

In Chapter 9, you'll be introduced to the communications features of Android. Starting with a look at the GTalk Service, you'll learn how to send and receive text and data messages to transmit data between devices. You'll then investigate the SMS functionality available for you to send and receive SMS text and data messages.

9

Peer-to-Peer Communication

In this chapter, you'll learn to use Android's peer-to-peer (P2P) text and data communication protocols, specifically, instant messaging and SMS (short messaging service). Using these technologies, you can create applications that can communicate between devices, including multiplayer games and collaborative mobile social applications.

When this chapter was originally written, the Android SDK included a comprehensive instant messaging (IM) service (powered by GTalk) that offered access to the instant messaging framework. This included the ability to send and receive text messages, set user status through presence, and determine the presence of IM contacts. Unfortunately, owing to security concerns the IM API has since been removed, though it's expected that later releases of Android will expose developer access to an IM framework. This chapter will show how earlier releases of Android allowed this technology to be used for sending text IM messages and as a mechanism for broadcasting Intents to remote Android devices — a mechanism that allowed you to create applications that interact between devices in real time.

Android still offers full access to SMS functionality, letting you send and receive SMS text messages within your applications. Using the Android APIs, you can create your own SMS client application to replace the native applications available as part of the software stack. Alternatively, you can incorporate the messaging functionality within your own applications.

At the end of this chapter, you'll use the SMS Manager in a detailed project that shows how to create an emergency SMS responder. In emergency situations, it will let users quickly, or automatically, respond to people asking after their safety.

Introducing Android Instant Messaging

> Largely as a result of security concerns, developer access to the GTalk IM Service has been restricted for Android SDK version 1.0. As a result, the functionality described in this section will not be available to developers using the first full release of the Android SDK.
>
> Rather than remove the affected sections, they have been left here in full as a guide for use with future Android releases.

Later releases of Android will expose a full suite of instant messaging functionality through an XMPP based IM Service. This will include management of contact rosters, presence notification, and the transmission and receipt of instant messages.

Google Talk (GTalk) is an instant messaging protocol for peer-to-peer (P2P) communication. Once connected, GTalk maintains a persistent socket connection with the GTalk server, meaning fast response times and low latency.

This section is based on an early SDK implementation that used GTalk. GTalk is based on the XMPP protocol, but it's a Google-specific variant that currently requires that users have a Gmail account.

What makes the GTalk Service particularly interesting for developers is the ability to broadcast Intents over the air (OTA) between Android devices using data messaging. Data messages received by a remote device are re-broadcast as Intents locally, meaning that this mechanism lets you broadcast an Intent on a remote device.

The GTalk Service can be used to create your own multi-user, social, or collaborative applications. It provides the framework for building a range of applications, including distributed emergency warning systems, dynamic route guidance applications, family social networks, and augmented reality gaming systems.

Android will eventually include all the interfaces needed to create a Google Talk Instant Messaging client, including full control over presence management and subscription handling. You can, if you're so inclined, build a replacement for the native client — or simply use the relevant components within your own applications.

Using the GTalk Service

Before you can access the GTalk Service, you need to import the `gtalkservice` library into your application with a `uses-library` tag inside the application node of the project manifest, as shown below:

```
<uses-library android:name="com.google.android.gtalkservice"/>
```

You also need to add the GTalk `uses-permission` tag, as shown in this XML snippet:

```
<uses-permission android:name="android.permission.GTALK"/>
```

Android Instant Messaging functionality is exposed through various interfaces as described below:

❑ `IGTalkService` Is used to create, access, and manage GTalk connections.

❑ `IGTalkConnection` A GTalk Connection represents a persistent socket connection between the device and the server it's connecting to. The GTalk Service creates a default connection upon start-up that you can access by calling `getDefaultConnection` on the GTalk Service object.

❑ `IImSession` Most instant messaging functionality is handled through the `IImSession` interface. It's used to retrieve the IM roster, set the user presence, obtain the presence of contacts, and manage chat sessions. Each GTalk Connection creates a default session, available through the `getDefaultSession` method.

❑ `IChatSession` All instant messaging chats are handled through the `IChatSession` interface. New Chat Sessions are created by initiating new chats, or joining existing ones, from an IM Session object. Using the Chat Session interface, you can send new chat messages, invite new participants to a group chat, and return a list of people involved in a chat.

❑ `IChatListener` Implement `IChatListener` to listen for messages in an IM Session or Chat Session. The `IChatListener` interface handlers listen for incoming messages, new chat participants, and people leaving a chat.

❑ `IGroupChatInvitationListener` Implement `IGroupChatInvitationListener` to listen for invitations to join group chats. The `onInvitationReceived` handler is passed a `GroupChatInvitation` that includes the username of the inviter, the room address, a "reason" (usually the room description), and the password you need in order to join the group chat.

❑ `IRosterListener` You can monitor your IM contacts roster, and the presence of the people on it, by implementing the `IRosterListener` interface. The Roster Listener includes event handlers that are fired when there are changes in a contact's presence as well as upon the addition and removal of contacts from the roster.

Binding to the GTalk Service

To use the GTalk Service, it must be bound to your application component using `bindService`.

The `bindService` method accepts two input parameters, an Intent, which specifies a component to bind to, and a `ServiceConnection` implementation. The following skeleton code demonstrates the pattern used to bind to the GTalk service:

```
IGTalkService gtalkService;

private void bindGTalk() {
    Intent i = new Intent();

    i.setComponent(GTalkServiceConstants.GTALK_SERVICE_COMPONENT);
    bindService(i, gTalkConnection, 0);
}

private ServiceConnection gTalkConnection = new ServiceConnection() {
```

```
      // When the service connects, get the default GTalk Session
      public void onServiceConnected(ComponentName className, IBinder service) {
        gtalkService = IGTalkService.Stub.asInterface(service);
      }

      // If the service disconnects
      public void onServiceDisconnected(ComponentName className) {
        gtalkService = null;
      }
    };
```

A bound GTalk Service represents a connection between your application and the GTalk Service APIs. Before you can use the Service to use Android's Instant Messaging functionality, you need to initiate a new `GTalkConnection`, as shown in the following section.

Making a GTalk Connection and Starting an IM Session

A GTalk Connection represents a conduit between the device and a GTalk server. An IM Session is the message pathway used to handle all the instant message traffic; all the instant messages for a given session flow through this pipe.

You can create several different connections and multiple IM Sessions connecting to different GTalk servers or IM providers.

Under normal circumstances, a device needs a single GTalk Connection supporting a single IM Session that uses the device owner's username. You can access the default connection and session using `getDefaultConnection` and `getDefaultSession` on the GTalk Service and default connection, respectively, as shown in the snippet below:

```
IGTalkConnection gTalkConnection = gtalkService.getDefaultConnection();
IImSession imSession = gTalkConnection.getDefaultImSession();
```

IM Sessions are used to send text and data messages, set user presence, manage the IM contact roster, and manage group chats.

The IM Session is your primary interface for handling instant messaging in Android applications. As a result, the following code snippet shows a more typical implementation of the `ServiceConnection` used to bind the GTalk Service to an application. It ensures that an IM Session object is always valid.

```
private IGTalkConnection gTalkConnection = null;
private IImSession imSession = null;

private ServiceConnection gTalkServiceConnection = new ServiceConnection() {

  // When the service connects, get the default GTalk session.
  public void onServiceConnected(ComponentName className, IBinder service) {
    IGTalkService gtalkService = IGTalkService.Stub.asInterface(service);
    try {
      gTalkConnection = gtalkService.getDefaultConnection();
      imSession = gTalkConnection.getDefaultImSession();
    } catch (RemoteException e) { }
```

```
    }

    // When the service disconnects, clear the GTalk session.
    public void onServiceDisconnected(ComponentName className) {
      gTalkConnection = null;
      imSession = null;
    }
  };
```

Introducing Presence and the Contact Roster

Presence is a lightweight mechanism used in instant messaging to broadcast a user's availability.

Originally, presence was represented as a simple flag that indicated when a user was logged on and available to chat. This has gradually evolved into a more detailed status indicator that lets users describe their availability more accurately by indicating if they're available, busy, away from the computer, or offline. The recent popularity of applications like FriendFeed and Twitter has resulted in presence being expanded to include custom messages that can describe anything from a user's current activity to the music they're listening to.

Users can see the presence of all the people in their contact roster. The *contact roster* is a list of all the contacts with whom a user has an agreement to exchange messages and share presence information.

When adding someone to their roster, users are implicitly subscribing to updates of that person's presence, and changes to their own presence are propagated to all the contacts on their roster.

Instant messaging is an inherently portable technology — a user's presence and contact roster are maintained by the GTalk server, so the roster on an Android device is synchronized with Gmail chat and any desktop IM clients.

Managing the Contact Roster

Developers can access the contact roster to determine the presence of any of a user's IM contacts, monitor presence updates, add new contacts, remove existing ones, and handle subscription requests.

Accessing the IM Contact Roster

When it's made available, the contact roster should be accessible through a native Content Provider using the helper class `android.provider.Im.Contacts`. You can query it as you would any other Content Provider.

In the following snippet, you can see how to iterate over the roster to find the presence of each IM contact:

```
Uri uri = android.provider.Im.Contacts.CONTENT_URI_CHAT_CONTACTS;
Cursor c = managedQuery(uri, null, null, null);
if (c.moveToFirst()) {
  do {
    String username = c.getString(c.getColumnIndexOrThrow(Contacts.USERNAME));
    int presence = c.getInt(c.getColumnIndexOrThrow(Contacts.PRESENCE_STATUS));

    if (presence == Contacts.AVAILABLE) {
```

```
      // TODO: Do something
    }

  } while (c.moveToNext());
}
```

Monitoring the Roster for Changes

To monitor the roster for changes and presence updates, implement an `IRosterListener` and register it with an IM Session using `addRemoteRosterListener`, as shown in the skeleton code below:

```
IRosterListener listener = new IRosterListener.Stub() {
    public void presenceChanged(String contact) throws RemoteException {
        // TODO Update the presence icon for the user.
    }

    public void rosterChanged() throws RemoteException {
        // TODO Update the roster UI.
    }

    public void selfPresenceChanged() throws RemoteException {
        // TODO Update the user's presence.
    }
};

try {
    imSession.addRemoteRosterListener(listener);
} catch (RemoteException e) { }
```

The Roster Listener includes event handlers that will be triggered when a contact has been added or removed from the current user's roster, when a contact's presence has changed, and if the user's presence has changed.

Adding Contacts to a Roster

To add a new contact to the user's roster, use `addContact`, specifying the contact username and a personal nickname to customize their entry on the roster, as shown below:

```
imSession.addContact("jim@dundermifflin.com", "Big Tuna", null);
```

The specified nickname is private and will only be visible to the device user.

People are only added to the roster after they've approved the request to become an instant messaging contact. After you attempt to add a contact, the target user receives an invitation (represented as a subscription request) that he or she can either approve or decline.

If the target user accepts the invitation, your user is placed in the target user's roster (and vice versa), and he or she will be able to exchange instant messages and receive presence updates.

Subscription requests are asynchronous, so you'll need to listen for changes in the roster to determine when a subscription request has been granted.

Handling Subscription Requests

Requests from others to add the device user to their contact lists should be presented to the user for his or her explicit approval or rejection.

Once the user has indicated his or her preference, you can approve or decline subscription requests using the `approveSubscriptionRequest` and `declineSubscriptionRequest` methods on an IM Session. As shown below, both methods take a contact name as a parameter; the `approve` method also accepts an optional nickname for the new contact being added.

```
imSession.approveSubscriptionRequest(sender, "nickname", null);
imSession.declineSubscriptionRequest(sender);
```

Removing and Blocking Contacts

In these times of fleeting attention and fickle friendships, there may come a time when a contact once added to a roster is no longer considered worthy of the honor. In extreme cases, users may choose to block all messages from a particular user.

Call `removeContact` from an IM Session to remove a contact from the user's roster and unsubscribe from his or her presence updates.

```
imSession.removeContact("whathaveyoudoneforme@lately.com");
```

When ignoring someone isn't enough, users can choose to block their messages entirely. The `blockContact` method effectively reverses the initial subscription-request approval and automatically denies any new subscription requests:

```
imSession.blockContact("ex@girlfriend.com");
```

Blocked contacts are added to the users "blocked list," which, like the roster itself, resides on the server. A contact blocked from Android will also be blocked in all other Google Talk clients.

Managing the User's Presence

The presence of the logged-in IM Session user is available using the `getPresence` method, as shown in the snippet below:

```
Presence p = imSession.getPresence();
```

This `Presence` object can be used to determine the user's IM visibility, his status, and any custom status message.

To change the user's presence, modify the `Presence` object and transmit it to the instant messaging server by calling `setPresence` on the IM Session.

The following code snippet shows how to set the user presence to DO_NOT_DISTURB and specifies a custom status message:

```
String customMessage = "Developing applications for Android. Professionally";
p.setStatus(Presence.Show.DND, customMessage);
imSession.setPresence(p);
```

Changes to a user's presence won't take effect until after they've been committed on the server. The best practice is to use a Roster Listener to react to the change in the user's presence once it's been applied on the server side.

Managing Chat Sessions

Chat Sessions are created within IM Sessions and are used to manage and participate in person-to-person chats and chat rooms. All text-based instant message chats are handled using the `IChatSession` interface, which offers methods for sending text or data messages and inviting new participants into a chat. You can attach a Chat Listener to a Chat Session to listen to the messages associated with it.

Handling Chat Sessions is particularly useful for integrating text messaging within your own applications. Using a Chat Session, you can create a chat room for multiplayer games, or integrate person-to-person messaging within a mobile social networking application.

Starting or Joining a Chat Session

A Chat Session represents the conduit through which all instant messaging communication with a target user passes, so you can only maintain a single Chat Session per contact per IM Session.

New Chat Sessions are created through an IM Session, using the `getChatSession` or `createChatSession` methods.

If a Chat Session already exists for a given contact, retrieve it by passing in the username of the person with whom you wish to converse, as shown in the following snippet. If there is no active Chat Session with the specified user, this method returns null.

```
IChatSession cs = imSession.getChatSession(targetContactEmailAddress);
```

If you haven't established a Chat Session with a particular user, create one using the `createChatSession` method, passing in the target contact's username. If the IM Session is unable to create a new Chat Session, this method will return null.

```
IChatSession chatSession = imSession.createChatSession(targetContactEmailAddress);
```

The following pattern checks to see if there is an existing Chat Session with a target user before creating a new one if necessary:

```
IChatSession chatSession = imSession.getChatSession(targetContactEmailAddress);
if (chatSession == null)
  chatSession = imSession.createChatSession(targetContactEmailAddress);
```

Group Chat Sessions are also represented using the `IChatSession` interface, but they're handled a little differently. Group chat functionality is explored in more detail later in this chapter.

Sending Instant Text Messages

Once you have an active Chat Session, use the `sendChatMessage` method to send messages to the contact(s) in that session, as shown in the following code snippet:

```
chatSession.sendChatMessage("Hello World!");
```

The message text specified will be transmitted to all the contacts involved in the current Chat Session.

Receiving Instant Text Messages

To listen for incoming messages, implement the `IChatListener` interface, overriding its `newMessageReceived` handler. You can register this interface with either a specific Chat Session or the more generic IM Session using the `addRemoteChatListener` method.

The following snippet shows the skeleton code for creating and registering a new Chat Listener interface for both a specific Chat Session and an IM Session. Note that the `IChatListener` interface includes a `Stub` class that you should extend when creating your own Chat Listener implementation.

```
IChatListener chatListener = new IChatListener.Stub() {

  public void newMessageReceived(String from, String body) {
    // TODO Handle incoming messages.
  }

  // Required group chat implementation stubs.
  public void convertedToGroupChat(String oldJid,
                                   String groupChatRoom,
                                   long groupId) {}
  public void participantJoined(String groupChatRoom, String nickname) {}
  public void participantLeft(String groupChatRoom, String nickname) {}
  public void chatClosed(String groupChatRoom) throws RemoteException {}
  public void chatRead(String arg0) throws RemoteException {}
};

  // Add Chat Listener to the chat session.
  chatSession.addRemoteChatListener(chatListener);

  // Add Chat Listener to the instant messaging session.
  imSession.addRemoteChatListener(chatListener);
```

Chat Listeners registered with an IM Session receive every message received by any Chat Session associated with that session, so the message handling here should be fairly generic. In contrast, listeners registered to a single Chat Session are only notified of messages and events relevant to that specific session.

Chat Rooms and Group Chats

Chat rooms are an excellent way to encourage a sense of community within a collaborative or multi-user application.

The GTalk Service supports chat rooms and group chats. They are managed using the same `IChatSession` interface used for simple P2P Chat Sessions.

To create a new chat room, use the `createGroupChatSession` method on an IM Session, passing in a nickname for the room and a list of users to invite, as shown in the following snippet:

```
String nickname = "Android Development";
String[] contacts = { "bill", "fred" };
imSession.createGroupChatSession(nickname, contacts);
```

Alternatively, you may want to join group chats that others have invited you to. Use the `IGroupChatInvitationListener` interface to listen for group chat invitations. Each invitation includes the address and password needed to join an existing chat room.

To join an existing chat room, use the `joinGroupChatSession` method from an active IM Session, passing in the address of the room you want to join, a nickname for you to identify it, and the password required to join, as shown in the following snippet:

```
imSession.joinGroupChatSession(address, nickname, password);
```

The following skeleton code shows how to register a Group Chat Invitation Listener on an active IM Session to listen for, and accept, invitations to join chat rooms.

```
IGroupChatInvitationListener listener = new IGroupChatInvitationListener.Stub() {
  public boolean onInvitationReceived(GroupChatInvitation _invite)
  throws RemoteException {
    String address = _invite.getRoomAddress();
    String password = _invite.getPassword();
    String nickname = _invite.getInviter();
    imSession.joinGroupChatSession(address, nickname, password);
    return true;
  }
};

try {
  imSession.addGroupChatInvitationListener(listener);
} catch (RemoteException e) { }
```

Managing Group Chat Sessions

You can get a list of participants in a Chat Session using the `getParticipants` method. You can also send text or data messages to each chat member as you would in a normal chat, as well as invite new members using `inviteContact`. The `leave` method lets you exit a chat room and end the session.

As with normal chats, you can listen to chat room messages by implementing and registering an `IChatListener`. As well as listening for chat messages, you can react to people joining or leaving the room.

The following skeleton code shows the implementation of a Chat Listener highlighting the group chat event handlers:

```
IChatListener groupChatListener = new IChatListener.Stub() {
  // Fired when a one-to-one chat becomes a group chat.
  public void convertedToGroupChat(String oldJid,
                                   String groupChatRoom,
                                   long groupId) throws RemoteException {
    // TODO Notify user that the conversation is now a group chat.
  }

  // Fired when a new person joins a chat room.
  public void participantJoined(String groupChatRoom, String nickname)
    throws RemoteException {
```

```
        // TODO Notify user that a new participant has joined the conversation.
    }

    // Fired when a participant leaves a chat room.
    public void participantLeft(String groupChatRoom, String nickname)
        throws RemoteException {
        // TODO Notify user a chat participant left.
    }

    // Fired when the group chat is closed
    public void chatClosed(String groupChatRoom) throws RemoteException {
        // TODO Close the chat.
    }

    public void chatRead(String arg0) throws RemoteException { }

    public void newMessageReceived(String from, String body) { }
};
```

Sending and Receiving Data Messages

The GTalk Service includes functionality to transmit data messages between applications running on different devices. These data messages are handled separately from normal text chat messages and are invisible to users.

> **The functionality described in this section was removed prior to the version 1.0 release of the Android SDK. This is largely because of the security implications associated with the ability to remotely execute code on a target device. It is expected that this API will be exposed for developer access in future releases of Android, although it may differ from the implementation described here.**

GTalk data messages are a mechanism that lets you broadcast Intents over the air (OTA) to remote user devices. On the target device, the GTalk Service extracts the Intent from the received message and re-broadcasts it locally, where it's handled by the Intent resolution mechanism in the same way as locally broadcast Intents. The process is illustrated in Figure 9-1.

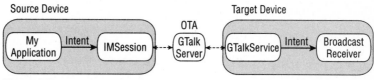

Figure 9-1

The result is an interface for broadcasting Intents on remote devices using instant messenger contacts. The broadcast Intent will be received by any Broadcast Receiver registered for the action represented by the Intent.

By extending the reach of your applications beyond the scope of the device on which they're running, you take on additional responsibilities to ensure that your applications are well behaved, and to take all possible precautions to ensure that your applications aren't open to exploitation by those looking to use this mechanism maliciously.

Data messages are an excellent way to support multi-user applications on distributed mobile devices, thanks to the low latency and rapid response times provided by the instant messaging architecture.

Transmitting Data Messages

The best practice is to create custom actions to use when broadcasting an Intent to a remote device, such as the one shown in the snippet below:

```
public static final String ACTION_OTA_ELIMINATE = "com.paad.ota_eliminate_action";
```

The next snippet shows how to create a simple Intent that will be packaged within a data message to transmit the above action to a remote device:

```
Intent intent = new Intent(ACTION_OTA_ELIMINATE);
```

As with normal broadcast Intents, you can package additional information within the Intent using the extras Bundle. These extras will be included in the Intent when it's re-broadcast on the remote device.

```
intent.putExtra("long", String.valueOf(location.getLatitude()));
intent.putExtra("lat", String.valueOf(location.getLatitude()));
intent.putExtra("target", "Sarah Conner");
intent.putExtra("sender", gTalk.getUsername());
```

Only String extras are currently supported in the OTA Intent broadcast mechanism. Non-string extras will be disregarded before transmission and won't be available on the target device.

Send the message using the `sendDataMessage` method, passing in the target username and the Intent to broadcast. The `sendDataMessage` is available on IM Session or Chat Session objects, as shown below:

```
String username = "T1000@sky.net";

// Send to target user.
imSession.sendDataMessage(username, intent);

// Send to all chat room participants.
chatSession.sendDataMessage(intent);
```

Receiving Data Messages

To listen for data messages, register a Broadcast Receiver that filters on the action String included in a transmitted Intent.

GTalk data messages are processed as normal broadcast Intents, so they have no sender information associated when they're received by a Broadcast Receiver. If you require such metadata, you should include them in the extras Bundle of the source Intent as was done in the code shown in the previous section.

The following skeleton code shows how to register a simple Broadcast Receiver implementation that can handle the Intent transmitted in the previous example:

```
BroadcastReceiver otaGTalkIntentReceiver = new BroadcastReceiver() {
  @Override
  public void onReceive(Context _context, Intent _intent) {
    if (_intent.getAction().equals(ACTION_OTA_ELIMINATE)) {
      String sender = _intent.getStringExtra("sender");
      String target = _intent.getStringExtra("target");

      String lat = _intent.getStringExtra("lat");
      String lng = _intent.getStringExtra("long");
      Location location = new Location(LocationManager.GPS_PROVIDER);
      location.setLatitude(Double.parseDouble(lat));
      location.setLongitude(Double.parseDouble(lng));

      // TODO: Do something with the data transmitted.
    }
  }
};

IntentFilter filter = new IntentFilter(ACTION_OTA_ELIMINATE);
registerReceiver(otaGTalkIntentReceiver, filter);
```

Introducing SMS

If you own a mobile phone that's less than two decades old, chances are you're familiar with SMS messaging. SMS (short messaging service) is now one of the most-used features on mobile phones, with many people favoring it over making phone calls.

SMS technology is designed to send short text messages between mobile phones. It provides support for sending both text messages (designed to be read by people) and data messages (meant to be consumed by applications).

As a mature mobile technology, there's a lot of information out there that describes the technical details of how an SMS message is constructed and transmitted over the air. Rather than rehash that here, the following sections focus on the practicalities of sending and receiving text and data messages within Android.

Using SMS in Your Application

Android offers full access to SMS functionality from within your applications with the SMSManager. Using the SMS Manager, you can replace the native SMS application or create new applications that send text messages, react to incoming texts, or use SMS as a data transport layer.

> SMS message delivery is not timely, so SMS is not really suitable for anything that requires real-time responsiveness. That said, the widespread adoption and resiliency of SMS networks make it a particularly good tool for delivering content to non-Android users and reducing the dependency on third-party servers.

As a ubiquitous technology, SMS offers a mechanism you can use to send text messages to other mobile phone users, irrespective of whether they have Android phones.

Compared to the instant messaging mechanism available through the GTalk Service, using SMS to pass data messages between applications is slow, possibly expensive, and suffers from high latency. On the other hand, SMS is supported by almost every phone on the planet, so where latency is not an issue, and updates are infrequent, SMS data messages are an excellent alternative.

Sending SMS Messages

SMS messaging in Android is handled by the `SmsManager`. You can get a reference to the SMS Manager using the static method `SmsManger.getDefault`, as shown in the snippet below.

```
SmsManager smsManager = SmsManager.getDefault();
```

To send SMS messages, your applications require the `SEND_SMS` permission. To request this permission, add it to the manifest using a `uses-permission` tag, as shown below:

```
<uses-permission android:name="android.permission.SEND_SMS"/>
```

Sending Text Messages

To send a text message, use `sendTextMessage` from the SMS Manager, passing in the address (phone number) of your recipient and the text message you want to send, as shown in the snippet below:

```
String sendTo = "5551234";
String myMessage = "Android supports programmatic SMS messaging!";

smsManager.sendTextMessage(sendTo, null, myMessage, null, null);
```

The second parameter can be used to specify the SMS service center to use; entering null as shown in the previous snippet uses the default service center for your carrier.

The final two parameters let you specify Intents to track the transmission and successful delivery of your messages.

To react to these Intents, create and register Broadcast Receivers as shown in the next section.

Tracking and Confirming SMS Message Delivery

To track the transmission and delivery success of your outgoing SMS messages, implement and register Broadcast Receivers that listen for the actions you specify when creating the Pending Intents you pass in to the `sendTextMessage` method.

The first Pending Intent parameter, `sentIntent`, is fired when the message is either successfully sent or fails to send. The result code for the Broadcast Receiver that receives this Intent will be one of:

❑   `Activity.RESULT_OK`   To indicate a successful transmission.

❑   `SmsManager.RESULT_ERROR_GENERIC_FAILURE`   To indicate a nonspecific failure.

❑   `SmsManager.RESULT_ERROR_RADIO_OFF`   When the connection radio is turned off.

❑   `SmsManager.RESULT_ERROR_NULL_PDU`   To indicate a PDU failure.

The second Pending Intent parameter, `deliveryIntent`, is fired only after the destination recipient receives your SMS message.

The following code snippet shows a typical pattern for sending an SMS and monitoring the success of its transmission and delivery:

```
String SENT_SMS_ACTION = "SENT_SMS_ACTION";
String DELIVERED_SMS_ACTION = "DELIVERED_SMS_ACTION";

// Create the sentIntent parameter
Intent sentIntent = new Intent(SENT_SMS_ACTION);
PendingIntent sentPI = PendingIntent.getBroadcast(getApplicationContext(),
                                        0,
                                        sentIntent,
                                        0);

// Create the deliveryIntent parameter
Intent deliveryIntent = new Intent(DELIVERED_SMS_ACTION);
PendingIntent deliverPI = PendingIntent.getBroadcast(getApplicationContext(),
                                        0,
                                        deliveryIntent,
                                        0);

// Register the Broadcast Receivers
registerReceiver(new BroadcastReceiver() {
                @Override
                public void onReceive(Context _context, Intent _intent) {
                  switch (getResultCode()) {
                    case Activity.RESULT_OK:
                      [… send success actions … ]; break;
                    case SmsManager.RESULT_ERROR_GENERIC_FAILURE:
                      [… generic failure actions … ]; break;
                    case SmsManager.RESULT_ERROR_RADIO_OFF:
                      [… radio off failure actions … ]; break;
                    case SmsManager.RESULT_ERROR_NULL_PDU:
                      [… null PDU failure actions … ]; break;
                  }
                }
              },
              new IntentFilter(SENT_SMS_ACTION));

registerReceiver(new BroadcastReceiver() {
                @Override
                public void onReceive(Context _context, Intent _intent) {
                  [… SMS delivered actions … ]
                }
              },
              new IntentFilter(DELIVERED_SMS_ACTION));

// Send the message
smsManager.sendTextMessage(sendTo, null, myMessage, sentPI, deliverPI);
```

Monitoring Outgoing SMS Messages

The Android debugging bridge supports sending SMS messages between multiple emulator instances. To send an SMS from one emulator to another, specify the port number of the target emulator as the "to" address when sending a new message.

Android will automatically route your message to the target emulator instance, where it'll be handled as a normal SMS.

Conforming to the Maximum SMS Message Size

SMS text messages are normally limited to 160 characters, so longer messages need to be broken into a series of smaller parts. The SMS Manager includes the `divideMessage` method, which accepts a string as an input and breaks it into an ArrayList of messages wherein each is less than the allowable size. Use `sendMultipartTextMessage` to transmit the array of messages, as shown in the snippet below:

```
ArrayList<String> messageArray = smsManager.divideMessage(myMessage);
ArrayList<PendingIntent> sentIntents = new ArrayList<PendingIntent>();
for (int i = 0; i < messageArray.size(); i++)
   sentIntents.add(sentPI);

smsManager.sendMultipartTextMessage(sendTo,
                                    null,
                                    messageArray,
                                    sentIntents, null);
```

The `sentIntent` and `deliveryIntent` parameters in the `sendMultipartTextMessage` method are ArrayLists that can be used to specify different Pending Intents to fire for each message part.

Sending Data Messages

You can send binary data via SMS using the `sendDataMessage` method on an SMS Manager. The `sendDataMessage` method works much like `sendTextMessage`, but includes additional parameters for the destination port and an array of bytes that constitute the data you want to send.

The following skeleton code shows the basic structure of sending a data message:

```
Intent sentIntent = new Intent(SENT_SMS_ACTION);
PendingIntent sentPI = PendingIntent.getBroadcast(getApplicationContext(),
                                                  0,
                                                  sentIntent,
                                                  0);

short destinationPort = 80;
byte[] data = [ … your data … ];
smsManager.sendDataMessage(sendTo, null, destinationPort, data, sentPI, null);
```

Listening for SMS Messages

When a new SMS message is received by the device, a new broadcast Intent is fired with the `android.provider.Telephony.SMS_RECEIVED` action. Note that this is a String literal, SDK 1.0 does not include a reference to this string so you must specify it explicitly when using it in your applications.

For an application to listen for SMS Intent broadcasts, it first needs to be have the RECEIVE_SMS permission granted. Request this permission by adding a uses-permission tag to the application manifest, as shown in the following snippet:

```
<uses-permission
  android:name="android.permission.RECEIVE_SMS"/>
```

The SMS broadcast Intent includes the incoming SMS details. To extract the array of SmsMessage objects packaged within the SMS broadcast Intent bundle, use the pdu key to extract an array of SMS pdus, each of which represents an SMS message. To convert each pdu byte array into an SMS Message object, call SmsMessage.createFromPdu, passing in each byte array as shown in the snippet below:

```
Bundle bundle = intent.getExtras();
if (bundle != null) {
  Object[] pdus = (Object[]) bundle.get("pdus");
  SmsMessage[] messages = new SmsMessage[pdus.length];
  for (int i = 0; i < pdus.length; i++)
    messages[i] = SmsMessage.createFromPdu((byte[]) pdus[i]);
}
```

Each SmsMessage object contains the SMS message details, including the originating address (phone number), time stamp, and the message body.

The following example shows a Broadcast Receiver implementation whose onReceive handler checks incoming SMS texts that start with the string @echo, and then sends the same text back to the phone that sent it:

```
public class IncomingSMSReceiver extends BroadcastReceiver {
  private static final String queryString = "@echo ";
  private static final String SMS_RECEIVED = "android.provider.Telephony.SMS_RECEIVED";

  public void onReceive(Context _context, Intent _intent) {
    if (_intent.getAction().equals(SMS_RECEIVED)) {
      SmsManager sms = SmsManager.getDefault();

      Bundle bundle = _intent.getExtras();
      if (bundle != null) {
        Object[] pdus = (Object[]) bundle.get("pdus");
        SmsMessage[] messages = new SmsMessage[pdus.length];
        for (int i = 0; i < pdus.length; i++)
          messages[i] = SmsMessage.createFromPdu((byte[]) pdus[i]);

        for (SmsMessage message : messages) {
          String msg = message.getMessageBody();
          String to = message.getOriginatingAddress();

          if (msg.toLowerCase().startsWith(queryString)) {
            String out = msg.substring(queryString.length());
            sms.sendTextMessage(to, null, out, null, null);
          }
        }
      }
    }
  }
}
```

To listen for incoming messages, register the Broadcast Receiver using an Intent Filter that listens for the `android.provider.Telephony.SMS_RECEIVED` action String, as shown in the code snippet below:

```
final String SMS_RECEIVED = "android.provider.Telephony.SMS_RECEIVED";
IntentFilter filter = new IntentFilter(SMS_RECEIVED);
BroadcastReceiver receiver = new IncomingSMSReceiver();
registerReceiver(receiver, filter);
```

Simulating Incoming SMS Messages

There are two techniques available for simulating incoming SMS messages in the emulator. The first was described previoulsy in this section; you can send an SMS message from one emulator to another by using its port number as the destination address.

Alternatively, you can use the Android debug tools introduced in Chapter 2 to simulate incoming SMS messages from arbitrary numbers, as shown in Figure 9-2.

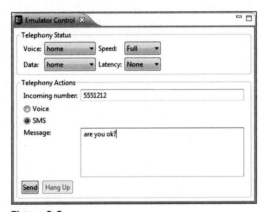

Figure 9-2

Handling Data SMS Messages

> For security reasons, the version 1 release has restricted access to receiving data messages. The following section has been left to indicate how likely future functionality may be made available.

Data messages are received in the same way as a normal SMS text message and are extracted in the same way as shown in the above section.

To extract the data transmitted within a data SMS, use the `getUserData` and `getUserDataHeader` methods, as shown in the following snippet:

```
byte[] data = msg.getUserData();
SmsHeader header = msg.getUserDataHeader();
```

The `getUserData` method returns a byte array of the data included in the message, while `getUserDataHeader` returns an array of metadata elements used to describe the data contained in the message.

Emergency Responder SMS Example

In this example, you'll create an SMS application that turns an Android phone into an emergency response beacon.

Once finished, the next time you're in unfortunate proximity to an alien invasion or find yourself in a robot-uprising scenario, you can set your phone to automatically respond to your friends' and family members' pleas for a status update with a friendly message (or a desperate cry for help).

To make things easier for your would-be saviors, you'll use location-based services to tell your rescuers exactly where to find you. The robustness of SMS network infrastructure makes SMS an excellent option for applications like this where reliability and accessibility are critical.

1. Start by creating a new `EmergencyResponder` project that features an `EmergencyResponder` Activity.

```
package com.paad.emergencyresponder;

import java.io.IOException;
import java.util.ArrayList;
import java.util.Locale;
import java.util.concurrent.locks.ReentrantLock;
import java.util.List;
import android.app.Activity;
import android.app.PendingIntent;
import android.content.Context;
import android.content.Intent;
import android.content.IntentFilter;

import android.content.BroadcastReceiver;
import android.content.SharedPreferences;
import android.location.Address;
import android.location.Geocoder;
import android.location.Location;
import android.location.LocationManager;

import android.os.Bundle;
import android.telephony.gsm.SmsManager;
import android.telephony.gsm.SmsMessage;
import android.view.View;
import android.view.View.OnClickListener;
import android.widget.ArrayAdapter;
import android.widget.Button;
import android.widget.CheckBox;
import android.widget.ListView;

public class EmergencyResponder extends Activity {

  @Override
```

```
        public void onCreate(Bundle icicle) {
          super.onCreate(icicle);
          setContentView(R.layout.main);
        }
      }
```

2. Add permissions for finding your location as well as sending and receiving incoming SMS messages to the project manifest.

```
<?xml version="1.0" encoding="utf-8"?>
<manifest xmlns:android="http://schemas.android.com/apk/res/android"
        package="com.paad.emergencyresponder">
  <application android:icon="@drawable/icon"
              android:label="@string/app_name">
    <activity android:name=".EmergencyResponder"
              android:label="@string/app_name">
      <intent-filter>
        <action android:name="android.intent.action.MAIN" />
        <category android:name="android.intent.category.LAUNCHER" />
      </intent-filter>
    </activity>
  </application>

  <uses-permission
    android:name="android.permission.ACCESS_GPS"/>

  <uses-permission
    android:name="android.permission.ACCESS_LOCATION"/>

  <uses-permission
    android:name="android.permission.RECEIVE_SMS"/>

  <uses-permission android:name="android.permission.SEND_SMS"/>

</manifest>
```

3. Modify the main.xml layout resource. Include a List View to show the people requesting a status update and a series of buttons that users can press to send response SMS messages. Use external resource references to fill in the button text; you'll create them in Step 4.

```
<?xml version="1.0" encoding="utf-8"?>
<RelativeLayout
  xmlns:android="http://schemas.android.com/apk/res/android"
  android:layout_width="fill_parent"
  android:layout_height="fill_parent">
  <TextView
    android:id="@+id/labelRequestList"
    android:layout_width="fill_parent"
    android:layout_height="wrap_content"
    android:text="These people want to know if you're ok"
    android:layout_alignParentTop="true"/>
  <LinearLayout
    android:id="@+id/buttonLayout"
```

```
          xmlns:android="http://schemas.android.com/apk/res/android"
          android:orientation="vertical"
          android:layout_width="fill_parent"
          android:layout_height="wrap_content"
          android:padding="5px"
          android:layout_alignParentBottom="true">
          <CheckBox
            android:id="@+id/checkboxSendLocation"
            android:layout_width="fill_parent"
            android:layout_height="wrap_content"
            android:text="Include Location in Reply"/>
          <Button
            android:id="@+id/okButton"
            android:layout_width="fill_parent"
            android:layout_height="wrap_content"
            android:text="@string/respondAllClearButtonText"/>
          <Button
            android:id="@+id/notOkButton"
            android:layout_width="fill_parent"
            android:layout_height="wrap_content"
            android:text="@string/respondMaydayButtonText"/>
          <Button
            android:id="@+id/autoResponder"
            android:layout_width="fill_parent"
            android:layout_height="wrap_content"
            android:text="Setup Auto Responder"/>
        </LinearLayout>
        <ListView
          android:id="@+id/myListView"
          android:layout_width="fill_parent"
          android:layout_height="fill_parent"
          android:layout_below="@id/labelRequestList"
          android:layout_above="@id/buttonLayout"/>
      </RelativeLayout>
```

4. Update the external strings.xml resource to include the text for each button and default
    response messages to use when responding, with "I'm safe" or "I'm in danger" messages.
    You should also define the incoming message text to use when detecting requests for status
    responses.

```
      <?xml version="1.0" encoding="utf-8"?>
      <resources>
        <string name="app_name">Emergency Responder</string>

        <string name="respondAllClearButtonText">I am Safe and Well</string>
        <string name="respondMaydayButtonText">MAYDAY! MAYDAY! MAYDAY!</string>

        <string name="respondAllClearText">I am safe and well. Worry not!</string>
        <string name="respondMaydayText">Tell my mother I love her.</string>

        <string name="querystring">are you ok?</string>
      </resources>
```

5. At this point, the GUI will be complete, so starting the application should show you the screen shown in Figure 9-3.

Figure 9-3

6. Create a new Array List of Strings within the `EmergencyResponder` Activity to store the phone numbers of the incoming requests for your status. Bind the Array List to the List View, using an Array Adapter in the Activity's `onCreate` method, and create a new `ReentrantLock` object to ensure thread safe handling of the Array List.

Take the opportunity to get a reference to the Check Box and to add Click Listeners for each of the response buttons. Each button should call the `respond` method, while the Setup Auto Responder button should call the `startAutoResponder` stub.

```
ReentrantLock lock;

CheckBox locationCheckBox;

ArrayList<String> requesters;
ArrayAdapter<String> aa;

@Override
public void onCreate(Bundle icicle) {
  super.onCreate(icicle);
  setContentView(R.layout.main);

  lock = new ReentrantLock();
  requesters = new ArrayList<String>();
  wireUpControls();
}

private void wireUpControls() {
  locationCheckBox = (CheckBox)findViewById(R.id.checkboxSendLocation);
```

```
ListView myListView = (ListView)findViewById(R.id.myListView);

int layoutID = android.R.layout.simple_list_item_1;
aa = new ArrayAdapter<String>(this, layoutID, requesters);

myListView.setAdapter(aa);

Button okButton = (Button)findViewById(R.id.okButton);
okButton.setOnClickListener(new OnClickListener() {
  public void onClick(View arg0) {
    respond(true, locationCheckBox.isChecked());
  }
});

Button notOkButton = (Button)findViewById(R.id.notOkButton);
notOkButton.setOnClickListener(new OnClickListener() {
  public void onClick(View arg0) {
    respond(false, locationCheckBox.isChecked());
  }
});

Button autoResponderButton = (Button)findViewById(R.id.autoResponder);
autoResponderButton.setOnClickListener(new OnClickListener() {
  public void onClick(View arg0) {
    startAutoResponder();
  }
});
}
```

```
public void respond(boolean _ok, boolean _includeLocation) {}
```

```
private void startAutoResponder() {}
```

7. Next, implement a Broadcast Receiver that will listen for incoming SMS messages.

   7.1 Start by creating a new static string variable to store the incoming SMS message intent action.

```
public static final String SMS_RECEIVED =
  "android.provider.Telephony.SMS_RECEIVED";
```

   7.2 Then create a new Broadcast Receiver as a variable in the EmergencyResponder Activity. The receiver should listen for incoming SMS messages and call the requestRecieved method when it sees SMS messages containing the "are you safe" String you defined as an external resource in Step 4.

```
BroadcastReceiver emergencyResponseRequestReceiver = new BroadcastReceiver() {

  @Override
  public void onReceive(Context _context, Intent _intent) {
    if (_intent.getAction().equals(SMS_RECEIVED)) {
      String queryString = getString(R.string.querystring);

      Bundle bundle = _intent.getExtras();
      if (bundle != null) {
```

```
            Object[] pdus = (Object[]) bundle.get("pdus");
            SmsMessage[] messages = new SmsMessage[pdus.length];
            for (int i = 0; i < pdus.length; i++)
              messages[i] = SmsMessage.createFromPdu((byte[]) pdus[i]);

            for (SmsMessage message : messages) {
              if (message.getMessageBody().toLowerCase().contains(queryString)) {
                requestReceived(message.getOriginatingAddress());
              }
            }
          }
        }
      }
    }

  };
```

```
      public void requestReceived(String _from) {}
```

8. Update the onCreate method of the Emergency Responder Activity to register the Broadcast Receiver created in Step 7.

```
@Override
public void onCreate(Bundle icicle) {
  super.onCreate(icicle);
  setContentView(R.layout.main);

  lock = new ReentrantLock();
  requesters = new ArrayList<String>();
  wireUpControls();

  IntentFilter filter = new IntentFilter(SMS_RECEIVED);
  registerReceiver(emergencyResponseRequestReceiver, filter);
}
```

9. Update the requestReceived method stub so that it adds the originating number of each status request's SMS to the "requesters" Array List.

```
public void requestReceived(String _from) {
  if (!requesters.contains(_from)) {
    lock.lock();
    requesters.add(_from);
    aa.notifyDataSetChanged();
    lock.unlock();
  }
}
```

10. The Emergency Responder Activity should now be listening for status request SMS messages and adding them to the List View as they arrive. Start the application and use the DDMS emulator control to simulate incoming SMS messages, as shown in Figure 9-4.

Figure 9-4

11. Now update the Activity to let users respond to these status requests.

Start by completing the `respond` method stub you created in Step 6. It should iterate over the Array List of status requesters and send a new SMS message to each. The SMS message text should be based on the response strings you defined as resources in Step 4. Fire the SMS using an overloaded `respond` method that you'll complete in the next step.

```
public void respond(boolean _ok, boolean _includeLocation) {
    String okString = getString(R.string.respondAllClearText);
    String notOkString = getString(R.string.respondMaydayText);

    String outString = _ok ? okString : notOkString;

    ArrayList<String> requestersCopy = (ArrayList<String>)requesters.clone();

    for (String to : requestersCopy)
      respond(to, outString, _includeLocation);
}
```

```
private void respond(String _to, String _response, boolean _includeLocation) {}
```

12. Update the `respond` method that handles the sending of each response SMS.

Start by removing each potential recipient from the "requesters" Array List before sending the SMS. If you are responding with your current location, use the Location Manager to find it before sending a second SMS with your current position as raw longitude/latitude points and a geocoded address.

```
public void respond(String _to, String _response, boolean _includeLocation) {
    // Remove the target from the list of people we need to respond to.
    lock.lock();
    requesters.remove(_to);
    aa.notifyDataSetChanged();
```

```
        lock.unlock();

        SmsManager sms = SmsManager.getDefault();

        // Send the message
        sms.sendTextMessage(_to, null, _response, null, null);

        StringBuilder sb = new StringBuilder();

        // Find the current location and send it as SMS messages if required.
        if (_includeLocation) {
          String ls = Context.LOCATION_SERVICE;
          LocationManager lm = (LocationManager)getSystemService(ls);
          Location l = lm.getLastKnownLocation(LocationManager.GPS_PROVIDER);

          sb.append("I'm @:\n");
          sb.append(l.toString() + "\n");

          List<Address> addresses;
          Geocoder g = new Geocoder(getApplicationContext(), Locale.getDefault());
          try {
            addresses = g.getFromLocation(l.getLatitude(), l.getLongitude(), 1);
            if (addresses != null) {
              Address currentAddress = addresses.get(0);
              if (currentAddress.getMaxAddressLineIndex() > 0) {
                for (int i = 0; i < currentAddress.getMaxAddressLineIndex(); i++) {
                  sb.append(currentAddress.getAddressLine(i));
                  sb.append("\n");
                }
              }
              else {
                if (currentAddress.getPostalCode() != null)
                  sb.append(currentAddress.getPostalCode());
              }
            }
          } catch (IOException e) {}

          ArrayList<String> locationMsgs = sms.divideMessage(sb.toString());
          for (String locationMsg : locationMsgs)
            sms.sendTextMessage(_to, null, locationMsg, null, null);
        }
      }
```

At the time of production, sendTextMessage *required a non-null value for the fourth parameter* (sentIntent). *In this example, this parameter is added in Step 13, so running the application now will cause it to throw an exception.*

13. In emergencies, it's important that messages get through. Improve the robustness of the application by including auto-retry functionality. Monitor the success of your SMS transmissions so that you can re-broadcast a message if it doesn't successfully send.

13.1. Start by creating a new public static String in the Emergency Responder Activity to be used as a local "SMS Sent" action.

```
public static final String SENT_SMS = "com.paad.emergencyresponder.SMS_SENT";
```

13.2. Update the `respond` method to include a new `PendingIntent` that broadcasts the action created in the previous step when the SMS transmission has completed. The packaged Intent should include the intended recipient's number as an extra.

```
public void respond(String _to, String _response, boolean _includeLocation) {
  // Remove the target from the list of people we need to respond to.
  lock.lock();
  requesters.remove(_to);
  aa.notifyDataSetChanged();
  lock.unlock();

  SmsManager sms = SmsManager.getDefault();

  Intent intent = new Intent(SENT_SMS);
  intent.putExtra("recipient", _to);

  PendingIntent sentIntent = PendingIntent.getBroadcast(getApplicationContext(),
                                                        0,
                                                        intent,
                                                        0);

  // Send the message
  sms.sendTextMessage(_to, null, _response, sentIntent, null);

  StringBuilder sb = new StringBuilder();

  if (_includeLocation) {
    [ … existing respond method that finds the current location … ]
    ArrayList<String> locationMsgs = sms.divideMessage(sb.toString());
    for (String locationMsg : locationMsgs)
      sms.sendTextMessage(_to, null, locationMsg, sentIntent, null);
  }
}
```

13.3. Then implement a new Broadcast Receiver to listen for this broadcast Intent. Override its `onReceive` handler to confirm that the SMS was successfully delivered; if it wasn't, then add the intended recipient back on to the requesters Array List.

```
private BroadcastReceiver attemptedDeliveryReceiver = new BroadcastReceiver()
{
  @Override
  public void onReceive(Context _context, Intent _intent) {
    if (_intent.getAction().equals(SENT_SMS)) {
      if (getResultCode() != Activity.RESULT_OK) {
        String recipient = _intent.getStringExtra("recipient");
        requestReceived(recipient);
      }
    }
  }
};
```

13.4. Finally, register the new Broadcast Receiver by extending the `onCreate` method of the Emergency Responder Activity.

```
@Override
public void onCreate(Bundle icicle) {
    super.onCreate(icicle);
    setContentView(R.layout.main);

    lock = new ReentrantLock();
    requesters = new ArrayList<String>();
    wireUpControls();

    IntentFilter filter = new IntentFilter(SMS_RECEIVED);
    registerReceiver(emergencyResponseRequestReceiver, filter);

    IntentFilter attemptedDeliveryfilter = new IntentFilter(SENT_SMS);
    registerReceiver(attemptedDeliveryReceiver, attemptedDeliveryfilter);
}
```

You can now run the application. To test it, you need to open two emulator instances with the application running in one of them.

Use the DDMS emulator controls to mimic sending an "are you safe" message from one emulator to the other (using its port number as the originating number). When you press one of the response buttons, you should see a new SMS message appear in the mimicked emulator.

Automating the Emergency Responder

In the following example, you'll fill in the code behind the Set up Auto Responder button added in the previous example, to let the Emergency Responder automatically respond to status update requests.

1. Start by creating a new autoresponder.xml layout resource that will be used to lay out the automatic response configuration window. Include an `EditText` for entering a status message to send, a `Spinner` to choose the auto-response expiry time, and a `CheckBox` to let users choose if they want to include their location in the automated responses.

```
<?xml version="1.0" encoding="utf-8"?>
<LinearLayout
  xmlns:android="http://schemas.android.com/apk/res/android"
  android:orientation="vertical"
  android:layout_width="fill_parent"
  android:layout_height="fill_parent">
<TextView
  android:layout_width="fill_parent"
  android:layout_height="wrap_content"
  android:text="Respond With"/>
<EditText
  android:id="@+id/responseText"
  android:layout_width="fill_parent"
  android:layout_height="wrap_content"/>
<CheckBox
  android:id="@+id/checkboxLocation"
```

```
    android:layout_width="fill_parent"
    android:layout_height="wrap_content"
    android:text="Transmit Location"/>
<TextView
    android:layout_width="fill_parent"
    android:layout_height="wrap_content"
    android:text="Auto Respond For"/>
<Spinner
    android:id="@+id/spinnerRespondFor"
    android:layout_width="fill_parent"
    android:layout_height="wrap_content"
    android:drawSelectorOnTop="true"/>
<LinearLayout
    xmlns:android="http://schemas.android.com/apk/res/android"
    android:orientation="horizontal"
    android:layout_width="fill_parent"
    android:layout_height="wrap_content">
    <Button
      android:id="@+id/okButton"
      android:layout_width="wrap_content"
      android:layout_height="wrap_content"
      android:text="Enable"/>
    <Button
      android:id="@+id/cancelButton"
      android:layout_width="wrap_content"
      android:layout_height="wrap_content"
      android:text="Disable"/>
  </LinearLayout>
</LinearLayout>
```

2. Update the application's string.xml resource to define a name for an application
`SharedPreference` and strings to use for each of its keys.

```
<?xml version="1.0" encoding="utf-8"?>
<resources>
  <string name="app_name">Emergency Responder</string>

  <string name="respondAllClearButtonText">I am Safe and Well</string>
  <string name="respondMaydayButtonText">MAYDAY! MAYDAY! MAYDAY!</string>

  <string name="respondAllClearText">I am safe and well. Worry not!</string>
  <string name="respondMaydayText">Tell my mother I love her.</string>

  <string name="querystring">"are you ok?"</string>

  <string name="user_preferences">com.paad.emergencyresponder.preferences</string>
  <string name="includeLocationPref">PREF_INCLUDE_LOC</string>
  <string name="responseTextPref">PREF_RESPONSE_TEXT</string>
  <string name="autoRespondPref">PREF_AUTO_RESPOND</string>
  <string name="respondForPref">PREF_RESPOND_FOR</string>
</resources>
```

You should also take this opportunity to externalize the strings used for labels within the layout.

3. Then create a new arrays.xml resource, and create arrays to use for populating the Spinner.

```xml
<resources>
  <string-array name="respondForDisplayItems">
    <item>- Disabled -</item>
    <item>Next 5 minutes</item>
    <item>Next 15 minutes</item>
    <item>Next 30 minutes</item>
    <item>Next hour</item>
    <item>Next 2 hours</item>
    <item>Next 8 hours</item>
  </string-array>

  <array name="respondForValues">
    <item>0</item>
    <item>5</item>
    <item>15</item>
    <item>30</item>
    <item>60</item>
    <item>120</item>
    <item>480</item>
  </array>
</resources>
```

4. Now create a new AutoResponder Activity, populating it with the layout you created in Step 1.

```java
package com.paad.emergencyresponder;

import android.app.Activity;
import android.app.AlarmManager;
import android.app.PendingIntent;
import android.content.res.Resources;
import android.content.Context;
import android.content.Intent;
import android.content.IntentFilter;
import android.content.BroadcastReceiver;
import android.content.SharedPreferences;
import android.content.SharedPreferences.Editor;
import android.os.Bundle;
import android.view.View;
import android.widget.ArrayAdapter;
import android.widget.Button;
import android.widget.CheckBox;
import android.widget.EditText;
import android.widget.Spinner;

public class AutoResponder extends Activity {

  @Override
  public void onCreate(Bundle icicle) {
      super.onCreate(icicle);
      setContentView(R.layout.autoresponder);
  }

}
```

5. Update `onCreate` further to get references to each of the controls in the layout and wire up the Spinner using the arrays defined in Step 3. Create two new stub methods, `savePreferences` and `updateUIFromPreferences`, that will be updated to save the auto-responder settings to a named `SharedPreference` and apply the saved `SharedPreferences` to the current UI, respectively.

```
Spinner respondForSpinner;
CheckBox locationCheckbox;
EditText responseTextBox;

@Override
public void onCreate(Bundle icicle) {
  super.onCreate(icicle);
  setContentView(R.layout.autoresponder);
```

5.1. Start by getting references to each View.

```
respondForSpinner = (Spinner)findViewById(R.id.spinnerRespondFor);
locationCheckbox = (CheckBox)findViewById(R.id.checkboxLocation);
responseTextBox = (EditText)findViewById(R.id.responseText);
```

5.2. Populate the Spinner to let users select the auto-responder expiry time.

```
ArrayAdapter<CharSequence> adapter = ArrayAdapter.createFromResource(
                                      this,
                                      R.array.respondForDisplayItems,
                                      android.R.layout.simple_spinner_item);

adapter.setDropDownViewResource(android.R.layout.simple_spinner_dropdown_item);
respondForSpinner.setAdapter(adapter);
```

5.3. Now wire up the OK and Cancel buttons to let users save or cancel setting changes.

```
Button okButton = (Button) findViewById(R.id.okButton);
okButton.setOnClickListener(new View.OnClickListener() {
  public void onClick(View view) {
    savePreferences();
    setResult(RESULT_OK, null);
    finish();
  }
});

Button cancelButton = (Button) findViewById(R.id.cancelButton);
cancelButton.setOnClickListener(new View.OnClickListener() {
  public void onClick(View view) {
    respondForSpinner.setSelection(-1);
    savePreferences();
    setResult(RESULT_CANCELED, null);
    finish();
  }
});
```

5.4. Finally, make sure that when the Activity starts, it updates the GUI to represent the current settings.

```
// Load the saved preferences and update the UI
updateUIFromPreferences();
```

5.5. Close off the `onCreate` method, and add the `updateUIFromPreferences` and `savePreferences` stubs.

```
}

private void updateUIFromPreferences() {}

private void savePreferences() {}
```

6. Next, complete the two stub methods from Step 5. Start with `updateUIFromPreferences`; it should read the current saved `AutoResponder` preferences and apply them to the UI.

```
private void updateUIFromPreferences() {
    // Get the saves settings
    String preferenceName = getString(R.string.user_preferences);
    SharedPreferences sp = getSharedPreferences(preferenceName, 0);

    boolean autoRespond = sp.getBoolean(getString(R.string.autoRespondPref), false);
    String respondText = sp.getString(getString(R.string.responseTextPref), "");
    boolean includeLoc = sp.getBoolean(getString(R.string.includeLocationPref),
                                       false);
    int respondForIndex = sp.getInt(getString(R.string.respondForPref), 0);

    // Apply the saved settings to the UI
    if (autoRespond)
      respondForSpinner.setSelection(respondForIndex);
    else
      respondForSpinner.setSelection(0);

    locationCheckbox.setChecked(includeLoc);
    responseTextBox.setText(respondText);
}
```

7. Complete the `savePreferences` stub to save the current UI settings to a Shared Preferences file.

```
private void savePreferences() {
    // Get the current settings from the UI
    boolean autoRespond = respondForSpinner.getSelectedItemPosition() > 0;
    int respondForIndex = respondForSpinner.getSelectedItemPosition();
    boolean includeLoc = locationCheckbox.isChecked();
    String respondText = responseTextBox.getText().toString();

    // Save them to the Shared Preference file
    String preferenceName = getString(R.string.user_preferences);
    SharedPreferences sp = getSharedPreferences(preferenceName, 0);

    Editor editor = sp.edit();
```

```
editor.putBoolean(getString(R.string.autoRespondPref), autoRespond);
editor.putString(getString(R.string.responseTextPref), respondText);
editor.putBoolean(getString(R.string.includeLocationPref), includeLoc );
editor.putInt(getString(R.string.respondForPref), respondForIndex );
editor.commit();

// Set the alarm to turn off the autoresponder
setAlarm(respondForIndex);
}
```

```
private void setAlarm(int respondForIndex) {}
```

8. The `setAlarm` stub from Step 8 is used to create a new Alarm that fires an Intent that should result in the AutoResponder being disabled.

You'll need to create a new `Alarm` object and a `BroadcastReceiver` that listens for it before disabling the auto-responder accordingly.

8.1. Start by creating the action String that will represent the Alarm Intent.

```
public static final String alarmAction =
  "com.paad.emergencyresponder.AUTO_RESPONSE_EXPIRED";
```

8.2. Then create a new Broadcast Receiver instance that listens for an Intent that includes the action specified in Step 7. When this Intent is received, it should modify the auto-responder settings to disable the automatic response.

```
private BroadcastReceiver stopAutoResponderReceiver = new BroadcastReceiver() {
  @Override
  public void onReceive(Context context, Intent intent) {
    if (intent.getAction().equals(alarmAction)) {
      String preferenceName = getString(R.string.user_preferences);
      SharedPreferences sp = getSharedPreferences(preferenceName, 0);

      Editor editor = sp.edit();
      editor.putBoolean(getString(R.string.autoRespondPref), false);
      editor.commit();
    }
  }
};
```

8.3. Finally, complete the `setAlarm` method. It should cancel the existing alarm if the auto-responder is turned off; otherwise, it should update it with the latest expiry time.

```
PendingIntent intentToFire;

private void setAlarm(int respondForIndex) {
  // Create the alarm and register the alarm intent receiver.

  AlarmManager alarms = (AlarmManager)getSystemService(ALARM_SERVICE);

  if (intentToFire == null) {
    Intent intent = new Intent(alarmAction);
```

```
        intentToFire = PendingIntent.getBroadcast(getApplicationContext(),
                                            0,intent,0);

        IntentFilter filter = new IntentFilter(alarmAction);

        registerReceiver(stopAutoResponderReceiver, filter);
    }

    if (respondForIndex < 1)
        // If "disabled" is selected, cancel the alarm.
        alarms.cancel(intentToFire);
    else {
        // Otherwise find the length of time represented by the selection and
        // and set the alarm to trigger after that time has passed.
        Resources r = getResources();
        int[] respondForValues = r.getIntArray(R.array.respondForValues);
        int respondFor = respondForValues [respondForIndex];

        long t = System.currentTimeMillis();
        t = t + respondFor*1000*60;

        // Set the alarm.
        alarms.set(AlarmManager.RTC_WAKEUP, t, intentToFire);
    }
}
```

9. That completes the `AutoResponder`, but before you can use it, you'll need to add it to your application manifest.

```xml
<?xml version="1.0" encoding="utf-8"?>
<manifest
  xmlns:android="http://schemas.android.com/apk/res/android"
  package="com.paad.emergencyresponder">
  <application
    android:icon="@drawable/icon"
    android:label="@string/app_name">
    <activity
      android:name=".EmergencyResponder"
      android:label="@string/app_name">
      <intent-filter>
        <action android:name="android.intent.action.MAIN" />
        <category android:name="android.intent.category.LAUNCHER" />
      </intent-filter>
    </activity>
    <activity
      android:name=".AutoResponder"
      android:label="Auto Responder Setup"/>
  </application>

  <uses-permission android:name="android.permission.ACCESS_GPS"/>
  <uses-permission android:name="android.permission.ACCESS_LOCATION"/>
  <uses-permission android:name="android.permission.RECEIVE_SMS"/>
  <uses-permission android:name="android.permission.SEND_SMS"/>

</manifest>
```

10. To enable the auto-responder, return to the Emergency Responder Activity and update the `startAutoResponder` method stub that you created in the previous example. It should open the `AutoResponder` Activity you just created.

```
private void startAutoResponder() {
    startActivityForResult(new Intent(EmergencyResponder.this,
                           AutoResponder.class), 0);
}
```

11. If you start your project, you should now be able to bring up the Auto Responder settings window to set the auto-response settings. It should appear as shown in Figure 9-5.

Figure 9-5

12. The final step is to update the `requestReceived` method in the Emergency Responder Activity to check if the auto-responder has been enabled.

If it has, the `requestReceived` method should automatically execute the `respond` method, using the message and location settings defined in the application's SharedPreferences.

```
public void requestReceived(String _from) {
    if (!requesters.contains(_from)) {
        lock.lock();
        requesters.add(_from);
        aa.notifyDataSetChanged();
        lock.unlock();

        // Check for auto-responder
        String preferenceName = getString(R.string.user_preferences);
        SharedPreferences prefs = getSharedPreferences(preferenceName, 0);

        String autoRespondPref = getString(R.string.autoRespondPref)
        boolean autoRespond = prefs.getBoolean(autoRespondPref, false);

        if (autoRespond) {
            String responseTextPref = getString(R.string.responseTextPref);
            String includeLocationPref = getString(R.string.includeLocationPref);

            String respondText = prefs.getString(responseTextPref, "");
```

```
            boolean includeLoc = prefs.getBoolean(includeLocationPref, false);

            respond(_from, respondText, includeLoc);
        }
    }
}
```

You should now have a fully functional interactive and automated emergency responder.

You can test it in the same way as described in the previous example by using a second emulator instance to receive the response messages, and the emulator controls to send the requests for status updates.

Summary

Technologies like SMS and instant messaging are providing an increasingly versatile platform for person-to-person communication.

Android lets you use these text-based communication channels to create applications that let users send messages using instant messengers and SMS texts, as well as supplying an invisible data conduit for your applications to exchange data between devices.

In this chapter, you learned how to connect to IM Sessions using the GTalk Service and how to send and receive text and data messages using these sessions. You learned about presence, how to set your own presence, and how to find the presence of the contacts on the IM roster.

You also used the SMS Manager to send and receive text and data messages from your applications.

This chapter also showed you how future SDK release may allow you to:

❑   Add and remove instant messaging contacts.

❑   Block contacts and monitor the roster for changes.

❑   Manage group chats and chat rooms.

Chapter 10 explores access to the low-level mobile hardware.

Using the phone's telephony services, you'll initiate new calls and monitor both outgoing and incoming calls. You'll be introduced to Android's multimedia capabilities and use the media API to play back and record a variety of media resources.

You'll also learn how to interact with the Sensor Manager to access the compass and accelerometer before investigating network management using the Wi-Fi and Bluetooth APIs.

10

Accessing Android Hardware

Android's application-neutral APIs provide low-level access to the increasingly diverse hardware commonly available on mobile devices. The ability to monitor and control these hardware features provides a great incentive for application development on the Android platform.

The hardware APIs available include:

❑ A telephony package that provides access to calls and phone status.

❑ A multimedia playback and recording library.

❑ Access to the device camera for taking pictures and previewing video.

❑ Extensible support for sensor hardware.

❑ Accelerometer and compass APIs to monitor orientation and movement.

❑ Communications libraries for managing Bluetooth, network, and Wi-Fi hardware.

In this chapter, you'll take a closer look at some of these hardware APIs. In particular, you'll learn how to play and record multimedia content including audio, video, and still images, as well as use the camera to capture images and preview and capture live video.

You'll also learn how to monitor hardware sensors using the Sensor Manager. The accelerometer and compass sensors will be used to determine changes in the device orientation and acceleration — which is extremely useful for creating motion-based User Interfaces — and lets you add new dimensions to your location-based applications.

Finally, you'll take a closer look at the communication hardware by examining the telephony package for monitoring phone state and phone calls, as well as seeing what's available in the Bluetooth, networking, and Wi-Fi APIs.

Using the Media APIs

The only modern technology that can compete with mobile phones for ubiquity is the portable digital media player. As a result, the multimedia capabilities of portable devices are a significant consideration for many consumers.

Android's open platform- and provider-agnostic philosophy ensures that it offers a multimedia library capable of playing and recording a wide range of media formats, both locally and streamed.

Android exposes this library to your applications, providing comprehensive multimedia functionality including recording and playback of audio, video, and still-image media stored locally, within an application, or streamed over a data connection.

At the time of print, Android supported the following multimedia formats:

- ❏ JPEG
- ❏ PNG
- ❏ OGG
- ❏ Mpeg 4
- ❏ 3GPP
- ❏ MP3
- ❏ Bitmap

Playing Media Resources

Multimedia playback in Android is handled by the `MediaPlayer` class. You can play back media stored as application resources, local files, or from a network URI.

To play a media resource, create a new Media Player instance, and assign it a media source to play using the `setDataSource` method. Before you can start playback, you need to call `prepare`, as shown in the following code snippet:

```
String MEDIA_FILE_PATH = Settings.System.DEFAULT_RINGTONE_URI.toString();
MediaPlayer mpFile = new MediaPlayer();

try {
  mpFile.setDataSource(MEDIA_FILE_PATH);
  mpFile.prepare();
  mpFile.start();
}
catch (IllegalArgumentException e) {}
catch (IllegalStateException e) {}
catch (IOException e) {}
```

Alternatively, the static `create` methods work as shortcuts, accepting media resources as a parameter and preparing them for playback, as shown in the following example, which plays back an application resource:

```
MediaPlayer mpRes = MediaPlayer.create(context, R.raw.my_sound);
```

Note that if you use a `create` method to generate your `MediaPlayer` object, `prepare` is called for you.

Once a Media Player is prepared, call `start` as shown below to begin playback of the associated media resource.

```
mpRes.start();

mpFile.start();
```

The Android Emulator simulates audio playback using the audio output of your development platform.

The Media Player includes `stop`, `pause`, and `seek` methods to control playback, as well as methods to find the duration, position, and image size of the associated media.

To loop or repeat playback, use the `setLooping` method.

When playing video resources, `getFrame` will take a screen grab of video media at the specified frame and return a bitmap resource.

Once you've finished with the Media Player, be sure to call `release` to free the associated resources, as shown below:

```
mpRes.release();
mpFile.release();
```

Since Android only supports a limited number of simultaneous Media Player objects, not releasing them can cause runtime exceptions.

On Android devices, the Media Player always plays audio using the standard output device — the speaker or connected Bluetooth headset. It's not currently possible to play audio into a phone conversation.

Recording Multimedia

Multimedia recording is handled by the aptly named `MediaRecorder` class. To record audio or video, create a new Media Recorder object, as shown in the following code snippet:

```
MediaRecorder mediaRecorder = new MediaRecorder();
```

Before you can record any media in Android, your application needs the `RECORD_AUDIO` and / or `RECORD_VIDEO` permissions. Add `uses-permission` tags for each of them, as appropriate, in your application manifest.

```
<uses-permission android:name="android.permission.RECORD_AUDIO"/>
<uses-permission android:name="android.permission.RECORD_VIDEO"/>
```

> **The ability to record video has been restricted for the version 1.0 release of Android; however, Audio recording is still available.**

The Media Recorder can be used to configure the video and audio sources (generally the camera and microphone), output format, video size and frame rate, and the video and audio encoders to use.

The following code snippet shows how to configure a Media Recorder to record audio from the microphone using the default format and encoder:

The emulator supports recording of audio using the microphone device attached to your development platform.

```
// Set the audio source.
mediaRecorder.setAudioSource(MediaRecorder.AudioSource.MIC);
// Set the output format.
mediaRecorder.setOutputFormat(MediaRecorder.OutputFormat.DEFAULT);
// Set the audio encoders to use.
mediaRecorder.setAudioEncoder(MediaRecorder.AudioEncoder.DEFAULT);
```

Once you've defined your input source and output format, assign a file to store the recorded media using the `setOutputFile` method as shown below:

```
mediaRecorder.setOutputFile("myoutputfile.mp4");
```

> **The `setOutputFile` method must be called before `prepare` and after `setOutputFormat` or it will throw an Illegal State Exception.**

To begin recording, call `prepare` followed by the `start` method, as shown below:

```
mediaRecorder.prepare();
mediaRecorder.start();
```

When you're finished, call `stop` to end the playback, followed by `release` to free the Media Recorder resources:

```
mediaRecorder.stop();
mediaRecorder.release();
```

When recording video, it's generally considered good practice to display a preview of the recorded video in real time. Using the `setPreviewDisplay` method, you can assign a `Surface` to display the video preview.

As with any other resource, media files created by your application will be unavailable to others. As a result, it's good practice to use the Media Store Content Provider to assign metadata, select a file location, and publish the recorded media to share recordings with other applications.

To do that, after recording new media create a new `ContentValues` object to add a new record to the Media Store. The metadata you specify here can include the details including the title, time stamp, and geocoding information for your new media file, as shown in the code snippet below:

```
ContentValues content = new ContentValues(3);
content.put(Audio.AudioColumns.TITLE, "TheSoundandtheFury");
```

```
content.put(Audio.AudioColumns.DATE_ADDED,
            System.currentTimeMillis() / 1000);
content.put(Audio.Media.MIME_TYPE, "audio/amr");
```

You must also specify the absolute path of the media file being added:

```
content.put(MediaStore.Audio.Media.DATA,
            "myoutputfile.mp4");
```

Get access to the application's `ContentResolver`, and use it to insert this new row into the Media Store as shown in the following code snippet:

```
ContentResolver resolver = getContentResolver();
Uri uri = resolver.insert(Audio.Media.EXTERNAL_CONTENT_URI, content);
```

Once the media file has been inserted into the media store you should announce it's availability using a broadcast Intent as shown below:

```
sendBroadcast(new Intent(Intent.ACTION_MEDIA_SCANNER_SCAN_FILE, uri));
```

Using the Camera

The popularity of digital cameras (particularly within phone handsets) has caused their prices to drop just as their size has shrunk dramatically. It's now becoming difficult to even find a mobile phone without a camera, and Android devices are unlikely to be exceptions.

To access the camera hardware, you need to add the CAMERA permission to your application manifest, as shown here:

```
<uses-permission android:name="android.permission.CAMERA"/>
```

This grants access to the Camera Service. The `Camera` class lets you adjust camera settings, take pictures, and manipulate streaming camera previews.

To access the Camera Service, use the static `open` method on the `Camera` class. When your application has finished with the camera, remember to relinquish your hold on the Service by calling `release` following the simple use pattern shown in the code snippet below:

```
Camera camera = Camera.open();
    [ … Do things with the camera … ]
camera.release();
```

Controlling Camera Settings

The current camera settings are available as a `Camera.Parameters` object. Call the `getParameters` method on the Camera to access the current parameters.

You can use the `set*` methods on the returned Parameters to modify the settings. To apply changes, call `setParameters`, passing in the modified values as shown below:

```
Camera.Parameters parameters = camera.getParameters();
parameters.setPictureFormat(PixelFormat.JPEG);
camera.setParameters(parameters);
```

The Camera Parameters can be used to specify the image and preview size, image format, and preview frame rate.

Using the Camera Preview

Access to the camera's streaming video means that you can incorporate live video into your applications. Some of the most exciting early Android applications have used this functionality as the basis for augmenting reality.

The camera preview can be displayed in real time onto a `Surface`, as shown in the code snippet below:

```
camera.setPreviewDisplay(mySurface);
camera.startPreview();
[ … ]
camera.stopPreview();
```

You'll learn more about Surfaces in the following chapter, although Android includes an excellent example of using a `SurfaceView` to display the camera preview in real time. This example is available in the `graphics/CameraPreview` project in the SDK API demos.

You can also assign a `PreviewCallback` to be fired for each preview frame, allowing you to manipulate or display each preview frame individually. Call the `setPreviewCallback` method on the `Camera` object, passing in a new `PreviewCallback` implementation overriding the `onPreviewFrame` method as shown here:

```
camera.setPreviewCallback(new PreviewCallback() {

  public void onPreviewFrame(byte[] _data, Camera _camera) {
    // TODO Do something with the preview image.
  }
});
```

Taking a Picture

Take a picture by calling `takePicture` on a `Camera` object, passing in a `ShutterCallback` and `PictureCallback` implementations for the RAW and JPEG-encoded images. Each picture callback will receive a byte array representing the image in the appropriate format, while the shutter callback is triggered immediately after the shutter is closed.

```
private void takePicture() {
  camera.takePicture(shutterCallback, rawCallback, jpegCallback);
}

ShutterCallback shutterCallback = new ShutterCallback() {
```

```
    public void onShutter() {
      // TODO Do something when the shutter closes.
    }
};

PictureCallback rawCallback = new PictureCallback() {
    public void onPictureTaken(byte[] _data, Camera _camera) {
      // TODO Do something with the image RAW data.
    }
};

PictureCallback jpegCallback = new PictureCallback() {
    public void onPictureTaken(byte[] _data, Camera _camera) {
      // TODO Do something with the image JPEG data.
    }
};
```

Introducing the Sensor Manager

The Sensor Manager is used to manage the sensor hardware available on an Android device. Use getSystemService to get a reference to the Sensor Service as shown in the code snippet below:

```
String service_name = Context.SENSOR_SERVICE;
SensorManager sensorManager = (SensorManager)getSystemService(service_name);
```

The following sections look closely at how to use the Sensor Manager to monitor orientation and acceleration, but the pattern shown here can be used to monitor sensor results from any available hardware sensor:

```
SensorListener mySensorListener = new SensorListener() {
    public void onSensorChanged(int sensor, float[] values) {
      // TODO Deal with sensor value changes
    }

    public void onAccuracyChanged(int sensor, int accuracy) {
      // TODO Auto-generated method stub
    }
};
```

The SensorListener interface is used to listen for Sensor value and accuracy changes.

Implement the onSensorChanged method to react to value changes. The sensor parameter identifies the sensor that triggered the event, while the values float array contains the new values detected by that sensor.

Implement onAccuracyChanged to react to changes in a sensor's accuracy. The sensor parameter again identifies the sensor that triggered the event, while the accuracy parameter indicates the new accuracy of that sensor using one of the constants:

❑ SensorManager.SENSOR_STATUS_ACCURACY_HIGH   Indicates that the sensor is reporting with the highest possible accuracy.

❑ SensorManager.SENSOR_STATUS_ACCURACY_LOW   Indicates that the sensor is reporting with low accuracy and needs to be calibrated.

❑   `SensorManager.SENSOR_STATUS_ACCURACY_MEDIUM`   Indicates that the sensor data is of average accuracy, and that calibration might improve the readings.

❑   `SensorManager.SENSOR_STATUS_UNRELIABLE`   Indicates that the sensor data is unreliable, meaning that either calibration is required or readings are not currently possible.

The Sensor Manager includes constants to help identify the sensor triggering the change event. The following list includes the sensors for which constants are currently defined. Some or all of these sensors will be available to your applications depending on the hardware available on the host device:

❑   `SensorManager.SENSOR_ACCELEROMETER`   Is an accelerometer sensor that returns the current acceleration along three axes in meters per second squared (m/s^2). The accelerometer is explored in greater detail later in this chapter.

❑   `SensorManager.SENSOR_ORIENTATION`   Is an orientation sensor that returns the current orientation on three axes in degrees. The orientation sensor is explored in greater detail later in this chapter.

❑   `SensorManager.SENSOR_LIGHT`   Is an ambient-light sensor that returns a single value describing the ambient illumination in lux.

❑   `SensorManager.SENSOR_MAGNETIC_FIELD`   Is a sensor used to determine the current magnetic field measured in microteslas (µT) along three axes.

❑   `SensorManager.SENSOR_PROXIMITY`   Is a proximity sensor that returns a single value describing the distance between the device and the target object in meters (m).

❑   `SensorManager.SENSOR_TEMPERATURE`   Is a thermometer sensor that returns the ambient temperature in degrees Celsius (°C).

To receive notifications of changes from a particular sensor, create a Sensor Listener as described previously, and register it with the Sensor Manager specifying the sensor that should trigger the Listener and the rate at which the sensor should update, as shown in the following code snippet:

```
sensorManager.registerListener(mySensorListener,
                    SensorManager.SENSOR_TRICORDER,
                    SensorManager.SENSOR_DELAY_FASTEST);
```

The Sensor Manager includes the following constants (shown in descending order of responsiveness) to let you select a suitable update rate:

❑   `SensorManager.SENSOR_DELAY_FASTEST`   Specifies the fastest possible sensor update rate.

❑   `SensorManager.SENSOR_DELAY_GAME`   Selects an update rate suitable for use in controlling games.

❑   `SensorManager.SENSOR_DELAY_NORMAL`   Specifies the default update rate.

❑   `SensorManager.SENSOR_DELAY_UI`   Specifies a rate suitable for updating UI features.

The rate you select is not binding; the Sensor Manager may return results faster or slower than you specify, though it will tend to be faster. To minimize the associated resource cost of using the sensor in your application you should try to select the slowest suitable rate.

An overloaded `registerListener` method is also available that applies the default (`SENSOR_DELAY_NORMAL`) update rate, as shown below:

```
sensorManager.registerListener(mySensorListener,
SensorManager.SENSOR_TRICORDER);
```

Using the Accelerometer and Compass

Input based on movement and orientation is an exciting innovation for mobile applications. It's a technique that has become possible thanks to the incorporation of compass and accelerometer sensors in modern devices.

Accelerometers and compasses are used to provide functionality based on changes in device orientation and movement. A recent trend is to use this functionality to provide alternative input techniques from more traditional touch-screen-, trackball-, and keyboard-based approaches. In recent years, these sensors have become increasingly common, having found their way into game controllers like the Nintendo Wii and mobile handsets like the Apple iPhone.

The availability of compass and accelerometer values depends on the hardware upon which your application runs. When available, they are exposed through the `SensorManager` class, allowing you to:

❑   Determine the current orientation of the hardware.

❑   Monitor for changes in orientation.

❑   Know which direction the user is facing.

❑   Monitor acceleration — changes in movement speed — in any direction: vertically, laterally, or longitudinally.

This opens some intriguing possibilities for your applications. By monitoring orientation, direction, and movement, you can:

❑   Use the compass and accelerometer to determine your speed and direction. Used with the maps and location-based services, you can create interfaces that incorporate direction and movement as well as location.

❑   Create User Interfaces that adjust dynamically to suit the orientation of your device. Android already alters the native screen orientation when the device is rotated from portrait to landscape or vice versa.

❑   Monitor for rapid acceleration to detect if a device has been dropped or thrown.

❑   Measure movement or vibration. For example, you could create an application that lets you lock your device; if any movement is detected while it's locked, it could send an alert IM message that includes its current location.

❑   Create User Interface controls that use physical gestures and movement as input.

Introducing Accelerometers

Accelerometers, as their name suggests, are used to measure acceleration.

Acceleration is defined as the rate of change of velocity, so they measure how quickly the speed of the device is changing in a given direction. Using an accelerometer, you can detect movement and, more usefully, the rate of change of the speed of that movement.

> *It's important to note that accelerometers do not measure velocity, so you can't measure speed directly based on a single accelerometer reading. Instead, you need to measure changes in acceleration over time.*

Generally, you'll be interested in acceleration changes relative to a rest state, or rapid movement (signified by rapid changes in acceleration) such as gestures used for user input. In the former case, you'll often need to calibrate the device to calculate the initial orientation and acceleration to take those effects into account in future results.

> *Accelerometers are unable to differentiate between acceleration due to movement and gravity. As a result, an accelerometer detecting acceleration on the Z-axis (up/down) will read –9.8 m/s² when it's at rest (this value is available as the* SensorManager.STANDARD_GRAVITY *constant).*

Detecting Acceleration Changes

Acceleration can be measured along three directional axes: forward–backward (longitudinal), left–right (lateral), and up–down (vertical). The Sensor Manager reports sensor changes in all three directions (as illustrated in Figure 10-1):

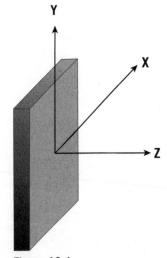

Figure 10-1

❏ **Vertical**   Upward or downward, where positive represents upward movement such as the device being lifted up.

❏ **Longitudinal**   Forward or backward acceleration, where forward acceleration is positive. This represents a device flat on its back, facing up, and in portrait orientation being moved along the desk in the direction of the top of the device.

❏ **Lateral**   Sideways (left or right) acceleration, where positive values represent movement toward the right of the device, and negative values show movement toward the left. In the same configuration as described in longitudinal movement, positive lateral movement would be created by moving the device along the surface to your right.

The Sensor Manager considers the device "at rest" when it is sitting face up on a flat surface in portrait orientation.

As described previously, you can monitor changes in acceleration using Sensor Listeners. Register an extension of the `SensorListener` class with the Sensor Manager, using the `SENSOR_ACCELEROMETER` flag to request updates of accelerometer values and a sensor update rate as shown in the following code snippet:

```
SensorManager sm = (SensorManager)getSystemService(Context.SENSOR_SERVICE);
sm.registerListener(mySensorListener,
                    SensorManager.SENSOR_ACCELEROMETER,
                    SensorManager.SENSOR_DELAY_UI);
```

Your Sensor Listener must implement the `onSensorChanged` method that will be triggered when the changes in acceleration along any of the three axes described previously are detected.

The `onSensorChanged` method receives a `float` array that contains the current acceleration along all three axes in smoothed and raw formats. The Sensor Manager includes index constants that you can use to extract the acceleration value you require, as shown in the following code snippet:

```
SensorListener mySensorListener = new SensorListener() {
    public void onSensorChanged(int sensor, float[] values) {
        if (sensor == SensorManager.SENSOR_ACCELEROMETER) {
            float xAxis = values[SensorManager.DATA_X];
            float yAxis = values[SensorManager.DATA_Y];
            float zAxis = values[SensorManager.DATA_Z];

            float raw_xAxis = values[SensorManager.RAW_DATA_X];
            float raw_yAxis = values[SensorManager.RAW_DATA_Y];
            float raw_zAxis = values[SensorManager.RAW_DATA_Z];

            // TODO apply the acceleration changes to your application.
        }
    }

    public void onAccuracyChanged(int sensor, int accuracy) { }
};
```

Creating a Speedometer

While an accelerometer won't tell you your current speed, you can calculate a rough estimate by monitoring changes in acceleration over time. In the following example, you'll create a simple speedometer using the accelerometers to determine the current speed based on acceleration changes.

The sensitivity and responsiveness of the hardware accelerometers will limit the accuracy and effectiveness of this application, but the techniques it uses should give you a better understanding of how to use the accelerometer sensors for something more useful.

Because accelerometers measure the change in velocity in a given direction, you can establish your current speed by determining how long each acceleration value has been applied. For those mathematically inclined, you're finding the second derivative of the acceleration changes.

For example, if you accelerate at a steady rate of 1 m/s^2 after 10 seconds, your speed will be 10 m/s (or 36 km/h). When your speed becomes steady, your acceleration should return to zero. In the real world, acceleration rarely stops and starts in an instant, nor does it remain constant, so you'll need to adjust your velocity calculations as the measured acceleration changes.

1. Start by creating a new `Speedometer` project with a Speedometer Activity. Modify the main.xml layout resource to display a single, centered line of large, bold text that will be used to display your current speed.

```xml
<?xml version="1.0" encoding="utf-8"?>
<LinearLayout
  xmlns:android="http://schemas.android.com/apk/res/android"
  android:orientation="vertical"
  android:layout_width="fill_parent"
  android:layout_height="fill_parent" >
  <TextView
    android:id="@+id/myTextView"
    android:gravity="center"
    android:layout_width="fill_parent"
    android:layout_height="fill_parent"
    android:textStyle="bold"
    android:textSize="40sp"
    android:text="CENTER"
    android:editable="false"
    android:singleLine="true"
    android:layout_margin="10px"/>
  />
</LinearLayout>
```

2. Within the Speedometer Activity, create instance variables to store references to the `TextView` and the `SensorManager`. Also create variables to record the current acceleration, velocity, and the last update time.

```
SensorManager sensorManager;
TextView myTextView;

float appliedAcceleration = 0;
float currentAcceleration = 0;
float velocity = 0;
Date lastUpdate;
```

3. Create a new `updateVelocity` method that calculates the velocity change since the last update based on the current acceleration.

```
private void updateVelocity() {
  // Calculate how long this acceleration has been applied.
  Date timeNow = new Date(System.currentTimeMillis());
  long timeDelta = timeNow.getTime()-lastUpdate.getTime();
  lastUpdate.setTime(timeNow.getTime());

  // Calculate the change in velocity at the
  // current acceleration since the last update.
  float deltaVelocity = appliedAcceleration * (timeDelta/1000);
  appliedAcceleration = currentAcceleration;

  // Add the velocity change to the current velocity.
  velocity += deltaVelocity;

  // Convert from meters per second to miles per hour.
  double mph = (Math.round(velocity / 1.6 * 3.6));

  myTextView.setText(String.valueOf(mph) + "mph");
}
```

4. Create a new `SensorListener` implementation that updates the current acceleration (and derived velocity) whenever a change in acceleration is detected.

    Because a speedometer will most likely be used while the device is mounted vertically, with the screen face perpendicular to the ground, measure negative acceleration along the Z-axis.

```
private final SensorListener sensorListener = new SensorListener() {

double calibration - Double.NAN;

  public void onSensorChanged(int sensor, float[] values) {
    double x = values[SensorManager.DATA_X];
    double y = values[SensorManager.DATA_Y];
    double z = values[SensorManager.DATA_Z];
    double a = -1*Math.sqrt(Math.pow(x, 2) +
                            Math.pow(y, 2) +
                            Math.pow(z, 2));
    if (calibration == Double.NaN)
      calibration = a;
    else {
      updateVelocity();
      currentAcceleration = (float)a;
    }
  }

  public void onAccuracyChanged(int sensor, int accuracy) {}

};
```

5. Update the `onCreate` method to register your new Listener for accelerometer updates using the `SensorManager`. Take the opportunity to get a reference to the Text View.

```
@Override
public void onCreate(Bundle icicle) {
```

```
                super.onCreate(icicle);
                setContentView(R.layout.main);

                myTextView = (TextView)findViewById(R.id.myTextView);
                lastUpdate = new Date(System.currentTimeMillis());

                sensorManager = (SensorManager)getSystemService(Context.SENSOR_SERVICE);
                sensorManager.registerListener(sensorListener,
                                        SensorManager.SENSOR_ACCELEROMETER,
                                        SensorManager.SENSOR_DELAY_FASTEST);
            }
```

6. Create a new `Timer` that updates the speed based on the current acceleration every second. Because this will update a GUI element, you'll need to create a new `updateGUI` method that synchronizes with the GUI thread using a `Handler` before updating the Text View.

```
            Handler handler = new Handler();

            @Override
            public void onCreate(Bundle icicle) {
                super.onCreate(icicle);
                setContentView(R.layout.main);

                myTextView = (TextView)findViewById(R.id.myTextView);
                lastUpdate = new Date(System.currentTimeMillis());

                sensorManager = (SensorManager)getSystemService(Context.SENSOR_SERVICE);
                sensorManager.registerListener(sensorListener,
                                    SensorManager.SENSOR_ACCELEROMETER,
                                    SensorManager.SENSOR_DELAY_FASTEST);

                Timer updateTimer = new Timer("velocityUpdate");
                updateTimer.scheduleAtFixedRate(new TimerTask() {
                                        public void run() {
                                            updateGUI();
                                        }
                                    }, 0, 1000);
            }

            private void updateGUI()}
                //Convert from m/s to mph
                final double mph = (Math.round(100*velocity / 1.6*3.6)) / 100;

                //Update the GUI
                handler.post(new Runnable() {
                    public void run() {
                        myTextView.setText(String.valueOf(mph) + "mph");
                    }
                });
            }
```

Once you're finished, you'll want to test this out. Given that keeping constant watch on your handset while, driving, cycling, or running is a Bad Idea, you should consider some further enhancements to the speedometer before you take it on the road.

Consider incorporating vibration or media player functionality to shake or beep with intensity proportional to your current speed, or simply log speed changes as they happen for later review.

If you're feeling particularly adventurous, consider integrating your speedometer into a map to track your speed along a journey using different colored lines to represent your speed along the way.

Determining Your Orientation

The *orientation sensors* are a combination of a built-in compass that provides the yaw (heading) and the accelerometers that help determine pitch and roll.

If you've done a bit of trigonometry, you've got the skills required to calculate the device orientation based on the accelerometer values along the three axes. If you enjoyed trig as much as I did, you'll be happy to learn that Android does these calculations for you.

The device orientation is reported along all three dimensions, as illustrated in Figure 10-2:

❑   **Heading**   The heading (also bearing or yaw) is the direction the device is facing around the Z-axis, where 0/360 degrees is North, 90 degrees is East, 180 degrees is South, and 270 degrees is West.

❑   **Pitch**   Pitch represents the angle of the device around the Y-axis. The tilt angle returned shows 0 degrees when the device is flat on its back, –90 degrees when standing upright (top of device pointing at the ceiling), 90 degrees when the device is upside down, and 180/–180 degrees when the device is face down.

❑   **Roll**   The roll represents the device's sideways tilt between –90 and 90 degrees on the X-axis. The tilt is 0 degrees when the device is flat on its back, –90 degrees when the screen faces left, and 90 degrees when the screen faces right.

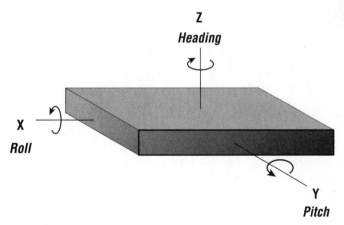

Figure 10-2

As implied by the preceding list, the Sensor Manager considers the device at rest (heading, pitch, roll at 0 degrees) when it is flat on its back. To monitor device orientation, register a Sensor Listener with the Sensor Manager, specifying the SENSOR_ORIENTATION flag, as shown in the following code snippet:

```
SensorManager sm = (SensorManager)getSystemService(Context.SENSOR_SERVICE);
sm.registerListener(myOrientationListener,
                    SensorManager.SENSOR_ORIENTATION,
                    SensorManager.SENSOR_DELAY_NORMAL);
```

The onSensorChanged method in your SensorListener implementation will receive a float array containing the current orientation, along the three axes described above, whenever the device's orientation changes.

Within this float array, use the Sensor Manager constants DATA_X, DATA_Y, and DATA_Z to find the roll, pitch, and heading (yaw) respectively. Use the corresponding RAW_DATA_* constants to find the unsmoothed / unfiltered values as shown in the following code snippet:

```
SensorListener myOrientationListener = new SensorListener() {
  public void onSensorChanged(int sensor, float[] values) {
    if (sensor == SensorManager.SENSOR_ORIENTATION) {
      float rollAngle = values[SensorManager.DATA_X];
      float pitchAngle = values[SensorManager.DATA_Y];
      float headingAngle =  values[SensorManager.DATA_Z];

      float raw_rollAngle = values[SensorManager.RAW_DATA_X];
      float raw_pitchAngle= values[SensorManager.RAW_DATA_Y];
      float raw_headingAngle = values[SensorManager.RAW_DATA_Z];
      // TODO apply the orientation changes to your application.
    }
  }

  public void onAccuracyChanged(int sensor, int accuracy) { }
};
```

Creating a Compass and Artificial Horizon

In Chapter 4, you created a simple CompassView to experiment with owner-drawn controls. In this example, you'll extend the functionality of the CompassView to display the device pitch and roll, before using it to display the current device orientation.

1. Open the Compass project you created in Chapter 4. You will be making changes to the CompassView as well as the Compass Activity used to display it. To ensure that the View and controller remain as decoupled as possible, the CompassView won't be linked to the sensors directly; instead, it will be updated by the Activity.

Start by adding field variables and get/set methods for pitch and roll to the CompassView.

```
float pitch = 0;
float roll = 0;


public float getPitch() {
  return pitch;
}
```

```
public void setPitch(float pitch) {
  this.pitch = pitch;
}

public float getRoll() {
  return roll;
}
public void setRoll(float roll) {
  this.roll = roll;
}
```

2. Update the onDraw method to include two circles that will be used to indicate the pitch and roll values.

```
@Override
protected void onDraw(Canvas canvas) {

  [ … Existing onDraw method … ]
```

2.1. Create a new circle that's half-filled and rotates in line with the sideways tilt.

```
RectF rollOval = new RectF((getMeasuredWidth()/3)-getMeasuredWidth()/7,
                           (getMeasuredHeight()/2)-getMeasuredWidth()/7,
                           (getMeasuredWidth()/3)+getMeasuredWidth()/7,
                           (getMeasuredHeight()/2)+getMeasuredWidth()/7
                          );
markerPaint.setStyle(Paint.Style.STROKE);
canvas.drawOval(rollOval, markerPaint);
markerPaint.setStyle(Paint.Style.FILL);
canvas.save();
canvas.rotate(roll, getMeasuredWidth()/3, getMeasuredHeight()/2);
canvas.drawArc(rollOval, 0, 180, false, markerPaint);

canvas.restore();
```

2.2. Create a new circle that starts half-filled and varies between full and empty based on the current pitch.

```
RectF pitchOval = new RectF((2*mMeasuredWidth/3)-mMeasuredWidth/7,
                            (getMeasuredHeight()/2)-getMeasuredWidth()/7,
                            (2*getMeasuredWidth()/3)+getMeasuredWidth()/7,
                            (getMeasuredHeight()/2)+getMeasuredWidth()/7
                           );
markerPaint.setStyle(Paint.Style.STROKE);
canvas.drawOval(pitchOval, markerPaint);
markerPaint.setStyle(Paint.Style.FILL);
canvas.drawArc(pitchOval, 0-pitch/2, 180+(pitch), false, markerPaint);
markerPaint.setStyle(Paint.Style.STROKE);
}
```

That completes the changes to the CompassView. If you run the application now, it should appear as shown in Figure 10-3. This screen capture was taken while the device was facing due East, with a 45-degree roll and 10-degree backward pitch.

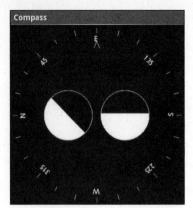

Figure 10-3

1. Now you'll be updating the `Compass` Activity to use the Sensor Manager to listen for orientation changes and pass them through to the `CompassView`. Start by adding local field variables to store the current roll, pitch, and heading as well as references to the `CompassView` and `SensorManager`.

```
float pitch = 0;
float roll = 0;
float heading = 0;

CompassView compassView;
SensorManager sensorManager;
```

2. Create a new `updateOrientation` method that takes new heading, pitch, and roll values to update the field variables and apply them to the `CompassView`.

```
private void updateOrientation(float _roll,
                               float _pitch,
                               float _heading) {
  heading = _heading;
  pitch = _pitch;
  roll = _roll;

  if (compassView!= null) {
    compassView.setBearing(heading);
    compassView.setPitch(pitch);
    compassView.setRoll(roll);
    compassView.invalidate();
  }
}
```

3. Update the `onCreate` method to get references to the `CompassView` and `SensorManager`, as well as initializing the heading, pitch, and roll values.

```
@Override
public void onCreate(Bundle icicle) {
  super.onCreate(icicle);
```

```
setContentView(R.layout.main);

compassView = (CompassView)this.findViewById(R.id.compassView);
sensorManager = (SensorManager)getSystemService(Context.SENSOR_SERVICE);
updateOrientation(0, 0, 0);
}
```

4. Create a new field variable that instantiates a new `SensorListener` implementation that calls the `updateOrientation` method.

```
private final SensorListener sensorListener = new SensorListener() {

public void onSensorChanged(int sensor, float[] values) {
  updateOrientation(values[SensorManager.DATA_X],
                    values[SensorManager.DATA_Y],
                    values[SensorManager.DATA_Z]);
}

public void onAccuracyChanged(int sensor, int accuracy) {}

};
```

5. Then override the `onResume` method to register the `SensorListener` to listen for orientation changes when the Activity is visible. Also override `onStop` to prevent updates when the Activity has been suspended.

```
@Override
protected void onResume()
{
  super.onResume();
  sensorManager.registerListener(sensorListener,
                                 SensorManager.SENSOR_ORIENTATION,
                                 SensorManager.SENSOR_DELAY_FASTEST);
}

@Override
protected void onStop()
{
  sensorManager.unregisterListener(sensorListener);
  super.onStop();
}
```

If you run the application now, you should see the three face dials update dynamically when the orientation of the device changes. Unfortunately, it's not currently possible to emulate the sensor hardware, so this application will only update when running on supported hardware.

Android Telephony

The telephony APIs let your applications access the underlying telephone hardware, making it possible to create your own dialer — or integrate call handling and phone state monitoring into your applications.

Due to security concerns, the current Android SDK does not allow you to create your own "in call" application — the screen that is displayed when an incoming call is received or an outgoing call has been initiated.

Rather than creating a new dialer implementation, the following sections focus on how to monitor and control phone, service, and cell events in your applications to augment and manage the native phone-handling functionality.

Making Phone Calls

The best practice is to use Intents to launch a dialer application to initiate new phone calls. There are two Intent actions you can use to dial a number; in both cases, you should specify the number to dial using the `tel:` schema as the data component of the Intent:

❑   `Intent.ACTION_CALL`   Automatically initiates the call, displaying the in-call application. You should only use this action if you are replacing the native dialer, otherwise you should use the `ACTION_DIAL` action as described below. Your application must have the `CALL_PHONE` permission granted to broadcast this action.

❑   `Intent.ACTION_DIAL`   Rather than dial the number immediately, this action starts a dialer application, passing in the specified number but allowing the dialer application to manage the call initialization (the default dialer asks the user to explicitly initiate the call). This action doesn't require any permissions and is the standard way applications should initiate calls.

The following skeleton code shows the basic technique for dialing a number:

```
Intent intent = new Intent(Intent.ACTION_DIAL, Uri.parse("tel:1234567"));
startActivity(intent);
```

By using Intents to announce your intention to dial a number, your application can remain fully decoupled from a particular hardware implementation used to initiate the call. For example, should you replace the existing dialer with a hybrid that allows IP-based telephony, using Intents to dial a number from other applications will let you leverage that new functionality without needing to change each application.

Monitoring Phone State and Phone Activity

The Android telephony API lets you monitor phone state, retrieve incoming phone numbers, and manage calls. Access to the telephony APIs is managed by the Telephony Manager, accessible using the `getSystemService` method as shown below:

```
String srvcName = Context.TELEPHONY_SERVICE;
TelephonyManager telephonyManager =
  (TelephonyManager)getSystemService(srvcName);
```

In order to monitor and manage phone state, your application will need a `READ_PHONE_STATE` permission, as shown in the following XML code snippet:

```
<uses-permission android:name="android.permission.READ_PHONE_STATE"/>
```

Changes to the phone state are announced to other components using the `PhoneStateListener` class. Extend the `PhoneStateListener` to listen for, and respond to, phone state change events including call state (ringing, off hook, etc.), cell location changes, voice-mail and call-forwarding status, phone service changes, and changes in mobile signal strength.

To react to phone state change events, create a new Phone State Listener implementation, and override the event handlers of the events you want to react to. Each handler receives parameters that indicate the new phone state, such as the current cell location, call state, or signal strength.

The following code highlights the available state change handlers in a skeleton Phone State Listener implementation:

```
PhoneStateListener phoneStateListener = new PhoneStateListener() {
    public void onCallForwardingIndicatorChanged(boolean cfi) {}
    public void onCallStateChanged(int state, String incomingNumber) {}
    public void onCellLocationChanged(CellLocation location) {}
    public void onDataActivity(int direction) {}
    public void onDataConnectionStateChanged(int state) {}
    public void onMessageWaitingIndicatorChanged(boolean mwi) {}
    public void onServiceStateChanged(ServiceState serviceState) {}
    public void onSignalStrengthChanged(int asu) {}
};
```

Once you've created your own Phone State Listener, register it with the Telephony Manager using a bit-mask to indicate the events you want to listen for, as shown in the following code snippet:

```
telephonyManager.listen(phoneStateListener,
                PhoneStateListener.LISTEN_CALL_FORWARDING_INDICATOR |
                PhoneStateListener.LISTEN_CALL_STATE |
                PhoneStateListener.LISTEN_CELL_LOCATION |
                PhoneStateListener.LISTEN_DATA_ACTIVITY |
                PhoneStateListener.LISTEN_DATA_CONNECTION_STATE |
                PhoneStateListener.LISTEN_MESSAGE_WAITING_INDICATOR |
                PhoneStateListener.LISTEN_SERVICE_STATE |
                PhoneStateListener.LISTEN_SIGNAL_STRENGTH);
```

To unregister a listener, call `listen` and pass in `PhoneStateListener.LISTEN_NONE` as the bit field parameter, as shown below:

```
telephonyManager.listen(phoneStateListener, PhoneStateListener.LISTEN_NONE);
```

In the following sections, you'll learn how to use the Phone State Listener to monitor incoming calls, track cell location changes, and monitor service changes.

Monitoring Phone Calls

One of the most popular reasons for monitoring phone state changes is to detect, and react to, incoming and outgoing phone calls.

Calls can be detected through changes in the phone's call state. Override the `onCallStateChanged` method in a Phone State Listener implementation, and register it as shown below to receive notifications when the call state changes:

```
PhoneStateListener callStateListener = new PhoneStateListener() {
  public void onCallStateChanged(int state, String incomingNumber) {
    // TODO React to incoming call.
  }
};

telephonyManager.listen(callStateListener,
PhoneStateListener.LISTEN_CALL_STATE);
```

The `onCallStateChanged` handler receives the phone number associated with incoming calls, and the state parameter represents the current call state as one of the following three values:

❑   `TelephonyManager.CALL_STATE_IDLE`   When the phone is neither ringing nor in a call

❑   `TelephonyManager.CALL_STATE_RINGING`   When the phone is ringing

❑   `TelephonyManager.CALL_STATE_OFFHOOK`   If the phone is currently on a call

Tracking Cell Location Changes

You can get notifications whenever the current cell location changes by overriding `onCellLocationChanged` on a Phone State Listener implementation. Before you can register to listen for cell location changes, you need to add the `ACCESS_COARSE_LOCATION` permission to your application manifest.

```
<uses-permission android:name="android.permission.ACCESS_COARSE_LOCATION"/>
```

The `onCellLocationChanged` handler receives a `CellLocation` object that includes methods for extracting the cell ID (`getCid`) and the current LAC (`getLac`).

The following code snippet shows how to implement a Phone State Listener to monitor cell location changes, displaying a Toast that includes the new location's cell ID:

```
PhoneStateListener cellLocationListener = new PhoneStateListener() {
  public void onCellLocationChanged(CellLocation location) {
    GsmCellLocation gsmLocation = (GsmCellLocation)location;
    Toast.makeText(getApplicationContext(),
                   String.valueOf(gsmLocation.getCid()),
                   Toast.LENGTH_LONG).show();
  }
};
telephonyManager.listen(cellLocationListener,
                        PhoneStateListener.LISTEN_CELL_LOCATION);
```

Tracking Service Changes

The `onServiceStateChanged` handler tracks the service details for the device's cell service. Use the `ServiceState` parameter to find details of the current service state.

The getState method on the Service State object returns the current service state as one of:

- ❏ ServiceState.STATE_IN_SERVICE   Normal phone service is available.

- ❏ ServiceState.STATE_EMERGENCY_ONLY   Phone service is available but only for emergency calls.

- ❏ ServiceState.STATE_OUT_OF_SERVICE   No cell phone service is currently available.

- ❏ ServiceState.STATE_POWER_OFF   The phone radio is turned off (usually when airplane mode is enabled).

A series of getOperator* methods is available to retrieve details on the operator supplying the cell phone service, while getRoaming tells you if the device is currently using a roaming profile.

The following example shows how to register for service state changes and displays a Toast showing the operator name of the current phone service:

```
PhoneStateListener serviceStateListener = new PhoneStateListener() {
  public void onServiceStateChanged(ServiceState serviceState) {
    if (serviceState.getState() == ServiceState.STATE_IN_SERVICE) {
      String toastText = serviceState.getOperatorAlphaLong();
      Toast.makeText(getApplicationContext(), toastText, Toast.LENGTH_SHORT);
    }
  }
};

telephonyManager.listen(serviceStateListener,
                        PhoneStateListener.LISTEN_SERVICE_STATE);
```

Monitoring Data Connectivity and Activity

As well as voice and service details, you can monitor changes in mobile data connectivity and mobile data transfer by implementing a PhoneStateListener.

The Phone State Listener includes two event handlers for monitoring the device data connection. Override onDataActivity to track data transfer activity, and onDataConnectionStateChanged to request notifications for data connection state changes.

The following skeleton code shows both handlers overridden, with switch statements demonstrating each of the possible values for the state and direction parameters passed in to each event:

```
PhoneStateListener dataStateListener = new PhoneStateListener() {
  public void onDataActivity(int direction) {
    switch (direction) {
      case TelephonyManager.DATA_ACTIVITY_IN : break;
      case TelephonyManager.DATA_ACTIVITY_OUT : break;
      case TelephonyManager.DATA_ACTIVITY_INOUT : break;
      case TelephonyManager.DATA_ACTIVITY_NONE : break;
    }
  }

  public void onDataConnectionStateChanged(int state) {
```

```
        switch (state) {
            case TelephonyManager.DATA_CONNECTED : break;
            case TelephonyManager.DATA_CONNECTING : break;
            case TelephonyManager.DATA_DISCONNECTED : break;
            case TelephonyManager.DATA_SUSPENDED : break;
        }
    }
};
```

```
    telephonyManager.listen(dataStateListener,
                            PhoneStateListener.LISTEN_DATA_ACTIVITY |
                            PhoneStateListener.LISTEN_DATA_CONNECTION_STATE);
```

Accessing Phone Properties and Status

The Telephony Manager also provides access to several static phone properties. You can obtain the current value of any of the phone state details described previously. The following code snippet shows how to extract the current incoming call number if the phone is ringing:

```
String incomingCall = null;
if (telephonyManager.getCallState() == TelephonyManager.CALL_STATE_RINGING)
    incomingCall = telephonyManager.getLine1Number();
```

You can also access SIM and network operator details, network information, and voice-mail details. The following code snippet shows the framework used to access the current network details:

```
String srvcName = Context.TELEPHONY_SERVICE;
TelephonyManager telephonyManager = (TelephonyManager)getSystemService(srvcName);

String networkCountry = telephonyManager.getNetworkCountryIso();
String networkOperatorId = telephonyManager.getNetworkOperator();
String networkName = telephonyManager.getNetworkOperatorName();
int networkType = telephonyManager.getNetworkType();
```

Controlling the Phone

There are times when you need access to the underlying phone hardware to effect changes rather than simply monitoring them.

> **Access to the underlying Phone hardware was removed shortly before the release of Android SDK version 1. It is expected that basic phone interaction including answering and hanging up the phone will be available in a subsequent API release.**
>
> **The following section is based on an earlier API release that included phone hardware interaction support. It has been included to serve as a guide for likely future implementations.**

The Phone class in Android provides this interface, letting you control hardware settings, handle incoming calls, initiate new outgoing calls, hang up calls in progress, handle conference calls, and a variety of other Phone functionalities.

Replacing the basic phone functionality is a complex process. Rather than delve into this in detail, this section focuses on some of the more useful functions that can be particularly powerful when used within applications that augment rather than replace the existing functionality.

To access the phone hardware, use the `Phone` class, available through the Telephony Manager using the `getPhone` method as shown in the following code snippet:

```
Phone phone = telephonyManager.getPhone();
```

Once you have a reference to the `Phone` object, you can initiate calls using the `call` or `dial` method or end them by calling `endCall`.

Answering, Dismissing, and Ending Calls

The following code snippet shows how to use the Phone State Listener to listen for incoming calls and reject them if they're from a particular place:

```
final String badPrefix = "+234";

PhoneStateListener callBlockListener = new PhoneStateListener() {
  public void onCallStateChanged(int state, String incomingNumber) {
    if (state == TelephonyManager.CALL_STATE_RINGING) {
      Phone phone = telephonyManager.getPhone();
      if (incomingNumber.startsWith(badPrefix)) {
        phone.endCall();
      }
    }
  }
};

telephonyManager.listen(callBlockListener,
PhoneStateListener.LISTEN_CALL_STATE);
```

Using Bluetooth

In this section, you'll learn how to interact directly with Bluetooth devices including other phones and Bluetooth headsets. Using Bluetooth, you can pair with other devices within range, initiate an `RFCOMMSocket`, and transmit and receive streams of data from or for your applications.

> The Bluetooth libraries have been removed for the Android version 1.0 release. The following sections are based on earlier SDK releases and are included as a guide to functionality that is expected to be made available in subsequent releases.

Introducing the Bluetooth Service

The Android Bluetooth service is represented by the `BluetoothDevice` class.

Bluetooth is a system service accessed using the `getSystemService` method. Get a reference to the `BluetoothDevice` by passing in the `Context.BLUETOOTH` constant as the service name parameter, as shown in the following code snippet:

```
String context = Context.BLUETOOTH_SERVICE;
final BluetoothDevice bluetooth = (BluetoothDevice)getSystemService(context);
```

To use the Bluetooth Service, your application needs to have the BLUETOOTH permission as shown here:

```
<uses-permission android:name="android.permission.BLUETOOTH"/>
```

Controlling the Local Bluetooth Device

The Bluetooth Device offers several methods that let you control the Bluetooth hardware.

The `enable` and `disable` methods let you enable or disable the Bluetooth adapter. The `getName` and `setName` methods let you modify the local device name, and `getAddress` can be used to determine the local device address. You can find and change the discovery mode and discovery time-out settings using the `getMode` and `getDiscoverableTimeout` methods and their setter equivalents.

The following code snippet enables the Bluetooth adapter and waits until it has connected before changing the device name and setting the mode to "discoverable":

```
bluetooth.enable(new IBluetoothDeviceCallback.Stub() {

  public void onCreateBondingResult(String _address, int _result)
               throws RemoteException
  {
    String friendlyName = bluetooth.getRemoteName(_address);
  }

  public void onEnableResult(int _result) throws RemoteException {
    if (_result == BluetoothDevice.RESULT_SUCCESS) {
      bluetooth.setName("BLACKFANG");
      bluetooth.setMode(BluetoothDevice.MODE_DISCOVERABLE);
    }
  }

});
```

Discovering and Bonding with Bluetooth Devices

Before you can establish a data communications socket, the local Bluetooth device must first discover, connect, and bond with the remote device.

Discovery

Looking for remote devices to connect to is called *discovery*. For other devices to discover your handset, you need to set the mode to "discoverable" or "connectable" using the `setMode` method as shown previously.

To discover other devices, initiate a discovery session using the `startDiscovery` or `startPeriodicDiscovery` methods, as shown below:

```
if (discoverPeriodically)
  bluetooth.startPeriodicDiscovery();
else
  bluetooth.startDiscovery(true);
```

Both of these calls are asynchronous, broadcasting a REMOTE_DEVICE_FOUND_ACTION whenever a new remote Bluetooth device is discovered.

To get a list of the remote devices that have been discovered, call `listRemoteDevices` on the Bluetooth device object. The returned String array contains the address of each remote device found. You can find their "friendly" names by passing in the device address to `getRemoteName`.

Bonding

Bonding, also known as *pairing*, lets you create an authenticated connection between two Bluetooth devices using a four-digit PIN. This ensures that your Bluetooth connections aren't hijacked.

Android requires you to bond with remote devices before you can establish application-layer communication sessions such as RFCOMM.

To bond with a remote device, call the `createBonding` method on the Bluetooth Device after using `setPin` to set the unique identifier PIN to use for this pairing request. To abort the bonding attempt, call `cancelBonding` and use `cancelPin` to re-set the PIN if required.

Once a remote device has been bonded, it will be added to the native database and will automatically bond with the local device if it is discovered in the future.

In the following code snippet, the Bluetooth Service is queried for a list of all the available remote devices. The list is then checked to see if any of these devices are not yet bonded with the local Bluetooth service, in which case, pairing is initiated.

```
String[] devices = bluetooth.listRemoteDevices();

for (String device : devices) {
  if (!bluetooth.hasBonding(device)) {
    // Set the pairing PIN. In real life it's probably a smart
    // move to make this user enterable and dynamic.
    bluetooth.setPin(device, new byte[] {1,2,1,2});
    bluetooth.createBonding(device, new IBluetoothDeviceCallback.Stub() {

      public void onCreateBondingResult(String _address, int _result)
                throws RemoteException {
        if (_result == BluetoothDevice.RESULT_SUCCESS) {
          String connectText = "Connected to " + bluetooth.getRemoteName(_address);
          Toast.makeText(getApplicationContext(), connectText, Toast.LENGTH_SHORT);
        }
```

```
        }

        public void onEnableResult(int _result) throws RemoteException {}

    });
  }
}
```

To listen for remote-device bonding requests, implement and register a `BroadcastListener` that filters for the `ACTION_PAIRING_REQUEST` Intent.

Managing Bluetooth Connections

Calling `listRemoteDevices` returns a list of the currently discovered devices, while `listBondings` returns the address of each remote device currently bonded to the local device. As a shortcut, `hasBonding` lets you specify a device address and returns `true` if you have bonded with it.

Further details on each device can be found using the `lastSeen` and `lastUsed` methods. These methods return the last time a device was seen (through discovery) or accessed.

Use `removeBonding` to sever a bond with a remote device. This will also close any application layer communications sockets you've established.

Communication with Bluetooth

The most likely reason for bonding to a remote Bluetooth device is to communicate with it.

Bluetooth data transfer is handled using the `RfcommSocket` class, which provides a wrapper for the Bluetooth radiofrequency communications (RFCOMM) protocol that supports RS232 serial communication over an underlying Logical Link Control and Adaptation Protocol (L2CAP) layer.

In practice, this alphabet soup provides a mechanism for opening communication sockets between two paired Bluetooth devices.

In order for an RFCOMM communication channel to be established, a listening port on one device must be connected to an outgoing port on the other. As a result, for bidirectional communication, two socket connections must be established.

Opening a Socket Connection

Before you can transfer data between Bluetooth devices, you need to open a new `RFCommSocket`.

Start by creating a new `RFCommSocket` object and calling its `create` method. This constructs a new socket for you to use on your Bluetooth device, returning a `FileDescriptor` for transferring data.

The `FileDescriptor` is the lowest-level representation of an I/O source. You can create any of the I/O class objects (`FileStream`, `DataOutputStream`, etc.) using a `FileDescriptor` as a constructor parameter. Later you'll use one of these I/O classes to transfer data with a remote device.

The following skeleton code shows the basic RFCommSocket implementation that creates a new socket connection ready to either initiate or respond to communications requests:

```
FileDescriptor localFile;
RfcommSocket localSocket = new RfcommSocket();
try {
  localFile = localSocket.create();
} catch (IOException e) { }
```

Once the socket has been created, you need to either bind it to the local device to listen for connection requests or initiate a connection with a remote device.

Listening for Data

To listen for incoming data, use the bind method to create a socket to use as a listening port for the local device. If this is successful, use the listen method to open the socket to start listening for incoming data transfer requests.

Once you've initialized your listener socket, use the accept method to check for, and respond to, any incoming socket connection requests.

The accept method takes a new RfcommSocket object that will be used to represent the remote socket connection, and a time-out for a connection request to be received. If a successful connection is made, accept returns a FileDescriptor that represents the input stream. Use this File Descriptor to process the incoming data stream from the remote device.

The following skeleton code shows how to configure a new socket that listens for, and accepts, an incoming socket connection:

```
FileDescriptor localFile;
FileDescriptor remoteFile;

RfcommSocket localSocket = new RfcommSocket();
try {
  localFile = localSocket.create();
  localSocket.bind(null);
  localSocket.listen(1);
  RfcommSocket remotesocket = new RfcommSocket();
  remoteFile = localSocket.accept(remotesocket, 10000);
}
catch (IOException e) { }
```

If no connection request is made within the time-out period, accept returns null.

Transmitting Data

To transmit data using an RfcommSocket, use the connect method to specify a bonded remote device address and port number to transmit data to. The connection request can also be made asynchronously using the connectAsync method to initiate the connection; waitForAsyncConnect can then be used to block on a separate thread until a response is received.

Once a connection has been established, you can transmit data with any of the I/O output classes using the local socket's `FileDescriptor` as a constructor parameter, as shown in the following code snippet:

```
FileDescriptor localFile;
String remoteAddress = bluetooth.listBondings()[0];

RfcommSocket localSocket = new RfcommSocket();
try {
  localFile = localSocket.create();
  // Select an unused port
  if (localSocket.connect(remoteAddress, 0)) {
    FileWriter output = new FileWriter(localFile);
    output.write("Hello, Android");
    output.close();
  }
} catch (IOException e) { }
```

Using a Bluetooth Headset

Wireless headsets are one of the most common uses of Bluetooth on mobile phones.

The `BluetoothHeadset` class provides specialized support for interacting with Bluetooth headsets. In this context, a headset includes any headset or hands-free device.

To use the Bluetooth headset API, create a new `BluetoothHeadset` object on your application context, as shown in the code snippet below:

```
BluetoothHeadset headset = new BluetoothHeadset(this);
```

This object will act as a proxy to the Bluetooth Headset Service that services any Bluetooth headsets bonded with the system.

Android only supports a single headset connection at a time, but you can change the connected headset using this API. Call `connectHeadset`, passing in the address of the headset to connect to, as shown in the code snippet below:

```
headset.connectHeadset(address, new IBluetoothHeadsetCallback.Stub() {

  public void onConnectHeadsetResult(String _address, int _resultCode)
              throws RemoteException {
    if (_resultCode == BluetoothHeadset.RESULT_SUCCESS) {
      // Connected to a new headset device.
    }
  }

});
```

The Headset Service is not guaranteed to be connected to a headset at all times, so it's good practice to use the `getState` method to confirm a valid connection before performing any actions, as shown in the code snippet below:

```
if (headset.getState() == BluetoothHeadset.STATE_CONNECTED) {
  // TODO Perform actions on headset.
}
```

When you've finished interacting with the headset, you should always call `close` on the `BluetoothHeadset` object to let the proxy unbind from the underlying service:

```
BluetoothHeadset headset = new BluetoothHeadset(this);
// [ … Perform headset actions … ]
headset.close();
```

Managing Network and Wi-Fi Connections

The incredible growth of Internet services and the ubiquity of mobile devices has made mobile Internet access an increasingly prevalent feature on mobile phones.

With the speed, reliability, and cost of Internet connectivity dependent on the network technology being used (Wi-Fi, GPRS, 3G), letting your applications know and manage these connections can help to ensure that they run efficiently and responsively.

Android provides access to the underlying network state, broadcasting Intents to notify application components of changes in network connectivity and offering control over network settings and connections.

Android networking is principally handled using the `ConnectivityManager`, a Service that lets you monitor the connectivity state, set your preferred network connection, and manage connectivity failover.

Later you'll learn how to use the `WifiManager` to monitor and control the device's Wi-Fi connectivity specifically. The Wi-Fi Manager lets you see and modify the configured Wi-Fi networks, manage the active connection, and perform access point scans.

Monitoring and Managing Your Internet Connectivity

The `ConnectivityManager` represents the Network Connectivity Service. It's used to monitor the state of network connections, configure failover settings, and control the network radios.

To access the Connectivity Manager, call `getSystemService`, passing in `Context.CONNECTIVITY_SERVICE` as the service name, as shown in the code snippet below:

```
String service = Context.CONNECTIVITY_SERVICE;
ConnectivityManager connectivity = (ConnectivityManager)getSystemService(service);
```

Before it can use the Connectivity Manager, your application will need Read and Write network state access permissions to be added to the manifest, as shown below:

```
<uses-permission android:name="android.permission.ACCESS_NETWORK_STATE"/>
<uses-permission android:name="android.permission.CHANGE_NETWORK_STATE"/>
```

Managing Active Connections

The Connectivity Manager provides a high-level view of the available network connections. Using the getActiveNetworkInfo or getNetworkInfo methods, you query NetworkInfo objects that include details on the currently active network or on an inactive network of the type specified.

In both cases, the NetworkInfo returned includes methods that indicate the connection status and network type of the specified network.

Configuring Network Preferences and Controlling Hardware

The Connectivity Manager can also be used to control network hardware and configure failover preferences.

Android will attempt to connect to the preferred network whenever an authorized application requests an Internet connection. You can set the preferred network using the setNetworkPreference method and specifying the network you would prefer to connect to, as shown in the code snippet below:

```
connectivity.setNetworkPreference(NetworkPreference.PREFER_WIFI);
```

If the preferred connection is unavailable, or connectivity on this network is lost, Android will automatically attempt to connect to the secondary network.

You can control the availability of the network types, using the setRadio method. This method lets you set the state of the radio associated with a particular network (Wi-Fi, mobile, etc.). For example, in the following code snippet, the Wi-Fi radio is turned off and the mobile radio is turned on:

```
connectivity.setRadio(NetworkType.WIFI, false);
connectivity.setRadio(NetworkType.MOBILE, true);
```

Monitoring Network Connectivity

One of the most useful functions of the Connectivity Manager is to notify applications of changes in network connectivity.

To monitor network connectivity, create your own Broadcast Receiver implementation that listens for ConnectivityManager.CONNECTIVITY_ACTION Intents. Such Intents include several extras that provide additional details on the change to the connectivity state:

❑ ConnectivityManager.EXTRA_IS_FAILOVER   Is a Boolean that returns true if the current connection is the result of a failover from a preferred network.

❑ ConnectivityManager.EXTRA_NO_CONNECTIVITY   Is a Boolean that returns true if the device is not connected to any network.

❑ ConnectivityManager.EXTRA_REASON   If this broadcast represents a connection failure, this string value includes a description of why the connection attempt failed.

❑ ConnectivityManager.EXTRA_NETWORK_INFO   This returns a NetworkInfo object containing more fine-grained details on the network associated with the current connectivity event.

❑ ConnectivityManager.EXTRA_OTHER_NETWORK_INFO   After a network disconnection, this value will return a NetworkInfo object populated with the details for the possible failover network connection.

❑ ConnectivityManager.EXTRA_EXTRA_INFO   Contains additional network-specific extra connection details.

Android SDK beta 0.9 included a NetworkConnectivityListener that encapsulated this functionality. This class has been removed for version 1.0.

Managing Your Wi-Fi

The WifiManager represents the Android Wi-Fi Connectivity Service. It can be used to configure Wi-Fi network connections, manage the current Wi-Fi connection, scan for access points, and monitor changes in Wi-Fi connectivity.

As with the Connectivity Manager, access the Wi-Fi Manager using the getSystemService method, passing in the Context.WIFI_SERVICE constant, as shown in the following code snippet:

```
String service = Context.WIFI_SERVICE;
final WifiManager wifi = (WifiManager)getSystemService(service);
```

To use the Wi-Fi Manager, your application must have uses-permissions for Read/Write Wi-Fi state access included in its manifest.

```
<uses-permission android:name="android.permission.ACCESS_WIFI_STATE"/>
<uses-permission android:name="android.permission.CHANGE_WIFI_STATE"/>
```

You can use the Wi-Fi Manager to enable or disable your Wi-Fi hardware using the setWifiEnabled method, or request the current Wi-Fi state using the getWifiState or isWifiEnabled methods as shown in the code snippet below:

```
if (!wifi.isWifiEnabled())
  if (wifi.getWifiState() != WifiManager.WIFI_STATE_ENABLING)
    wifi.setWifiEnabled(true);
```

The following sections begin with tracking the current Wi-Fi connection status and monitoring changes in signal strength. Later you'll also learn how to scan for and connect to specific access points.

While these functions may be sufficient for most developers, the WifiManager also provides low-level access to the Wi-Fi network configurations, giving you full control over each configuration setting and allowing you to completely replace the native Wi-Fi management application. Later in the section, you'll be introduced to the API used to create, delete, and modify network configurations.

Monitoring Wi-Fi Connectivity

The Wi-Fi Manager broadcasts Intents whenever the connectivity status of the Wi-Fi network changes, using the following actions:

❑ `WifiManager.WIFI_STATE_CHANGED_ACTION` Indicates that the Wi-Fi hardware status has changed, moving between enabling, enabled, disabling, disabled, and unknown. It includes two extra values keyed on `EXTRA_WIFI_STATE` and `EXTRA_PREVIOUS_STATE` that provide the previous and new Wi-Fi states.

❑ `WifiManager.SUPPLICANT_CONNECTION_CHANGE_ACTION` This Intent is broadcast whenever the connection state with the active supplicant (access point) changes. It is fired when a new connection is established or an existing connection is lost using the `EXTRA_NEW_STATE` Boolean extra that returns `true` in the former case.

❑ `WifiManager.NETWORK_STATE_CHANGED_ACTION` The network state change broadcast is fired whenever the Wi-Fi connectivity state changes. This Intent includes two extras — the first `EXTRA_NETWORK_INFO` includes a `NetworkInfo` object that details the current network state, while the second `EXTRA_BSSID` includes the BSSID of the access point you're connected to.

❑ `WifiManager.RSSI_CHANGED_ACTION` You can monitor the current signal strength of the connected Wi-Fi network by listening for the `RSSI_CHANGED_ACTION` Intent. This Broadcast Intent includes an integer extra, `EXTRA_NEW_RSSI`, that holds the current signal strength. To use this signal strength, you should use the `calculateSignalLevel` static method on the Wi-Fi Manager to convert it to an integer value on a scale you specify.

Creating and Managing Wi-Fi Connections and Configurations

You can use the Wi-Fi Manager to manage the configured network settings and control which networks to connect to. Once connected, you can interrogate the active network connection to get additional details of its configuration and settings.

Get a list of the current network configurations using `getConfiguredNetworks`. The list of `WifiConfiguration` objects returned includes the network ID, SSID, and other details for each configuration.

To use a particular network configuration, use the `enableNetwork` method, passing in the network ID to use and specifying `true` for the `disableAllOthers` parameter as shown below:

```
// Get a list of available configurations
List<WifiConfiguration> configurations = wifi.getConfiguredNetworks();
// Get the network ID for the first one.
if (configurations.size() > 0) {
  int netID = configurations.get(0).networkId;
  // Enable that network.
  boolean disableAllOthers = true;
  wifi.enableNetwork(netID, disableAllOtherstrue);
}
```

Once an active network connection has been established, use the `getConnectionInfo` method to return information on the active connection's status. The returned `WifiInfo` object includes the BSSID, Mac address, and IP address of the current access point, as well as the current link speed and signal strength.

The following code snippet queries the currently active Wi-Fi connection and displays a Toast showing the connection speed and signal strength:

```
WifiInfo info = wifi.getConnectionInfo();
if (info.getBSSID() != null) {
  int strength = WifiManager.calculateSignalLevel(info.getRssi(), 5);
  int speed = info.getLinkSpeed();
  String units = WifiInfo.LINK_SPEED_UNITS;
  String ssid = info.getSSID();

  String toastText = String.format("Connected to {0} at {1}{2}. Strength {3}/5",
                                   ssid, speed, units, strength);

  Toast.makeText(this, toastText, Toast.LENGTH_LONG);
}
```

Scanning for Hotspots

You can use the Wi-Fi Manager to conduct access point scans using the startScan method.

An Intent with the SCAN_RESULTS_AVAILABLE_ACTION action will be broadcast to asynchronously announce that the scan is complete and results are available.

Call getScanResults to get those results as a list of ScanResult objects.

Each ScanResult includes the details retrieved for each access point detected, including link speed, signal strength, SSID, and the authentication techniques supported.

The following skeleton code shows how to initiate a scan for access points that displays a Toast indicating the total number of access points found and the name of the Access Point with the strongest signal:

```
// Register a broadcast receiver that listens for scan results.
registerReceiver(new BroadcastReceiver() {

  @Override
  public void onReceive(Context context, Intent intent) {
    List<ScanResult> results = wifi.getScanResults();
    ScanResult bestSignal = null;
    for (ScanResult result : results) {
      if (bestSignal == null ||
          WifiManager.compareSignalLevel(bestSignal.level, result.level) < 0)
        bestSignal = result;
    }

    String toastText = String.format("{0} networks found. {1} is the strongest.",
                                     results.size(), bestSignal.SSID);

    Toast.makeText(getApplicationContext(), toastText, Toast.LENGTH_LONG);
  }

}, new IntentFilter(WifiManager.SCAN_RESULTS_AVAILABLE_ACTION));

// Initiate a scan.
wifi.startScan();
```

Managing Wi-Fi Network Configurations

To connect to a Wi-Fi network, you need to create and register a configuration. Normally your users would do this using the native Wi-Fi configuration settings, but there's no reason you can't expose the same functionality within your own applications, or for that matter replace the native Wi-Fi configuration Activity entirely.

Network configurations are stored as `WifiConfiguration` objects. The following is a non-exhaustive list of some of the public fields available for each Wi-Fi Configuration:

- ❑ `BSSID`   Specifies the BSSID for an access point.
- ❑ `SSID`   The SSID for a particular network
- ❑ `networkId`   A unique identifier used to identify this network configuration on the current device
- ❑ `priority`   The priority of each network configuration when choosing which of several access points to connect to
- ❑ `status`   The current status of this network connection, will be one of `WifiConfiguration.Status.ENABLED`, `WifiConfiguration.Status.DISABLED`, or `WifiConfiguration.Status.CURRENT`

The configuration object also contains the supported authentication technique, as well as the keys used previously to authenticate with this access point.

The `addNetwork` method lets you specify a new configuration to add to the current list; similarly, `updateNetwork` lets you update a network configuration by passing in a `WifiConfiguration` that's sparsely populated with a network ID and the values you want to change.

You can also use `removeNetwork`, passing in a network ID, to remove a configuration.

To persist any changes made to the network configurations, you must call `saveConfiguration`.

Controlling Device Vibration

In Chapter 8, you learned how to create Notifications that can trigger vibration to provide additional user feedback when signaling events. In some circumstances, you may wish to vibrate the device independently of Notifications. Vibrating the device is an excellent way to provide haptic user feedback and is particularly popular as a feedback mechanism for games.

To control device vibration, your applications need the `VIBRATE` permission. Add this to your application manifest using the code snippet below:

```
<uses-permission android:name="android.permission.VIBRATE"/>
```

Device vibration is controlled through the `Vibrator` class, accessible using the `getSystemService` method, as shown in the following code snippet:

```
String vibratorService = Context.VIBRATOR_SERVICE;
Vibrator vibrator = (Vibrator)getSystemService(vibratorService);
```

Call `vibrate` to start device vibration; you can pass in either a vibration duration or pattern of alternating vibration/pause sequences along with an optional index parameter that will repeat the pattern starting at the index specified. Both techniques are demonstrated below:

```
long[] pattern = {1000, 2000, 4000, 8000, 16000 };
vibrator.vibrate(pattern, 0);
vibrator.vibrate(1000); // Vibrate for 1 second
```

To cancel vibration, you can call `cancel`. Alternatively, exiting your application will automatically cancel any vibration it has initiated.

Summary

In this chapter, you learned how to monitor and control some of the hardware services available on Android devices.

Beginning with the media APIs, you learned about Android's multimedia capabilities including playback and recording using the Media Player and Media Recorder classes.

You were introduced to the Camera APIs that can be used to change camera settings, initiate live camera previews, and take photos.

With the Sensor Manager, you used the accelerometer and compass hardware to determine the device's orientation and acceleration, as well as monitoring and interpreting changes to detect device movement.

Finally, you examined the underlying communications hardware APIs available in Android. This included an introduction to the telephony APIs and an overview of the Bluetooth, network, and Wi-Fi managers for monitoring and controlling device connectivity.

This chapter also included:

- ❑ Monitoring phone state information, including cell location, phone state, and service state.
- ❑ Controlling the Bluetooth device to discover, bond, and transmit information between local and remote Bluetooth devices.
- ❑ Managing Bluetooth headsets.
- ❑ Managing Wi-Fi configurations, searching for access points, and managing Wi-Fi connections.
- ❑ Controlling device vibration to provide haptic feedback.

In the final chapter, you'll be introduced to some of the advanced Android features. You'll learn more about security and how to use AIDL to facilitate interprocess communication. You'll learn about Android's User Interface and graphics capabilities by exploring animations and advanced Canvas drawing techniques. Finally, you'll be introduced to the `SurfaceView` and touch-screen input functionality.

11

Advanced Android Development

In this chapter, you'll be returning to some of the possibilities touched on in previous chapters and explore some of the topics that deserve more attention.

In the first six chapters, you learned the fundamentals of creating mobile applications for Android devices. In Chapters 7 through 10, you were introduced to some of the more powerful optional APIs, including location-based services, maps, instant messaging, and hardware monitoring and control.

You'll start this chapter by taking a closer look at security, in particular, how permissions work and how to use them to secure your own applications.

Next you'll examine the Android Interface Definition Language (AIDL) and learn how to create rich application interfaces that support full object-based interprocess communication (IPC) between Android applications running in different processes.

You'll then take a closer look at the rich toolkit available for creating User Interfaces for your Activities. Starting with animations, you'll learn how to apply tweened animations to Views and View Groups, and construct frame-by-frame cell-based animations.

Next is an in-depth examination of the possibilities available with Android's raster graphics engine. You'll be introduced to the drawing primitives available before learning some of the more advanced possibilities available with Paint. You'll learn how to use transparency and create gradient Shaders and bitmap brushes. You'll be introduced to mask and color filters, as well as Path Effects and the possibilities of using different transfer modes.

You'll then delve a little deeper into the design and execution of more complex User Interface Views, learning how to create three-dimensional and high frame-rate interactive controls using the Surface View, and how to use the touch screen, trackball, and device keys to create intuitive input possibilities for your UIs.

Paranoid Android

Much of Android's security is native to the underlying Linux kernel. Resources are sandboxed to their owner applications, making them inaccessible from other applications. Android provides broadcast Intents, Services, and Content Providers to let you relax these strict process boundaries, using the permission mechanism to maintain application-level security.

You've already used the permission system to request access to native system services — notably the location-based services and contacts Content Provider — for your applications.

The following sections provide a more detailed look at the security available. For a comprehensive view, the Android documentation provides an excellent resource that describes the security features in depth at `code.google.com/android/devel/security.html`.

Linux Kernel Security

Each Android package has a unique Linux userID assigned to it during installation. This has the effect of sandboxing the process and the resources it creates, so that it can't affect (or be affected by) other applications.

Because of this kernel-level security, you need to take additional steps to communicate between applications. Enter Content Providers, broadcast Intents, and AIDL interfaces. Each of these mechanisms opens a tunnel for information to flow between applications. Android permissions act as border guards at either end to control the traffic allowed through these tunnels.

Introducing Permissions

Permissions are an application-level security mechanism that lets you restrict access to application components. Permissions are used to prevent malicious applications from corrupting data, gaining access to sensitive information, or making excessive (or unauthorized) use of hardware resources or external communication channels.

As you've learned in earlier chapters, many of Android's native components have permission requirements. The native permission strings used by native Android Activities and Services can be found as static constants in the `android.Manifest.permission` class.

To use permission-protected components, you need to add `uses-permission` tags to application manifests, specifying the permission string that each application requires.

When an application package is installed, the permissions requested in its manifest are analyzed and granted (or denied) by checks with trusted authorities and user feedback.

Unlike many existing mobile platforms, all Android permission checks are done at installation. Once an application is installed, the user will not be prompted to reevaluate those permissions.

> *There's no guarantee that your application will be granted the permissions it requests, so it's good practice to write defensive code that ensures it fails gracefully in these circumstances.*

Declaring and Enforcing Permissions

Before you can assign a permission to an application component, you need to define it within your manifest using the `permission` tag as shown in the following code snippet:

```
<permission
  android:name="com.paad.DETONATE_DEVICE"
  android:protectionLevel="dangerous"
  android:label="Self Destruct"
  android:description="@string/detonate_description">
</permission>
```

Within the permission tag, you can specify the level of access that the permission will permit (`normal`, `dangerous`, `signature`, `signatureOrSystem`), a label, and an external resource containing the description that explains the risks of granting this permission.

To include permission requirements for your own application components, use the `permission` attribute in the application manifest. Permission constraints can be enforced throughout your application, most usefully at application interface boundaries, for example:

❑ **Activities** Add a permission to limit the ability of other applications to launch an Activity.

❑ **Broadcast Receivers** Control which applications can send broadcast Intents to your receiver.

❑ **Content Providers** Limit Read access and Write operations on Content Providers.

❑ **Services** Limit the ability of other applications to start, or bind to, a Service.

In each case, you can add a `permission` attribute to the application component in the manifest, specifying a required permission string to access each component, as shown below in a manifest excerpt that shows a permission requirement for an Activity:

```
<activity
  android:name=".MyActivity"
  android:label="@string/app_name"
  android:permission="com.paad.DETONATE_DEVICE">
</activity>
```

Content Providers let you set `readPermission` and `writePermission` attributes to offer a more granular control over Read/Write access.

Enforcing Permissions with Broadcasting Intents

As well as requiring permissions for Intents to be received by your Broadcast Receivers, you can also attach a permission string to each Intent you broadcast.

When calling `sendIntent`, you can supply a permission string required by Broadcast Receivers before they can receive the Intent. This process is shown below:

```
sendBroadcast(myIntent, REQUIRED_PERMISSION);
```

Using AIDL to Support IPC for Services

One of the more interesting possibilities of Services is the idea of running independent background processes to supply processing, data lookup, or other useful functionality to multiple independent applications.

In Chapter 8, you learned how to create Services for your applications. Here, you'll learn how to use the Android Interface Definition Language (AIDL) to support interprocess communication (IPC) between Services and application components. This will give your Services the ability to support multiple applications across process boundaries.

To pass objects between processes, you need to deconstruct them into OS-level primitives that the underlying operating system (OS) can then marshal across application boundaries.

AIDL is used to simplify the code that lets your processes exchange objects. It's similar to interfaces like COM or Corba in that it lets you create public methods within your Services that can accept and return object parameters and return values between processes.

Implementing an AIDL Interface

AIDL supports the following data types:

❑ Java language primitives (`int`, `boolean`, `float`, `char`, etc.)

❑ `String` and `CharSequence` values

❑ `List` (including generic) objects, where each element is a supported type. The receiving class will always receive the List object instantiated as an `ArrayList`.

❑ `Map` (*not* including generic) objects in which each key and element is a supported type. The receiving class will always receive the `Map` object instantiated as a `HashMap`.

❑ AIDL-generated interfaces (covered later). An import statement is always needed for these.

❑ Classes that implement the `Parcelable` interface (covered next). An import statement is always needed for these.

The following sections demonstrate how to make your application classes AIDL-compatible by implementing the `Parcelable` interface, before creating an AIDL interface definition and implementing that interface within your Service.

Passing Custom Class Objects

To pass non-native objects between processes, they must implement the `Parcelable` interface. This lets you decompose your objects into primitive types stored within a `Parcel` that can be marshaled across process boundaries.

Implement the `writeToParcel` method to decompose your class object, then implement the public static `Creator` field (which implements a new `Parcelable.Creator` class), which will create a new object based on an incoming Parcel.

The following code snippet shows a basic example of using the `Parcelable` interface for the `Quake` class you've been using in the ongoing Earthquake example:

```
package com.paad.earthquake;

import java.util.Date;
import android.location.Location;
import android.os.Parcel;
import android.os.Parcelable;

public class Quake implements Parcelable {
    private Date date;
    private String details;
    private Location location;
    private double magnitude;
    private String link;

    public Date getDate() { return date; }
    public String getDetails() { return details; }
    public Location getLocation() { return location; }
    public double getMagnitude() { return magnitude; }
    public String getLink() { return link; }

    public Quake(Date _d, String _det, Location _loc, double _mag, String _link) {
        date = _d;
        details = _det;
        location = _loc;
        magnitude = _mag;
        link = _link;
    }

    @Override
    public String toString(){
        SimpleDateFormat sdf = new SimpleDateFormat("HH.mm");
        String dateString = sdf.format(date);
        return dateString + ":" + magnitude + " " + details;
    }

    private Quake(Parcel in) {
        date.setTime(in.readLong());
        details = in.readString();
        magnitude = in.readDouble();
        Location location = new Location("gps");
        location.setLatitude(in.readDouble());
        location.setLongitude(in.readDouble());
        link= in.readString();
    }

    public void writeToParcel(Parcel out, int flags) {
        out.writeLong(date.getTime());
        out.writeString(details);
        out.writeDouble(magnitude);
```

```
        out.writeDouble(location.getLatitude());
        out.writeDouble(location.getLongitude());
        out.writeString(link);
    }
```

```
    public static final Parcelable.Creator<Quake> CREATOR =
        new Parcelable.Creator<Quake>() {
            public Quake createFromParcel(Parcel in) {
                return new Quake(in);
            }

            public Quake[] newArray(int size) {
                return new Quake[size];
            }
        };
```

```
    public int describeContents() {
        return 0;
    }
```

```
}
```

Now that you've got a Parcelable class, you need to create an AIDL definition to make it available when defining your Service's AIDL interface.

The following code snippet shows the contents of the Quake.aidl file you need to create for the Quake class defined above:

```
package com.paad.earthquake;

parcelable Quake;
```

Remember that when you're passing class objects between processes, the client process must understand the definition of the object being passed.

Creating the AIDL Definition

In this section, you will be defining a new AIDL interface definition for a Service you'd like to use across processes.

Start by creating a new .aidl file within your project. This will define the methods and fields to include in an Interface that your Service will implement.

The syntax for creating AIDL definitions is similar to that used for standard Java interface definitions.

Start by specifying a fully qualified package name, then `import` all the packages required. Unlike normal Java interfaces, AIDL definitions need to import packages for any class or interface that isn't a native Java type even if it's defined in the same project.

Define a new `interface`, adding the properties and methods you want to make available.

Methods can take zero or more parameters and return void or a supported type. If you define a method that takes one or more parameters, you need to use a directional tag to indicate if the parameter is a value or reference type using the in, out, and inout keywords.

Where possible, you should limit the direction of each parameter, as marshaling parameters is an expensive operation.

The following sample shows a basic AIDL definition for the IEarthquakeService.aidl file:

```
package com.paad.earthquake;

import com.paad.earthquake.Quake;

interface IEarthquakeService {
  List<Quake> getEarthquakes();

  void refreshEarthquakes();
}
```

Implementing and Exposing the IPC Interface

If you're using the ADT plug-in, saving the AIDL file will automatically code-generate a Java interface file. This interface will include an inner Stub class that implements the interface as an abstract class.

Have your Service extend the Stub and implement the functionality required. Typically, this will be done using a private field variable within the Service whose functionality you'll be exposing.

The following code snippet shows an implementation of the IEarthquakeService AIDL definition created above:

```
IBinder myEarthquakeServiceStub = new IEarthquakeService.Stub() {
  public void refreshEarthquakes() throws RemoteException {
    EarthquakeService.this.refreshEarthquakes();
  }

  public List<Quake> getEarthquakes() throws RemoteException {
    ArrayList<Quake> result = new ArrayList<Quake>();

    ContentResolver cr = EarthquakeService.this.getContentResolver();
    Cursor c = cr.query(EarthquakeProvider.CONTENT_URI, null, null, null, null);
    if (c.moveToFirst())
      do {

        Double lat = c.getDouble(EarthquakeProvider.LATITUDE_COLUMN);
        Double lng = c.getDouble(EarthquakeProvider.LONGITUDE_COLUMN);
        Location location = new Location("dummy");
        location.setLatitude(lat);
        location.setLongitude(lng);

        String details = c.getString(EarthquakeProvider.DETAILS_COLUMN);
```

```
                String link =  c.getString(EarthquakeProvider.LINK_COLUMN);

                double magnitude = c.getDouble(EarthquakeProvider.MAGNITUDE_COLUMN);

                long datems =  c.getLong(EarthquakeProvider.DATE_COLUMN);
                Date date = new Date(datems);

                result.add(new Quake(date, details, location, magnitude, link));
            } while(c.moveToNext());

        return result;
      }
  };
```

There are several considerations when implementing these methods:

❑   All exceptions will remain local to the implementing process; they will not be propagated to the calling application.

❑   All IPC calls are synchronous. If you know that the process is likely to be time-consuming, you should consider wrapping the synchronous call in an asynchronous wrapper or moving the processing on the receiver side onto a background thread.

With the functionality implemented, you need to expose this interface to client applications. Expose the IPC-enabled Service interface by overriding the onBind method within our service implementation to return an instance of the interface.

The code snippet below demonstrates the onBind implementation for the EarthquakeService:

```
@Override
public IBinder onBind(Intent intent) {
  return myEarthquakeServiceStub;
}
```

To use the IPC Service from within an Activity, you must bind it as shown in the following code snippet taken from the Earthquake Activity:

```
IEarthquakeService earthquakeService = null;

private void bindService() {
  bindService(new Intent(IEarthquakeService.class.getName()),
          serviceConnection, Context.BIND_AUTO_CREATE);
}

private ServiceConnection serviceConnection = new ServiceConnection() {
  public void onServiceConnected(ComponentName className,
                                 IBinder service) {
    earthquakeService = IEarthquakeService.Stub.asInterface(service);
  }

  public void onServiceDisconnected(ComponentName className) {
```

```
        earthquakeService = null;
    }
};
```

Using Internet Services

Software as a service, or cloud computing, is becoming increasingly popular as companies try to reduce the cost overheads associated with installation, upgrades, and maintenance of deployed software. The result is a range of rich Internet services with which you can build thin mobile applications that enrich online services with the personalization available from your mobile.

The idea of using a middle tier to reduce client-side load is not a novel one, and happily there are many Internet-based options to supply your applications with the level of service you need.

The sheer volume of Internet services available makes it impossible to list them all here (let alone look at them in any detail), but the following list shows some of the more mature and interesting Internet services currently available:

❑ **Google's gData Services** As well as the native Google applications, Google offers Web APIs for access to their calendar, spreadsheet, Blogger, and Picasaweb platforms. These APIs collectively make use of Google's standardized gData framework, a form of Read/Write XML data communication.

❑ **Yahoo! Pipes** Yahoo! Pipes offers a graphical web-based approach to XML feed manipulation. Using pipes, you can filter, aggregate, analyze, and otherwise manipulate XML feeds and output them in a variety of formats to be consumed by your applications.

❑ **The Google App Engine** Using the Google App Engine, you can create cloud-hosted web services that shift complex processing away from your mobile client. Doing so reduces the load on your system resources but comes at the price of Internet-connection dependency.

❑ **Amazon Web Services** Amazon offers a range of cloud-based services, including a rich API for accessing its media database of books, CDs, and DVDs. Amazon also offers a distributed storage solution (S3) and an elastic compute cloud (EC2).

Building Rich User Interfaces

Mobile phone User Interfaces have improved dramatically in recent years, thanks not least of all to the iPhone's innovative take on mobile UI.

In this section, you'll learn how to use more advanced UI visual effects like Shaders, translucency, animations, touch screens, and OpenGL to add a level of polish to your Activities and Views.

Working with Animations

Back in Chapter 3, you learned how to define animations as external resources. Now, eight chapters later, you get the opportunity to put them to use.

Android offers two kinds of animation:

❑ **Frame-by-Frame Animations**   Traditional cell-based animations in which a different Drawable is displayed in each frame. Frame-by-frame animations are displayed within a View, using its Canvas as a projection screen.

❑ **Tweened Animations**   Tweened animations are applied to Views, letting you define a series of changes in position, size, rotation, and opacity that animate the View contents.

Both animation types are restricted to the original bounds of the View they're applied to. Rotations, translations, and scaling transformations that extend beyond the original boundaries of the View will result in the contents being clipped.

Introducing Tweened Animations

Tweened Animations offer a simple way to provide depth, movement, or feedback to your users at a minimal resource cost.

Using animations to apply a set of orientation, scale, position, and opacity changes is much less resource-intensive than manually redrawing the Canvas to achieve similar effects, not to mention far simpler to implement.

Tweened animations are commonly used to:

❑ Transition between Activities.

❑ Transition between layouts within an Activity.

❑ Transition between different content displayed within the same View.

❑ Provide user feedback such as:

  ❑ A rotating hourglass View to indicate progress

    or

  ❑ "Shaking" an input box to indicate an incorrect or invalid data entry.

Creating Tweened Animations

Tweened animations are created using the Animation class. The following list explains the animation types available:

❑ AlphaAnimation   Lets you animate a change in the Views transparency (opacity or alpha blending).

❑ RotateAnimation   Lets you spin the selected View canvas in the *XY* plane.

❑ ScaleAnimation   Allows you to zoom in to or out from the selected View.

❑ TranslateAnimation   Lets you move the selected View around the screen (although it will only be drawn within its original bounds).

Android offers the AnimationSet class to group and configure animations to be run as a set. You can define the start time and duration of each animation used within a set to control the timing and order of the animation sequence.

It's important to set the start offset and duration for each child animation, or they will all start and complete at the same time.

The following code and XML snippets demonstrate how to create the same animation sequence in code or as an external resource:

```java
// Create the AnimationSet
AnimationSet myAnimation = new AnimationSet(true);

// Create a rotate animation.
RotateAnimation rotate = new RotateAnimation(0, 360,
                                RotateAnimation.RELATIVE_TO_SELF,0.5f,
                                RotateAnimation.RELATIVE_TO_SELF,0.5f
                                );
rotate.setFillAfter(true);
rotate.setDuration(1000);

// Create a scale animation
ScaleAnimation scale = new ScaleAnimation(1, 0,
                            1, 0,
                            ScaleAnimation.RELATIVE_TO_SELF, 0.5f,
                            ScaleAnimation.RELATIVE_TO_SELF, 0.5f
                            );
scale.setFillAfter(true);
scale.setDuration(500);
scale.setStartOffset(500);

// Create an alpha animation
AlphaAnimation alpha = new AlphaAnimation(1, 0);
scale.setFillAfter(true);
scale.setDuration(500);
scale.setStartOffset(500);

// Add each animation to the set
myAnimation.addAnimation(rotate);
myAnimation.addAnimation(scale);
myAnimation.addAnimation(alpha);
```

The code snippet above implements the same animation sequence shown in the following XML snippet:

```xml
<?xml version="1.0" encoding="utf-8"?>
<set
  xmlns:android="http://schemas.android.com/apk/res/android"
  android:shareInterpolator="true">
  <rotate
    android:fromDegrees="0"
    android:toDegrees="360"
    android:pivotX="50%"
    android:pivotY="50%"
    android:startOffset="0"
    android:duration="1000" />
  <scale
    android:fromXScale="1.0"
    android:toXScale="0.0"
```

```
      android:fromYScale="1.0"
      android:toYScale="0.0"
      android:pivotX="50%"
      android:pivotY="50%"
      android:startOffset="500"
      android:duration="500" />
  <alpha
      android:fromAlpha="1.0"
      android:toAlpha="0.0"
      android:startOffset="500"
      android:duration="500" />
</set>
```

As you can see, it's generally both easier and more intuitive to create your animation sequences using an external animation resource.

Applying Tweened Animations

Animations can be applied to any View by calling its `startAnimation` method and passing in the Animation or Animation Set to apply.

Animation sequences will run once and then stop, unless you modify this behavior using the `setRepeatMode` and `setRepeatCount` methods on the Animation or Animation Set. You can force an animation to loop or ping-pong by setting the repeat mode of RESTART or REVERSE. Setting the repeat count controls the number of times the animation will repeat.

The following code snippet shows an Animation that repeats indefinitely:

```
myAnimation.setRepeatMode(Animation.RESTART);
myAnimation.setRepeatCount(Animation.INFINITE);

myView.startAnimation(myAnimation);
```

Using Animation Listeners

The `AnimationListener` lets you create an event handler that's fired when an animation begins or ends. This lets you perform actions before or after an animation has completed, such as changing the View contents or chaining multiple animations.

Call `setAnimationListener` on an Animation object, and pass in a new implementation of `AnimationListener`, overriding `onAnimationEnd`, `onAnimationStart`, and `onAnimationRepeat` as required.

The following skeleton code shows the basic implementation of an Animation Listener:

```
myAnimation.setAnimationListener(new AnimationListener() {

  public void onAnimationEnd(Animation _animation) {
   // TODO Do something after animation is complete.
  }


  public void onAnimationRepeat(Animation _animation) {
```

```
    // TODO Do something when the animation repeats.
  }

  public void onAnimationStart(Animation _animation) {
    // TODO Do something when the animation starts.
  }

});
```

Animated Sliding User Interface Example

In this example, you'll create a new Activity that uses an Animation to smoothly change the content of the User Interface based on the direction pressed on the D-pad.

1. Start by creating a new ContentSlider project featuring a `ContentSlider` Activity.

```
package com.paad.contentslider;

import android.app.Activity;
import android.view.KeyEvent;
import android.os.Bundle;
import android.view.animation.Animation;
import android.view.animation.Animation.AnimationListener;
import android.view.animation.AnimationUtils;
import android.widget.TextView;

public class ContentSlider extends Activity {
  @Override
  public void onCreate(Bundle icicle) {
    super.onCreate(icicle);
    setContentView(R.layout.main);
  }
}
```

2. Next, modify the main.xml layout resource. It should contain a single `TextView` with the text bold, centered, and relatively large.

```
<?xml version="1.0" encoding="utf-8"?>
<LinearLayout
  xmlns:android="http://schemas.android.com/apk/res/android"
  android:orientation="vertical"
  android:layout_width="fill_parent"
  android:layout_height="fill_parent">
  <TextView
    android:id="@+id/myTextView"
    android:layout_width="fill_parent"
    android:layout_height="fill_parent"
    android:gravity="center"
    android:textStyle="bold"
    android:textSize="30sp"
    android:text="CENTER"
    android:editable="false"
    android:singleLine="true"
    android:layout_margin="10px"
  />
</LinearLayout>
```

365

3. Then create a series of animations that slides the current View out of, and the next View into, the frame for each direction: left, right, up, and down. Each animation should have its own file.

3.1. Create `slide_bottom_in.xml`.

```xml
<set xmlns:android="http://schemas.android.com/apk/res/android"
    android:interpolator="@android:anim/accelerate_interpolator">
  <translate
    android:fromYDelta="-100%p"
    android:toYDelta="0"
    android:duration="700"
  />
</set>
```

3.2. Create `slide_bottom_out.xml`.

```xml
<set xmlns:android="http://schemas.android.com/apk/res/android"
    android:interpolator="@android:anim/accelerate_interpolator">
  <translate
    android:fromYDelta="0"
    android:toYDelta="100%p"
    android:duration="700"
  />
</set>
```

3.3. Create `slide_top_in.xml`.

```xml
<set xmlns:android="http://schemas.android.com/apk/res/android"
    android:interpolator="@android:anim/accelerate_interpolator">
  <translate
    android:fromYDelta="100%p"
    android:toYDelta="0"
    android:duration="700"
  />
</set>
```

3.4. Create `slide_top_out.xml`.

```xml
<set xmlns:android="http://schemas.android.com/apk/res/android"
    android:interpolator="@android:anim/accelerate_interpolator">
  <translate
    android:fromYDelta="0"
    android:toYDelta="-100%p"
    android:duration="700"
  />
</set>
```

3.5. Create `slide_left_in.xml`.

```xml
<set xmlns:android="http://schemas.android.com/apk/res/android"
    android:interpolator="@android:anim/accelerate_interpolator">
  <translate
    android:fromXDelta="100%p"
    android:toXDelta="0"
    android:duration="700"
  />
</set>
```

3.6.   Create `slide_left_out.xml`.

```xml
<set xmlns:android="http://schemas.android.com/apk/res/android"
     android:interpolator="@android:anim/accelerate_interpolator">
  <translate
    android:fromXDelta="0"
    android:toXDelta="-100%p"
    android:duration="700"
  />
</set>
```

3.7.   Create `slide_right_in.xml`.

```xml
<set xmlns:android="http://schemas.android.com/apk/res/android"
     android:interpolator="@android:anim/accelerate_interpolator">
  <translate
    android:fromXDelta="-100%p"
    android:toXDelta="0"
    android:duration="700"
  />
</set>
```

3.8.   Create `slide_right_out.xml`.

```xml
<set xmlns:android="http://schemas.android.com/apk/res/android"
     android:interpolator="@android:anim/accelerate_interpolator">
  <translate
    android:fromXDelta="0"
    android:toXDelta="100%p"
    android:duration="700"
  />
</set>
```

4.   Return to the `ContentSlider` Activity and get references to the TextView and each of the animations you created in Step 3.

```java
Animation slideInLeft;
Animation slideOutLeft;
Animation slideInRight;
Animation slideOutRight;
Animation slideInTop;
Animation slideOutTop;
Animation slideInBottom;
Animation slideOutBottom;
TextView myTextView;

@Override
public void onCreate(Bundle icicle) {
  super.onCreate(icicle);
  setContentView(R.layout.main);

  slideInLeft = AnimationUtils.loadAnimation(this, R.anim.slide_left_in);
  slideOutLeft = AnimationUtils.loadAnimation(this, R.anim.slide_left_out);
  slideInRight = AnimationUtils.loadAnimation(this, R.anim.slide_right_in);
  slideOutRight = AnimationUtils.loadAnimation(this, R.anim.slide_right_out);
  slideInTop = AnimationUtils.loadAnimation(this, R.anim.slide_top_in);
  slideOutTop = AnimationUtils.loadAnimation(this, R.anim.slide_top_out);
```

```
    slideInBottom = AnimationUtils.loadAnimation(this, R.anim.slide_bottom_in);
    slideOutBottom = AnimationUtils.loadAnimation(this,
                                        R.anim.slide_bottom_out);

    myTextView = (TextView)findViewById(R.id.myTextView);
}
```

Each screen transition consists of two animations chained together: sliding out the old text before sliding in the new text. Rather than create multiple Views, you can change the value of the View once it's "off screen" before sliding it back in from the opposite side.

5. Create a new method that applies a slide-out animation and waits for it to complete before modifying the text and initiating the slide-in animation.

```
private void applyAnimation(Animation _out, Animation _in, String _newText) {
    final String text = _newText;
    final Animation in = _in;

    // Ensure the text stays out of screen when the slide-out
    // animation has completed.
    _out.setFillAfter(true);

    // Create a listener to wait for the slide-out animation to complete.
    _out.setAnimationListener(new AnimationListener() {

      public void onAnimationEnd(Animation _animation) {
        // Change the text
        myTextView.setText(text);
        // Slide it back in to view
        myTextView.startAnimation(in);
      }

      public void onAnimationRepeat(Animation _animation) {}

      public void onAnimationStart(Animation _animation) {}
    });

    // Apply the slide-out animation
    myTextView.startAnimation(_out);
}
```

6. The text displayed can represent nine positions. To keep track of the current location, create an enum for each position and an instance variable to track it.

```
TextPosition textPosition = TextPosition.Center;
enum TextPosition { UpperLeft, Top, UpperRight,
                    Left, Center, Right,
                    LowerLeft, Bottom, LowerRight };
```

7. Create a new method movePosition that takes the current position, and the direction to move, and calculates the new position. It should then execute the appropriate animation sequence created in Step 5.

```
private void movePosition(TextPosition _current,
                          TextPosition _directionPressed) {
```

```
    Animation in;
    Animation out;
    TextPosition newPosition;

    if (_directionPressed == TextPosition.Left){
      in = slideInLeft;
      out = slideOutLeft;
    }
    else if (_directionPressed == TextPosition.Right){
      in = slideInRight;
      out = slideOutRight;
    }
    else if (_directionPressed == TextPosition.Top){
      in = slideInTop;
      out = slideOutTop;
    }
    else {
      in = slideInBottom;
      out = slideOutBottom;
    }


    int newPosValue = _current.ordinal();
    int currentValue = _current.ordinal();

    // To simulate the effect of 'tilting' the device moving in one
    // direction should make text for the opposite direction appear.
    // Ie. Tilting right should make left appear.
    if (_directionPressed == TextPosition.Bottom)
      newPosValue = currentValue - 3;
    else if (_directionPressed == TextPosition.Top)
      newPosValue = currentValue + 3;
    else if (_directionPressed == TextPosition.Right) {
      if (currentValue % 3 != 0)
        newPosValue = currentValue - 1;
    }
    else if (_directionPressed == TextPosition.Left) {
      if ((currentValue+1) % 3 != 0)
        newPosValue = currentValue + 1;
    }

    if (newPosValue != currentValue &&
        newPosValue > -1 &&
        newPosValue < 9){
        newPosition = TextPosition.values()[newPosValue];

      applyAnimation(in, out, newPosition.toString());
      textPosition = newPosition;
    }
  }
```

8. Wire up the D-pad by overriding the Activity's onKeyDown handler to listen for key presses and trigger movePosition accordingly.

```
@Override
public boolean onKeyDown(int _keyCode, KeyEvent _event) {
```

```
            if (super.onKeyDown(_keyCode, _event))
              return true;

            if (_event.getAction() == KeyEvent.ACTION_DOWN){
              switch (_keyCode) {
                case (KeyEvent.KEYCODE_DPAD_LEFT):
                  movePosition(textPosition, TextPosition.Left); return true;
                case (KeyEvent.KEYCODE_DPAD_RIGHT):
                  movePosition(textPosition, TextPosition.Right); return true;
                case (KeyEvent.KEYCODE_DPAD_UP):
                  movePosition(textPosition, TextPosition.Top); return true;
                case (KeyEvent.KEYCODE_DPAD_DOWN):
                  movePosition(textPosition, TextPosition.Bottom); return true;
              }
            }
            return false;
          }
```

Running the application now will show a screen displaying "Center"; pressing any of the four directions will slide out this text and display the appropriate new position.

As an extra step, you could wire up the accelerometer sensor rather than relying on pressing the D-pad.

Animating Layouts and View Groups

A LayoutAnimation is used to animate View Groups, applying a single Animation (or Animation Set) to each child View in a predetermined sequence.

Use a LayoutAnimationController to specify an Animation (or Animation Set) that's applied to each child View in a View Group. Each View it contains will have the same animation applied, but you can use the Layout Animation Controller to specify the order and start time for each View.

Android includes two LayoutAnimationController classes.

❑ LayoutAnimationController   Lets you select the start offset of each View (in milliseconds) and the order (forward, reverse, and random) to apply the animation to each child View.

❑ GridLayoutAnimationController   Is a derived class that lets you assign the animation sequence of the child Views using grid row and column references.

Creating Layout Animations

To create a new Layout Animation, start by defining the Animation to apply to each child view. Then create a new LayoutAnimation, either in code or as an external animation resource, that references the animation to apply and defines the order and timing in which to apply it.

The following XML snippets show the definition of a simple animation stored as popin.xml in the res/anim folder, and a layout animation stored as popinlayout.xml.

The Layout Animation applies a simple "pop-in" animation randomly to each child View of any View Group it's assigned to.

res/anim/popin.xml

```
<set xmlns:android="http://schemas.android.com/apk/res/android"
    android:interpolator="@android:anim/accelerate_interpolator">
  <scale
    android:fromXScale="0.0" android:toXScale="1.0"
    android:fromYScale="0.0" android:toYScale="1.0"
    android:pivotX="50%"
    android:pivotY="50%"
    android:duration="400"
  />
</set>
```

res/anim/popinlayout.xml

```
<layoutAnimation xmlns:android="http://schemas.android.com/apk/res/android"
                 android:delay="0.5"
                 android:animationOrder="random"
                 android:animation="@anim/popin" />
```

Using Layout Animations

Once you've defined a Layout Animation, you can apply it to a ViewGroup either in code or in the layout XML resource. In XML this is done using the `android:layoutAnimation` tag in the layout definition, as shown in the following XML snippet:

```
android:layoutAnimation="@anim/popinlayout"
```

To set a Layout Animation in code, call `setLayoutAnimation` on the View Group, passing in a reference to the `LayoutAnimation` object you want to apply.

In both cases, the Layout Animation will execute once, when the View Group is first laid out. You can force it to execute again by calling `scheduleLayoutAnimation` on the `ViewGroup` object. The animation will be executed the next time the View Group is laid out.

Layout Animations also support Animation Listeners.

In the following code snippet, a ViewGroup's animation is re-run with a listener attached to trigger additional actions once it's complete:

```
aViewGroup.setLayoutAnimationListener(new AnimationListener() {

  public void onAnimationEnd(Animation _animation) {
    // TODO: Actions on animation complete.
  }

  public void onAnimationRepeat(Animation _animation) {}

  public void onAnimationStart(Animation _animation) {}
});

aViewGroup.scheduleLayoutAnimation();
```

Creating and Using Frame-by-Frame Animations

Frame-by-frame animations are akin to traditional cell-based cartoons where an image is chosen for each frame. Where tweened animations use the target View to supply the content of the animation, frame-by-frame animations let you specify a series of `Drawable` objects that are used as the background to a View.

The `AnimationDrawable` class is used to create a new frame-by-frame animation presented as a `Drawable` resource.

You can define your Animation Drawable resource as an external resource in your project's `drawable` folder using XML. Use the `animation-list` tag to group a collection of `item` tags, each of which uses a `drawable` attribute to define an image to display, and a `duration` attribute to specify the time (in milliseconds) to display it.

The following XML snippet shows how to create a simple animation that displays a rocket taking off (rocket images not included). The file is stored as res/drawable/animated_rocket.xml:

```xml
<animation-list xmlns:android="http://schemas.android.com/apk/res/android"
                android:oneshot="false">
  <item android:drawable="@drawable/rocket1" android:duration="500" />
  <item android:drawable="@drawable/rocket2" android:duration="500" />
  <item android:drawable="@drawable/rocket3" android:duration="500" />
</animation-list>
```

To display your animation, set it as the background to a View using the `setBackgroundResource` method, as shown in the following code snippet:

```java
ImageView image = (ImageView)findViewById(R.id.my_animation_frame);
image.setBackgroundResource(R.drawable.animated_rocket);
```

Alternatively, use the `setBackgroundDrawable` to use a Drawable instance instead of a resource reference. Run the animation calling its `start` method, as shown in the code snippet below:

```java
AnimationDrawable animation = (AnimationDrawable)image.getBackground();
animation.start();
```

Using Themes to Skin Your Applications

The multifunction nature of a mobile device means users will be running and switching between many applications created by a range of different developers. Themes are a way of ensuring that your applications present a consistent look and feel.

To apply a theme, set the `android:theme` attribute on either the `application` or an individual `activity` tag in the manifest, as shown in the code snippet below:

```xml
<manifest xmlns:android="http://schemas.android.com/apk/res/android"
    package="com.google.android.home">
    <application
        android:theme="@android:style/Theme.Light" >
        <activity
            android:theme="@android:style/Theme.Black" >
```

```
      </activity>
    </application>
  </manifest>
```

Android includes several predefined themes as part of the base package, including:

❑   `Theme.Black`   Features a black background with white foreground controls and text.

❑   `Theme.Light`   Features a white background with dark borders and text.

❑   `Theme.Translucent`   Features a partially transparent Form.

You can set the theme of an Activity at run time, but it's generally not recommended, as Android uses your Activity's theme for intra-Activity animations, which happens before your application is loaded. If you do apply a theme programmatically, be sure to do so before you lay out the Activity as shown in the code snippet below:

```
protected void onCreate(Bundle icicle) {
    super.onCreate(icicle);
    setTheme(android.R.style.Theme_Translucent);
    setContentView(R.layout.main);
}
```

If you don't apply a theme to your application or any of its Activities, it will use the default theme
`android.R.style.Theme`.

Advanced Canvas Drawing

You were introduced to the `Canvas` class in Chapter 4, where you learned how to create your own Views. The Canvas was also used in Chapter 7 to annotate Overlays for `MapViews`.

The concept of the Canvas is a common metaphor used in graphics programming and generally consists of three basic drawing components:

❑   `Canvas`   Supplies the draw methods that paint drawing primitives onto the underlying bitmap.

❑   `Paint`   Also referred to as a "brush," `Paint` lets you specify how a primitive is drawn on the bitmap.

❑   `Bitmap`   Is the surface being drawn on.

Most of the advanced techniques described in this chapter involve variations and modifications to the `Paint` object that let you add depth and texture to otherwise flat raster drawings.

The Android drawing API supports translucency, gradient fills, rounded rectangles, and anti-aliasing. Unfortunately, owing to resource limitations, it does not yet support vector graphics; instead, it uses traditional raster-style repaints.

The result of this raster approach is improved efficiency, but changing a `Paint` object will not affect primitives that have already been drawn; it will only affect new elements.

If you've got a Windows development background, the two-dimensional (2D) drawing capabilities of Android are roughly equivalent to those available in GDI+.

Chapter 11: Advanced Android Development

What Can You Draw?

The `Canvas` class wraps up the bitmap that's used as a surface for your artistic endeavors; it also exposes the `draw*` methods used to implement your designs.

Without going into detail on each of the `draw` methods, the following list provides a taste of the primitives available:

- ❏ `drawARGB` / `drawRGB` / `drawColor`   Fill the canvas with a single color.
- ❏ `drawArc`   Draws an arc between two angles within an area bounded by a rectangle.
- ❏ `drawBitmap`   Draws a bitmap on the Canvas. You can alter the appearance of the target bitmap by specifying a target size or using a matrix to transform it.
- ❏ `drawBitmapMesh`   Draws a bitmap using a mesh that lets you manipulate the appearance of the target by moving points within it.
- ❏ `drawCircle`   Draws a circle of a specified radius centered on a given point.
- ❏ `drawLine(s)`   Draws a line (or series of lines) between two points.
- ❏ `drawOval`   Draws an oval bounded by the rectangle specified.
- ❏ `drawPaint`   Fills the entire Canvas with the specified Paint.
- ❏ `drawPath`   Draws the specified Path. A `Path` object is often used to hold a collection of drawing primitives within a single object.
- ❏ `drawPicture`   Draws a `Picture` object within the specified rectangle.
- ❏ `drawPosText`   Draws a text string specifying the offset of each character.
- ❏ `drawRect`   Draws a rectangle.
- ❏ `drawRoundRect`   Draws a rectangle with rounded edges.
- ❏ `drawText`   Draws a text string on the Canvas. The text font, size, color, and rendering properties are all set in the `Paint` object used to render the text.
- ❏ `drawTextOnPath`   Draws text that follows along a specified path.
- ❏ `drawVertices`   Draws a series of tri-patches specified as a series of vertex points.

Each of these drawing methods lets you specify a `Paint` object to render it. In the following sections, you'll learn how to create and modify `Paint` objects to get the most out of your drawing.

Getting the Most from Your Paint

The `Paint` class represents a paint brush and palette. It lets you choose how to render the primitives you draw onto the canvas using the draw methods described above. By modifying the `Paint` object, you can control the color, style, font, and special effects used when drawing. Most simply, `setColor` lets you select the color of a Paint while the style of a `Paint` object (controlled using `setStyle`) lets you decide if you want to draw only the outline of a drawing object (STROKE), just the filled portion (FILL), or both (STROKE_AND_FILL).

Beyond these simple controls, the `Paint` class also supports transparency and can also be modified using a variety of Shaders, filters, and effects to provide a rich palette of complex paints and brushes.

The Android SDK includes several excellent projects that demonstrate most of the features available in the `Paint` class. They are available in the graphics subfolder of the API demos at

```
[sdk root folder]\samples\ApiDemos\src\com\android\samples\graphics
```

In the following sections, you'll learn what some of these features are and how to use them. These sections outline what can be achieved (such as gradients and edge embossing) without exhaustively listing all possible alternatives.

Using Translucency

All colors in Android include an opacity component (alpha channel).

You define an alpha value for a color when you create it using the `argb` or `parseColor` methods shown below:

```
// Make color red and 50% transparent
int opacity = 127;
int intColor = Color.argb(opacity, 255, 0, 0);
int parsedColor = Color.parseColor("#7FFF0000");
```

Alternatively, you can set the opacity of an existing `Paint` object using the `setAlpha` method:

```
// Make color 50% transparent
int opacity = 127;
myPaint.setAlpha(opacity);
```

Creating a paint color that's not 100 percent opaque means that any primitive drawn with it will be partially transparent — making whatever is drawn beneath it partially visible.

You can use transparency effects in any class or method that uses colors including Paint colors, Shaders, and Mask Filters.

Introducing Shaders

Extensions of the `Shader` class let you create Paints that fill drawn objects with more than a single solid color.

The most common use of Shaders is to define gradient fills; gradients are an excellent way to add depth and texture to 2D drawings. Android includes three gradient Shaders as well as a Bitmap Shader and a Compose Shader.

Trying to describe painting techniques seems inherently futile, so have a look at Figure 11-1 to get an idea of how each of the Shaders works. Represented from left to right are `LinearGradient`, `RadialGradient`, and `SweepGradient`.

Not included in the image in Figure 11-1 is the ComposeShader, *which lets you create a composite of multiple Shaders and the* BitmapShader *that lets you create a paint brush based on a bitmap image.*

To use a Shader when drawing, apply it to a Paint using the setShader method, as shown in the following code snippet:

```
Paint shaderPaint = new Paint();
shaderPaint.setShader(myLinearGradient);
```

Anything you draw with this Paint will be filled with the Shader you specified rather than the paint color.

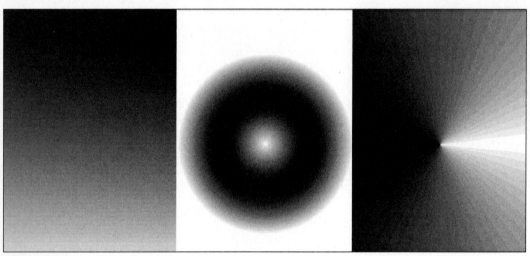

Figure 11-1

Defining Gradient Shaders

As shown above, using gradient Shaders lets you fill drawings with an interpolated color range; you can define the gradient as either a simple transition between two colors, as shown in the LinearGradientShader in the following code snippet:

```
int colorFrom = Color.BLACK;
int colorTo = Color.WHITE;

LinearGradient linearGradientShader = new LinearGradient(x1, y1, x2, y2,
                                          colorFrom,
                                          colorTo,
                                          TileMode.CLAMP);
```

or as a more complex series of colors distributed at set proportions, as shown in the following example of a RadialGradientShader:

```
int[] gradientColors = new int[3];
gradientColors[0] = Color.GREEN;
```

```
gradientColors[1] = Color.YELLOW;
gradientColors[2] = Color.RED;

float[] gradientPositions = new float[3];
gradientPositions[0] = 0.0f;
gradientPositions[1] = 0.5f;
gradientPositions[2] = 1.0f;

RadialGradient radialGradientShader = new RadialGradient(centerX, centerY, radius,
                                           gradientColors,
                                           gradientPositions,
                                           TileMode.CLAMP);
```

Each of the gradient Shaders (linear, radial, and sweep) lets you define the gradient fill using either of these techniques.

Using Shader Tile Modes

The brush sizes of the gradient Shaders are defined using explicit bounding rectangles or center points and radius lengths; the Bitmap Shader implies a brush size through its bitmap size.

If the area defined by your Shader brush is smaller than the area being filled, the `TileMode` determines how the remaining area will be covered.

❑ CLAMP   Uses the edge colors of the Shader to fill the extra space.

❑ MIRROR   Flips the Shader image horizontally and vertically so that each image seams with the last.

❑ REPEAT   Repeats the Shader image horizontally and vertically, but doesn't flip it.

Using `MaskFilters`

The `MaskFilter` classes let you assign edge effects to your Paint.

Extensions to `MaskFilter` apply transformations to the alpha-channel of a Paint along its outer edge. Android includes the following Mask Filters:

❑ BlurMaskFilter   Specifies a blur style and radius to feather the edges of your Paint.

❑ EmbossMaskFilter   Specifies the direction of the light source and ambient light level to add an embossing effect.

To apply a Mask Filter, use the `setMaskFilter` method, passing in a `MaskFilter` object. The following code snippet applies an `EmbossMaskFilter` to an existing Paint:

```
// Set the direction of the light source
float[] direction = new float[]{ 1, 1, 1 };
// Set the ambient light level
float light = 0.4f;
// Choose a level of specularity to apply
float specular = 6;
```

```
// Apply a level of blur to apply to the mask
float blur = 3.5f;
EmbossMaskFilter emboss = new EmbossMaskFilter(direction, light, specular, blur);

// Apply the mask
myPaint.setMaskFilter(emboss);
```

The `FingerPaint` API demo included in the SDK is an excellent example of how to use `MaskFilters`. It demonstrates the effect of both the emboss and blur filters.

Using `ColorFilters`

Where `MaskFilters` are transformations of the alpha-channel of a Paint, a `ColorFilter` applies a transformation to each of the RGB channels. All `ColorFilter`-derived classes ignore the alpha-channel when performing their transformations.

Android includes three Color Filters:

❏ `ColorMatrixColorFilter` Lets you specify a 4 × 5 `ColorMatrix` to apply to a Paint. `ColorMatrixes` are commonly used to perform image processing programmatically and are useful as they support chaining transformations using matrix multiplication.

❏ `LightingColorFilter` Multiplies the RGB channels by the first color before adding the second. The result of each transformation will be clamped to between 0 and 255.

❏ `PorterDuffColorFilter` Lets you use any one of the 16 Porter-Duff rules for digital image compositing to apply a specified color to the Paint.

Apply `ColorFilters` using the `setColorFilter` method as shown below:

```
myPaint.setColorFilter(new LightingColorFilter(Color.BLUE, Color.RED));
```

There is an excellent example of using a Color Filter and Color Matrixes in the `ColorMatrixSample` API example.

Using `PathEffects`

The effects so far have affected the way the Paint *fills* a drawing; `PathEffects` are used to control how its outline (or stroke) is drawn.

Path Effects are particularly useful for drawing Path primitives, but they can be applied to any Paint to affect the way the stroke is drawn.

Using Path Effects, you can change the appearance of a shape's corners and control the appearance of the outline. Android includes several Path Effects including:

❏ `CornerPathEffect` Lets you smooth sharp corners in the shape of a primitive by replacing sharp edges with rounded corners.

❏ `DashPathEffect` Rather than drawing a solid outline, you can use the `DashPathEffect` to create an outline of broken lines (dashes/dots). You can specify any repeating pattern of solid/ empty line segments.

❑ `DiscretePathEffect`   Similar to the `DashPathEffect`, but with added randomness. Specifies the length of each segment and a degree of deviation from the original path to use when drawing it.

❑ `PathDashPathEffect`   This effect lets you define a new shape (path) to use as a stamp to outline the original path.

The following effects let you combine multiple Path Effects to a single Paint.

❑ `SumPathEffect`   Adds two effects to a path in sequence, such that each effect is applied to the original path and the two results are combined.

❑ `ComposePathEffect`   Compose applies first one effect and then applies the second effect to the result of the first.

Path Effects that modify the shape of the object being drawn will change the area of the affected shape. This ensures that any fill effects being applied to the same shape are drawn within the new bounds.

Path Effects are applied to `Paint` objects using the `setPathEffect` method as shown below:

```
borderPaint.setPathEffect(new CornerPathEffect(5));
```

The Path Effects API sample gives an excellent guide to how to apply each of these effects.

Changing the `Xfermode`

Change a Paint's `Xfermode` to affect the way it paints new colors on top of what's already on the Canvas.

Under normal circumstances, painting on top of an existing drawing will layer the new shape on top. If the new Paint is fully opaque, it will totally obscure the paint underneath; if it's partially transparent, it will tint the colors underneath.

The following `Xfermode` subclasses let you change this behavior:

❑ `AvoidXfermode`   Specifies a color and tolerance to force your Paint to avoid drawing over (or only draw over) it.

❑ `PixelXorXfermode`   Applies a simple pixel XOR operation when covering existing colors.

❑ `PorterDuffXfermode`   This is a very powerful transfer mode with which you can use any of the 16 Porter-Duff rules for image composition to control how the paint interacts with the existing canvas image.

To apply transfer modes, use the `setXferMode` method as shown in the sample below:

```
AvoidXfermode avoid = new AvoidXfermode(Color.BLUE, 10, AvoidXfermode.Mode.AVOID);
borderPen.setXfermode(avoid);
```

Improving Paint Quality with Anti-Aliasing

When you create a new `Paint` object, you can pass in several flags that affect the way the Paint will be rendered. One of the most interesting is the `ANTI_ALIAS_FLAG`, which ensures that diagonal lines drawn with this paint are anti-aliased to give a smooth appearance (at the cost of performance).

Anti-aliasing is particularly important when drawing text, as anti-aliased text can be significantly easier to read. To create even smoother text effects, you can apply the SUBPIXEL_TEXT_FLAG, which will apply subpixel anti-aliasing.

You can also set both of these flags manually using the setSubpixelText and setAntiAlias methods, as shown below:

```
myPaint.setSubpixelText(true);
myPaint.setAntiAlias(true);
```

Hardware Acceleration for 2D Graphics

In a boon for 2D graphics enthusiasts everywhere, Android lets you request that your application always be rendered using hardware acceleration.

If hardware acceleration is available on the device, setting this flag will cause every View within the Activity to be rendered using hardware. This has the side effect of dramatically improving the speed of your graphics while reducing the load on the system processor.

Turn it on by applying the Window.FEATURE_OPENGL flag to your Activity using the requestWindowFeature method, as shown below:

```
myActivity.requestWindowFeature(Window.FEATURE_OPENGL);
```

Unfortunately, Good Things seldom come for free, and this is no exception.

Not all the 2D drawing primitives available in Android are supported by hardware (notably most of the Path Effects described previously).

Also, as your entire Activity is being effectively rendered as a single Canvas, invalidate requests on any View will cause the whole Activity to be redrawn.

Canvas Drawing Best Practice

2D owner-draw operations tend to be expensive in terms of processor use; inefficient drawing routines can block the GUI thread and have a detrimental effect on application responsiveness. This is particularly true in a resource-constrained environment with a single, limited processor.

You need to be aware of the resource drain and CPU-cycle cost of your onDraw methods, to ensure you don't end up with an attractive application that's completely unresponsive.

A lot of techniques exist to help minimize the resource drain associated with owner-drawn controls. Rather than focus on general principles, I'll describe some Android specific considerations for ensuring that you can create activities that look good and remain interactive (note that this list is not exhaustive):

❏ **Consider Hardware Acceleration** OpenGL hardware acceleration support for 2D graphics is a Good Thing, so you should always consider if it's suitable for your Activity. Good candidates are Activities consisting of a single View with rapid, time-consuming updates. Be sure that the primitives you use are supported by hardware.

❏ **Consider Size and Orientation** When you're designing your Views and Overlays, be sure to consider (and test!) how they will look at different resolutions and sizes.

❏ **Create Static Objects Once** Object creation in Android is particularly expensive. Where possible, create drawing objects like `Paint` objects, Paths, and Shaders once, rather than recreating them each time the View is invalidated.

❏ **Remember onDraw Is Expensive** Performing the `onDraw` method is an expensive process that forces Android to perform several image composition and bitmap construction operations. Many of the following points suggest ways to modify the appearance of your Canvas without having to redraw it:

  ❏ **Use Canvas Transforms** Use canvas transforms like `rotate` and `translate` to simplify complex relational positioning of elements on your canvas. For example, rather than positioning and rotating each text element around a clock face, simply rotate the canvas 22.5 degrees, and draw the text in the same place.

  ❏ **Use Animations** Consider using Animations to perform pre-set transformations of your View rather than manually redrawing it. Scale, rotation, and translation Animations can be performed on any View within an Activity and provide a resource-efficient way to provide zoom, rotate, or shake effects.

  ❏ **Consider Using Bitmaps and 9 Patches** If your Views feature static backgrounds, you should consider using a Drawable like a bitmap or scalable 9 patch rather than manually drawing it.

Advanced Compass Face Example

Early in Chapter 4, you created a simple compass. In the last chapter, you returned to it, extending it to display the pitch and roll using the accelerometer hardware.

The UI of the View used in those examples was kept simple to keep the code in those chapters as clear as possible.

In the following example, you'll make some significant changes to the `CompassView`'s `onDraw` method to change it from a simple, flat compass into a dynamic artificial horizon, as shown in Figure 11-2.

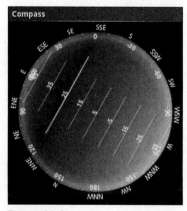

Figure 11-2

As the previous image is limited to black and white, you'll need to create the control in order to see the full effect.

1. Start by modifying the `colors.xml` resource file to include color values for the border gradient, the glass compass shading, the sky, and the ground. Also update the colors used for the border and the face markings.

```xml
<?xml version="1.0" encoding="utf-8"?>
<resources>
  <color name="text_color">#FFFF</color>
  <color name="background_color">#F000</color>
  <color name="marker_color">#FFFF</color>
  <color name="shadow_color">#7AAA</color>

  <color name="outer_border">#FF444444</color>
  <color name="inner_border_one">#FF323232</color>
  <color name="inner_border_two">#FF414141</color>
  <color name="inner_border">#FFFFFFFF</color>

  <color name="horizon_sky_from">#FFA52A2A</color>
  <color name="horizon_sky_to">#FFFFC125</color>
  <color name="horizon_ground_from">#FF5F9EA0</color>
  <color name="horizon_ground_to">#FF00008B</color>
</resources>
```

2. The `Paint` and `Shader` objects used for the sky and ground in the artificial horizon are created based on the size of the current View, so they're not static like the `Paint` objects you created in Chapter 4. Instead of creating `Paint` objects, construct the gradient arrays and colors they use.

```java
int[] borderGradientColors;
float[] borderGradientPositions;

int[] glassGradientColors;
float[] glassGradientPositions;

int skyHorizonColorFrom;
int skyHorizonColorTo;
int groundHorizonColorFrom;
int groundHorizonColorTo;
```

3. Update the `CompassView`'s `initCompassView` method to initialize the variables created in Step 2 using the resources from Step 1. The existing method code can be left largely intact, with some changes to the `textPaint`, `circlePaint`, and `markerPaint` variables, as highlighted below:

```java
protected void initCompassView() {
  setFocusable(true);
  // Get external resources
  Resources r = this.getResources();

  circlePaint = new Paint(Paint.ANTI_ALIAS_FLAG);
  circlePaint.setColor(R.color.background_color);
  circlePaint.setStrokeWidth(1);
  circlePaint.setStyle(Paint.Style.STROKE);

  northString = r.getString(R.string.cardinal_north);
```

```
eastString = r.getString(R.string.cardinal_east);
southString = r.getString(R.string.cardinal_south);
westString = r.getString(R.string.cardinal_west);

textPaint = new Paint(Paint.ANTI_ALIAS_FLAG);
textPaint.setColor(r.getColor(R.color.text_color));
textPaint.setFakeBoldText(true);
textPaint.setSubpixelText(true);
textPaint.setTextAlign(Align.LEFT);

textHeight = (int)textPaint.measureText("yY");

markerPaint = new Paint(Paint.ANTI_ALIAS_FLAG);
markerPaint.setColor(r.getColor(R.color.marker_color));
markerPaint.setAlpha(200);
markerPaint.setStrokeWidth(1);
markerPaint.setStyle(Paint.Style.STROKE);
markerPaint.setShadowLayer(2, 1, 1, r.getColor(R.color.shadow_color));
```

3.1. Create the color and position arrays that will be used by a radial Shader to paint the outer border.

```
borderGradientColors = new int[4];
borderGradientPositions = new float[4];

borderGradientColors[3] = r.getColor(R.color.outer_border);
borderGradientColors[2] = r.getColor(R.color.inner_border_one);
borderGradientColors[1] = r.getColor(R.color.inner_border_two);
borderGradientColors[0] = r.getColor(R.color.inner_border);
borderGradientPositions[3] = 0.0f;
borderGradientPositions[2] = 1-0.03f;
borderGradientPositions[1] = 1-0.06f;
borderGradientPositions[0] = 1.0f;
```

3.2. Now create the radial gradient color and position arrays that will be used to create the semitransparent "glass dome" that sits on top of the View to give it the illusion of depth.

```
glassGradientColors = new int[5];
glassGradientPositions = new float[5];

int glassColor = 245;
glassGradientColors[4] = Color.argb(65, glassColor, glassColor, glassColor);
glassGradientColors[3] = Color.argb(100, glassColor, glassColor, glassColor);
glassGradientColors[2] = Color.argb(50, glassColor, glassColor, glassColor);
glassGradientColors[1] = Color.argb(0, glassColor, glassColor, glassColor);
glassGradientColors[0] = Color.argb(0, glassColor, glassColor, glassColor);
glassGradientPositions[4] = 1-0.0f;
glassGradientPositions[3] = 1-0.06f;
glassGradientPositions[2] = 1-0.10f;
glassGradientPositions[1] = 1-0.20f;
glassGradientPositions[0] = 1-1.0f;
```

3.3. Finally, get the colors you'll use to create the linear gradients that will represent the sky and the ground in the artificial horizon.

```
skyHorizonColorFrom = r.getColor(R.color.horizon_sky_from);
skyHorizonColorTo = r.getColor(R.color.horizon_sky_to);

groundHorizonColorFrom = r.getColor(R.color.horizon_ground_from);
groundHorizonColorTo = r.getColor(R.color.horizon_ground_to);
}
```

4. Before you start drawing the face, create a new `enum` that stores each of the cardinal directions.

```
private enum CompassDirection { N, NNE, NE, ENE,
                                E, ESE, SE, SSE,
                                S, SSW, SW, WSW,
                                W, WNW, NW, NNW }
```

Now you need to completely replace the existing `onDraw` method. You'll start by figuring out some size-based values including the center of the View, the radius of the circular control, and the rectangles that will enclose the outer (heading) and inner (tilt and roll) face elements.

```
@Override
protected void onDraw(Canvas canvas) {
```

1. Calculate the width of the outer (heading) ring based on the size of the font used to draw the heading values.

```
float ringWidth = textHeight + 4;
```

2. Then calculate the height and width of the View, and use those values to establish the radius of the inner and outer face dials, as well as create the bounding boxes for each face.

```
int height = getMeasuredHeight();
int width =getMeasuredWidth();

int px = width/2;
int py = height/2;
Point center = new Point(px, py);

int radius = Math.min(px, py)-2;

RectF boundingBox = new RectF(center.x - radius,
                              center.y - radius,
                              center.x + radius,
                              center.y + radius);

RectF innerBoundingBox = new RectF(center.x - radius + ringWidth,
                                   center.y - radius + ringWidth,
                                   center.x + radius - ringWidth,
                                   center.y + radius - ringWidth);

float innerRadius = innerBoundingBox.height()/2;
```

3. With the dimensions of the View established, it's time to start drawing the faces.

Start from the bottom layer at the outside, and work your way in and up, starting with the outer face (heading). Create a new `RadialGradient` Shader using the colors and positions you defined in Step 3.2 in the previous code sample, and assign that Shader to a new Paint before using it to draw a circle.

```
RadialGradient borderGradient = new RadialGradient(px, py, radius,
                                                   borderGradientColors,
                                                   borderGradientPositions,
                                                   TileMode.CLAMP);

Paint pgb = new Paint();
pgb.setShader(borderGradient);

Path outerRingPath = new Path();
outerRingPath.addOval(boundingBox, Direction.CW);

canvas.drawPath(outerRingPath, pgb);
```

4. Next you need to draw the artificial horizon. The horizon is created by dividing the circular face into two sections, one representing the sky and the other the ground. The proportion of each section depends on the current pitch.

Start by creating the `Shader` and `Paint` objects that will be used to draw the sky and earth.

```
LinearGradient skyShader = new LinearGradient(center.x,
                                              innerBoundingBox.top,
                                              center.x,
                                              innerBoundingBox.bottom,
                                              skyHorizonColorFrom,
                                              skyHorizonColorTo,
                                              TileMode.CLAMP);
Paint skyPaint = new Paint();
skyPaint.setShader(skyShader);

LinearGradient groundShader = new LinearGradient(center.x,
                                                 innerBoundingBox.top,
                                                 center.x,
                                                 innerBoundingBox.bottom,
                                                 groundHorizonColorFrom,
                                                 groundHorizonColorTo,
                                                 TileMode.CLAMP);
Paint groundPaint = new Paint();
groundPaint.setShader(groundShader);
```

5. Now normalize the pitch and roll values to clamp them within ±90 degrees and ±180 degrees, respectively.

```
float tiltDegree = pitch;
while (tiltDegree > 90 || tiltDegree < -90)
{
  if (tiltDegree > 90) tiltDegree = -90 + (tiltDegree - 90);
    if (tiltDegree < -90) tiltDegree = 90 - (tiltDegree + 90);
}

float rollDegree = roll;
```

```
while (rollDegree > 180 || rollDegree < -180)
{
  if (rollDegree > 180) rollDegree = -180 + (rollDegree - 180);
   if (rollDegree < -180) rollDegree = 180 - (rollDegree + 180);
}
```

6. Create paths that will fill each segment of the circle (ground and sky). The proportion of each segment should be related to the clamped pitch.

```
Path skyPath = new Path();
skyPath.addArc(innerBoundingBox,
               -tiltDegree,
               (180 + (2 * tiltDegree)));
```

7. Spin the canvas around the center in the opposite direction to the current roll, and draw the sky and ground paths using the Paints you created in Step 4.

```
canvas.rotate(-rollDegree, px, py);
canvas.drawOval(innerBoundingBox, groundPaint);
canvas.drawPath(skyPath, skyPaint);
canvas.drawPath(skyPath, markerPaint);
```

8. Next is the face marking. Start by calculating the start and end points for the horizontal horizon markings.

```
int markWidth = radius / 3;
int startX = center.x - markWidth;
int endX = center.x + markWidth;
```

9. To make the horizon values easier to read, you should ensure that the pitch scale always starts at the current value. The following code calculates the position of the interface between the ground and sky on the horizon face:

```
double h = innerRadius*Math.cos(Math.toRadians(90-tiltDegree));
double justTiltY = center.y - h;
```

10. Find the number of pixels that represents each degree of tilt.

```
float pxPerDegree = (innerBoundingBox.height()/2)/45f;
```

11. Now iterate over 180 degrees, centered on the current tilt value, to give a sliding scale of possible pitch.

```
for (int i = 90; i >= -90; i -= 10)
{
  double ypos = justTiltY + i*pxPerDegree;

  // Only display the scale within the inner face.
  if ((ypos < (innerBoundingBox.top + textHeight)) ||
      (ypos > innerBoundingBox.bottom - textHeight))
    continue;

  // Draw a line and the tilt angle for each scale increment.
  canvas.drawLine(startX, (float)ypos, endX, (float)ypos, markerPaint);
  int displayPos = (int)(tiltDegree - i);
```

```
String displayString = String.valueOf(displayPos);
float stringSizeWidth = textPaint.measureText(displayString);
canvas.drawText(displayString,
                (int)(center.x-stringSizeWidth/2),
                (int)(ypos)+1,
                textPaint);
}
```

12. Now draw a thicker line at the earth/sky interface. Change the stroke thickness of the `markerPaint` object before drawing the line (then set it back to the previous value).

```
markerPaint.setStrokeWidth(2);
canvas.drawLine(center.x - radius / 2,
                (float)justTiltY,
                center.x + radius / 2,
                (float)justTiltY,
                markerPaint);
markerPaint.setStrokeWidth(1);
```

13. To make it easier to read the exact roll, you should draw an arrow and display a text string that shows the exact value.

Create a new `Path`, and use the `moveTo` / `lineTo` methods to construct an open arrow that points straight up. Draw the path and a text string that shows the current roll.

```
// Draw the arrow
Path rollArrow = new Path();
rollArrow.moveTo(center.x - 3, (int)innerBoundingBox.top + 14);
rollArrow.lineTo(center.x, (int)innerBoundingBox.top + 10);
rollArrow.moveTo(center.x + 3, innerBoundingBox.top + 14);
rollArrow.lineTo(center.x, innerBoundingBox.top + 10);
canvas.drawPath(rollArrow, markerPaint);
// Draw the string
String rollText = String.valueOf(rollDegree);
double rollTextWidth = textPaint.measureText(rollText);
canvas.drawText(rollText,
                (float)(center.x - rollTextWidth / 2),
                innerBoundingBox.top + textHeight + 2,
                textPaint);
```

14. Spin the canvas back to upright so that you can draw the rest of the face markings.

```
canvas.restore();
```

15. Draw the roll dial markings by rotating the canvas 10 degrees at a time to draw either a mark or a value. When you've completed the face, restore the canvas to its upright position.

```
canvas.save();
canvas.rotate(180, center.x, center.y);
for (int i = -180; i < 180; i += 10)
{
  // Show a numeric value every 30 degrees
  if (i % 30 == 0) {
    String rollString = String.valueOf(i*-1);
    float rollStringWidth = textPaint.measureText(rollString);
```

```
                    PointF rollStringCenter = new PointF(center.x-rollStringWidth / 2,
                                                 innerBoundingBox.top+1+textHeight);

                    canvas.drawText(rollString,
                                    rollStringCenter.x, rollStringCenter.y,
                                    textPaint);
                }
                // Otherwise draw a marker line
                else {
                    canvas.drawLine(center.x, (int)innerBoundingBox.top,
                                    center.x, (int)innerBoundingBox.top + 5,
                                    markerPaint);
                }

                canvas.rotate(10, center.x, center.y);
            }
            canvas.restore();
```

16. The final step in creating the face is drawing the heading markers around the outside edge.

```
            canvas.save();
            canvas.rotate(-1*(bearing), px, py);

            double increment = 22.5;

            for (double i = 0; i < 360; i += increment)
            {
                CompassDirection cd = CompassDirection.values()[(int)(i / 22.5)];
                String headString = cd.toString();

                float headStringWidth = textPaint.measureText(headString);
                PointF headStringCenter = new PointF(center.x - headStringWidth / 2,
                                                boundingBox.top + 1 + textHeight);

                if (i % increment == 0)
                    canvas.drawText(headString,
                                    headStringCenter.x, headStringCenter.y,
                                    textPaint);
                else
                    canvas.drawLine(center.x, (int)boundingBox.top,
                                    center.x, (int)boundingBox.top + 3,
                                    markerPaint);

                canvas.rotate((int)increment, center.x, center.y);
            }
            canvas.restore();
```

17. With the face complete, you get to add some finishing touches.

Start by adding a "glass dome" over the top to give the illusion of a watch face. Using the radial gradient array you constructed earlier, create a new Shader and Paint object. Use them to draw a circle over the inner face that makes it look like it's covered in glass.

```
            RadialGradient glassShader = new RadialGradient(px, py,
                                                        (int)innerRadius,
```

```
                                              glassGradientColors,
                                              glassGradientPositions,
                                              TileMode.CLAMP);

    Paint glassPaint = new Paint();
    glassPaint.setShader(glassShader);

    canvas.drawOval(innerBoundingBox, glassPaint);
```

18. All that's left is to draw two more circles as clean borders for the inner and outer face boundaries. Then restore the canvas to upright, and finish the onDraw method.

```
    // Draw the outer ring
    canvas.drawOval(boundingBox, circlePaint);

    // Draw the inner ring
    circlePaint.setStrokeWidth(2);
    canvas.drawOval(innerBoundingBox, circlePaint);

    canvas.restore();
  }
```

Bringing Map Overlays to Life

In Chapter 7, you learned how to use Overlays to add annotation layers to MapViews. The Canvas used for annotating MapView Overlays is the same class as the one used to draw new View controls. As a result, all of the advanced features described so far in this section can be used to enhance map Overlays.

That means you can use any of the draw methods, transparency, Shaders, Color Masks, and Filter Effects to create rich Overlays using the Android graphics framework.

Interacting with Overlays

Touch-screen interaction in MapViews is handled individually by each of its Overlays. To handle map taps within an Overlay, override the onTap event.

The following code snippet shows an onTap implementation that receives the map coordinates of the tap and the MapView on which the tap occurred:

```
@Override
public boolean onTap(GeoPoint point, MapView map) {
  // Get the projection to convert to and from screen coordinates
  Projection projection = map.getProjection();

  // Return true if we handled this onTap()
  return [ … hit test passed … ];
}
```

The MapView can be used to obtain the Projection of the map when it was tapped. Used in conjunction with the GeoPoint parameter, you can determine the position on screen of the real-world longitude and latitude pressed.

The `onTap` method of an Overlay derived class should return `true` if it has handled the tap (and `false` otherwise). If none of the Overlays assigned to a MapView return true, the tap event will be handled by the MapView itself, or failing that, by the Activity.

Introducing `SurfaceView`

Under normal circumstances, your applications' Views are all drawn on the same GUI thread. This main application thread is also used for all user interaction (such as button clicks or text entry).

In Chapter 8, you learned how to move blocking processes onto background threads. Unfortunately, you can't do this with the `onDraw` method of a View, as modifying a GUI element from a background thread is explicitly disallowed.

When you need to update the View's UI rapidly, or the rendering code blocks the GUI thread for too long, the `SurfaceView` class is the answer. A Surface View wraps a `Surface` object rather than a `Canvas`. This is important because Surfaces can be drawn onto from background threads. This is particularly useful for resource-intensive operations, or where rapid updates or high frame rates are required, such as when using 3D graphics, creating games, or previewing the camera in real time.

The ability to draw independently of the GUI thread comes at the price of additional memory consumption, so while it's a useful — sometimes necessary — way to create custom Views, Surface Views should be used with caution.

When Should You Use the `SurfaceView`?

A `SurfaceView` can be used in exactly the same way as any View-derived class. You can apply animations and place them in layouts as you would any other View.

The `Surface` encapsulated by the SurfaceView supports drawing, using most of the standard Canvas methods described previously in this chapter, and also supports the full OpenGL ES library.

Using OpenGL, you can draw any supported 2D or 3D object onto the Surface, relying on hardware acceleration (where available) to significantly improve performance compared to simulating the same effects on a 2D canvas.

SurfaceViews are particularly useful for displaying dynamic 3D images, such as those featured in applications like Google Earth, or featured in interactive games that provide immersive experiences. It's also the best choice for displaying real-time camera previews.

Creating a New `SurfaceView` Control

To create a new `SurfaceView`, create a new class that extends `SurfaceView` and implements `SurfaceHolder.Callback`.

The `SurfaceHolder` callback notifies the View when the underlying Surface is created and destroyed, passing a reference to the `SurfaceHolder` object that contains the currently valid Surface.

A typical Surface View design pattern includes a `Thread`-derived class that accepts a reference to the current `SurfaceHolder` and independently updates it.

The following skeleton code shows a Surface View implementation for drawing using the Canvas. A new Thread-derived class is created within the Surface View control, and all UI updates are handled within this new class.

```java
import android.content.Context;
import android.graphics.Canvas;
import android.view.SurfaceHolder;
import android.view.SurfaceView;

public class MySurfaceView extends SurfaceView implements SurfaceHolder.Callback {

  private SurfaceHolder holder;
  private MySurfaceViewThread mySurfaceViewThread;
  private boolean hasSurface;

  MySurfaceView(Context context) {
    super(context);
    init();
  }

  private void init() {
    // Create a new SurfaceHolder and assign this class as its callback.
    holder = getHolder();
    holder.addCallback(this);
    hasSurface = false;
  }

  public void resume() {
    // Create and start the graphics update thread.
    if (mySurfaceViewThread == null) {
      mySurfaceViewThread = new MySurfaceViewThread();

      if (hasSurface == true)
        mySurfaceViewThread.start();
    }
  }

  public void pause() {
    // Kill the graphics update thread
    if (mySurfaceViewThread != null) {
      mySurfaceViewThread.requestExitAndWait();
      mySurfaceViewThread = null;
    }
  }

  public void surfaceCreated(SurfaceHolder holder) {
    hasSurface = true;
    if (mySurfaceViewThread != null)
      mySurfaceViewThread.start();
  }

  public void surfaceDestroyed(SurfaceHolder holder) {
    hasSurface = false;
```

```
      pause();
   }

   public void surfaceChanged(SurfaceHolder holder, int format, int w, int h) {
      if (mySurfaceViewThread != null)
         mySurfaceViewThread.onWindowResize(w, h);
   }

   class MySurfaceViewThread extends Thread {
      private boolean done;

      MySurfaceViewThread() {
         super();
         done = false;
      }

      @Override
      public void run() {
         SurfaceHolder surfaceHolder = holder;

         // Repeat the drawing loop until the thread is stopped.
         while (!done) {
            // Lock the surface and return the canvas to draw onto.
            Canvas canvas = surfaceHolder.lockCanvas();

            // TODO: Draw on the canvas!

            // Unlock the canvas and render the current image.
            surfaceHolder.unlockCanvasAndPost(canvas);
         }
      }

      public void requestExitAndWait() {
         // Mark this thread as complete and combine into
         // the main application thread.
         done = true;
         try {
            join();
         } catch (InterruptedException ex) { }
      }

      public void onWindowResize(int w, int h) {
         // Deal with a change in the available surface size.
      }
   }
}
```

Creating 3D Controls with SurfaceView

Android includes full support for the OpenGL ES 3D rendering framework including support for hardware acceleration on devices that offer it. The SurfaceView control provides a Surface onto which you can render your OpenGL scenes.

OpenGL is commonly used in desktop applications to provide dynamic 3D interfaces and animations. Resource-constrained devices don't have the capacity for polygon handling that's available on desktop PCs and gaming devices that feature dedicated 3D graphics processors. Within your applications, consider the load your 3D SurfaceView will be placing on your processor, and attempt to keep the total number of polygons being displayed, and the rate at which they're updated, as low as possible.

Creating a Doom clone for Android is well out of the scope of this book, so I'll leave it to you to test the limits of what's possible in a mobile 3D User Interface. Check out the GLSurfaceView API Demo example included in the SDK distribution to see an example of the OpenGL ES framework in action.

Creating Interactive Controls

Anyone who's used a mobile phone will be painfully aware of the challenges associated with designing intuitive User Interfaces for mobile devices. Touch screens have been available on mobiles for many years, but it's only recently that touch-enabled devices have been designed to be used by fingers rather than styluses.

Full physical keyboards have also become common, with the compact size of the slide-out or flip-out keyboard introducing its own challenges.

As an open framework, Android is expected to be available on a wide variety of devices featuring many different permutations of input technologies including touch screens, D-pads, trackballs, and keyboards.

The challenge for you as a developer is to create intuitive User Interfaces that make the most of the whatever input hardware is available, while introducing as little hardware dependence as possible.

The techniques described in this section show how to listen for (and react to) user input from key presses, trackball events, and touch-screen taps using the following event handlers in Views and Activities:

- ❑ onKeyDown Called when any hardware key is pressed.
- ❑ onKeyUp Called when any hardware key is released.
- ❑ onTrackballEvent Triggered by movement on the trackball.
- ❑ onTouchEvent The touch-screen event handler, triggered when the touch screen is touched, released, or dragged.

Using the Touch Screen

Mobile touch screens have existed since the days of the Apple Newton and the Palm Pilot, although their usability has had mixed reviews. Recently this technology has enjoyed a popular resurgence, with devices like the Nintendo DS and the Apple iPhone using touch screens in innovative ways.

Modern mobiles are all about finger input — a design principle that assumes users will be using their fingers rather than a specialized stylus to touch the screen.

Finger-based touch makes interaction less precise and is often based more on movement than simple contact. Android's native applications make extensive use of finger-based touch-screen interfaces, including the use of dragging motions to scroll lists or perform actions.

To create a View or Activity that uses touch-screen interaction, override the onTouchEvent handler as shown in the skeleton code below:

```
@Override
public boolean onTouchEvent(MotionEvent event) {
  return super.onTouchEvent(event);
}
```

Return true if you have handled the screen press; otherwise, return false to pass events through a stack of Views and Activities until the touch has been successfully handled.

Processing Touch Events

The onTouchEvent handler is fired when the user first touches the screen, once each time the position changes, and again when the contact ends.

The action property of the MotionEvent parameter reflects which of these event types has triggered the handler. To determine the initiating touch action, call getAction on the Motion Event parameter, and compare it to the static MotionEvent action values, as shown in the following skeleton code:

```
@Override
public boolean onTouchEvent(MotionEvent event) {

  int action = event.getAction();

  switch (action) {
    case (MotionEvent.ACTION_DOWN)   : // Touch screen pressed
                                       break;
    case (MotionEvent.ACTION_UP)     : // Touch screen touch ended
                                       break;
    case (MotionEvent.ACTION_MOVE)   : // Contact has moved across screen
                                       break;
    case (MotionEvent.ACTION_CANCEL) : // Touch event cancelled
                                       break;
  }

  return super.onTouchEvent(event);
}
```

The Motion Event also includes the coordinates of the current screen contact. You can access these coordinates using the getX and getY methods. These methods return the coordinate relative to the responding View or Activity; alternatively, getRawX and getRawY return the absolute screen coordinates. Both techniques are shown in the following code snippet:

```
// Relative screen coordinates.
int xPos = (int)event.getX();
int yPos = (int)event.getY();
```

```
// Absolute screen coordinates.
int xPosRaw = (int)event.getRawX();
int yPosRaw = (int)event.getRawY();
```

The Motion Event parameter also includes the pressure being applied to the screen using `getPressure`, a method that returns a value usually between 0 (no pressure) and 1 (normal pressure).

Depending on the calibration of the hardware, it's possible to return values greater than 1.

Finally, you can also determine the normalized size of the current contact area using the `getSize` method. This method returns a value between 0 and 1, where 0 suggests a very precise measurement and 1 indicates a possible "fat touch" event in which the user may not have intended to press anything.

Tracking Movement

Whenever the current touch contact position, pressure, or size changes, a new `onTouchEvent` is triggered with an `ACTION_MOVE` action.

As well as the fields described previously, the Motion Event parameter can include historical values. This history represents all the movement events that have occurred between the previous `onTouchEvent` and this one, allowing Android to buffer rapid movement changes to provide fine-grained capture of movement data.

You can find the size of the history by calling `getHistorySize`, which returns the number of movement positions available for the current event. You can then obtain the times, pressures, sizes, and positions of each of the historical events, using a series of `getHistorical*` methods and passing in the position index, as shown in the following code snippet:

```
int historySize = event.getHistorySize();

for (int i = 0; i < historySize; i++) {
  long time = event.getHistoricalEventTime(i);
  float pressure = event.getHistoricalPressure(i);
  float x = event.getHistoricalX(i);
  float y = event.getHistoricalY(i);
  float size = event.getHistoricalSize(i);

  // TODO: Do something with each point
}
```

The normal pattern used for handling movement events is to process each of the historical events first, followed by the current Motion Event values, as shown in the following code snippet:

```
@Override
public boolean onTouchEvent(MotionEvent event) {

  int action = event.getAction();

  switch (action) {
    case (MotionEvent.ACTION_MOVE)
    {
      int historySize = event.getHistorySize();
```

```
        for (int i = 0; i < historySize; i++) {
          float x = event.getHistoricalX(i);
          float y = event.getHistoricalY(i);
          processMovement(x, y);
        }

        float x = event.getX();
        float y = event.getY();
        processMovement(x, y);

        return true;
      }
    }

    return super.onTouchEvent(event);
  }

  private void processMovement(float _x, float _y) {
    // Todo: Do something on movement.
  }
```

Android includes two excellent examples of using the touch screen in the `Fingerpaint` and `Touch Paint` API Demos.

Using the `OnTouchListener`

You can listen for touch events without subclassing an existing View by attaching an `OnTouchListener` to any `View` object, using the `setOnTouchListener` method. The following code snippet demonstrates how to assign a new `OnTouchListener` implementation to an existing View within an Activity:

```
myView.setOnTouchListener(new OnTouchListener() {

  public boolean onTouch(View _view, MotionEvent _event) {
    // TODO Respond to motion events
    return false;
  }

});
```

Using the Device Keys and Buttons (Including D-Pad)

Button and key-press events for all hardware keys are handled by the `onKeyDown` and `onKeyUp` handlers of the active Activity or the focused view. This includes keyboard keys, D-pad, volume, back, dial, and hang-up buttons. The only exception is the Home key, which is reserved to ensure that users can never get locked within an application.

To have your View or Activity react to button presses, override the `onKeyUp` and `onKeyDown` event handlers as shown in the following skeleton code:

```
@Override
public boolean onKeyDown(int _keyCode, KeyEvent _event) {
  // Perform on key pressed handling, return true if handled
```

```
    return false
}

@Override
public boolean onKeyUp(int _keyCode, KeyEvent _event) {
    // Perform on key released handling, return true if handled
    return false;
}
```

The keyCode parameter contains the value of the key being pressed; compare it to the static key code values available from the KeyEvent class to perform key-specific processing.

The KeyEvent parameter also includes the isAltPressed, isShiftPressed, and isSymPressed methods to determine if the function, shift, and symbol metakeys are also being held. The static isModifierKey method accepts the keyCode and determines if this key event was triggered by the user pressing one of these modifier keys.

Using the OnKeyListener

To respond to key presses within Views in your Activity, implement an OnKeyListener, and assign it to a View using the setOnKeyListener method. Rather than implementing a separate method for key-press and key-release events, the OnKeyListener uses a single onKey event, as shown below:

```
myView.setOnKeyListener(new OnKeyListener() {

    public boolean onKey(View v, int keyCode, KeyEvent event)
    {
        // TODO Process key press event, return true if handled
        return false;
    }
});
```

Use the keyCode parameter to find the key pressed. The KeyEvent parameter is used to determine if the key has been pressed or released, where ACTION_DOWN represents a key press, and ACTION_UP signals its release.

Using the Trackball

Many mobile devices offer a trackball as a useful alternative (or addition) to the touch screen and D-pad. Trackball events are handled by overriding the onTrackballEvent method in your View or Activity.

Like touch events, trackball movement is included in a MotionEvent parameter. In this case, the MotionEvent contains the relative movement of the trackball since the last trackball event, normalized so that 1 represents the equivalent movement caused by the user pressing the D-pad key.

Vertical change can be obtained using the getY method, and horizontal scrolling is available through the getX method, as shown in the following skeleton code:

```
@Override
public boolean onTrackballEvent(MotionEvent _event) {
```

```
    float vertical = _event.getY();
    float horizontal = _event.getX();

    // TODO: Process trackball movement.

    return false;
}
```

Summary

This final chapter has served as a catch-all for some of the more complex Android features that were glossed over in earlier chapters.

You learned more about Android's security mechanisms, in particular, examining the permissions mechanism used to control access to Content Providers, Services, Activities, Intent Receivers, and broadcast Intents.

You explored the possibilities of interprocess communication using the Android Interface Definition Language to create rich interfaces between application components.

Much of the last part of the chapter focused on the Canvas class, as some of the more complex features available in the 2D drawing library were exposed. This included an examination of the drawing primitives available and a closer look at the possibilities of the Paint class.

You learned to use transparency and create gradient Shaders before looking at Mask Filters, Color Filters, and Path Effects. You also learned how to use hardware acceleration on 2D canvas-based Views, as well as some Canvas drawing best-practice techniques.

You were then introduced to the SurfaceView — a graphical control that lets you render graphics onto a surface from a background thread. This led to an introduction of rendering 3D graphics using the OpenGL ES framework and using the Surface View to provide live camera previews.

Finally, you learned the details for providing interactivity within your Activities and View by listening for and interpreting touch screen, track ball, and key press events.

In particular, you learned:

- ❑ Some of the possibilities of using the Internet as a data source, or processing middle tier, to keep your applications lightweight and information-rich.
- ❑ How to animate Views and ViewGroups using tweened animations.
- ❑ How to create frame-by-frame animations.
- ❑ Which drawing primitives you can use to draw on a canvas.
- ❑ How to get the most out of the Paint object using translucency, Shaders, Mask Filters, Color Filters, and Path Effects.
- ❑ Some of the best-practice techniques for drawing on the canvas.
- ❑ That you can apply hardware acceleration to 2D graphics drawing.

Index